CAT'S
Matchless
ESTATE
SALES
TODAY
9 AM - 2PM

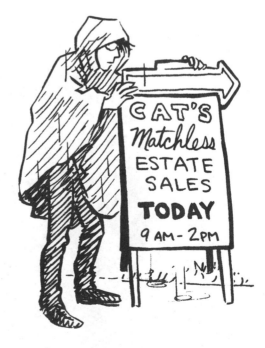

BAD HOUSES ™

Written by
SARA RYAN

Illustrated by
CARLA SPEED MCNEIL

DARK HORSE BOOKS

FROM SARA: Special thanks to my agent and friend Barry Goldblatt; to early *Bad Houses* supporters Joan Hilty, Rachel Edidin, and Jemiah Jefferson; to Sierra Hahn, Freddye Lins, and the whole team at Dark Horse for their hard work getting the book into the world; to Steve Lieber for providing the ideal blend of encouragement and crackdowns; and most of all to Carla, for bringing people and places from inside my head to such vibrant life on the pages.

FROM CARLA: Special thanks to Joan Hilty, Rachel Edidin, Jemiah Jefferson, Sierra Hahn, and Freddye Lins: for carrying the torch!

editors Rachel Edidin, Sierra Hahn / *assistant editors* Jemiah Jefferson, Freddye Lins / *collection designer* Tina Alessi

president and publisher Mike Richardson / *executive vice president* Neil Hankerson / *chief financial officer* Tom Weddle / *vice president of publishing* Randy Stradley / *vice president of book trade sales* Michael Martens / *vice president of business affairs* Anita Nelson / *editor in chief* Scott Allie / *vice president of marketing* Matt Parkinson / *vice president of product development* David Scroggy / *vice president of information technology* Dale LaFountain / *senior director of print, design, and production* Darlene Vogel / *general counsel* Ken Lizzi / *editorial director* Davey Estrada / *senior books editor* Chris Warner / *executive editor* Diana Schutz / *director of print and development* Cary Grazzini / *art director* Lia Ribacchi / *director of scheduling* Cara Niece / *director of international licensing* Tim Wiesch / *director of digital publishing* Mark Bernardi

Published by Dark Horse Books, a division of Dark Horse Comics, Inc.
10956 SE Main Street, Milwaukie, OR 97222 I DarkHorse.com

International Licensing: 503-905-2377
To find a comics shop in your area, call the Comic Shop Locator Service toll-free at 1-888-266-4226

LIBRARY OF CONGRESS CATALOGING-IN-PUBLICATION DATA
Ryan, Sara, author.
  Bad Houses / written by Sara Ryan ; illustrated by Carla Speed McNeil. -- First edition.
      pages cm
  Summary: "Teenagers Anne and Lewis cross paths and together refuse to succumb to the fate of the older generation as they discover the secrets of their hometown and their own families"-- Provided by publisher.
  ISBN 978-1-59582-993-1
  1. Graphic novels. I. McNeil, Carla Speed, illustrator. II. Title.
  PN6727.R95B33 2013
  741.5'973--dc23
                                    2013022081

First edition: October 2013 / ISBN 978-1-59582-993-1
10 9 8 7 6 5 4 3 2 1
Printed in the United States of America

FOR MY MOM, who did not inspire any of the characters in this book, but who does inspire me.

—SARA

TO EVERYONE who has trouble letting go.

—CARLA

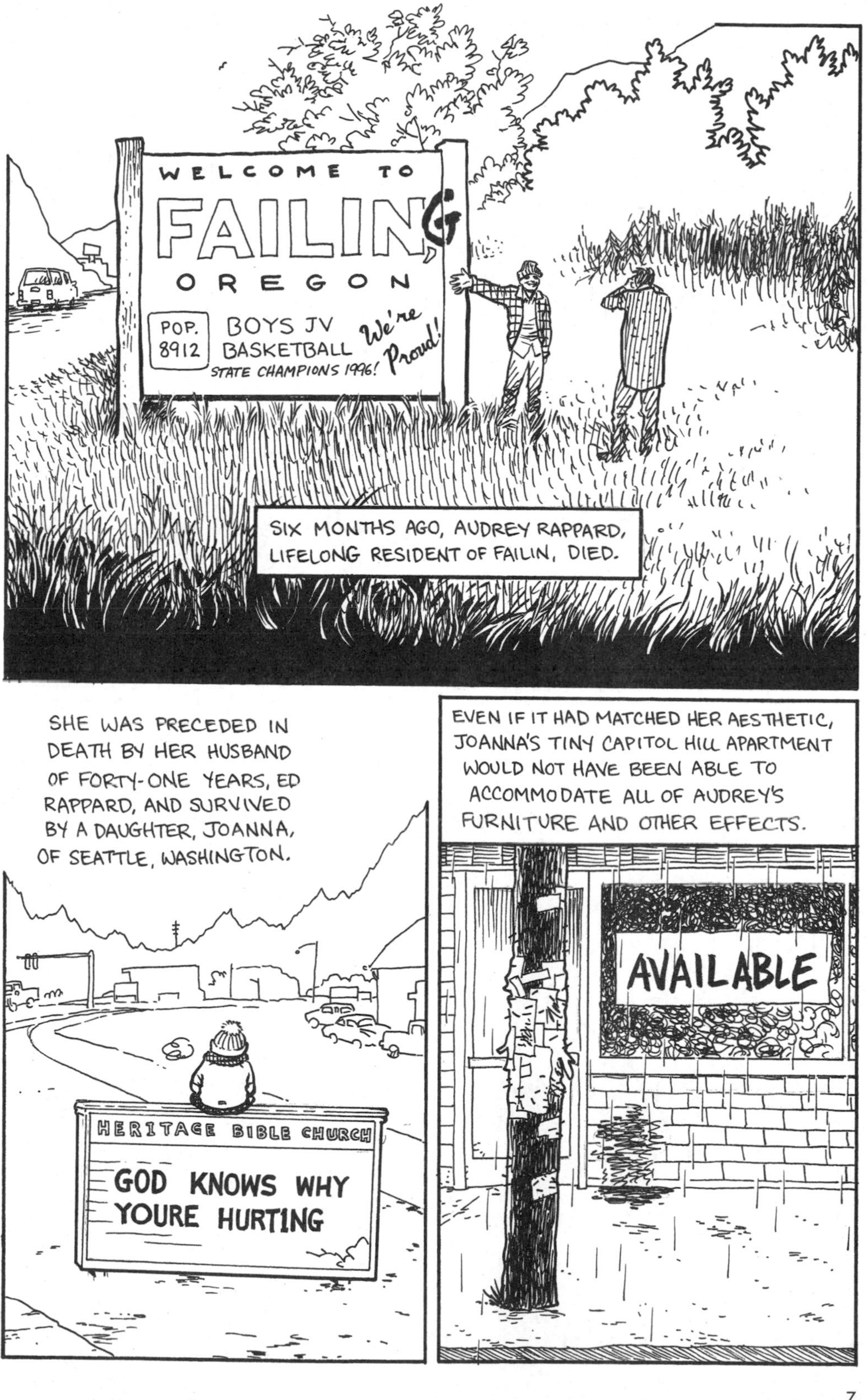
WELCOME TO
FAILING
OREGON
POP. 8912
BOYS JV BASKETBALL STATE CHAMPIONS 1996!
We're Proud!
SIX MONTHS AGO, AUDREY RAPPARD, LIFELONG RESIDENT OF FAILIN, DIED.
SHE WAS PRECEDED IN DEATH BY HER HUSBAND OF FORTY-ONE YEARS, ED RAPPARD, AND SURVIVED BY A DAUGHTER, JOANNA, OF SEATTLE, WASHINGTON.
HERITAGE BIBLE CHURCH
GOD KNOWS WHY YOURE HURTING
EVEN IF IT HAD MATCHED HER AESTHETIC, JOANNA'S TINY CAPITOL HILL APARTMENT WOULD NOT HAVE BEEN ABLE TO ACCOMMODATE ALL OF AUDREY'S FURNITURE AND OTHER EFFECTS.
AVAILABLE

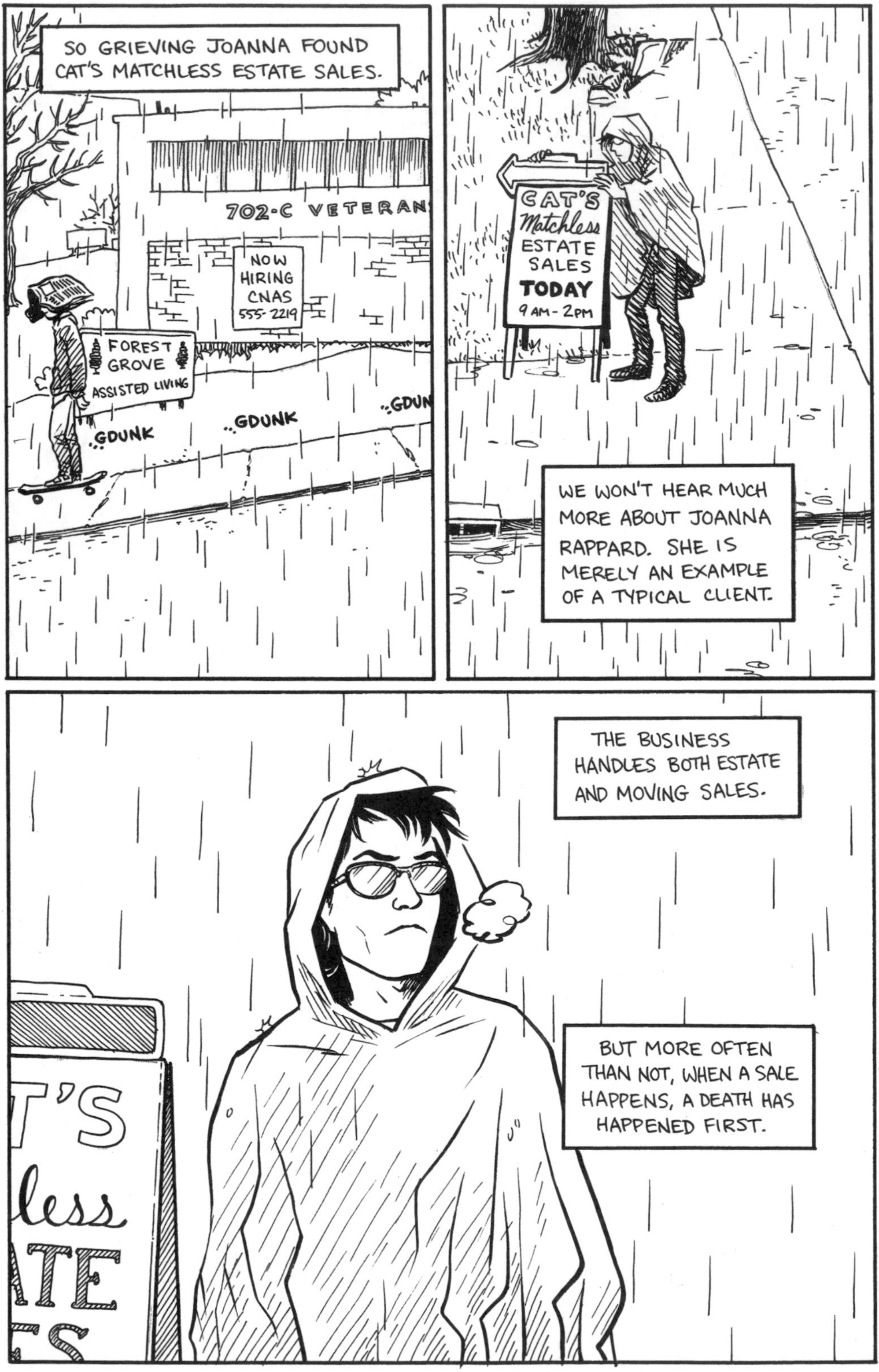
SO GRIEVING JOANNA FOUND CAT'S MATCHLESS ESTATE SALES.
702-C VETERAN
NOW HIRING CNAS 555-2219
FOREST GROVE ASSISTED LIVING
GDUNK
GDUNK
GDUN
CAT'S Matchless ESTATE SALES TODAY 9 AM - 2 PM
WE WON'T HEAR MUCH MORE ABOUT JOANNA RAPPARD. SHE IS MERELY AN EXAMPLE OF A TYPICAL CLIENT.
THE BUSINESS HANDLES BOTH ESTATE AND MOVING SALES.
BUT MORE OFTEN THAN NOT, WHEN A SALE HAPPENS, A DEATH HAS HAPPENED FIRST.

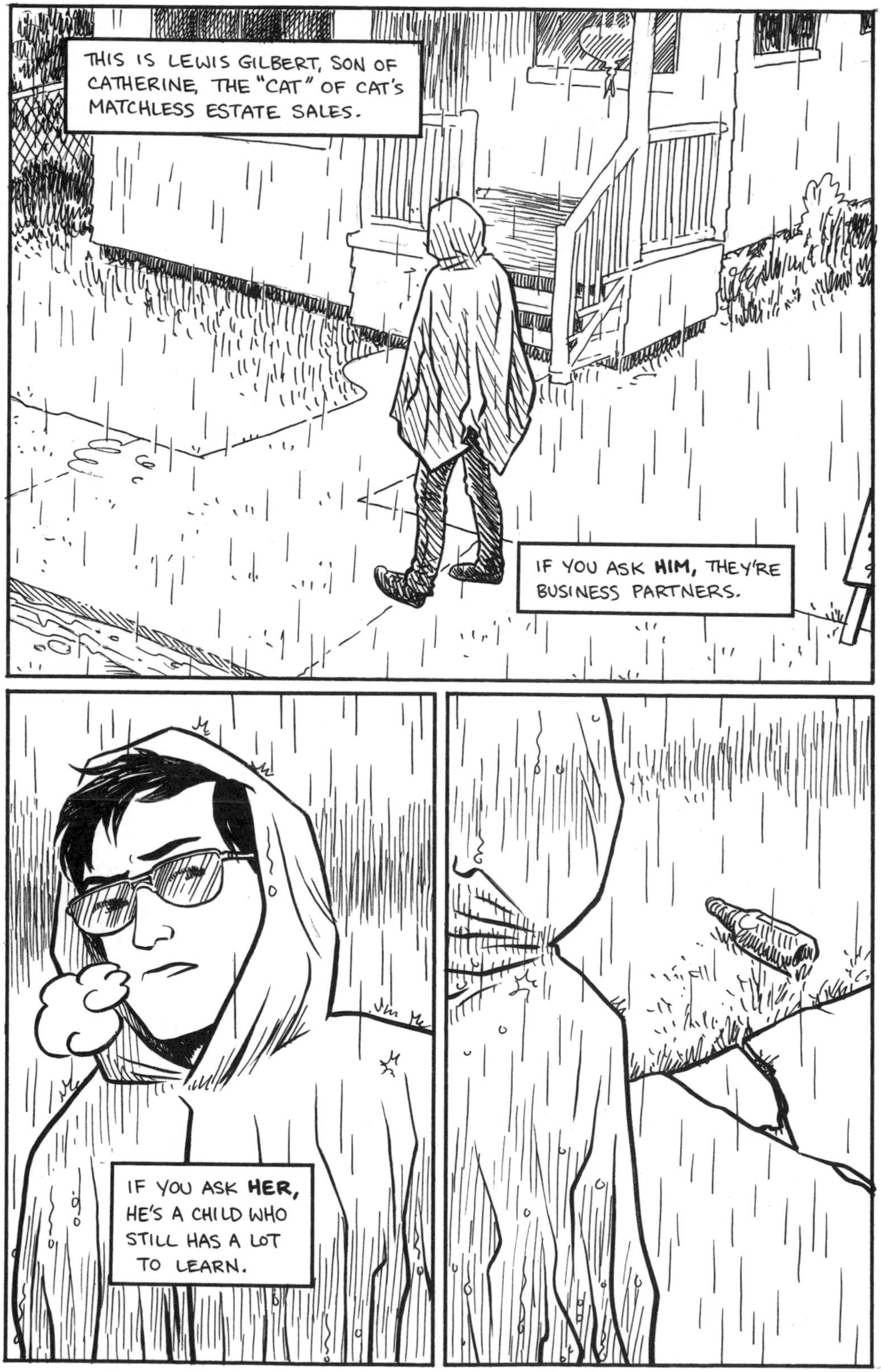
THIS IS LEWIS GILBERT, SON OF CATHERINE, THE "CAT" OF CAT'S MATCHLESS ESTATE SALES.
IF YOU ASK **HIM,** THEY'RE BUSINESS PARTNERS.
IF YOU ASK **HER,** HE'S A CHILD WHO STILL HAS A LOT TO LEARN.

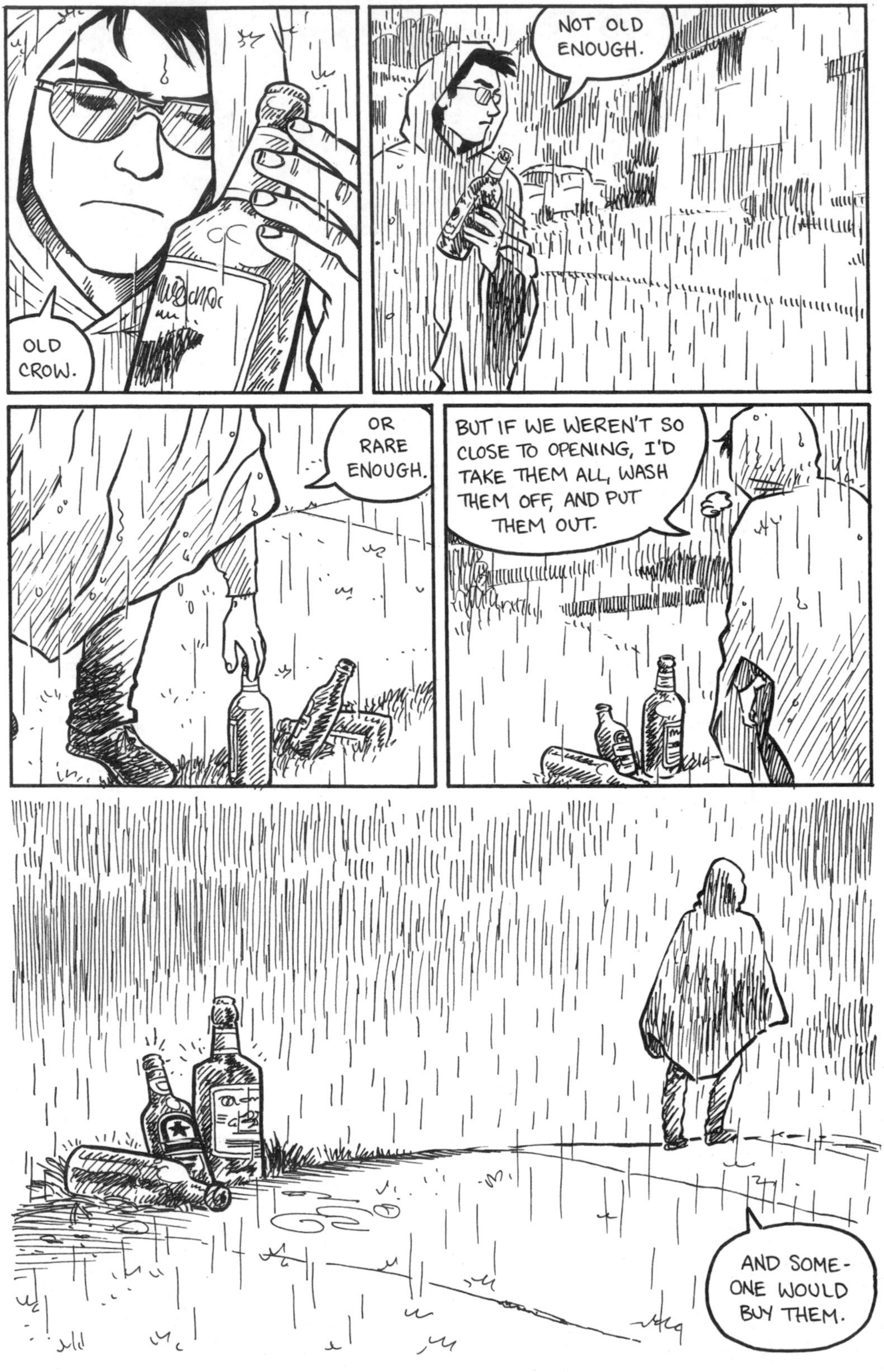
OLD CROW.
NOT OLD ENOUGH.
OR RARE ENOUGH.
BUT IF WE WEREN'T SO CLOSE TO OPENING, I'D TAKE THEM ALL, WASH THEM OFF, AND PUT THEM OUT.
AND SOME-ONE WOULD BUY THEM.

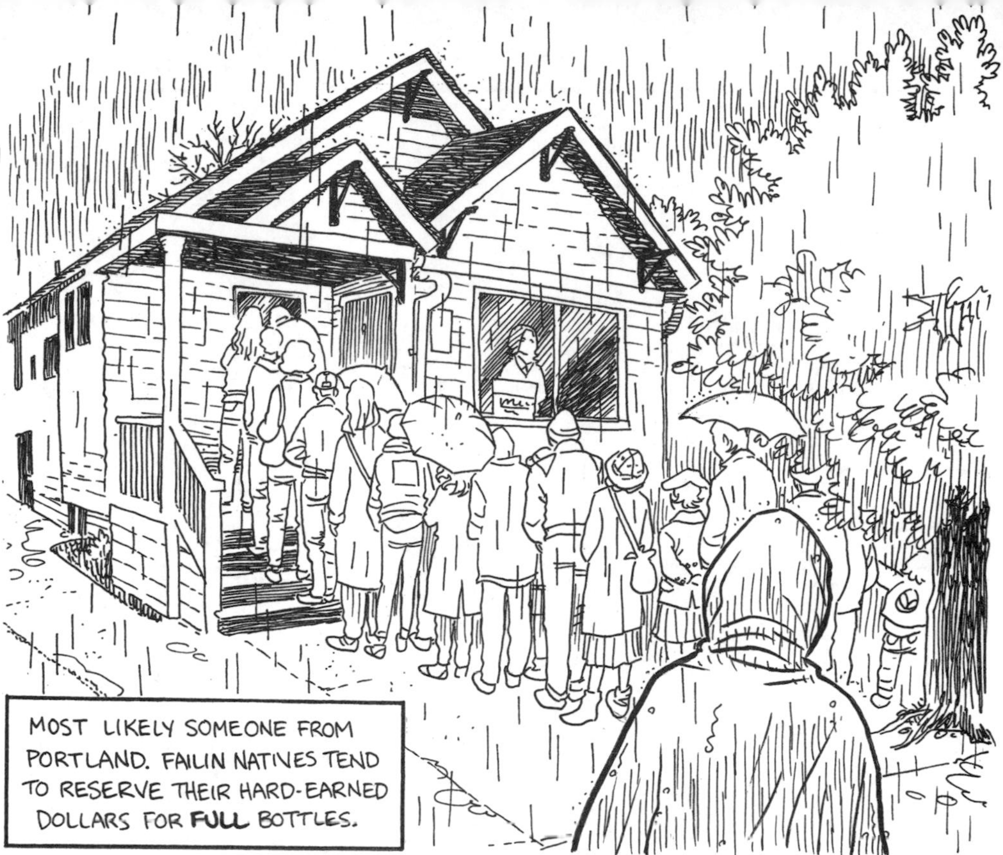
MOST LIKELY SOMEONE FROM PORTLAND. FAILIN NATIVES TEND TO RESERVE THEIR HARD-EARNED DOLLARS FOR **FULL** BOTTLES.

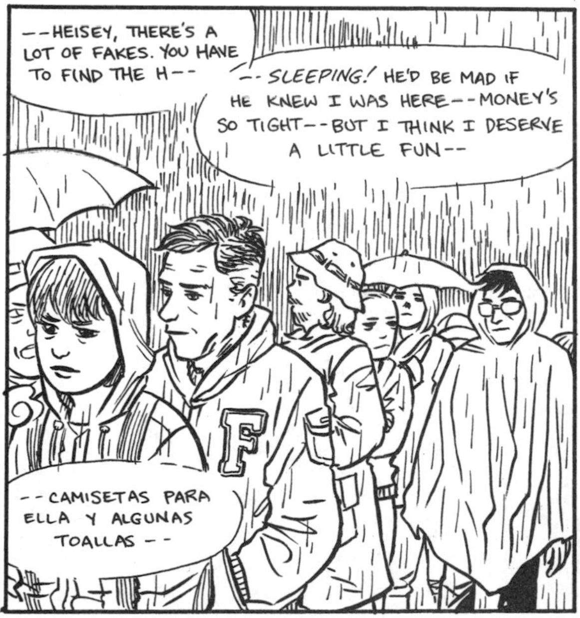
--HEISEY, THERE'S A LOT OF FAKES. YOU HAVE TO FIND THE H--
--*SLEEPING!* HE'D BE MAD IF HE KNEW I WAS HERE--MONEY'S SO TIGHT--BUT I THINK I DESERVE A LITTLE FUN--
F
--CAMISETAS PARA ELLA Y ALGUNAS TOALLAS --

LEWIS BELIEVES THAT IT'S NOT SO MUCH THAT THERE'S A SUCKER BORN EVERY MINUTE — ALTHOUGH HE DOESN'T NECESSARILY DISAGREE WITH BARNUM — BUT THAT THERE'S SOMEONE OUT THERE WHO WILL FETISHIZE EVERY OBJECT.

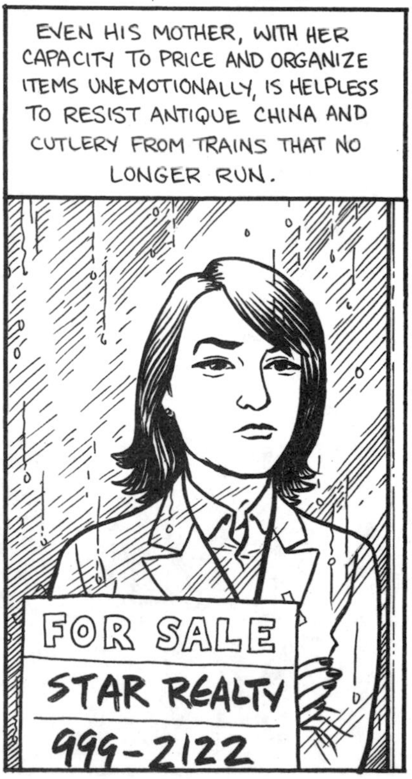
EVEN HIS MOTHER, WITH HER CAPACITY TO PRICE AND ORGANIZE ITEMS UNEMOTIONALLY, IS HELPLESS TO RESIST ANTIQUE CHINA AND CUTLERY FROM TRAINS THAT NO LONGER RUN.
FOR SALE
STAR REALTY
999-2122

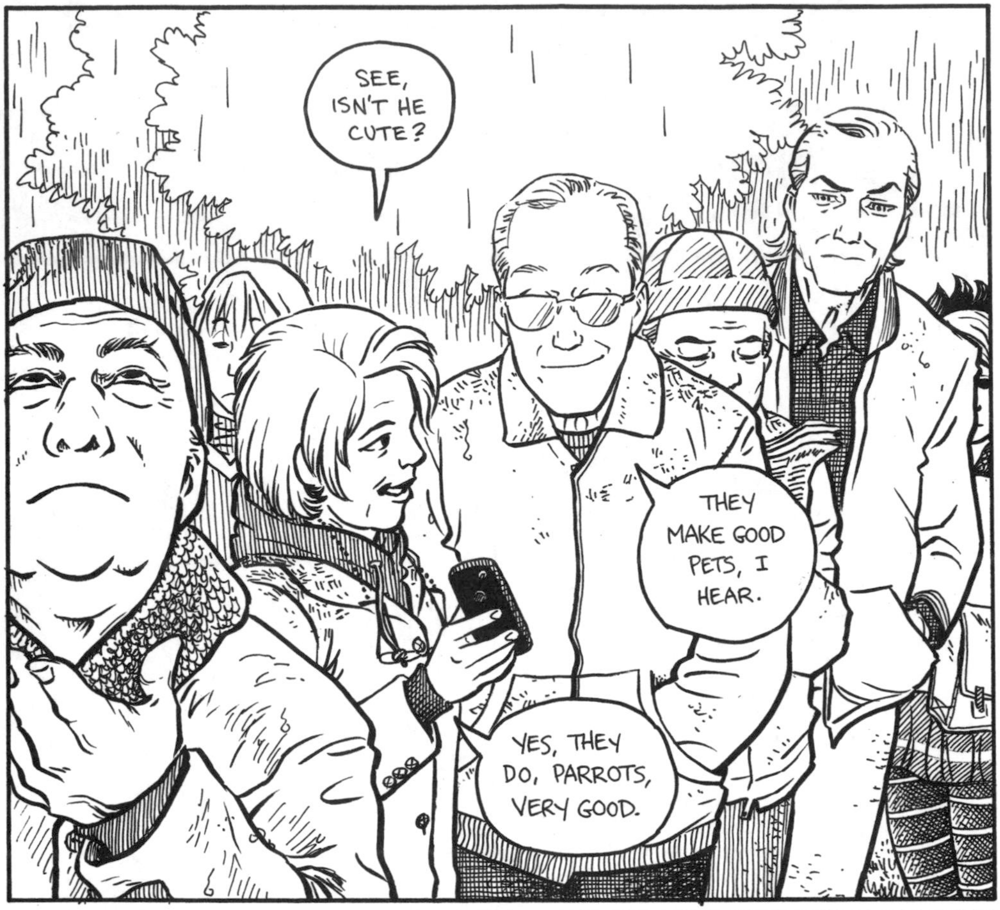
SEE, ISN'T HE CUTE?
THEY MAKE GOOD PETS, I HEAR.
YES, THEY DO, PARROTS, VERY GOOD.

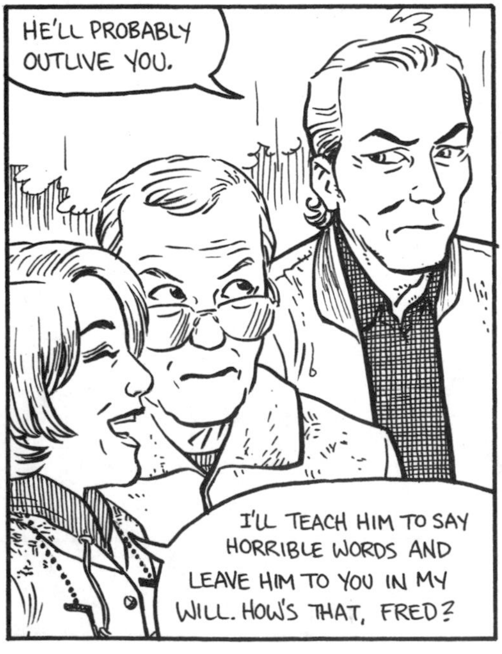
HE'LL PROBABLY OUTLIVE YOU.
I'LL TEACH HIM TO SAY HORRIBLE WORDS AND LEAVE HIM TO YOU IN MY WILL. HOW'S THAT, FRED?

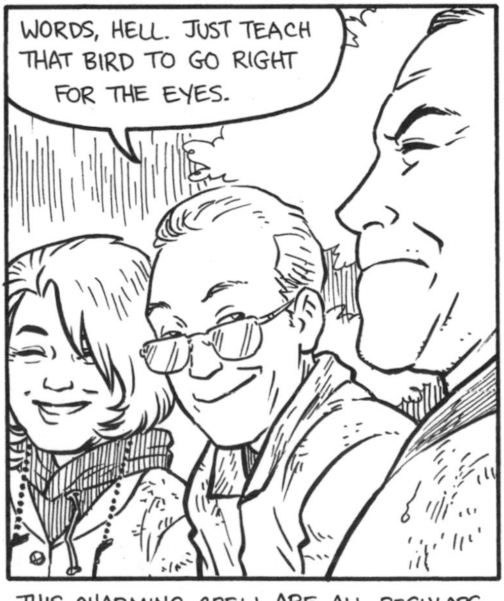
WORDS, HELL. JUST TEACH THAT BIRD TO GO RIGHT FOR THE EYES.

THIS CHARMING CREW ARE ALL REGULARS, ANTIQUE DEALERS AND SERIOUS COLLECTORS.

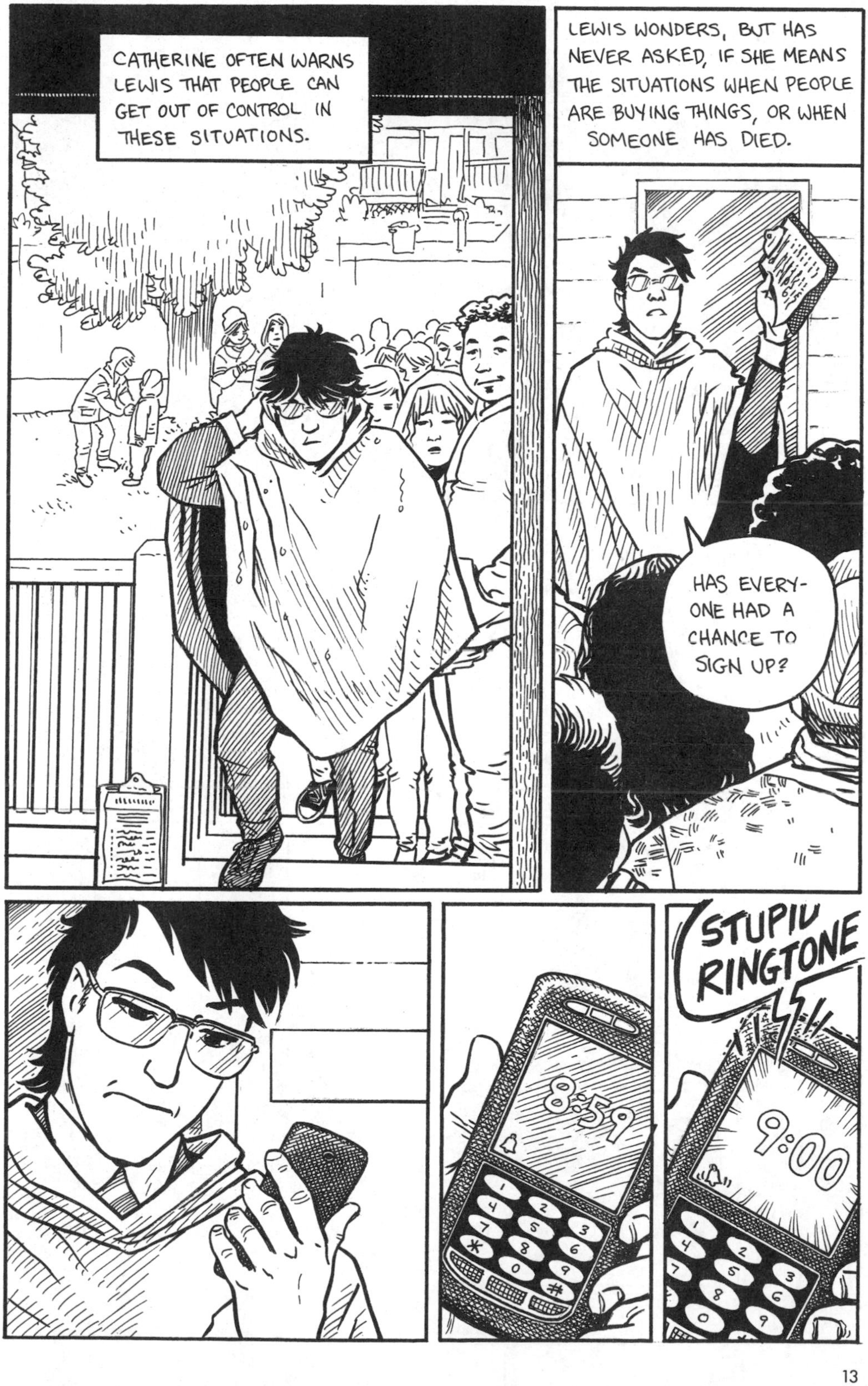
CATHERINE OFTEN WARNS LEWIS THAT PEOPLE CAN GET OUT OF CONTROL IN THESE SITUATIONS.
LEWIS WONDERS, BUT HAS NEVER ASKED, IF SHE MEANS THE SITUATIONS WHEN PEOPLE ARE BUYING THINGS, OR WHEN SOMEONE HAS DIED.
HAS EVERY-ONE HAD A CHANCE TO SIGN UP?
8:59
STUPID RINGTONE
9:00

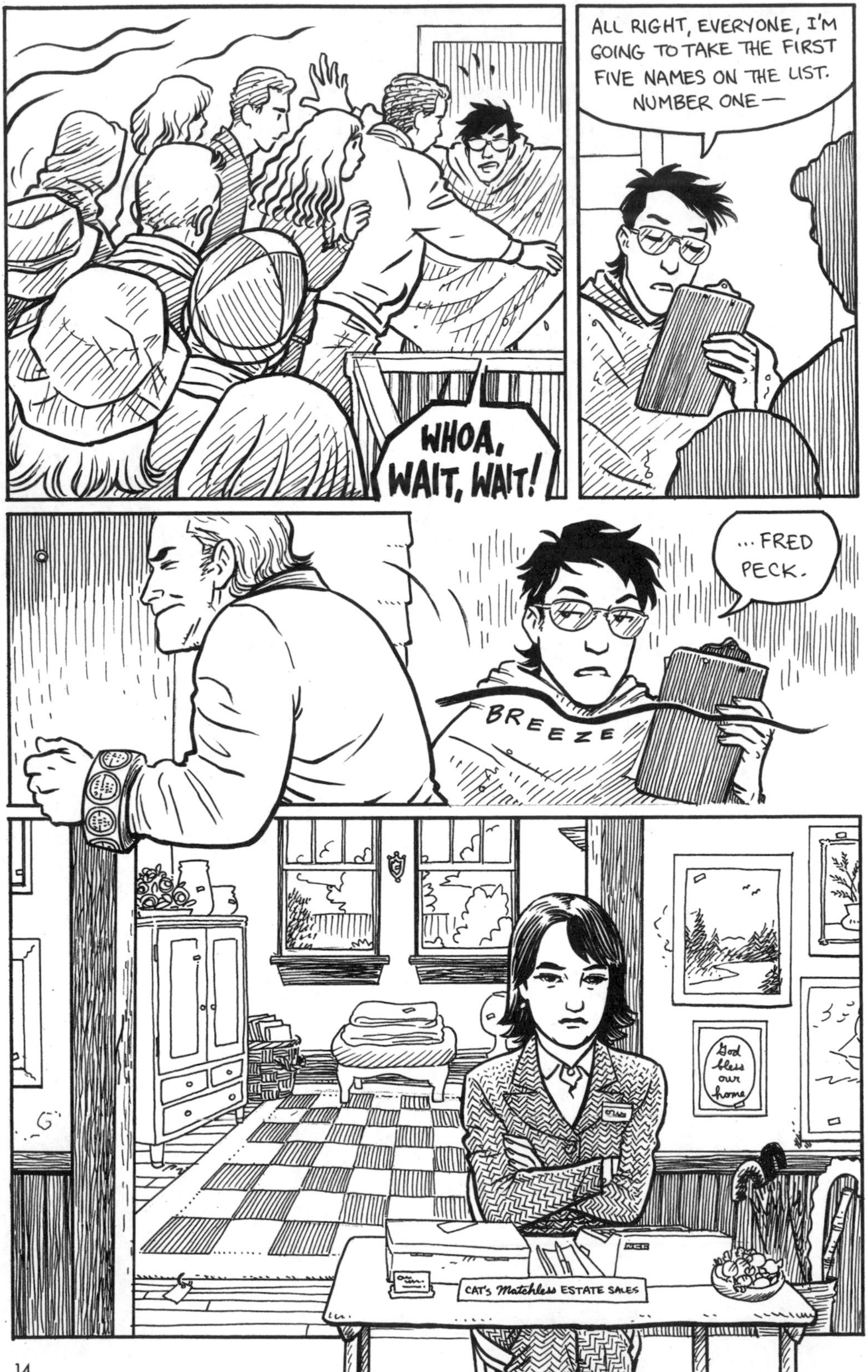
WHOA, WAIT, WAIT!
ALL RIGHT, EVERYONE, I'M GOING TO TAKE THE FIRST FIVE NAMES ON THE LIST. NUMBER ONE—
...FRED PECK.
BREEZE
God bless our home
CAT's Matchless ESTATE SALES

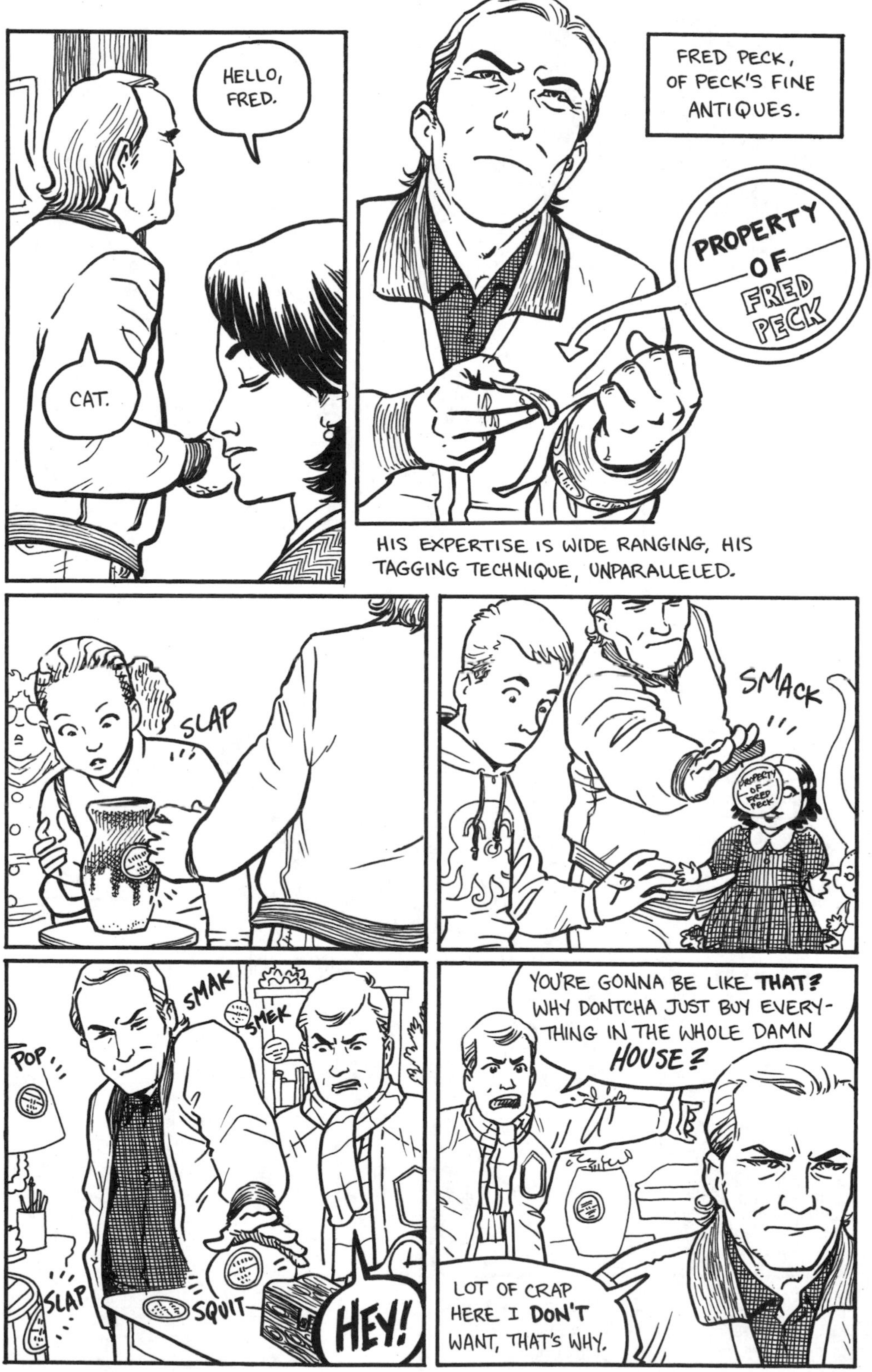
HELLO, FRED.
CAT.
FRED PECK, OF PECK'S FINE ANTIQUES.
PROPERTY OF FRED PECK
HIS EXPERTISE IS WIDE RANGING, HIS TAGGING TECHNIQUE, UNPARALLELED.
SLAP
SMACK
POP
SMAK
SMEK
SLAP
SQUIT
HEY!
YOU'RE GONNA BE LIKE **THAT?** WHY DONTCHA JUST BUY EVERYTHING IN THE WHOLE DAMN ***HOUSE?***
LOT OF CRAP HERE I **DON'T** WANT, THAT'S WHY.

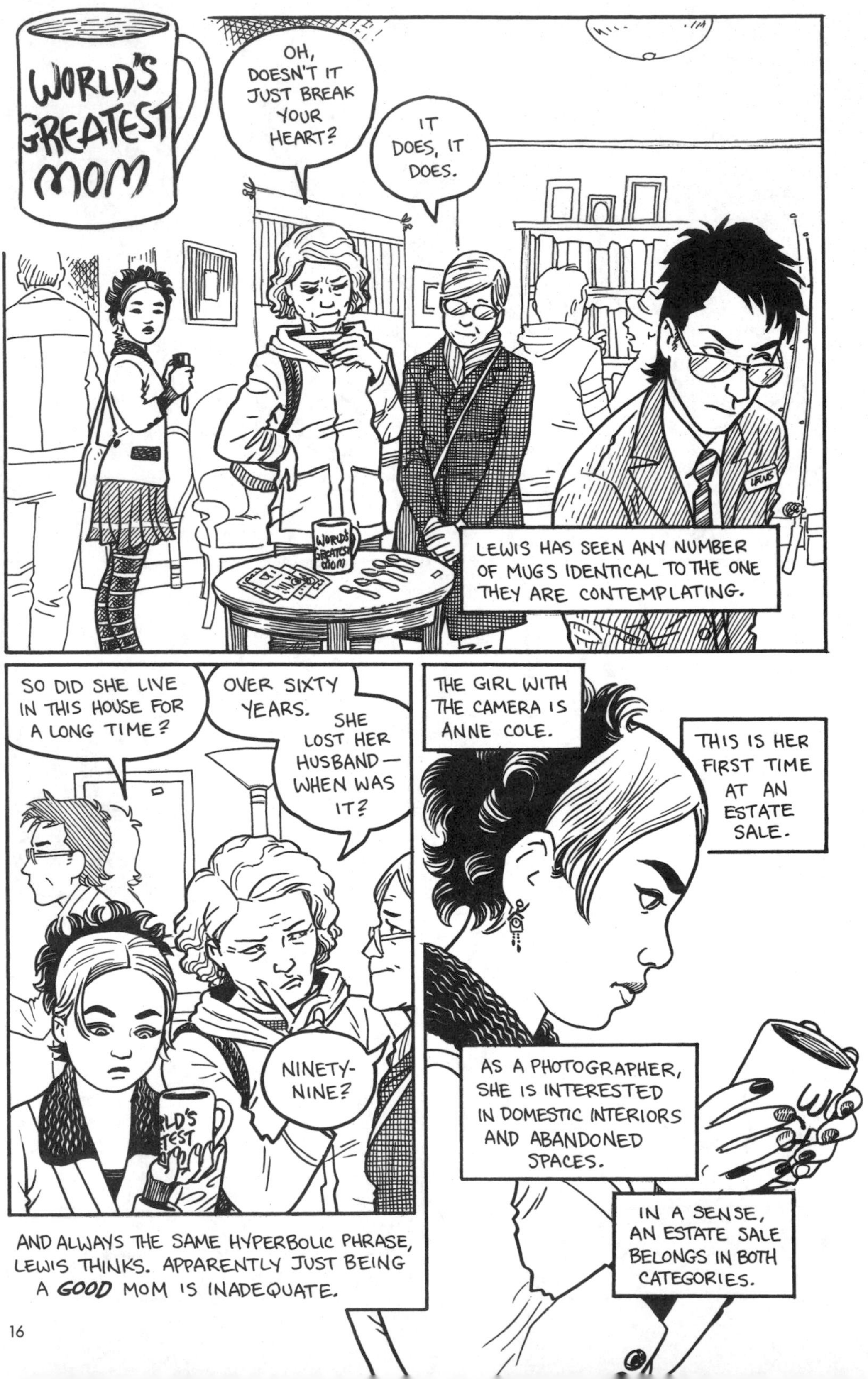
WORLD'S GREATEST MOM
OH, DOESN'T IT JUST BREAK YOUR HEART?
IT DOES, IT DOES.
WORLD'S GREATEST MOM
LEWIS
LEWIS HAS SEEN ANY NUMBER OF MUGS IDENTICAL TO THE ONE THEY ARE CONTEMPLATING.
SO DID SHE LIVE IN THIS HOUSE FOR A LONG TIME?
OVER SIXTY YEARS.
SHE LOST HER HUSBAND— WHEN WAS IT?
NINETY-NINE?
THE GIRL WITH THE CAMERA IS ANNE COLE.
THIS IS HER FIRST TIME AT AN ESTATE SALE.
AS A PHOTOGRAPHER, SHE IS INTERESTED IN DOMESTIC INTERIORS AND ABANDONED SPACES.
AND ALWAYS THE SAME HYPERBOLIC PHRASE, LEWIS THINKS. APPARENTLY JUST BEING A ***GOOD*** MOM IS INADEQUATE.
IN A SENSE, AN ESTATE SALE BELONGS IN BOTH CATEGORIES.

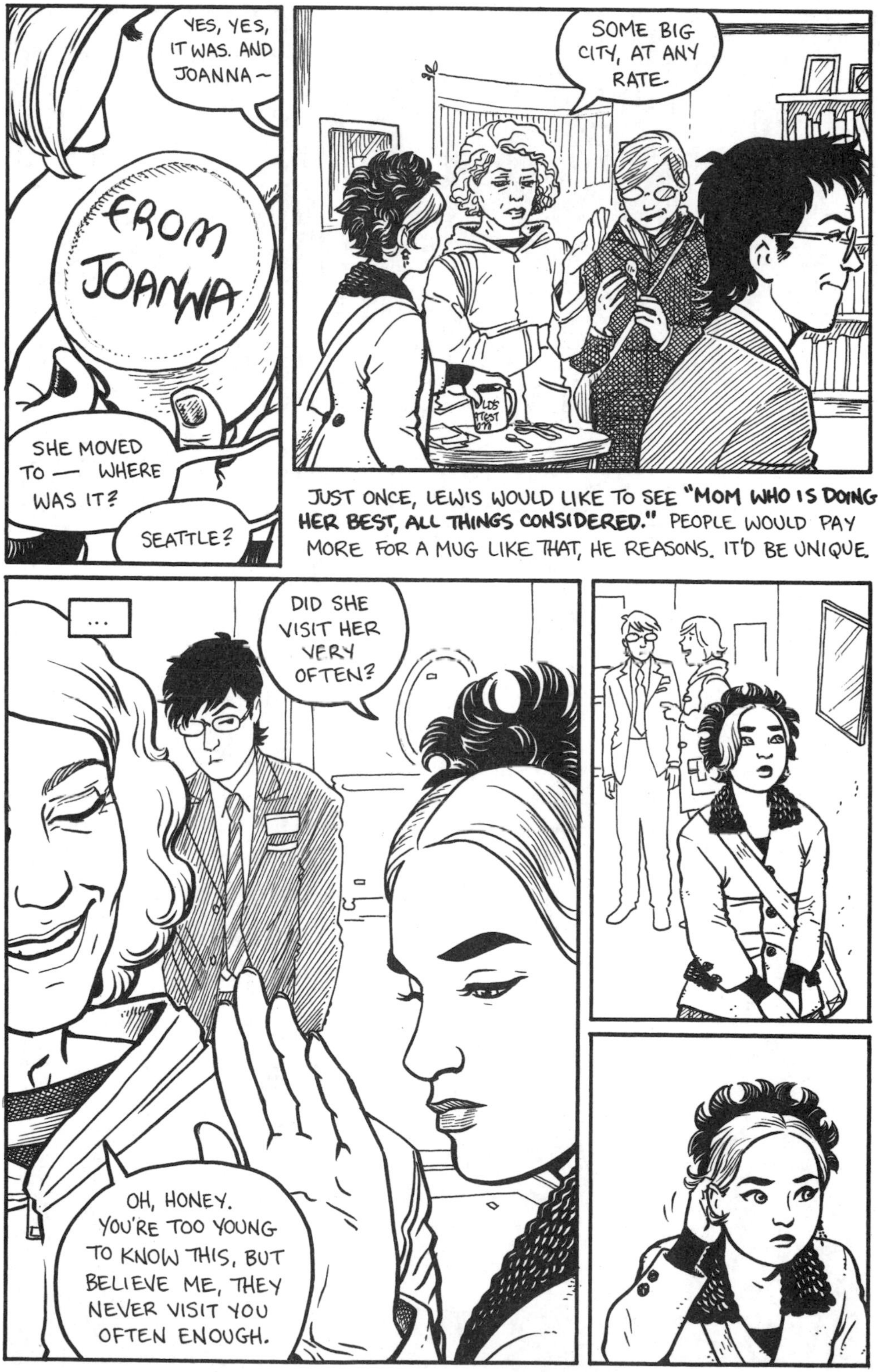
YES, YES, IT WAS. AND JOANNA~
FROM JOANNA
SHE MOVED TO — WHERE WAS IT?
SEATTLE?
SOME BIG CITY, AT ANY RATE.
JUST ONCE, LEWIS WOULD LIKE TO SEE "MOM WHO IS DOING HER BEST, ALL THINGS CONSIDERED." PEOPLE WOULD PAY MORE FOR A MUG LIKE THAT, HE REASONS. IT'D BE UNIQUE.
...
DID SHE VISIT HER VERY OFTEN?
OH, HONEY. YOU'RE TOO YOUNG TO KNOW THIS, BUT BELIEVE ME, THEY NEVER VISIT YOU OFTEN ENOUGH.

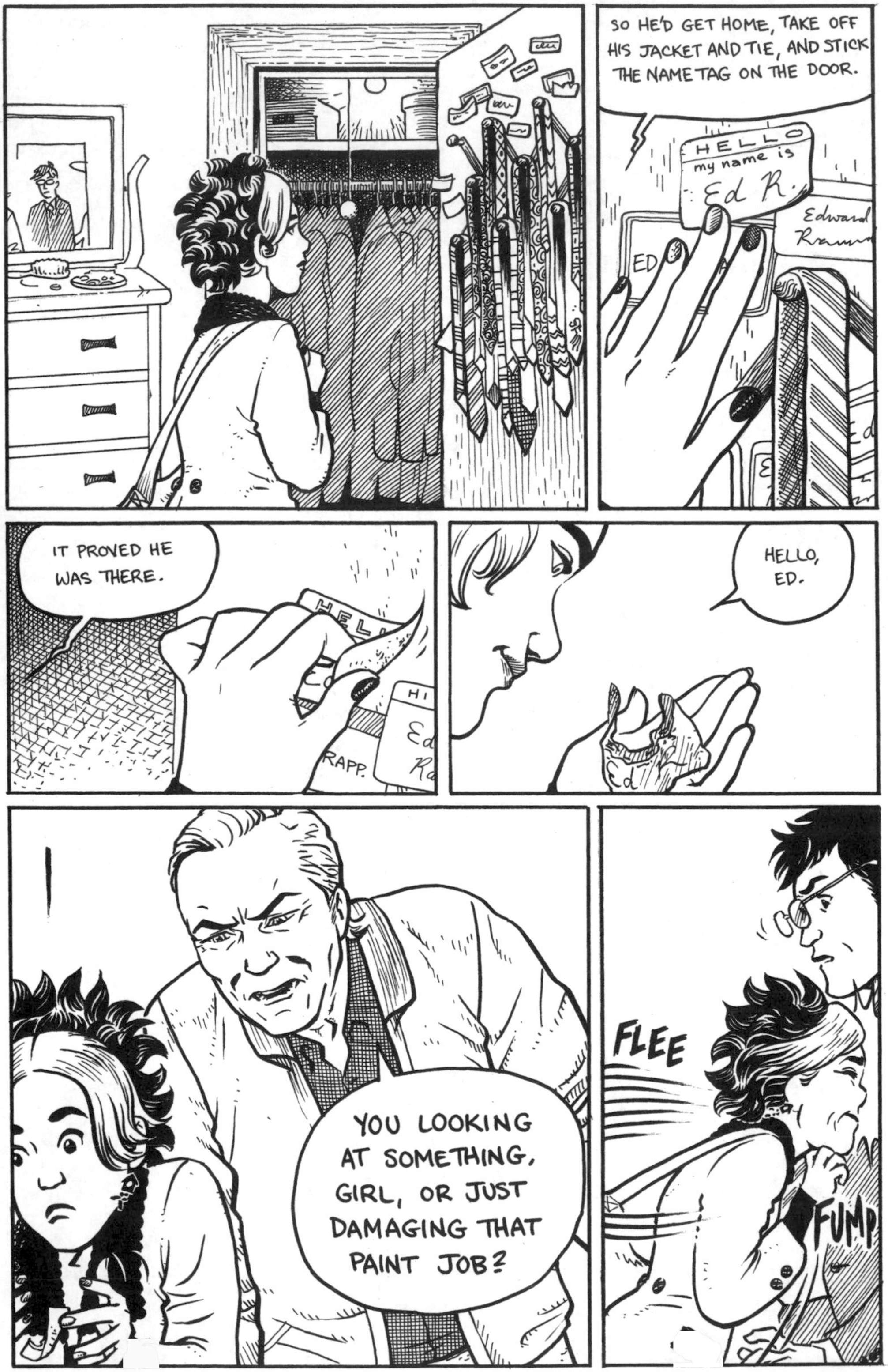
SO HE'D GET HOME, TAKE OFF HIS JACKET AND TIE, AND STICK THE NAME TAG ON THE DOOR.
HELLO my name is Ed R.
Edward
ED
IT PROVED HE WAS THERE.
RAPP.
HELLO, ED.
YOU LOOKING AT SOMETHING, GIRL, OR JUST DAMAGING THAT PAINT JOB?
FLEE
FUMP

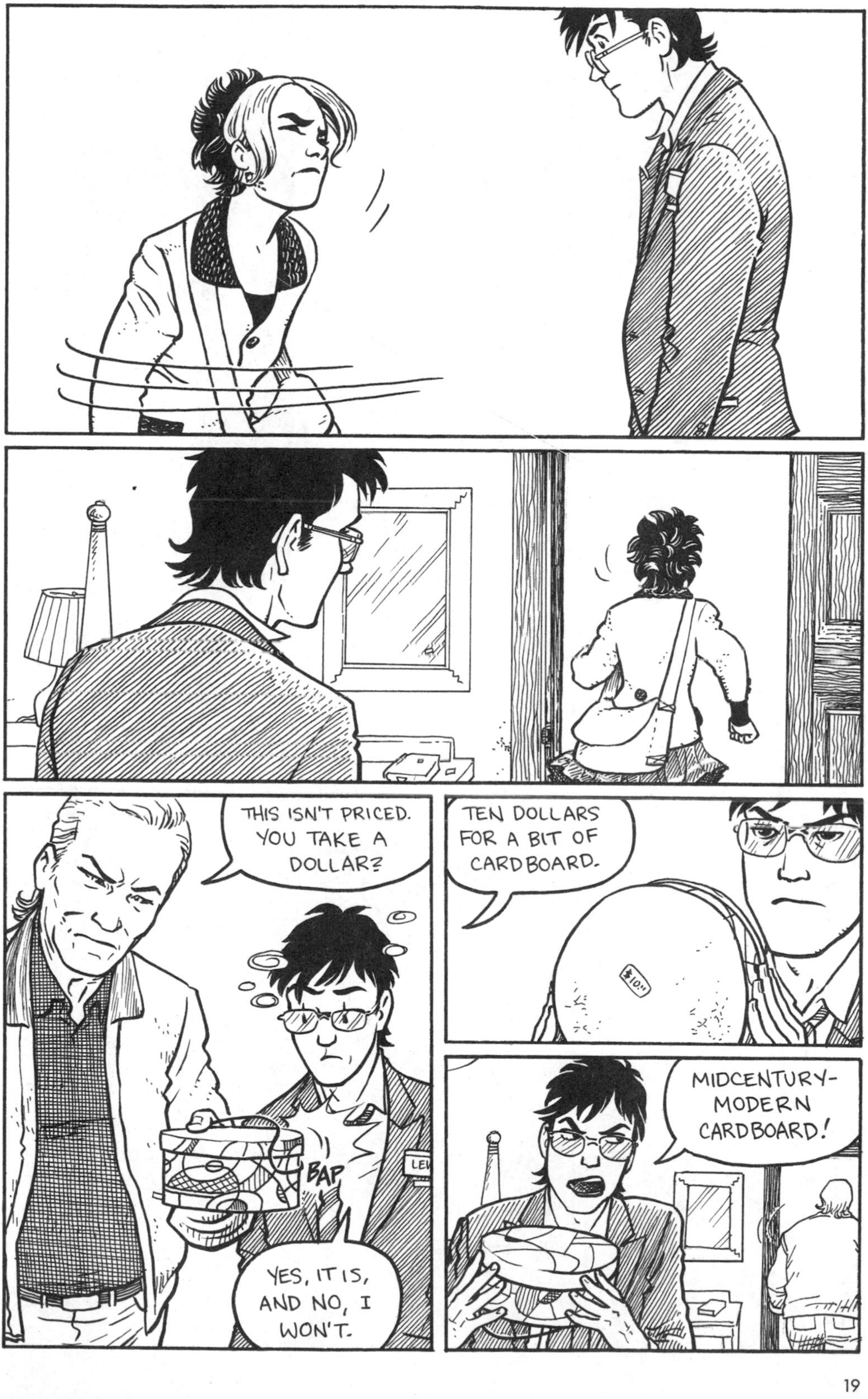
THIS ISN'T PRICED. YOU TAKE A DOLLAR?
BAP
LEW
YES, IT IS, AND NO, I WON'T.
TEN DOLLARS FOR A BIT OF CARDBOARD.
$10.00
MIDCENTURY-MODERN CARDBOARD!

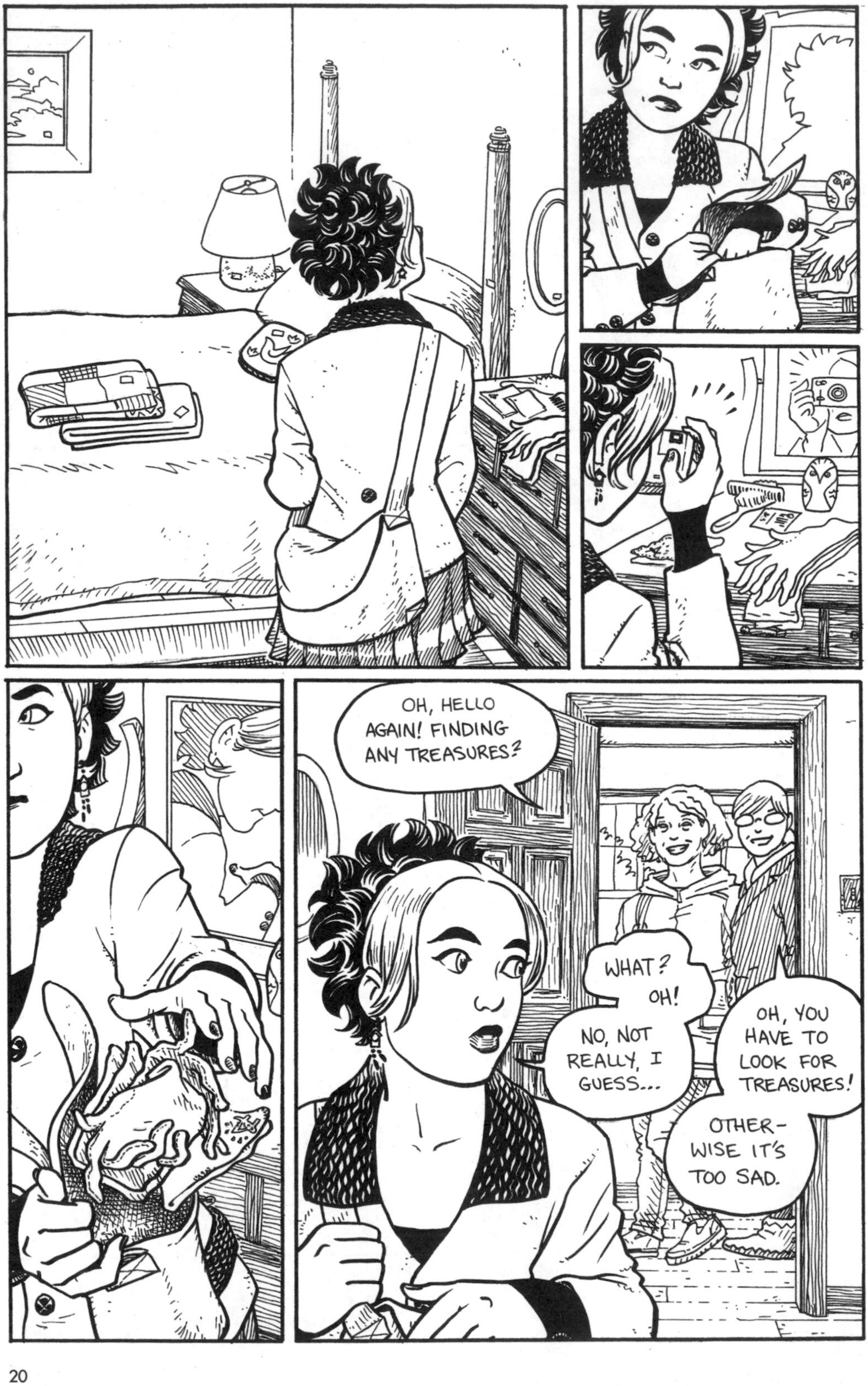

OH, HELLO AGAIN! FINDING ANY TREASURES?
WHAT? OH!
NO, NOT REALLY, I GUESS...
OH, YOU HAVE TO LOOK FOR TREASURES!
OTHER-WISE IT'S TOO SAD.

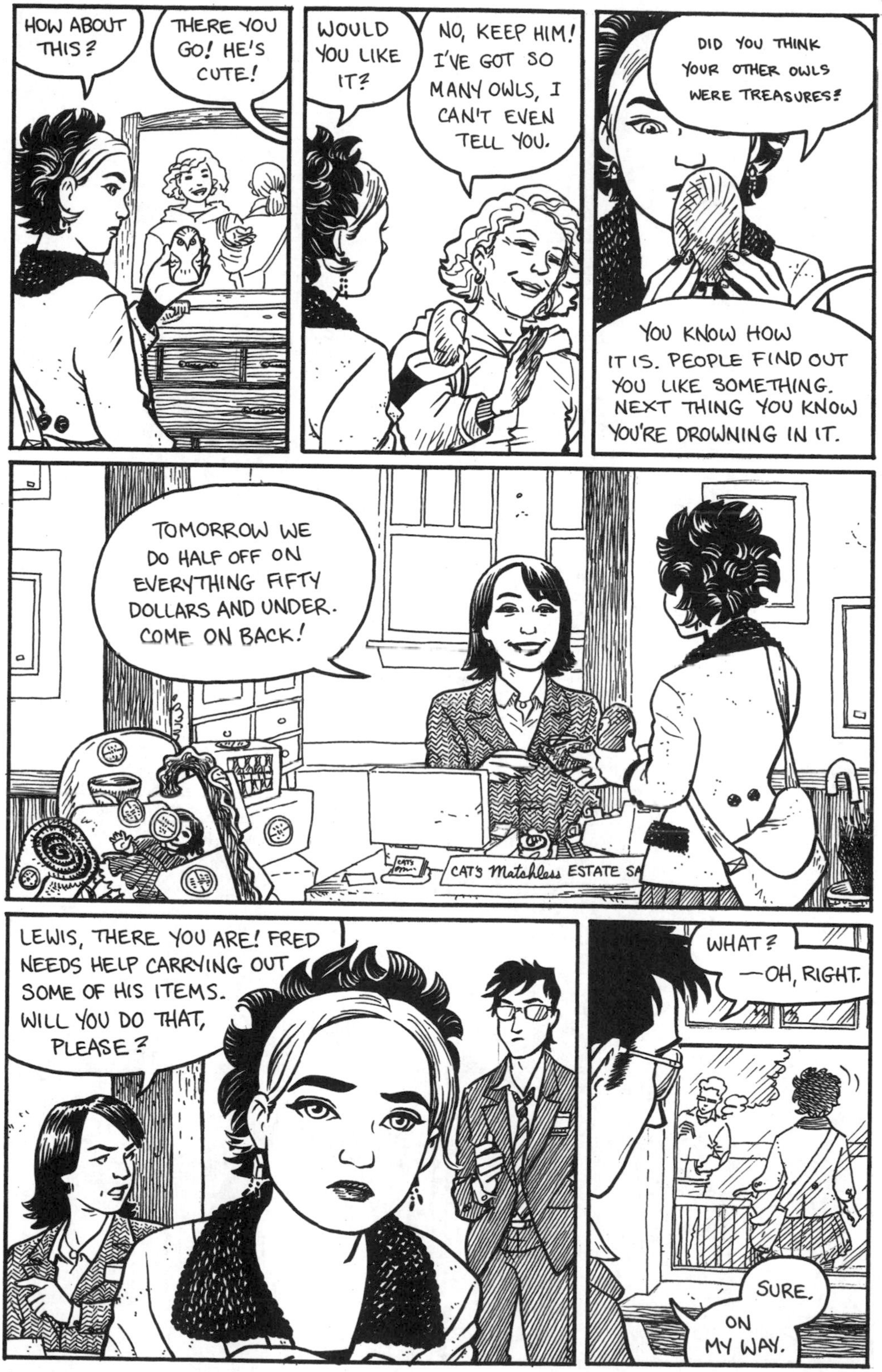
HOW ABOUT THIS?
THERE YOU GO! HE'S CUTE!
WOULD YOU LIKE IT?
NO, KEEP HIM! I'VE GOT SO MANY OWLS, I CAN'T EVEN TELL YOU.
DID YOU THINK YOUR OTHER OWLS WERE TREASURES?
YOU KNOW HOW IT IS. PEOPLE FIND OUT YOU LIKE SOMETHING. NEXT THING YOU KNOW YOU'RE DROWNING IN IT.
TOMORROW WE DO HALF OFF ON EVERYTHING FIFTY DOLLARS AND UNDER. COME ON BACK!
CAT'S Matchless ESTATE SA
LEWIS, THERE YOU ARE! FRED NEEDS HELP CARRYING OUT SOME OF HIS ITEMS. WILL YOU DO THAT, PLEASE?
WHAT? —OH, RIGHT.
SURE.
ON MY WAY.

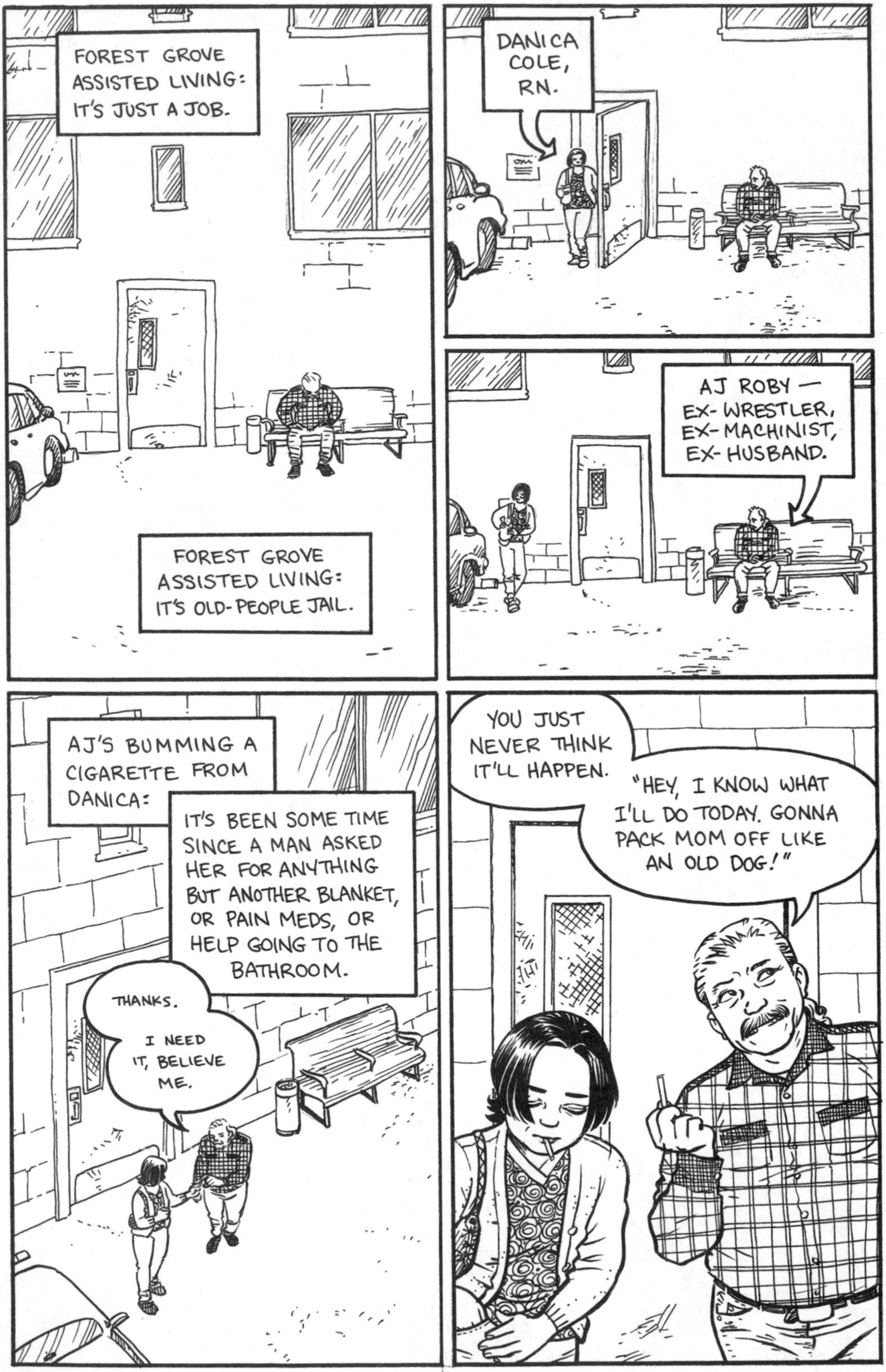

FOREST GROVE ASSISTED LIVING: IT'S JUST A JOB.
FOREST GROVE ASSISTED LIVING: IT'S OLD-PEOPLE JAIL.
DANICA COLE, RN.
AJ ROBY — EX-WRESTLER, EX-MACHINIST, EX-HUSBAND.
AJ'S BUMMING A CIGARETTE FROM DANICA:
IT'S BEEN SOME TIME SINCE A MAN ASKED HER FOR ANYTHING BUT ANOTHER BLANKET, OR PAIN MEDS, OR HELP GOING TO THE BATHROOM.
THANKS. I NEED IT, BELIEVE ME.
YOU JUST NEVER THINK IT'LL HAPPEN.
"HEY, I KNOW WHAT I'LL DO TODAY. GONNA PACK MOM OFF LIKE AN OLD DOG!"

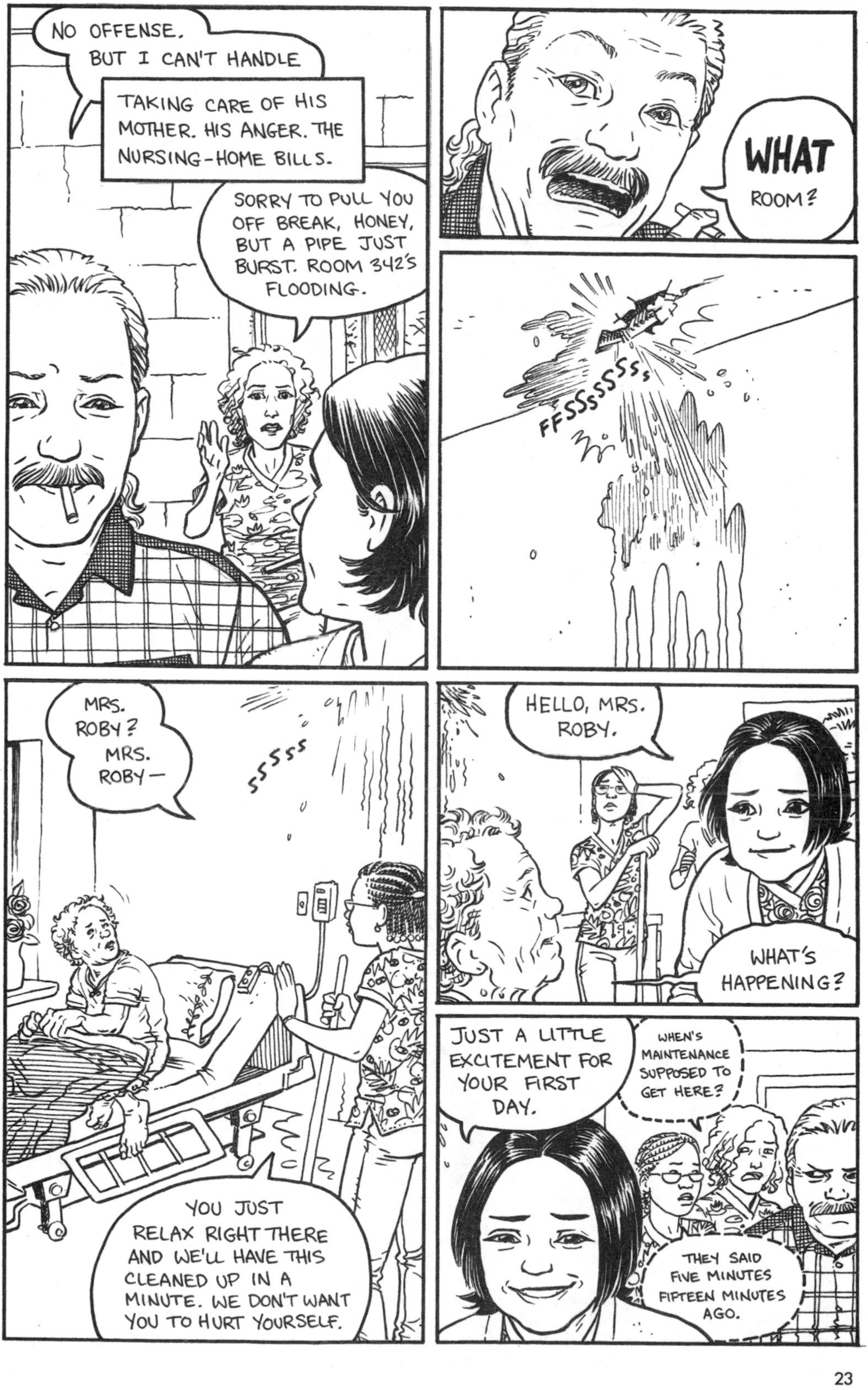
NO OFFENSE. BUT I CAN'T HANDLE
TAKING CARE OF HIS MOTHER. HIS ANGER. THE NURSING-HOME BILLS.
SORRY TO PULL YOU OFF BREAK, HONEY, BUT A PIPE JUST BURST. ROOM 342'S FLOODING.
WHAT ROOM?
FFSSSSSSSs
MRS. ROBY? MRS. ROBY—
SSSSS
YOU JUST RELAX RIGHT THERE AND WE'LL HAVE THIS CLEANED UP IN A MINUTE. WE DON'T WANT YOU TO HURT YOURSELF.
HELLO, MRS. ROBY.
WHAT'S HAPPENING?
JUST A LITTLE EXCITEMENT FOR YOUR FIRST DAY.
WHEN'S MAINTENANCE SUPPOSED TO GET HERE?
THEY SAID FIVE MINUTES FIFTEEN MINUTES AGO.

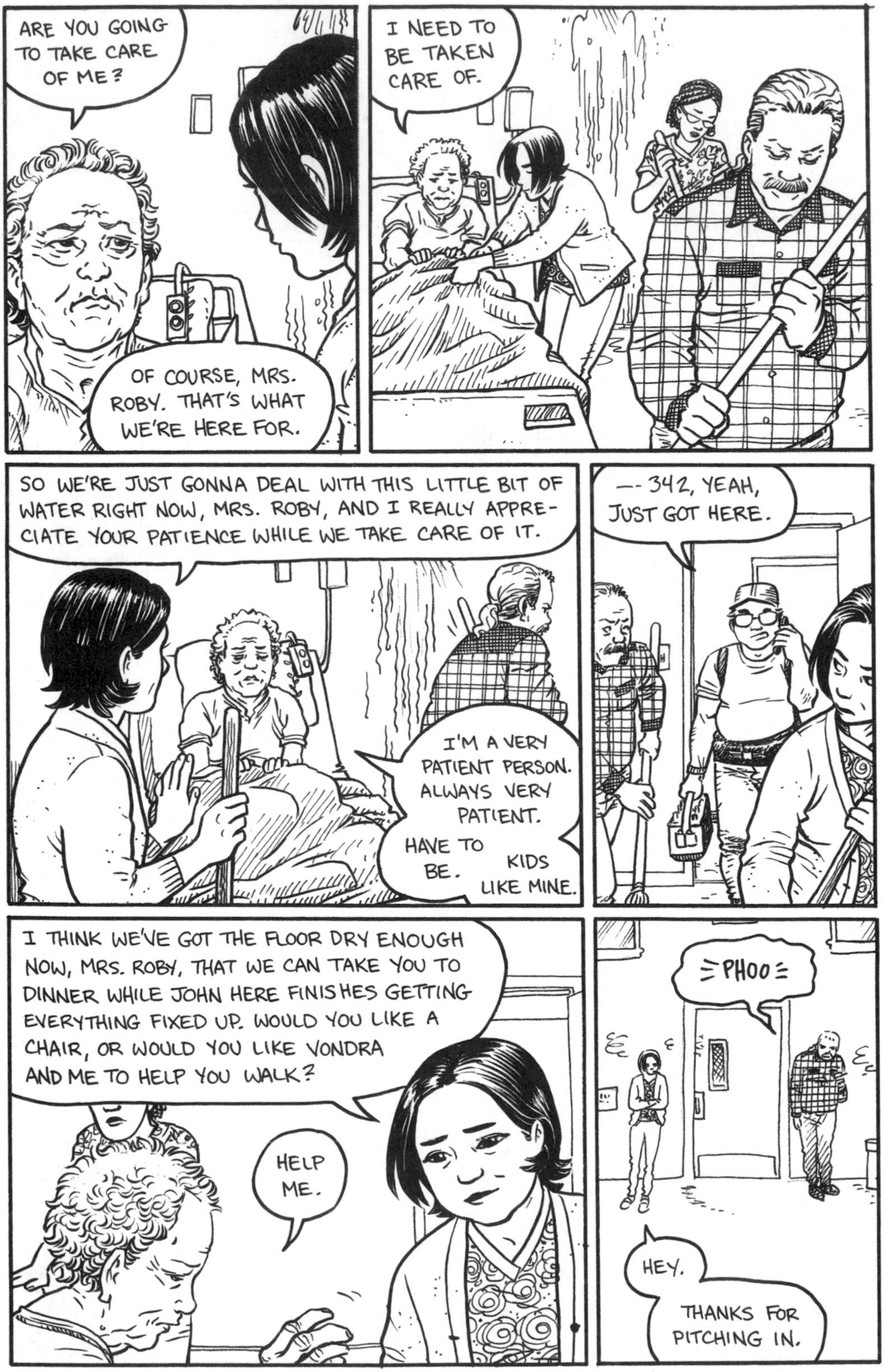
ARE YOU GOING TO TAKE CARE OF ME?
OF COURSE, MRS. ROBY. THAT'S WHAT WE'RE HERE FOR.
I NEED TO BE TAKEN CARE OF.
SO WE'RE JUST GONNA DEAL WITH THIS LITTLE BIT OF WATER RIGHT NOW, MRS. ROBY, AND I REALLY APPRECIATE YOUR PATIENCE WHILE WE TAKE CARE OF IT.
I'M A VERY PATIENT PERSON. ALWAYS VERY PATIENT.
HAVE TO BE. KIDS LIKE MINE.
—-342, YEAH, JUST GOT HERE.
I THINK WE'VE GOT THE FLOOR DRY ENOUGH NOW, MRS. ROBY, THAT WE CAN TAKE YOU TO DINNER WHILE JOHN HERE FINISHES GETTING EVERYTHING FIXED UP. WOULD YOU LIKE A CHAIR, OR WOULD YOU LIKE VONDRA AND ME TO HELP YOU WALK?
HELP ME.
PHOO
HEY.
THANKS FOR PITCHING IN.

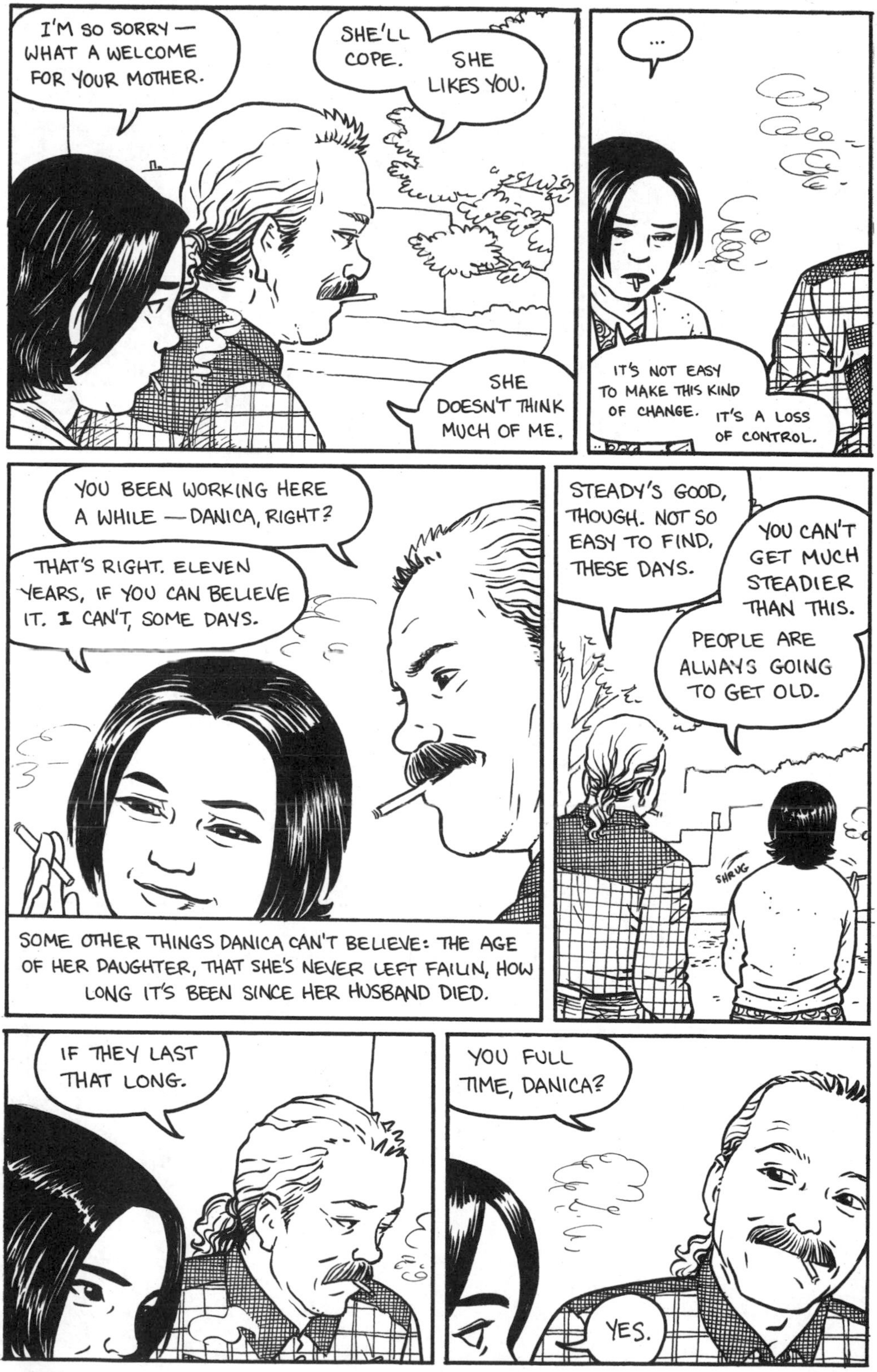
I'M SO SORRY — WHAT A WELCOME FOR YOUR MOTHER.
SHE'LL COPE.
SHE LIKES YOU.
SHE DOESN'T THINK MUCH OF ME.
...
IT'S NOT EASY TO MAKE THIS KIND OF CHANGE.
IT'S A LOSS OF CONTROL.
YOU BEEN WORKING HERE A WHILE — DANICA, RIGHT?
THAT'S RIGHT. ELEVEN YEARS, IF YOU CAN BELIEVE IT. I CAN'T, SOME DAYS.
SOME OTHER THINGS DANICA CAN'T BELIEVE: THE AGE OF HER DAUGHTER, THAT SHE'S NEVER LEFT FAILIN, HOW LONG IT'S BEEN SINCE HER HUSBAND DIED.
STEADY'S GOOD, THOUGH. NOT SO EASY TO FIND, THESE DAYS.
YOU CAN'T GET MUCH STEADIER THAN THIS.
PEOPLE ARE ALWAYS GOING TO GET OLD.
SHRUG
IF THEY LAST THAT LONG.
YOU FULL TIME, DANICA?
YES.

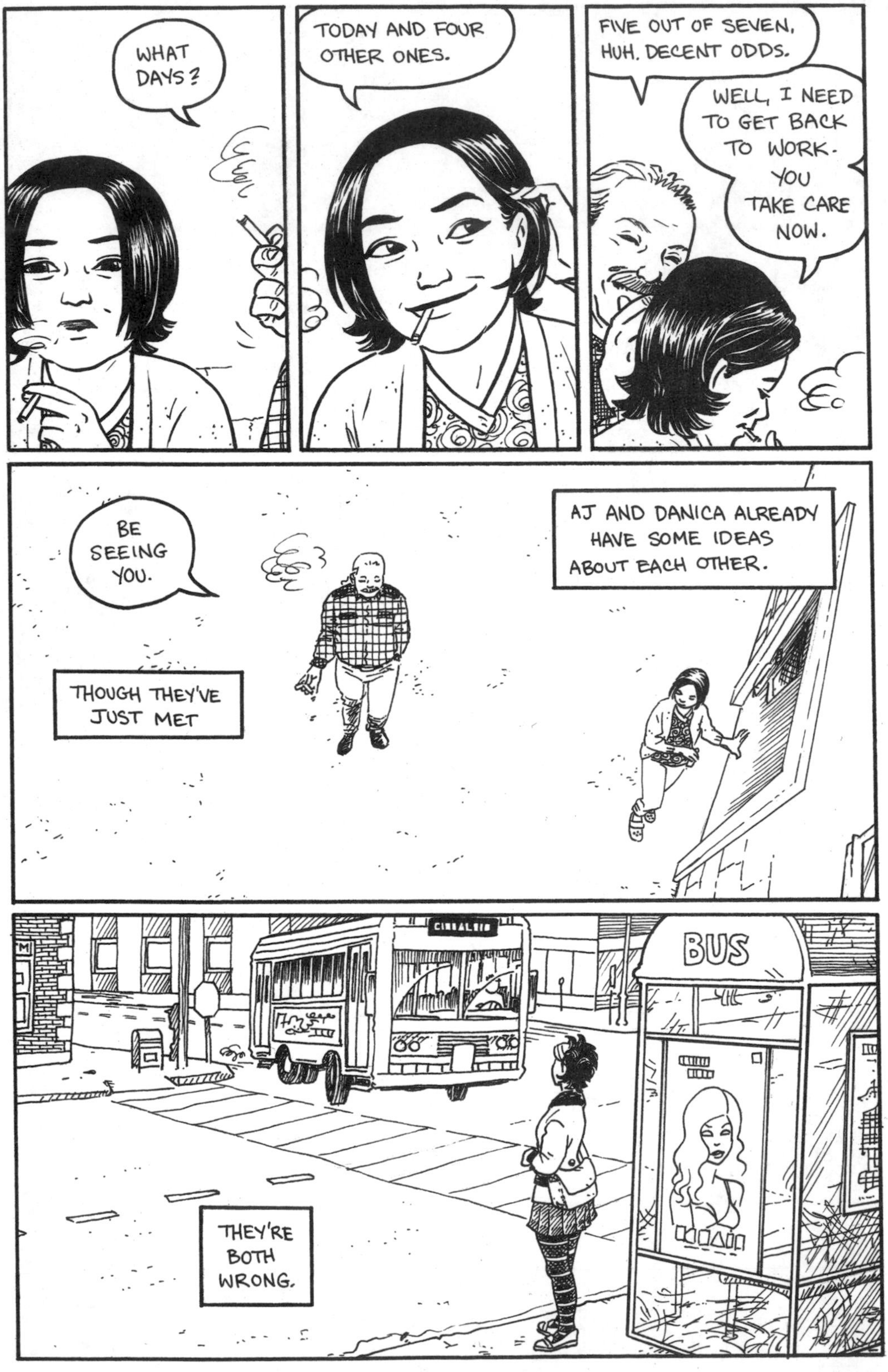
WHAT DAYS?
TODAY AND FOUR OTHER ONES.
FIVE OUT OF SEVEN, HUH. DECENT ODDS.
WELL, I NEED TO GET BACK TO WORK. YOU TAKE CARE NOW.
BE SEEING YOU.
AJ AND DANICA ALREADY HAVE SOME IDEAS ABOUT EACH OTHER.
THOUGH THEY'VE JUST MET
BUS
THEY'RE BOTH WRONG.

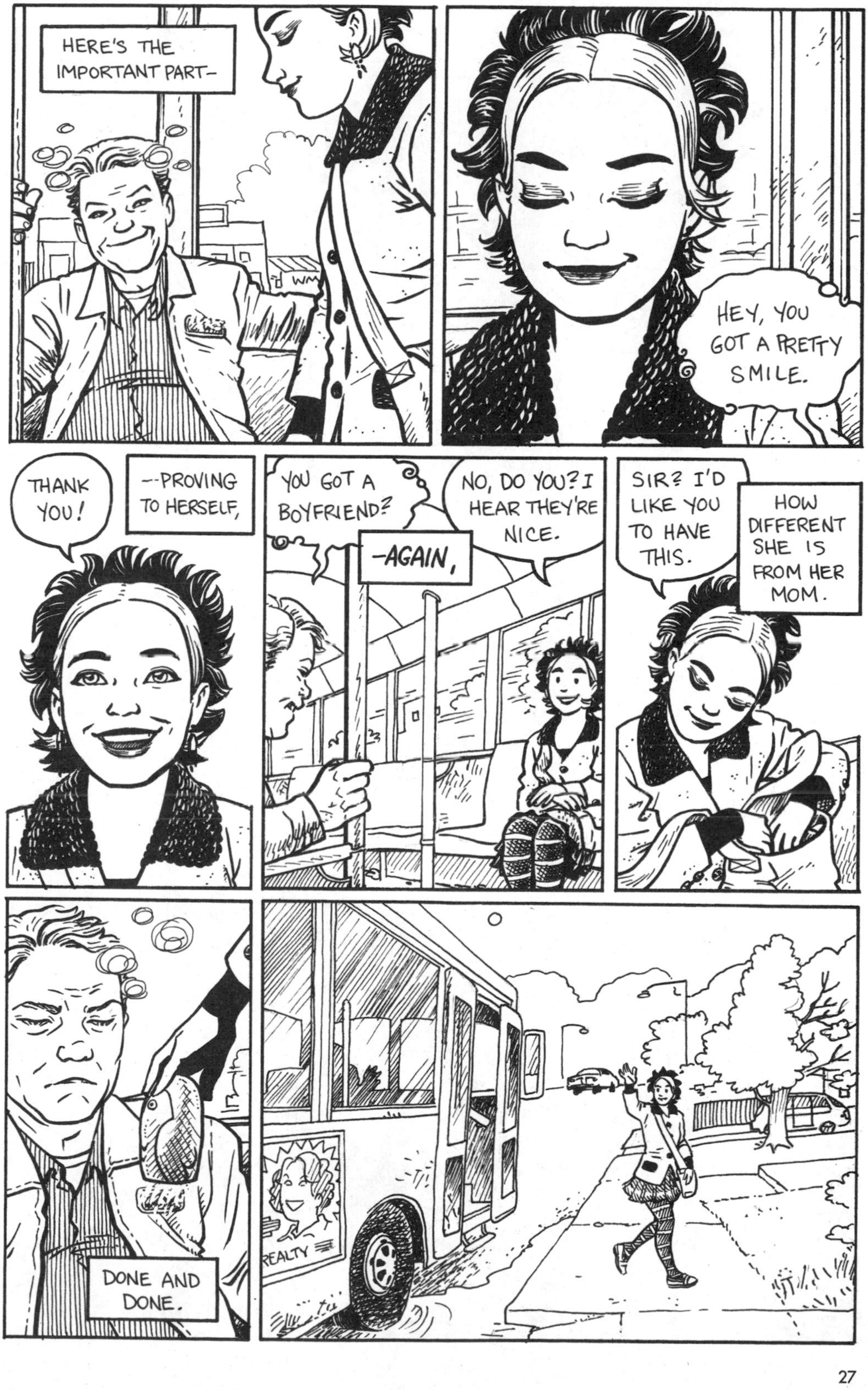
HERE'S THE IMPORTANT PART-
HEY, YOU GOT A PRETTY SMILE.
THANK YOU!
--PROVING TO HERSELF,
YOU GOT A BOYFRIEND?
-AGAIN,
NO, DO YOU? I HEAR THEY'RE NICE.
SIR? I'D LIKE YOU TO HAVE THIS.
HOW DIFFERENT SHE IS FROM HER MOM.
DONE AND DONE.
REALTY

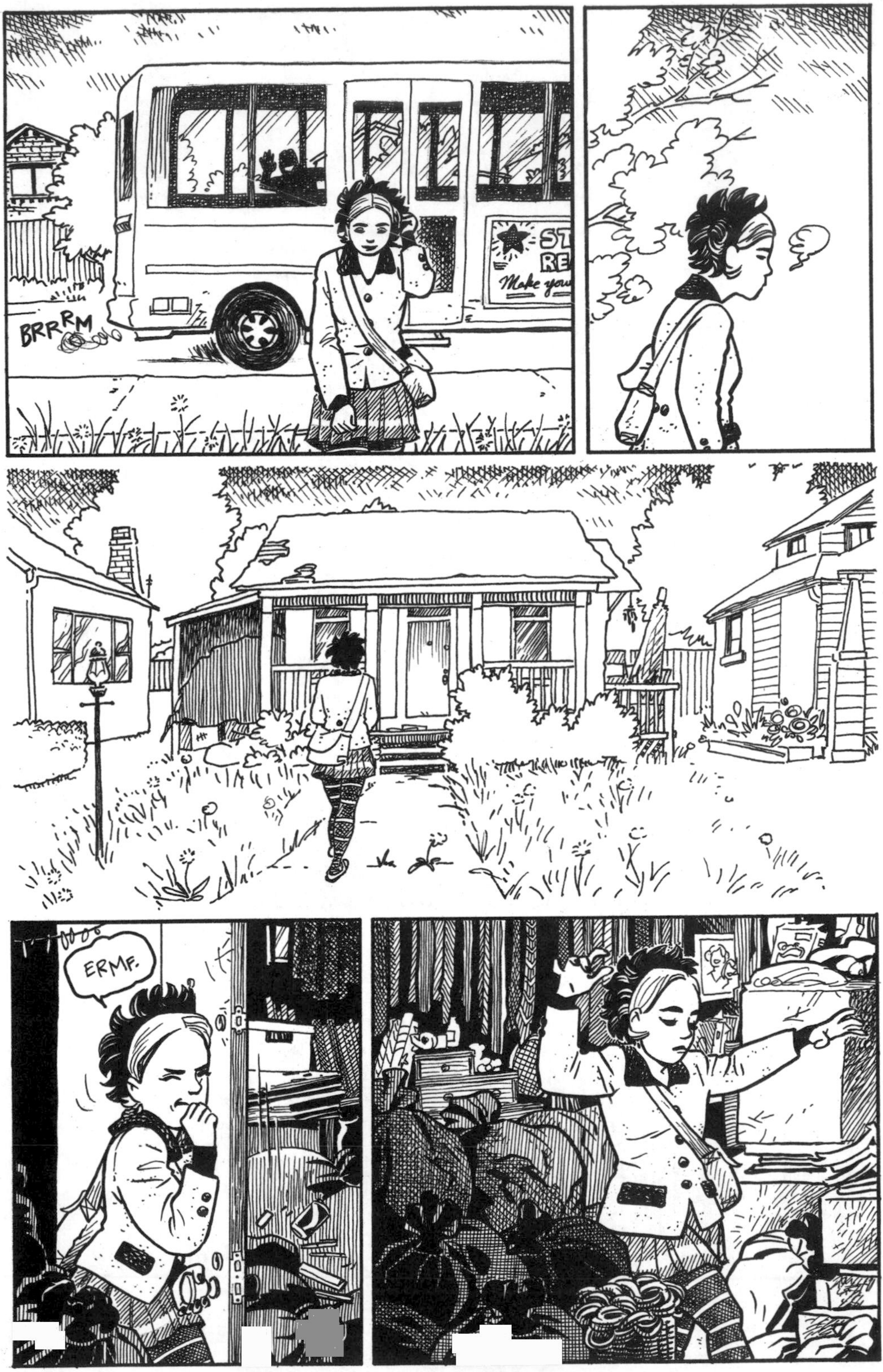
BRRRM
ERMF.

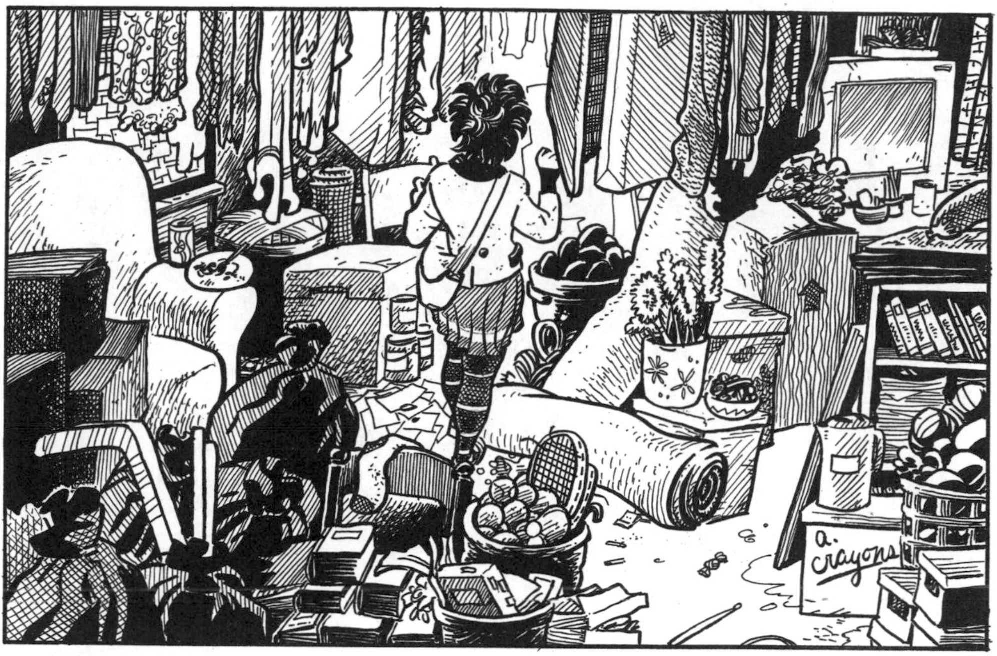

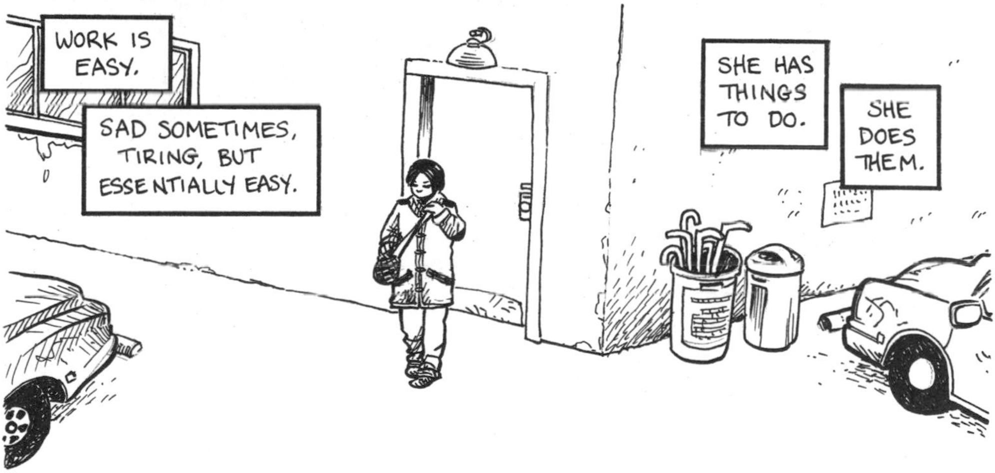
WORK IS EASY.
SAD SOMETIMES, TIRING, BUT ESSENTIALLY EASY.
SHE HAS THINGS TO DO.
SHE DOES THEM.

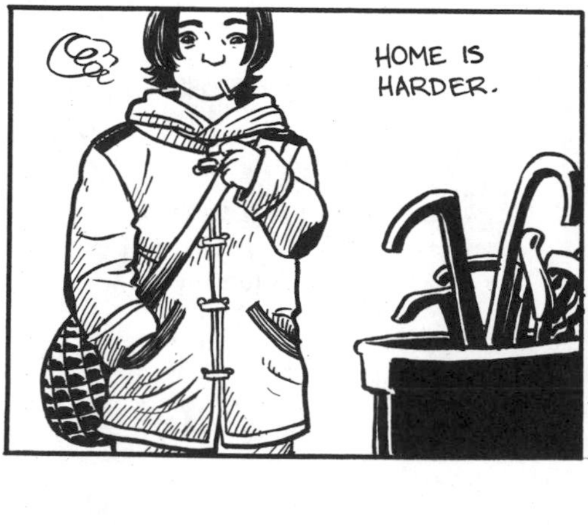
HOME IS HARDER.

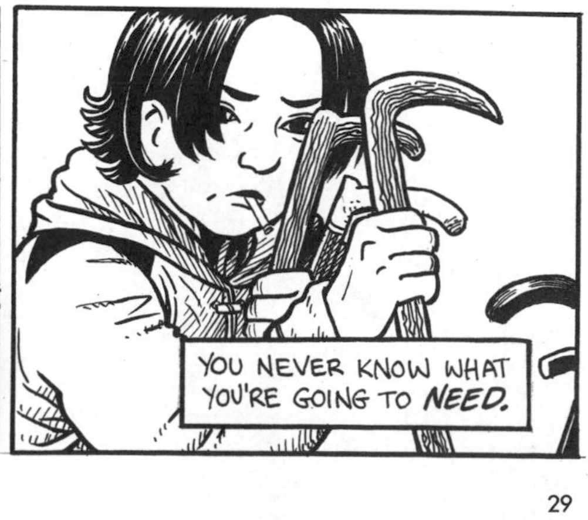
YOU NEVER KNOW WHAT YOU'RE GOING TO NEED.

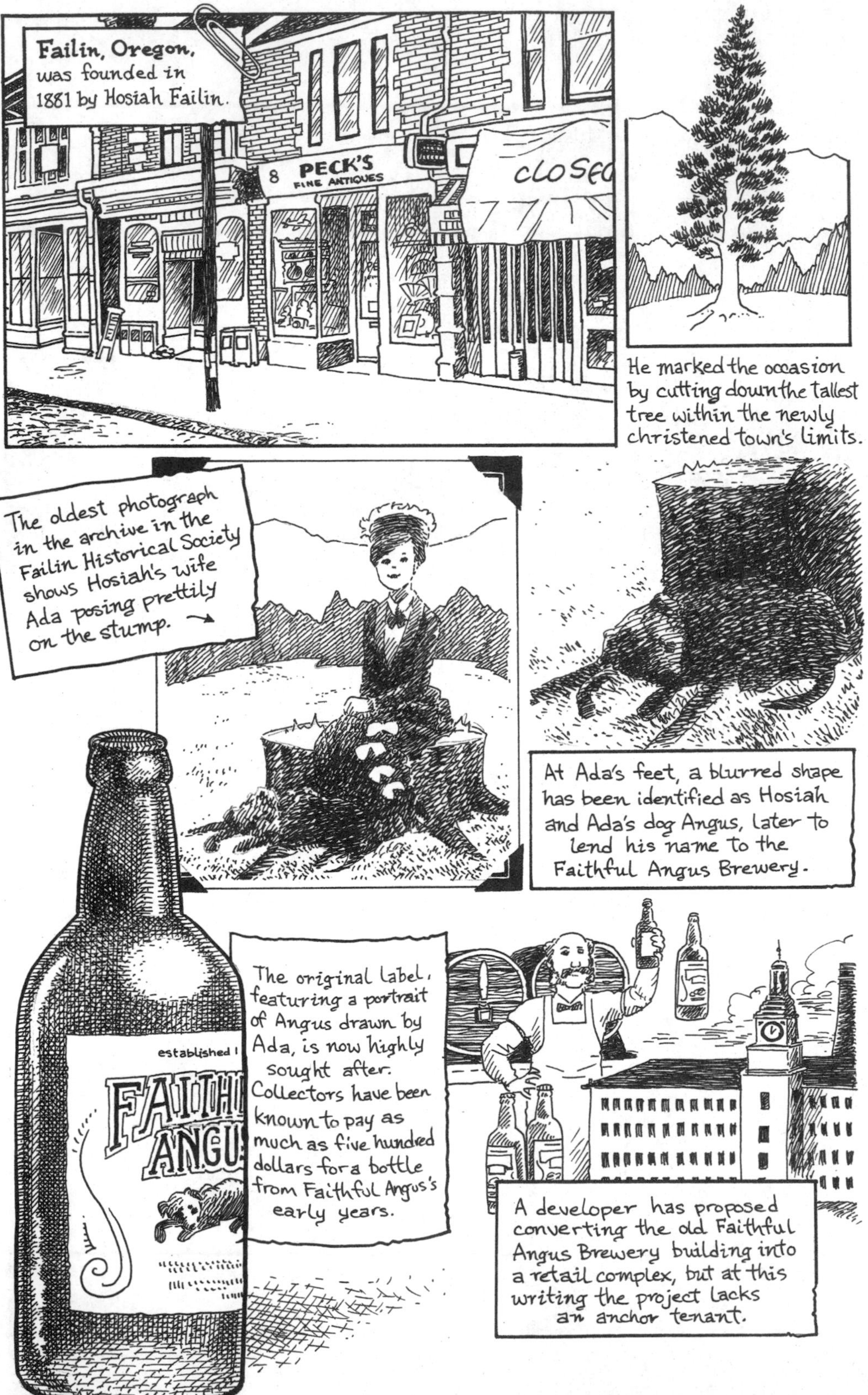
Failin, Oregon, was founded in 1881 by Hosiah Failin.
8 PECK'S FINE ANTIQUES
CLOSED
He marked the occasion by cutting down the tallest tree within the newly christened town's limits.
The oldest photograph in the archive in the Failin Historical Society shows Hosiah's wife Ada posing prettily on the stump.
At Ada's feet, a blurred shape has been identified as Hosiah and Ada's dog Angus, later to lend his name to the Faithful Angus Brewery.
established 1
FAITH
ANGUS
The original label, featuring a portrait of Angus drawn by Ada, is now highly sought after. Collectors have been known to pay as much as five hundred dollars for a bottle from Faithful Angus's early years.
A developer has proposed converting the old Faithful Angus Brewery building into a retail complex, but at this writing the project lacks an anchor tenant.

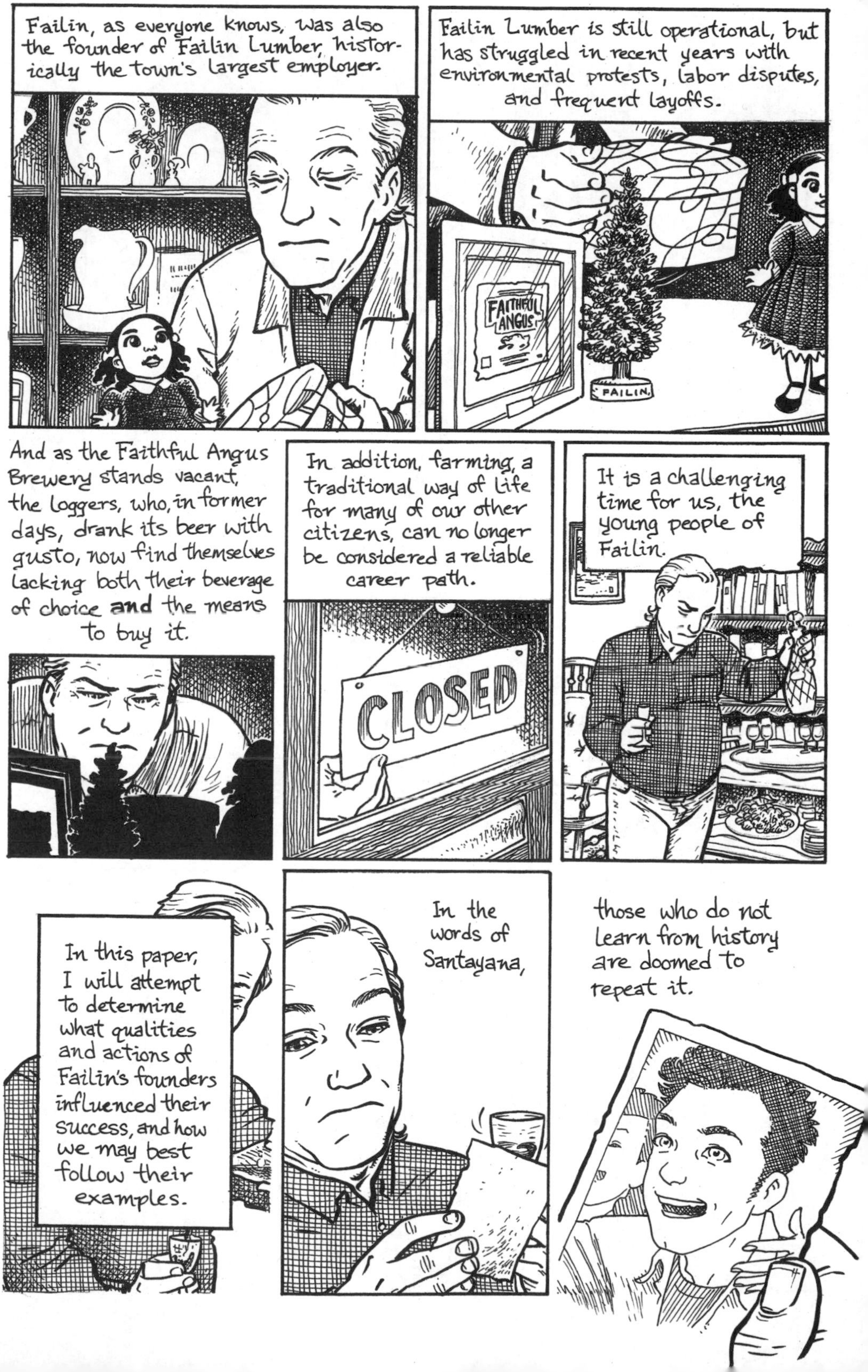
Failin, as everyone knows, was also the founder of Failin Lumber, historically the town's largest employer.
Failin Lumber is still operational, but has struggled in recent years with environmental protests, labor disputes, and frequent layoffs.
FAITHFUL ANGUS
FAILIN
And as the Faithful Angus Brewery stands vacant, the loggers, who, in former days, drank its beer with gusto, now find themselves lacking both their beverage of choice **and** the means to buy it.
In addition, farming, a traditional way of life for many of our other citizens, can no longer be considered a reliable career path.
CLOSED
It is a challenging time for us, the young people of Failin.
In this paper, I will attempt to determine what qualities and actions of Failin's founders influenced their success, and how we may best follow their examples.
In the words of Santayana,
those who do not learn from history are doomed to repeat it.

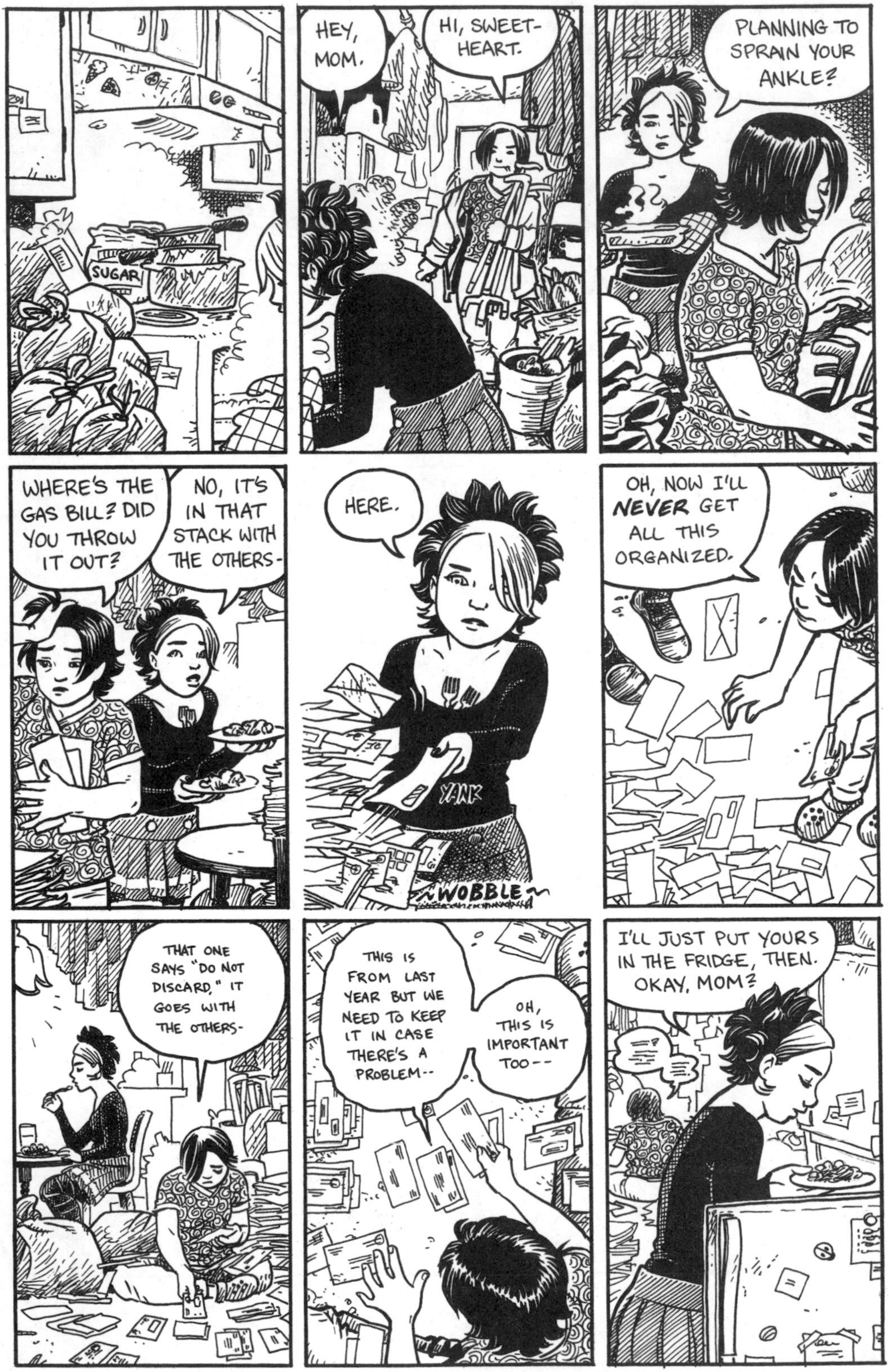
SUGAR
HEY, MOM.
HI, SWEET-HEART.
PLANNING TO SPRAIN YOUR ANKLE?
WHERE'S THE GAS BILL? DID YOU THROW IT OUT?
NO, IT'S IN THAT STACK WITH THE OTHERS-
HERE.
YANK
WOBBLE
OH, NOW I'LL NEVER GET ALL THIS ORGANIZED.
THAT ONE SAYS "DO NOT DISCARD," IT GOES WITH THE OTHERS-
THIS IS FROM LAST YEAR BUT WE NEED TO KEEP IT IN CASE THERE'S A PROBLEM--
OH, THIS IS IMPORTANT TOO--
I'LL JUST PUT YOURS IN THE FRIDGE, THEN. OKAY, MOM?

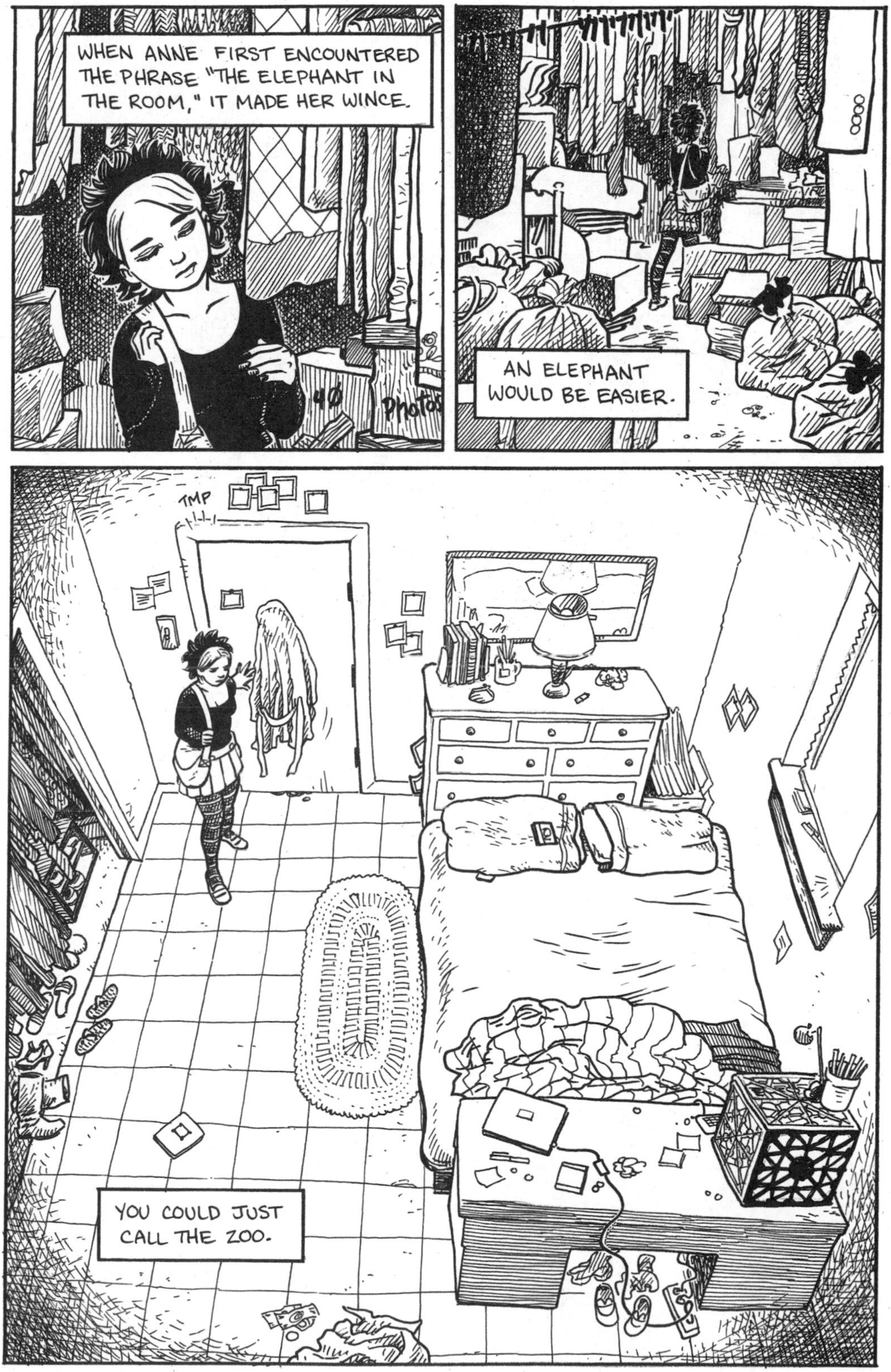
WHEN ANNE FIRST ENCOUNTERED THE PHRASE "THE ELEPHANT IN THE ROOM," IT MADE HER WINCE.
40
PHOTOS
AN ELEPHANT WOULD BE EASIER.
TMP
YOU COULD JUST CALL THE ZOO.

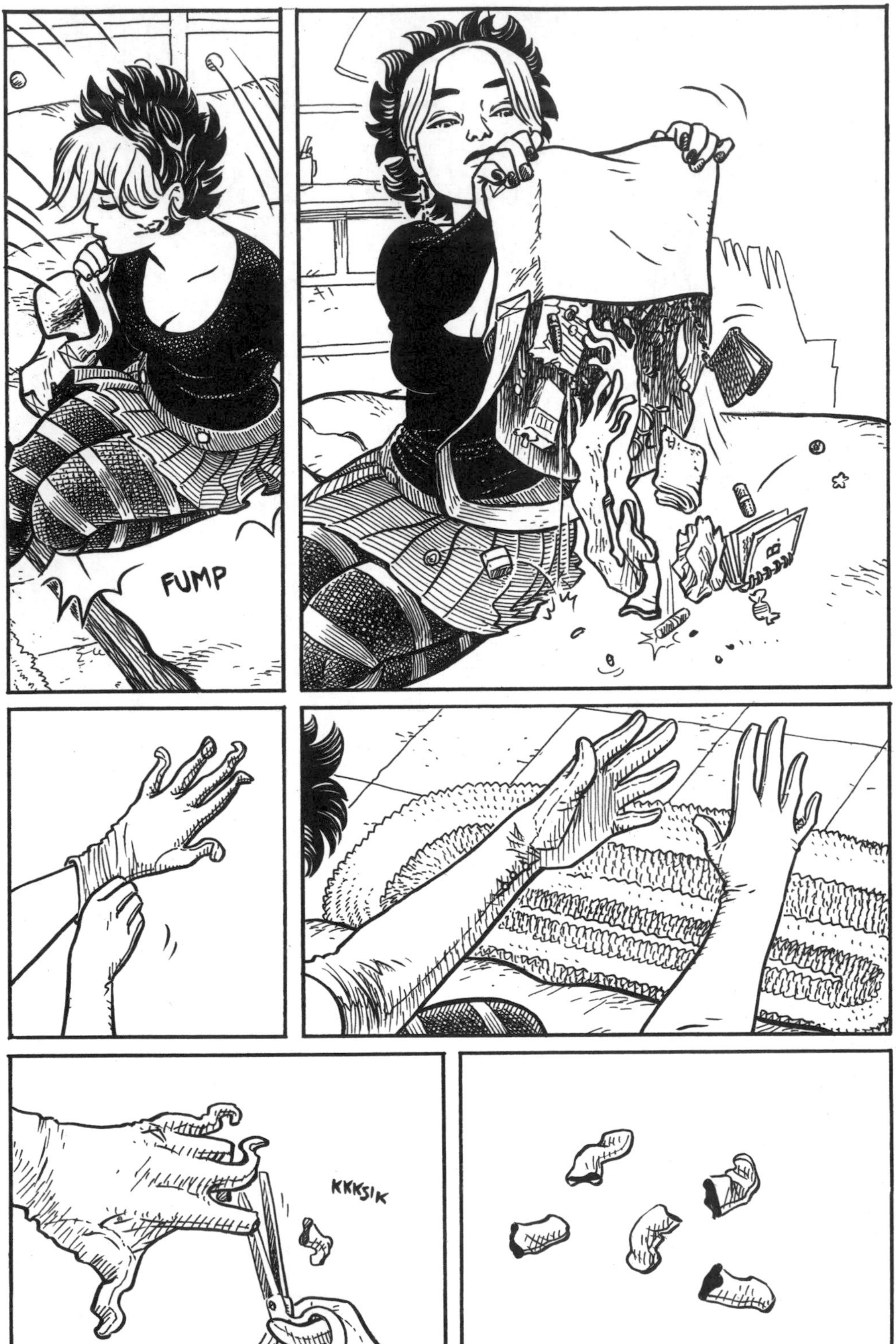
FUMP
KKKSIK

THIS PRIVATE CLUB
(SO DESIGNATED BECAUSE THAT
ENABLES THEM TO GET AROUND
OREGON'S SMOKING BAN)

IS THE FAVORED DESTINATION OF FAILIN'S
MACHINISTS' LOCAL, INCLUDING BOTH THE
EMPLOYED AND THE UNEMPLOYED MEMBERS.

TONIGHT AJ'S HERE
WITH BOB, HIS FORMER COWORKER
AND FREQUENT DRINKING COMPANION.

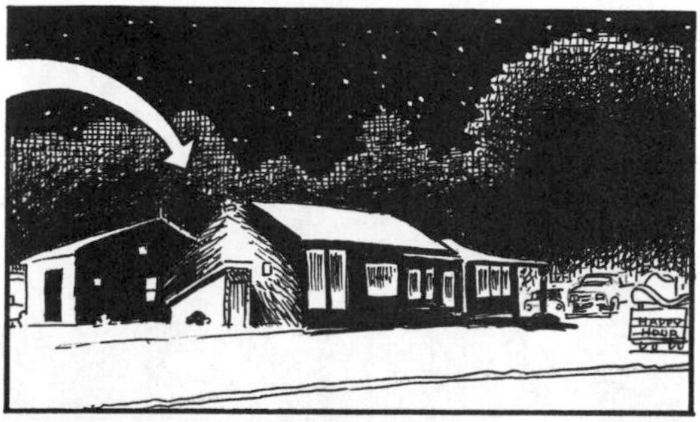

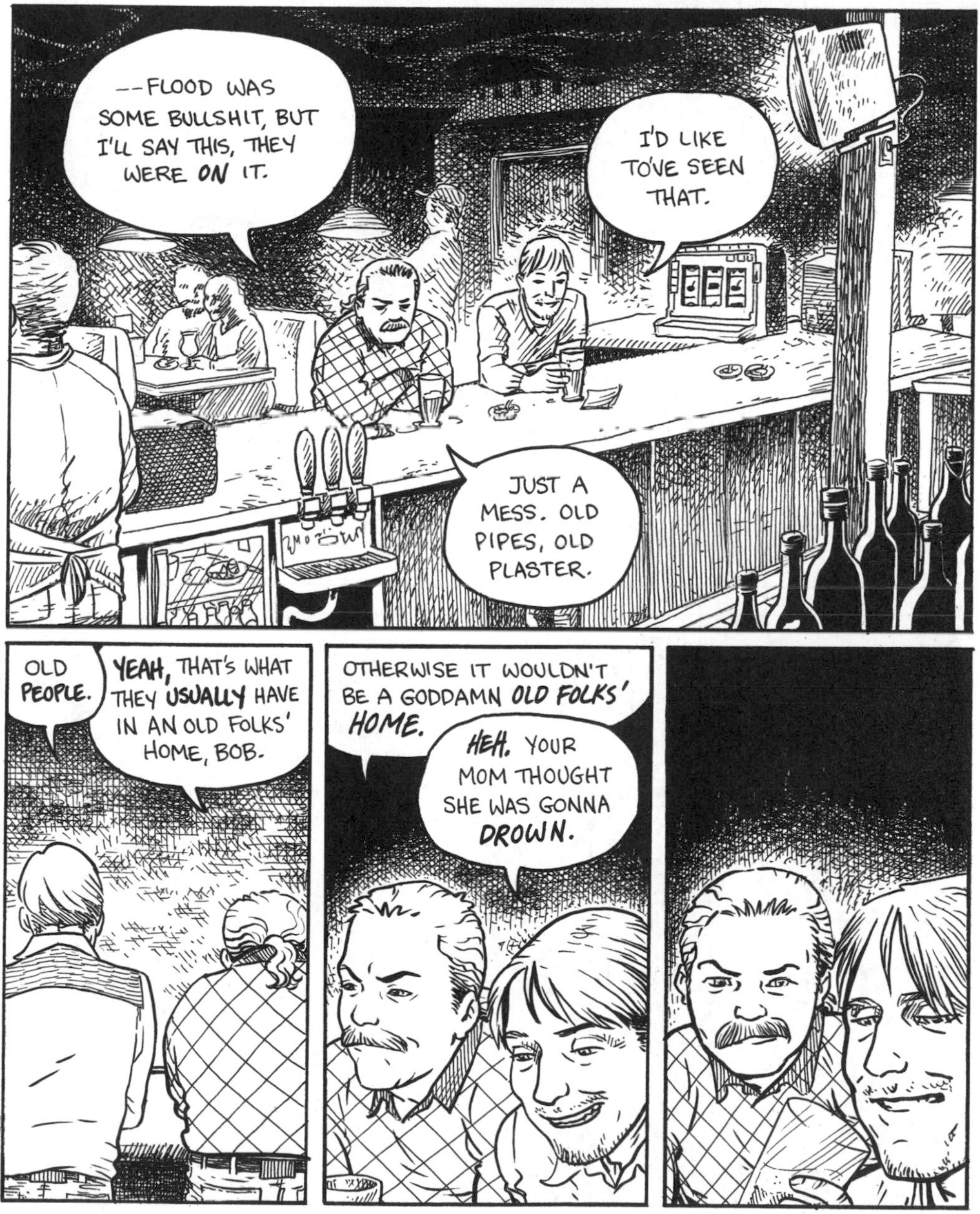
--FLOOD WAS SOME BULLSHIT, BUT I'LL SAY THIS, THEY WERE ON IT.
I'D LIKE TO'VE SEEN THAT.
JUST A MESS. OLD PIPES, OLD PLASTER.
OLD PEOPLE.
YEAH, THAT'S WHAT THEY USUALLY HAVE IN AN OLD FOLKS' HOME, BOB.
OTHERWISE IT WOULDN'T BE A GODDAMN OLD FOLKS' HOME.
HEH. YOUR MOM THOUGHT SHE WAS GONNA DROWN.

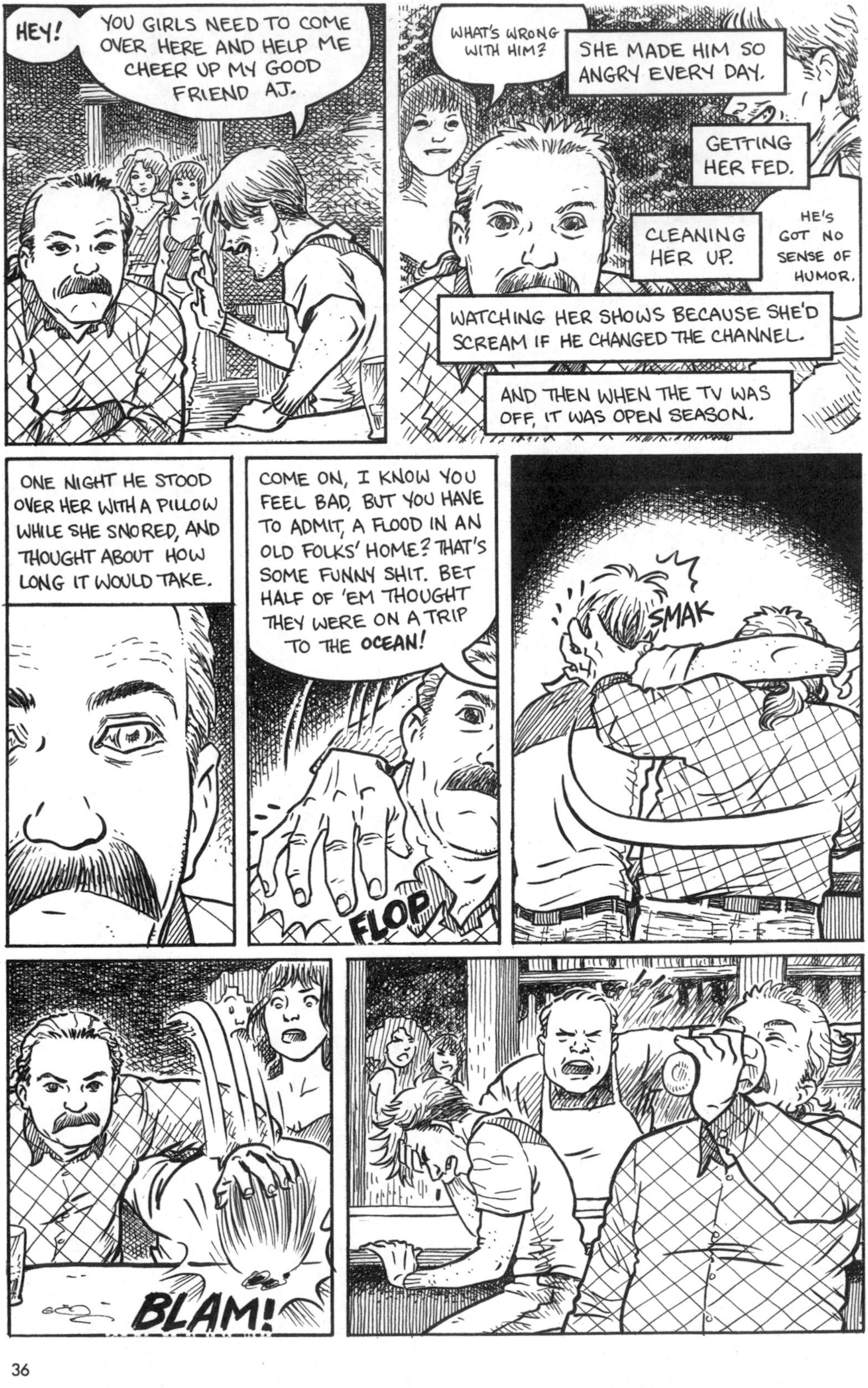
HEY!
YOU GIRLS NEED TO COME OVER HERE AND HELP ME CHEER UP MY GOOD FRIEND AJ.
WHAT'S WRONG WITH HIM?
SHE MADE HIM SO ANGRY EVERY DAY.
GETTING HER FED.
CLEANING HER UP.
HE'S GOT NO SENSE OF HUMOR.
WATCHING HER SHOWS BECAUSE SHE'D SCREAM IF HE CHANGED THE CHANNEL.
AND THEN WHEN THE TV WAS OFF, IT WAS OPEN SEASON.
ONE NIGHT HE STOOD OVER HER WITH A PILLOW WHILE SHE SNORED, AND THOUGHT ABOUT HOW LONG IT WOULD TAKE.
COME ON, I KNOW YOU FEEL BAD, BUT YOU HAVE TO ADMIT, A FLOOD IN AN OLD FOLKS' HOME? THAT'S SOME FUNNY SHIT. BET HALF OF 'EM THOUGHT THEY WERE ON A TRIP TO THE OCEAN!
FLOP
SMAK
BLAM!

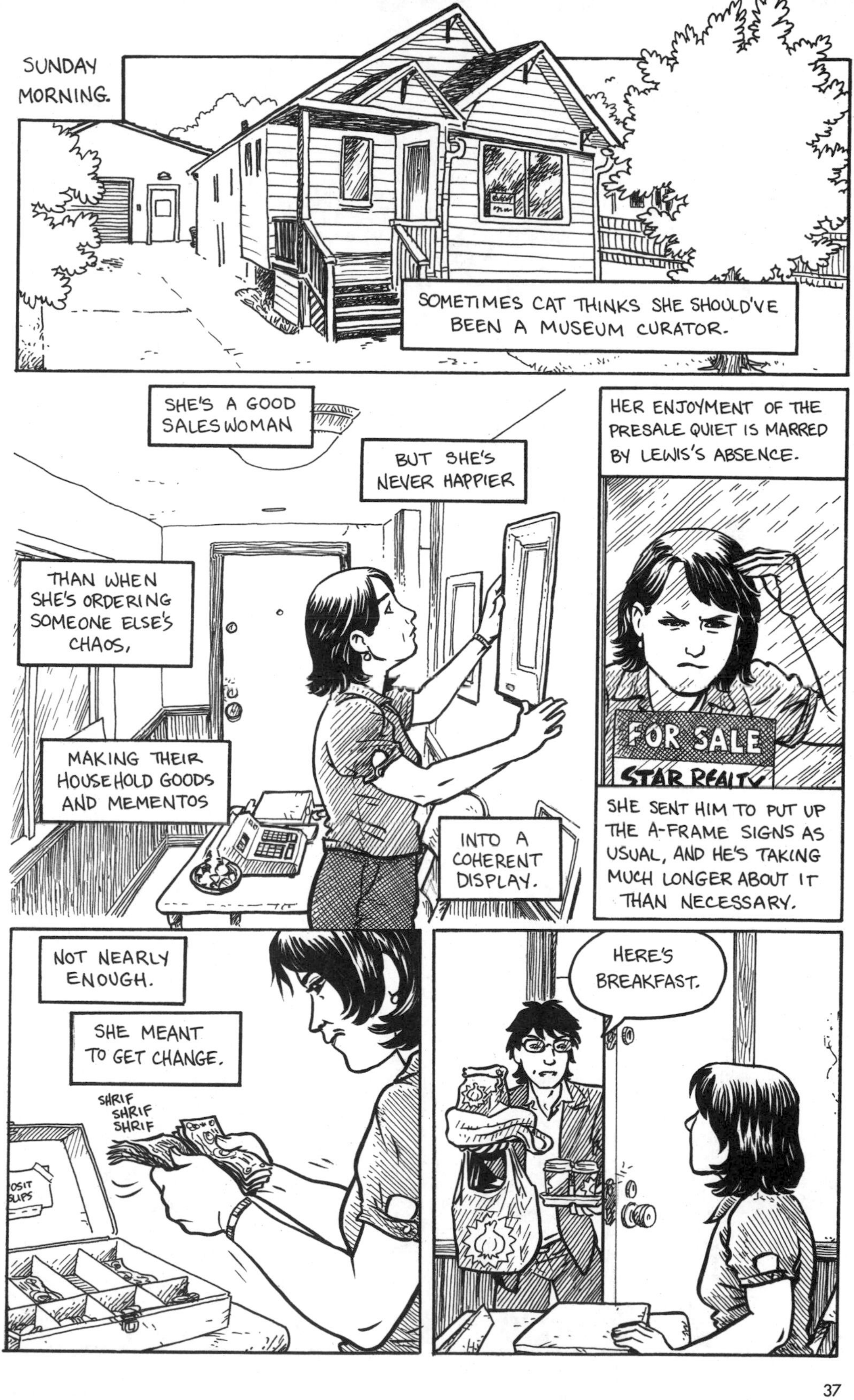
SUNDAY MORNING.
SOMETIMES CAT THINKS SHE SHOULD'VE BEEN A MUSEUM CURATOR.
SHE'S A GOOD SALESWOMAN
BUT SHE'S NEVER HAPPIER
THAN WHEN SHE'S ORDERING SOMEONE ELSE'S CHAOS,
MAKING THEIR HOUSEHOLD GOODS AND MEMENTOS
INTO A COHERENT DISPLAY.
HER ENJOYMENT OF THE PRESALE QUIET IS MARRED BY LEWIS'S ABSENCE.
FOR SALE
STAR REALTY
SHE SENT HIM TO PUT UP THE A-FRAME SIGNS AS USUAL, AND HE'S TAKING MUCH LONGER ABOUT IT THAN NECESSARY.
NOT NEARLY ENOUGH.
SHE MEANT TO GET CHANGE.
SHRIF SHRIF SHRIF
HERE'S BREAKFAST.

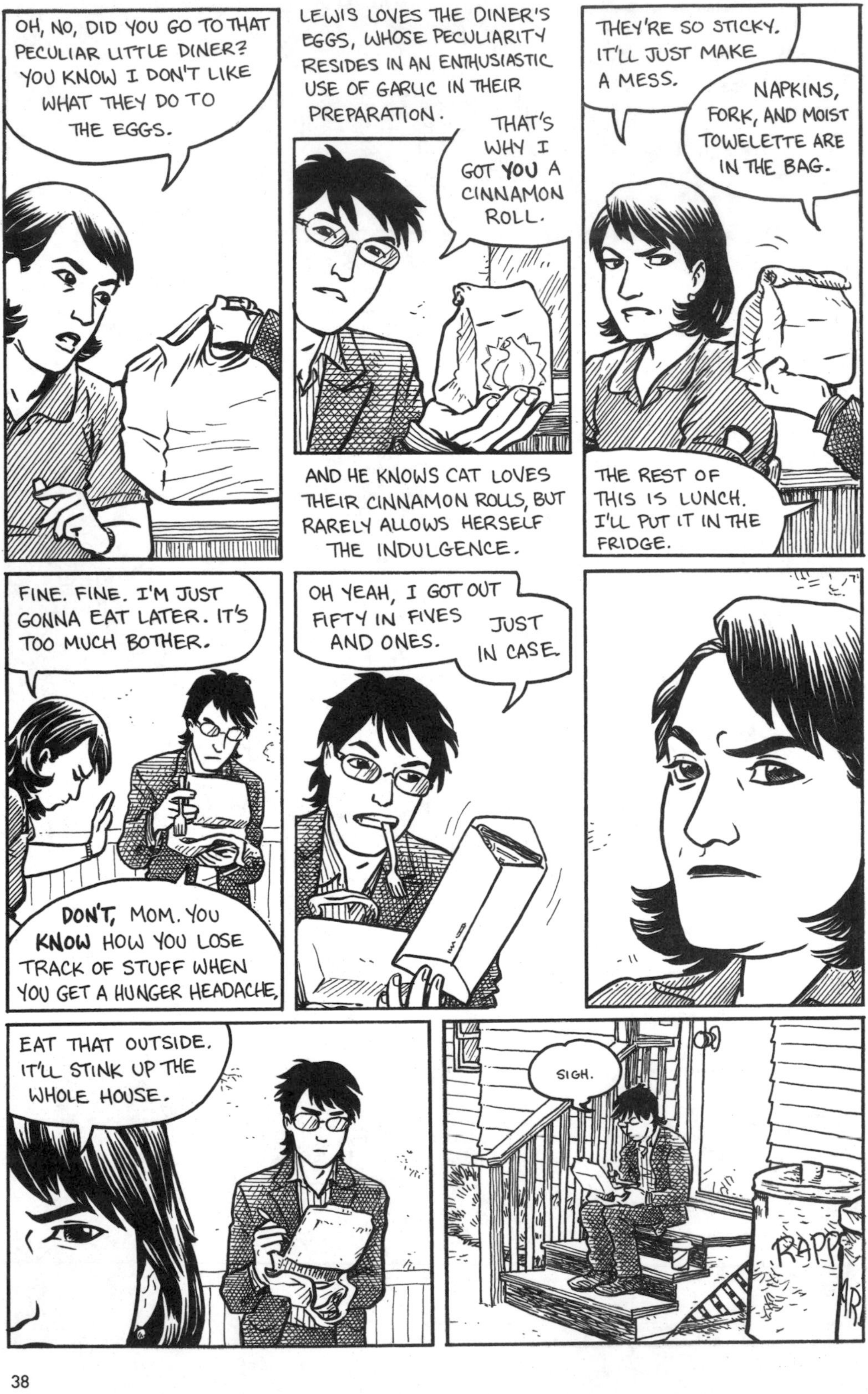
OH, NO, DID YOU GO TO THAT PECULIAR LITTLE DINER? YOU KNOW I DON'T LIKE WHAT THEY DO TO THE EGGS.
LEWIS LOVES THE DINER'S EGGS, WHOSE PECULIARITY RESIDES IN AN ENTHUSIASTIC USE OF GARLIC IN THEIR PREPARATION.
THAT'S WHY I GOT YOU A CINNAMON ROLL.
AND HE KNOWS CAT LOVES THEIR CINNAMON ROLLS, BUT RARELY ALLOWS HERSELF THE INDULGENCE.
THEY'RE SO STICKY. IT'LL JUST MAKE A MESS.
NAPKINS, FORK, AND MOIST TOWELETTE ARE IN THE BAG.
THE REST OF THIS IS LUNCH. I'LL PUT IT IN THE FRIDGE.
FINE. FINE. I'M JUST GONNA EAT LATER. IT'S TOO MUCH BOTHER.
DON'T, MOM. YOU KNOW HOW YOU LOSE TRACK OF STUFF WHEN YOU GET A HUNGER HEADACHE.
OH YEAH, I GOT OUT FIFTY IN FIVES AND ONES.
JUST IN CASE.
EAT THAT OUTSIDE. IT'LL STINK UP THE WHOLE HOUSE.
SIGH.
RAPP

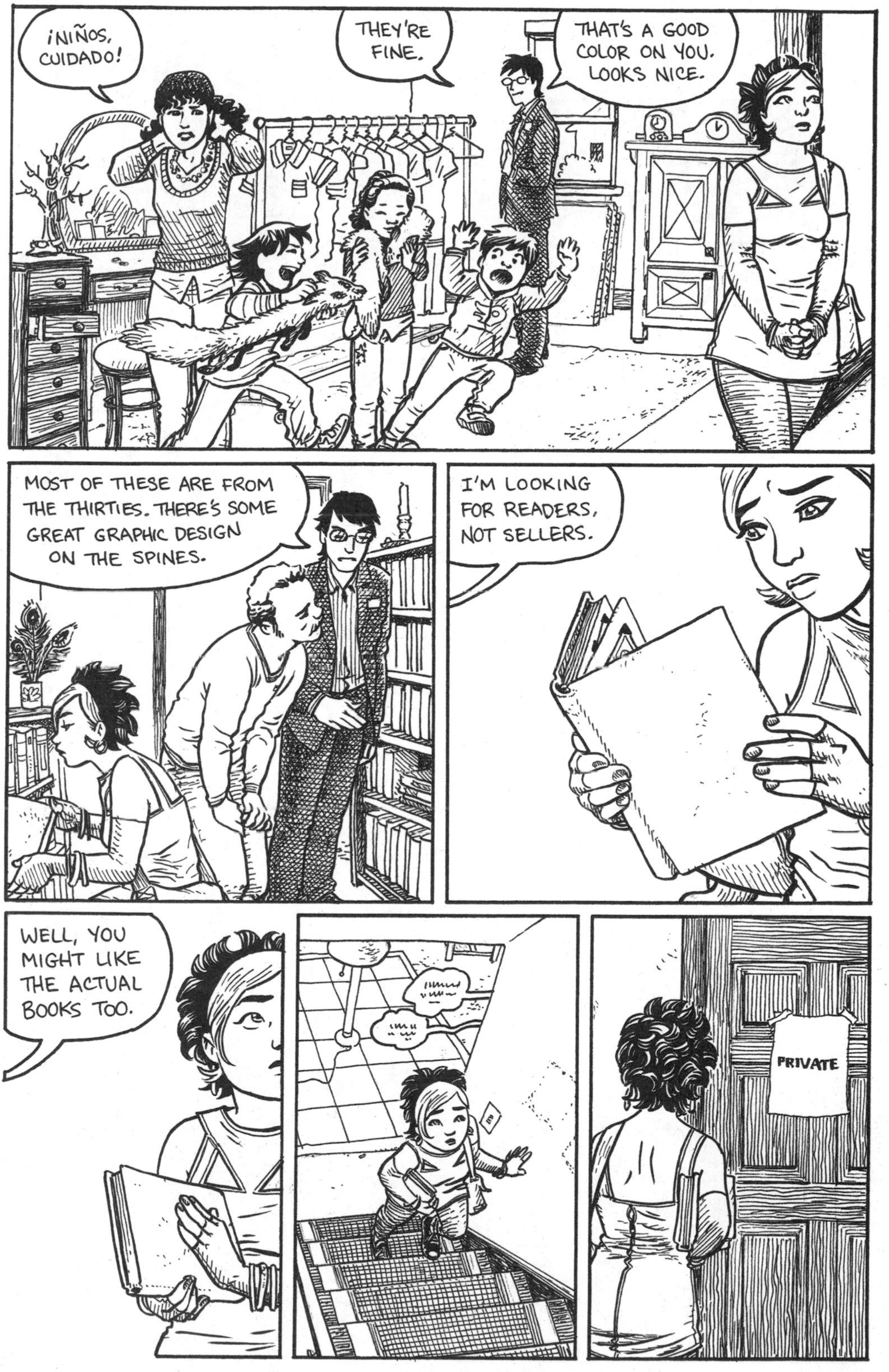
¡NIÑOS, CUIDADO!
THEY'RE FINE.
THAT'S A GOOD COLOR ON YOU. LOOKS NICE.
MOST OF THESE ARE FROM THE THIRTIES. THERE'S SOME GREAT GRAPHIC DESIGN ON THE SPINES.
I'M LOOKING FOR READERS, NOT SELLERS.
WELL, YOU MIGHT LIKE THE ACTUAL BOOKS TOO.
PRIVATE

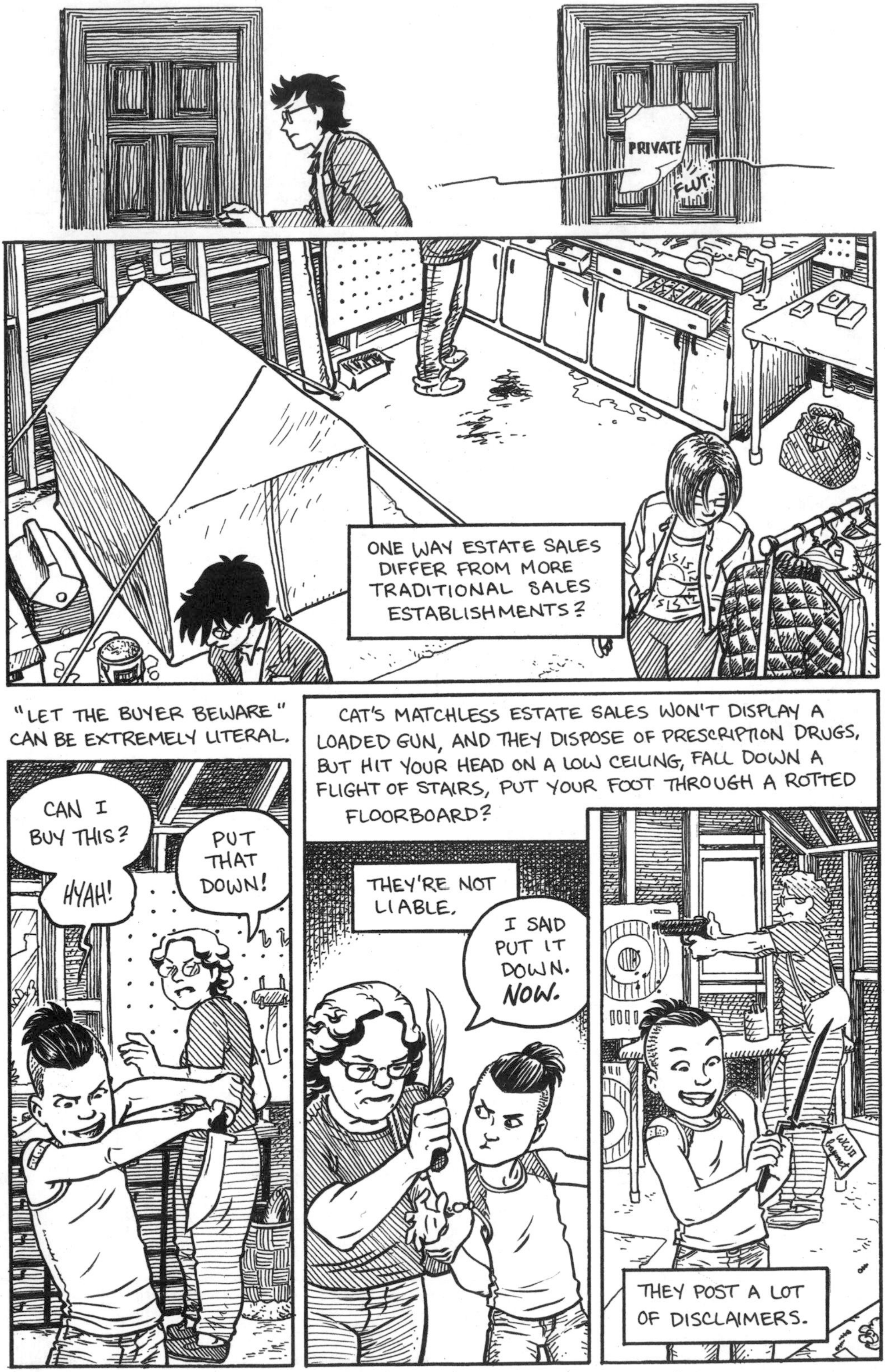
PRIVATE
FLUT
ONE WAY ESTATE SALES DIFFER FROM MORE TRADITIONAL SALES ESTABLISHMENTS?
"LET THE BUYER BEWARE" CAN BE EXTREMELY LITERAL.
CAT'S MATCHLESS ESTATE SALES WON'T DISPLAY A LOADED GUN, AND THEY DISPOSE OF PRESCRIPTION DRUGS, BUT HIT YOUR HEAD ON A LOW CEILING, FALL DOWN A FLIGHT OF STAIRS, PUT YOUR FOOT THROUGH A ROTTED FLOORBOARD?
CAN I BUY THIS?
HYAH!
PUT THAT DOWN!
THEY'RE NOT LIABLE.
I SAID PUT IT DOWN. NOW.
THEY POST A LOT OF DISCLAIMERS.

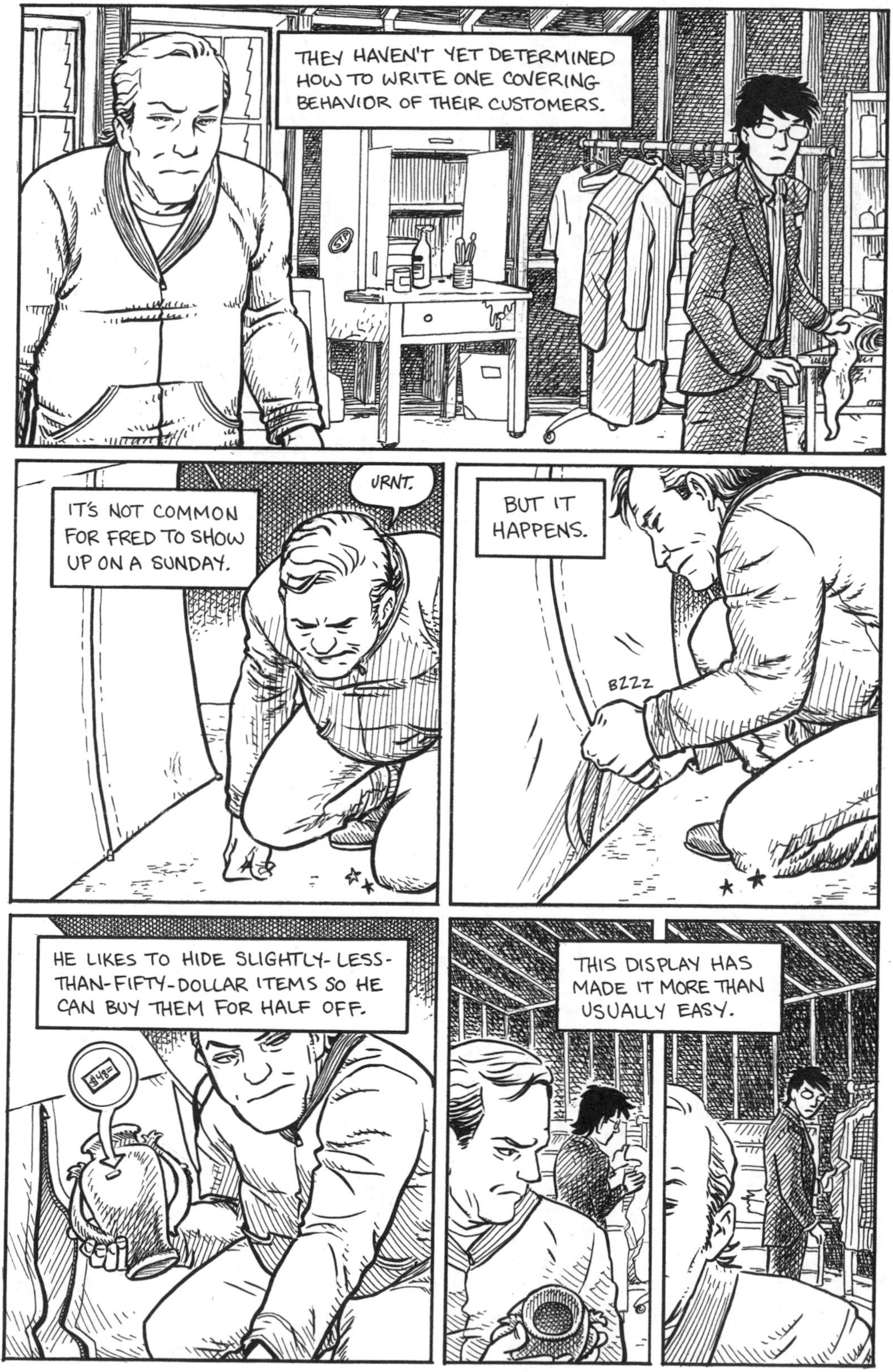
THEY HAVEN'T YET DETERMINED HOW TO WRITE ONE COVERING BEHAVIOR OF THEIR CUSTOMERS.
IT'S NOT COMMON FOR FRED TO SHOW UP ON A SUNDAY.
URNT.
BUT IT HAPPENS.
BZZz
HE LIKES TO HIDE SLIGHTLY-LESS-THAN-FIFTY-DOLLAR ITEMS SO HE CAN BUY THEM FOR HALF OFF.
THIS DISPLAY HAS MADE IT MORE THAN USUALLY EASY.

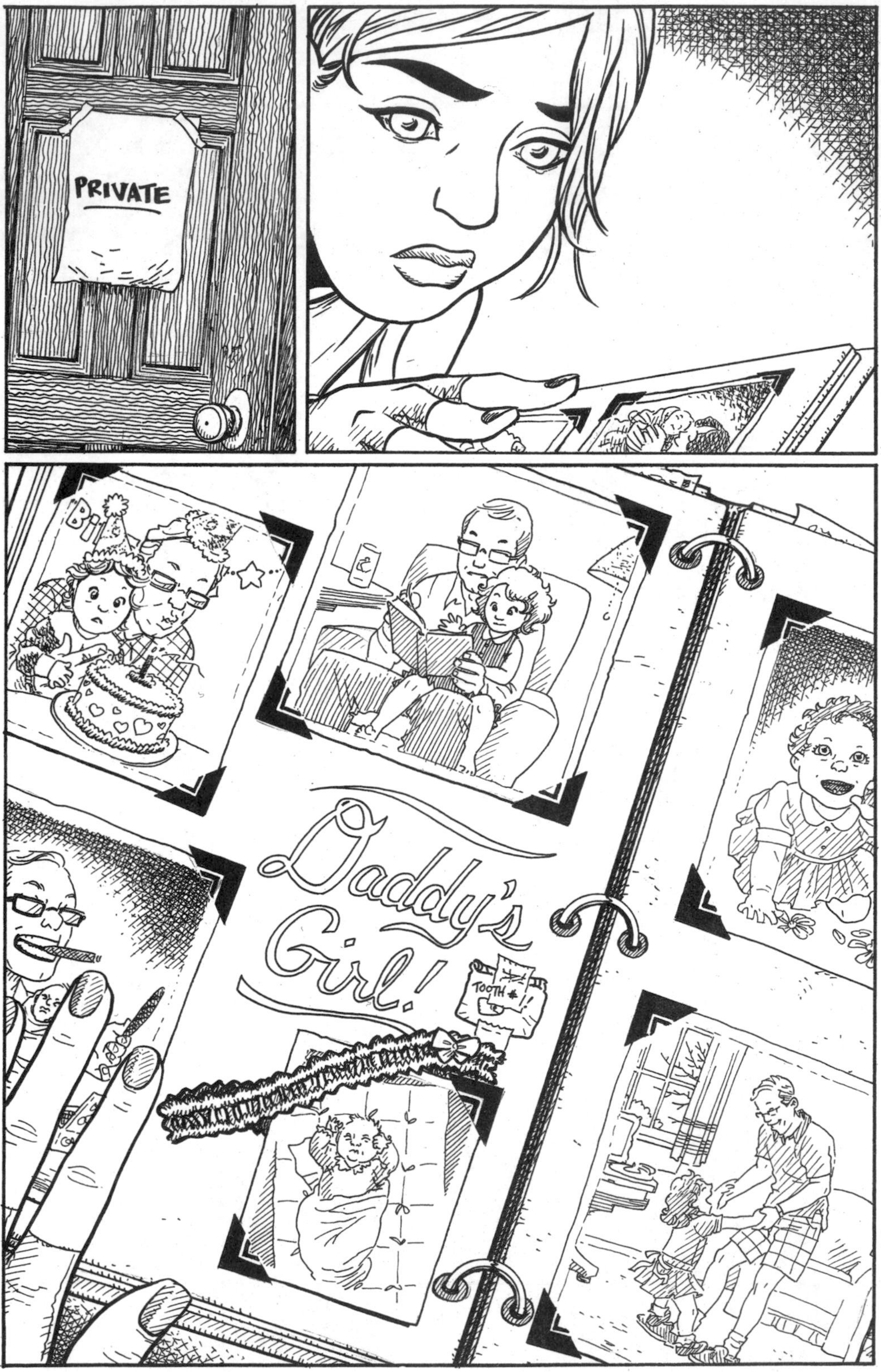
PRIVATE
Daddy's Girl!
TOOTH #

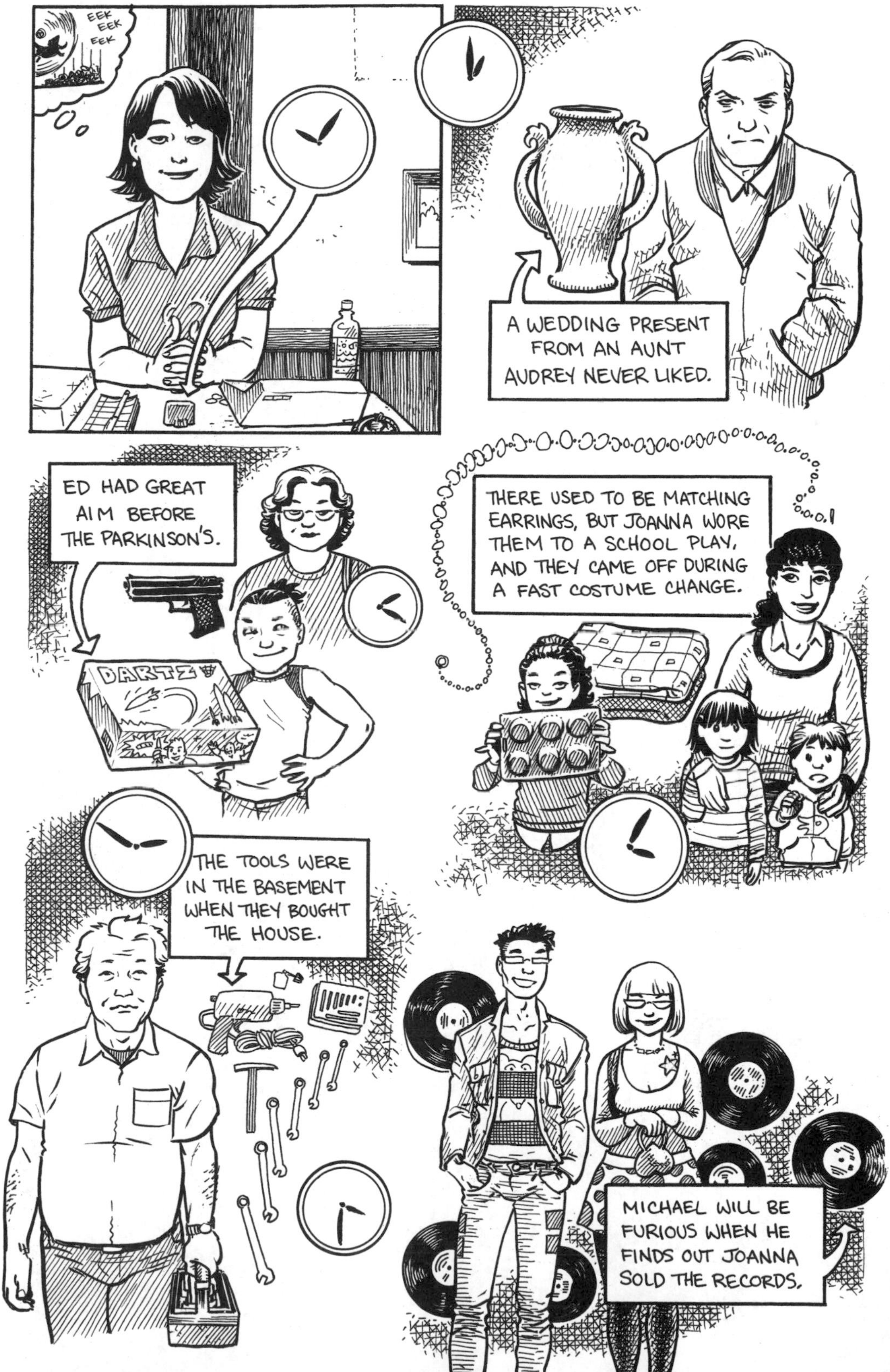
EEK EEK EEK
A WEDDING PRESENT FROM AN AUNT AUDREY NEVER LIKED.
ED HAD GREAT AIM BEFORE THE PARKINSON'S.
DARTZ
THERE USED TO BE MATCHING EARRINGS, BUT JOANNA WORE THEM TO A SCHOOL PLAY, AND THEY CAME OFF DURING A FAST COSTUME CHANGE.
THE TOOLS WERE IN THE BASEMENT WHEN THEY BOUGHT THE HOUSE.
MICHAEL WILL BE FURIOUS WHEN HE FINDS OUT JOANNA SOLD THE RECORDS.

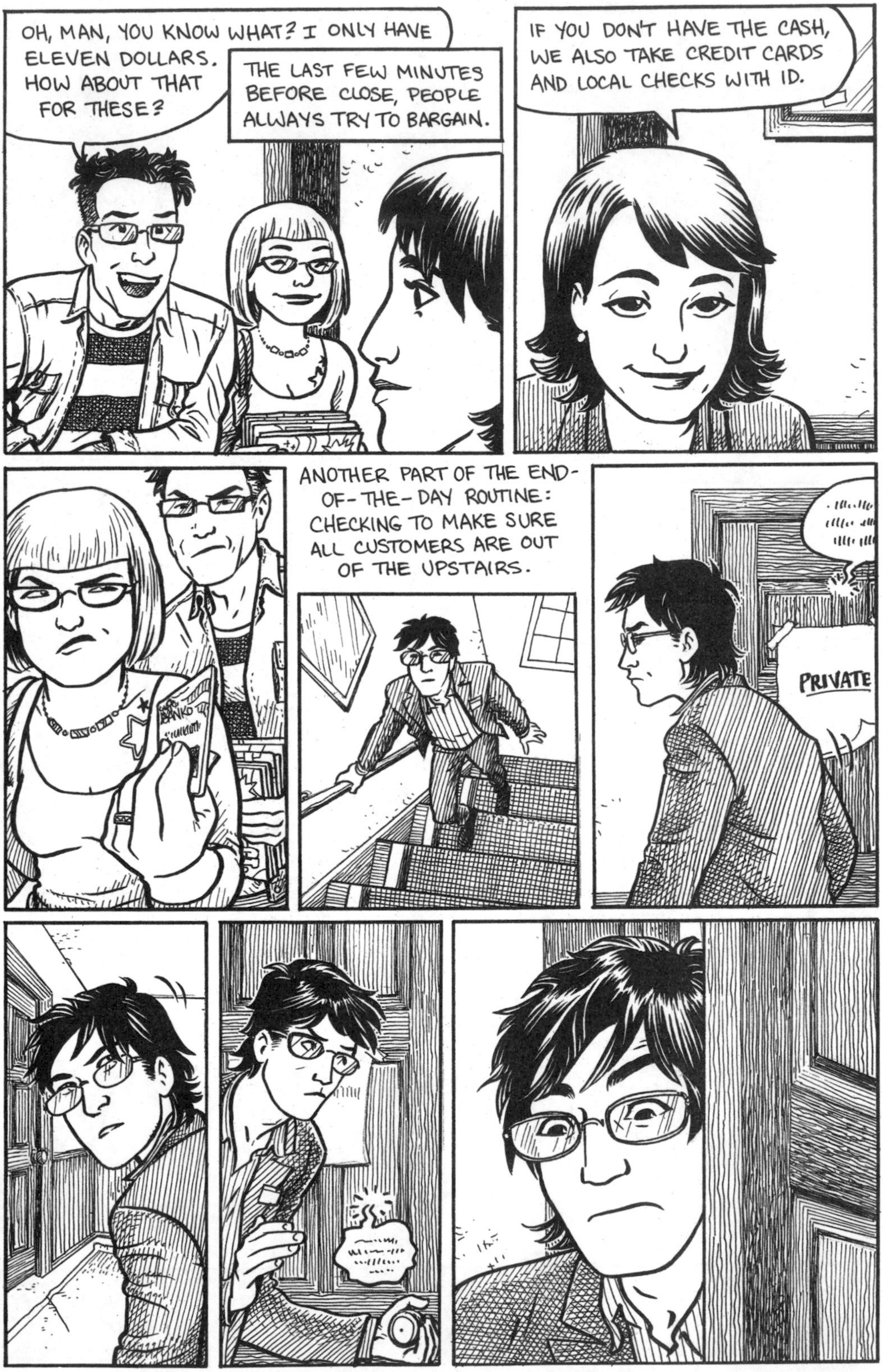
OH, MAN, YOU KNOW WHAT? I ONLY HAVE ELEVEN DOLLARS. HOW ABOUT THAT FOR THESE?
THE LAST FEW MINUTES BEFORE CLOSE, PEOPLE ALWAYS TRY TO BARGAIN.
IF YOU DON'T HAVE THE CASH, WE ALSO TAKE CREDIT CARDS AND LOCAL CHECKS WITH ID.
ANOTHER PART OF THE END-OF-THE-DAY ROUTINE: CHECKING TO MAKE SURE ALL CUSTOMERS ARE OUT OF THE UPSTAIRS.
PRIVATE

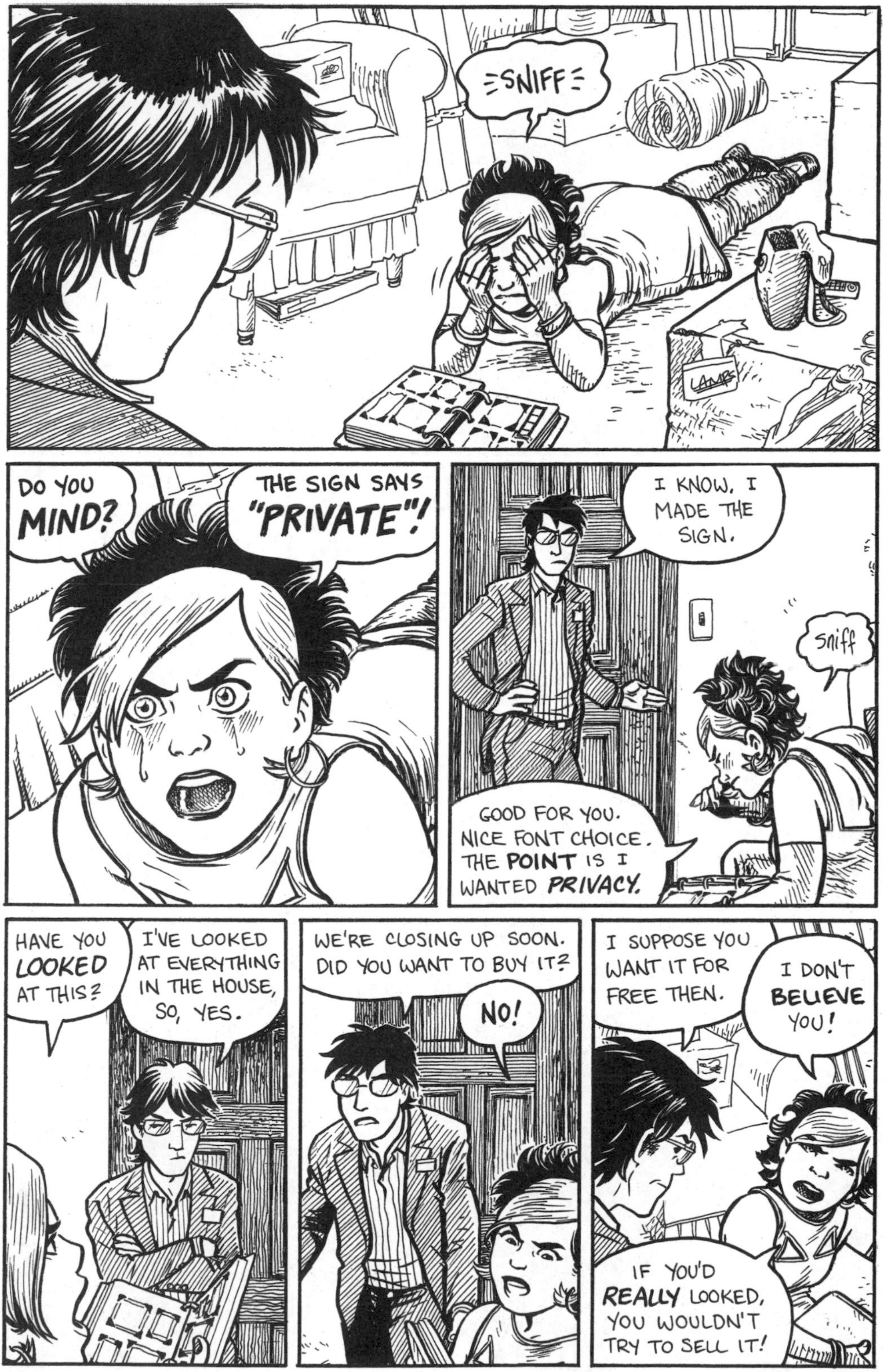
SNIFF
DO YOU MIND?
THE SIGN SAYS "PRIVATE"!
I KNOW, I MADE THE SIGN.
sniff
GOOD FOR YOU. NICE FONT CHOICE. THE POINT IS I WANTED PRIVACY.
HAVE YOU LOOKED AT THIS?
I'VE LOOKED AT EVERYTHING IN THE HOUSE, SO, YES.
WE'RE CLOSING UP SOON. DID YOU WANT TO BUY IT?
NO!
I SUPPOSE YOU WANT IT FOR FREE THEN.
I DON'T BELIEVE YOU!
IF YOU'D REALLY LOOKED, YOU WOULDN'T TRY TO SELL IT!

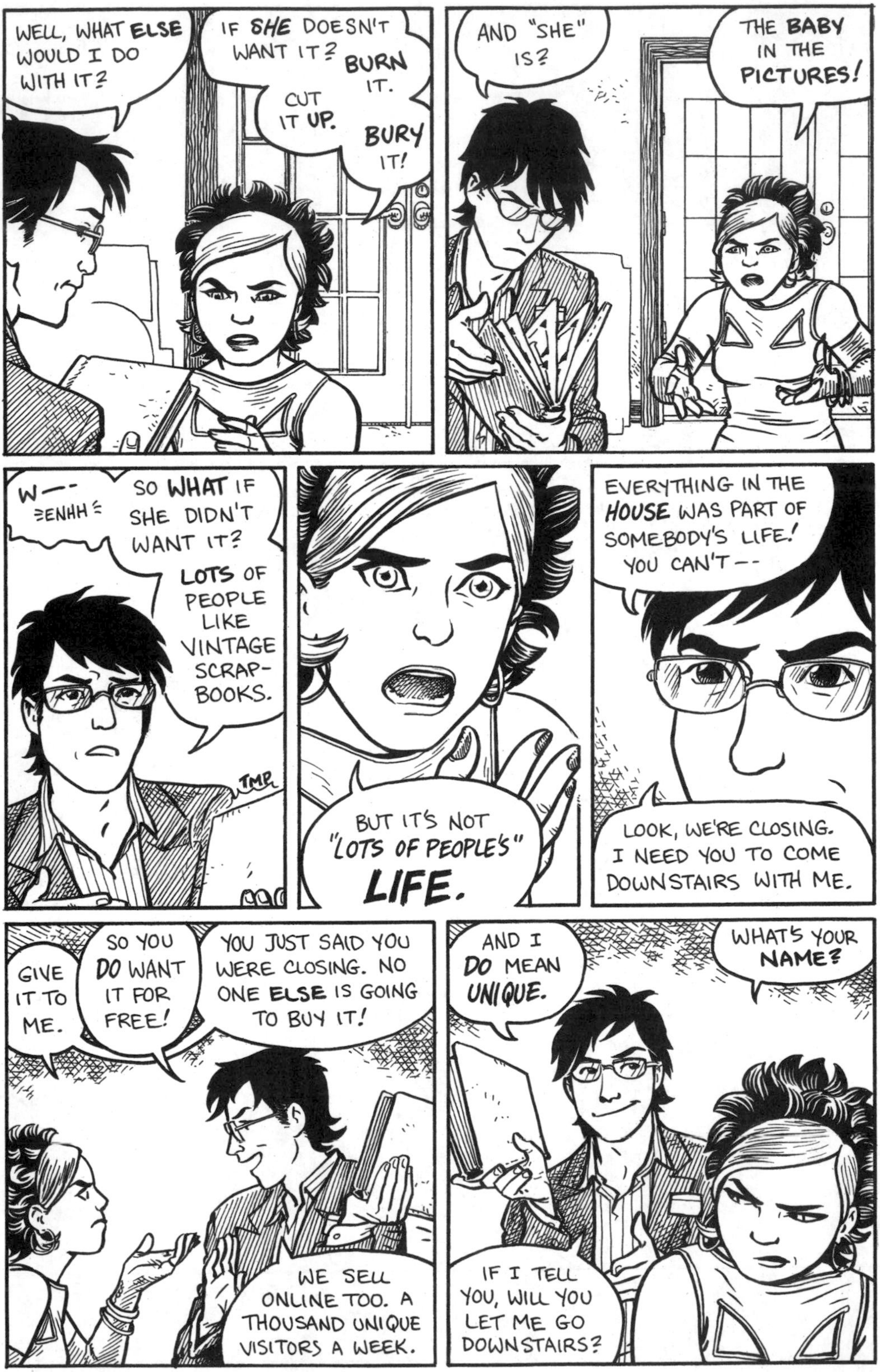
WELL, WHAT ELSE WOULD I DO WITH IT?
IF SHE DOESN'T WANT IT? BURN IT.
CUT IT UP.
BURY IT!
AND "SHE" IS?
THE BABY IN THE PICTURES!
W-- ENHH
SO WHAT IF SHE DIDN'T WANT IT? LOTS OF PEOPLE LIKE VINTAGE SCRAP-BOOKS.
TMP
BUT IT'S NOT "LOTS OF PEOPLE'S" LIFE.
EVERYTHING IN THE HOUSE WAS PART OF SOMEBODY'S LIFE! YOU CAN'T --
LOOK, WE'RE CLOSING. I NEED YOU TO COME DOWNSTAIRS WITH ME.
GIVE IT TO ME.
SO YOU DO WANT IT FOR FREE!
YOU JUST SAID YOU WERE CLOSING. NO ONE ELSE IS GOING TO BUY IT!
WE SELL ONLINE TOO. A THOUSAND UNIQUE VISITORS A WEEK.
AND I DO MEAN UNIQUE.
WHAT'S YOUR NAME?
IF I TELL YOU, WILL YOU LET ME GO DOWNSTAIRS?

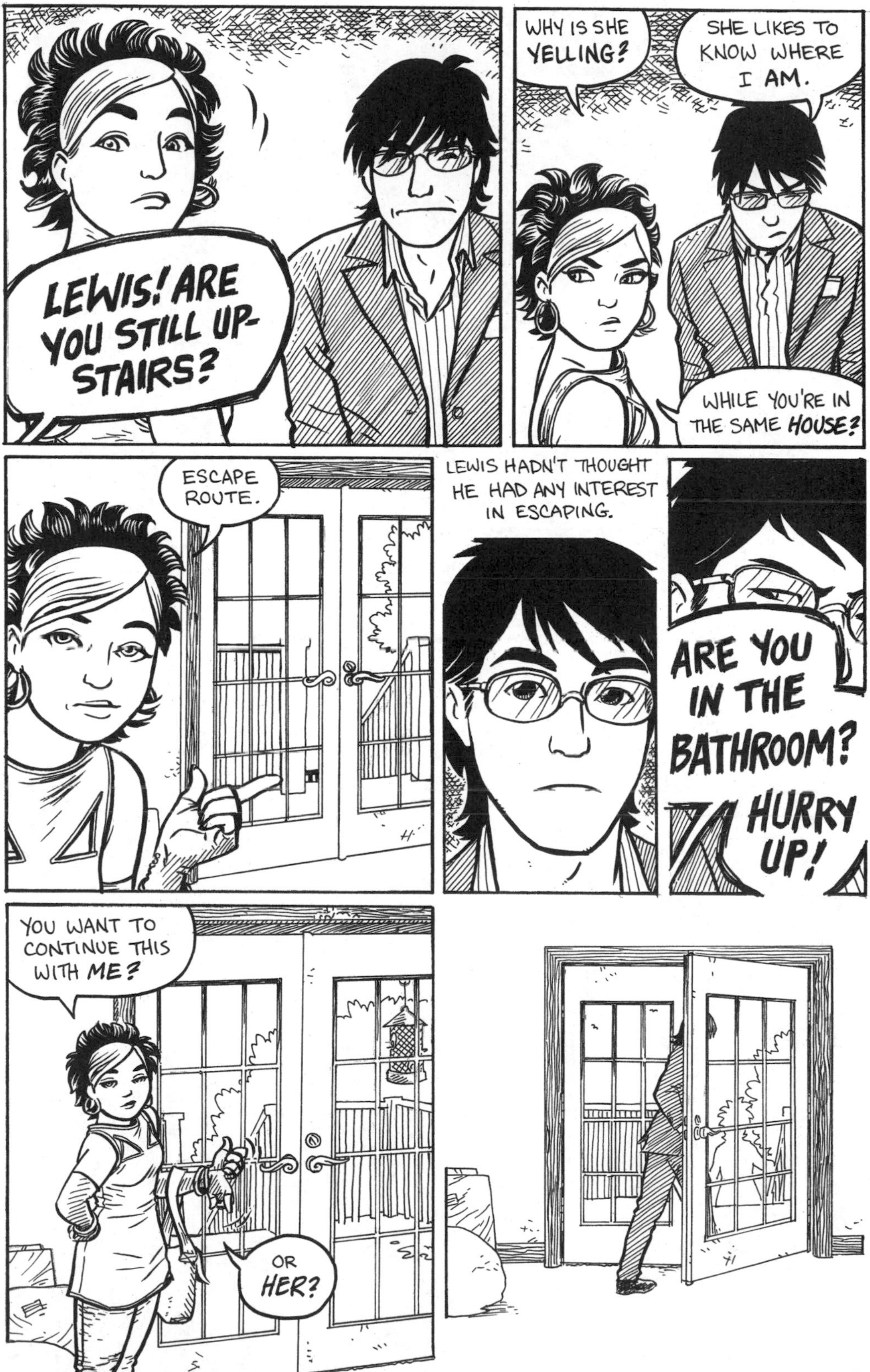
LEWIS! ARE YOU STILL UP-STAIRS?
WHY IS SHE YELLING?
SHE LIKES TO KNOW WHERE I AM.
WHILE YOU'RE IN THE SAME HOUSE?
ESCAPE ROUTE.
LEWIS HADN'T THOUGHT HE HAD ANY INTEREST IN ESCAPING.
ARE YOU IN THE BATHROOM?
HURRY UP!
YOU WANT TO CONTINUE THIS WITH ME?
OR HER?

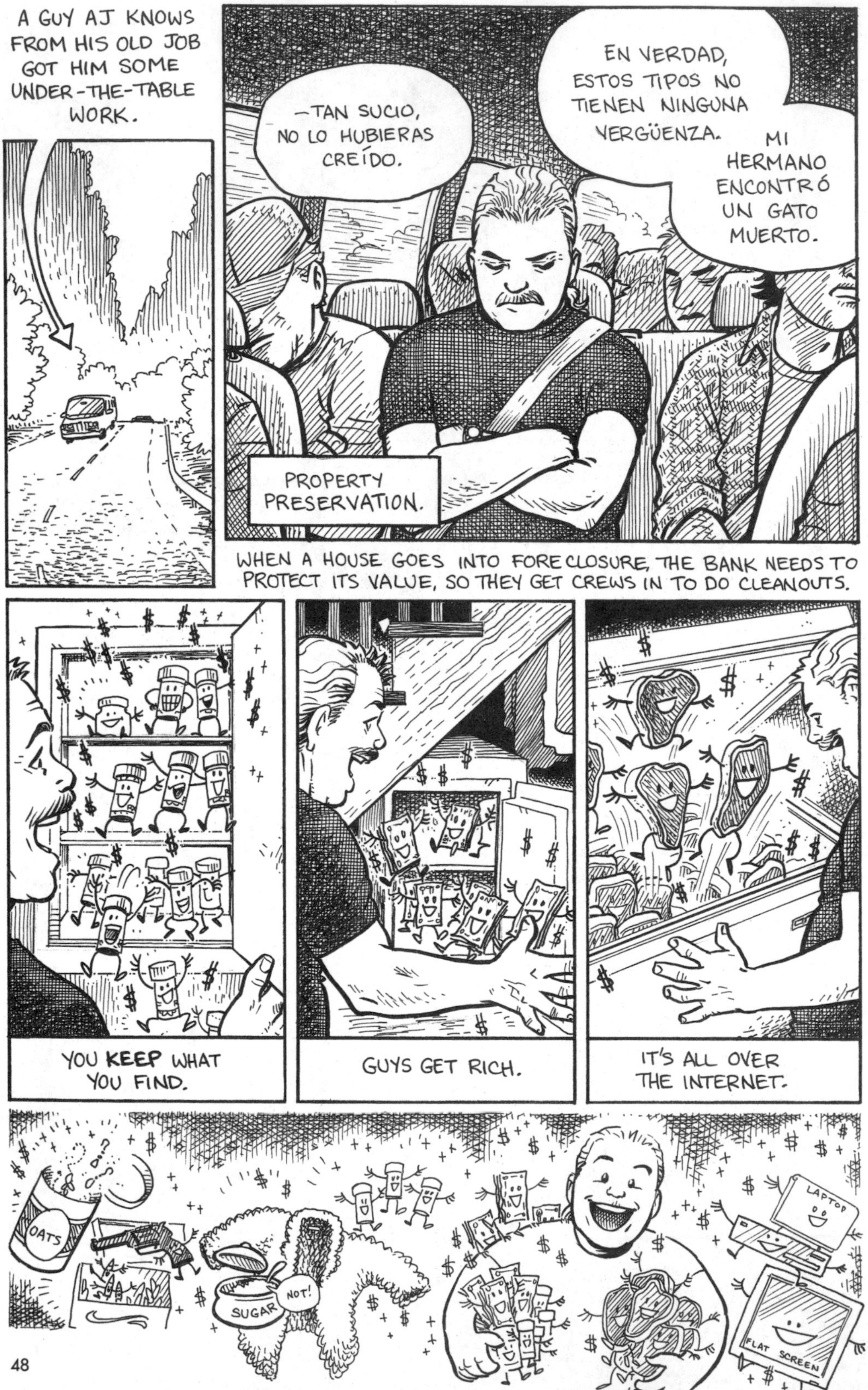

A GUY AJ KNOWS FROM HIS OLD JOB GOT HIM SOME UNDER-THE-TABLE WORK.
—TAN SUCIO, NO LO HUBIERAS CREÍDO.
EN VERDAD, ESTOS TIPOS NO TIENEN NINGUNA VERGÜENZA.
MI HERMANO ENCONTRÓ UN GATO MUERTO.
PROPERTY PRESERVATION.
WHEN A HOUSE GOES INTO FORECLOSURE, THE BANK NEEDS TO PROTECT ITS VALUE, SO THEY GET CREWS IN TO DO CLEANOUTS.
YOU **KEEP** WHAT YOU FIND.
GUYS GET RICH.
IT'S ALL OVER THE INTERNET.
OATS
SUGAR
NOT!
LAPTOP
FLAT SCREEN

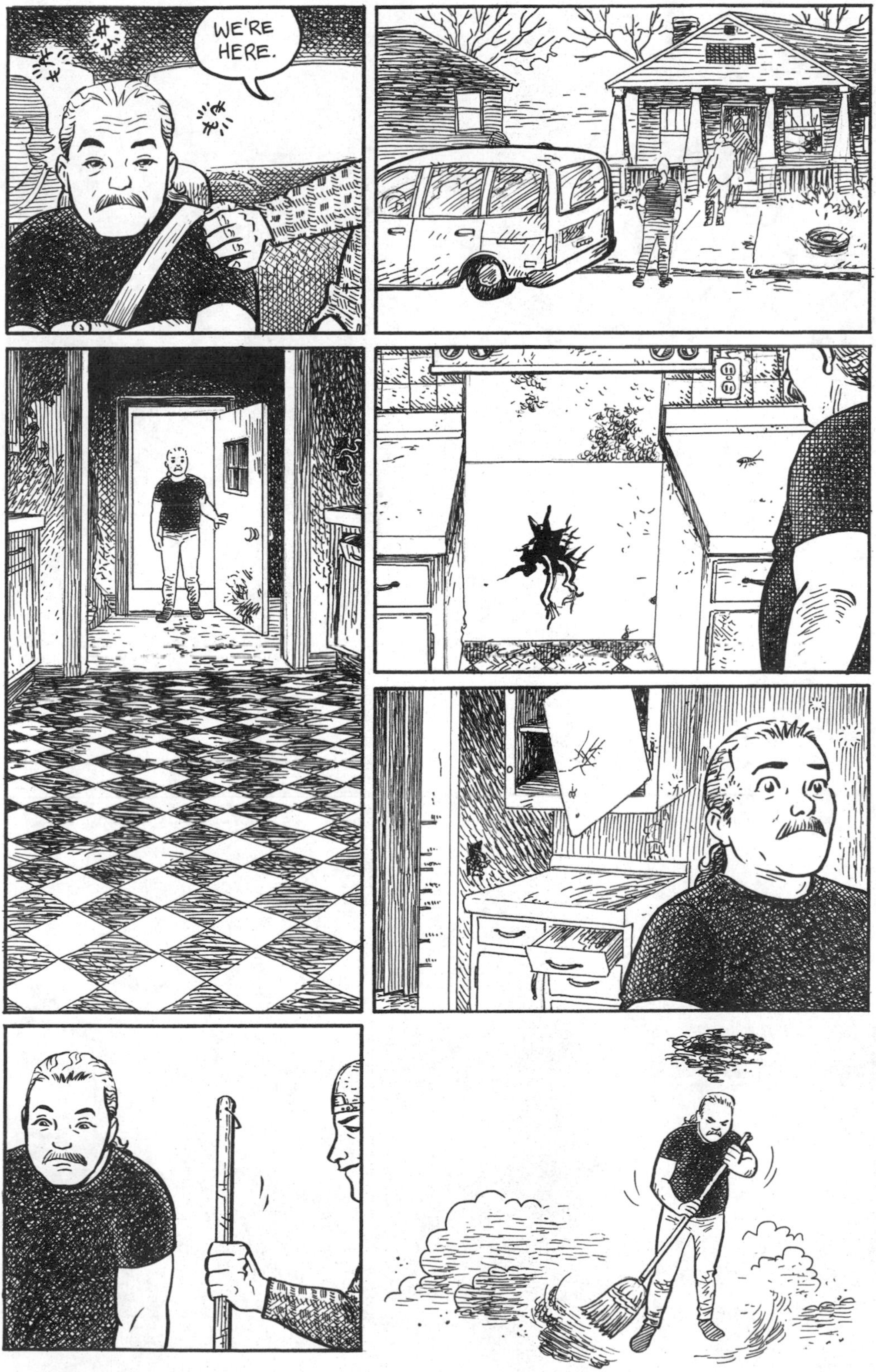
WE'RE HERE.

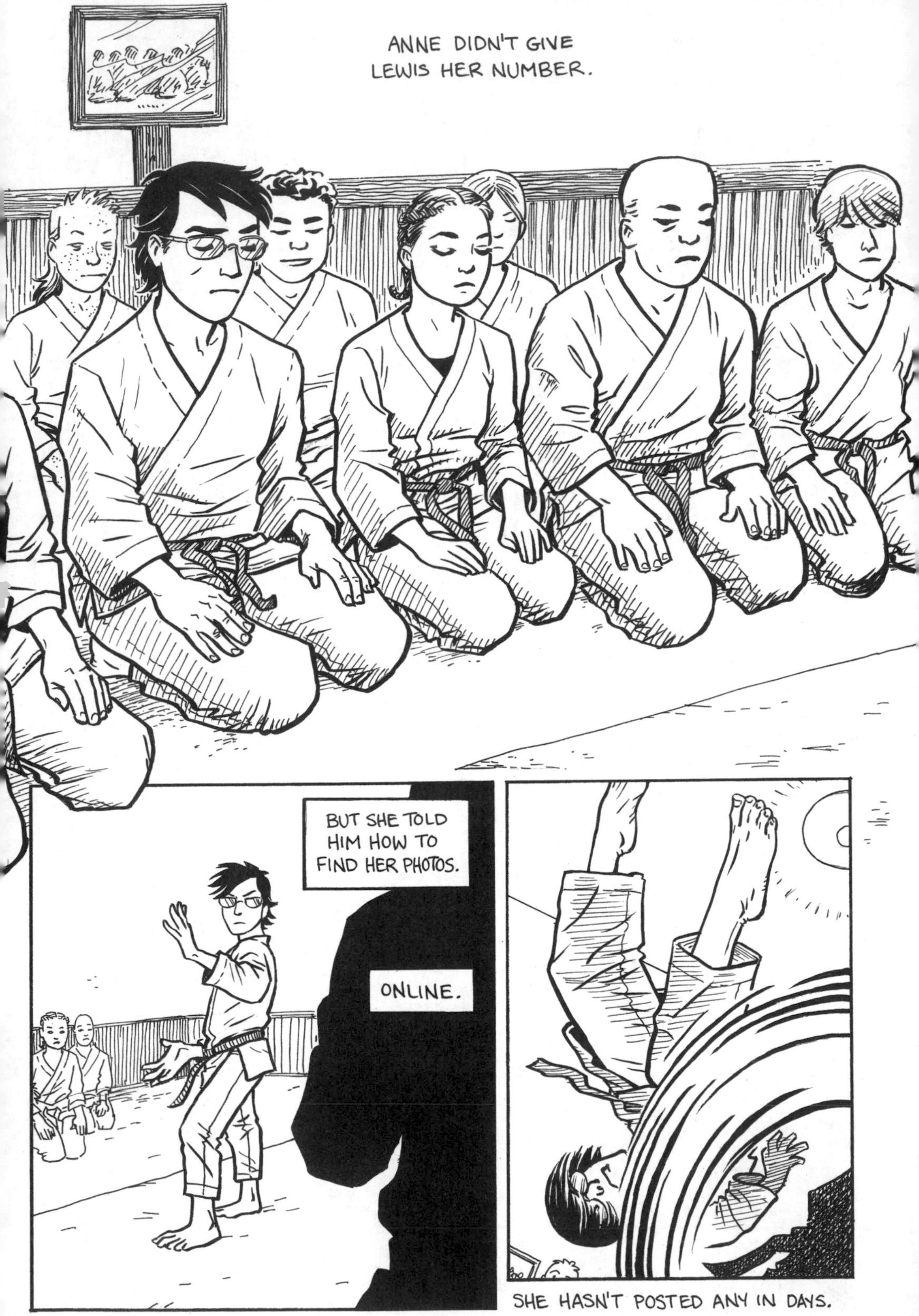
ANNE DIDN'T GIVE LEWIS HER NUMBER.
BUT SHE TOLD HIM HOW TO FIND HER PHOTOS.
ONLINE.
SHE HASN'T POSTED ANY IN DAYS.

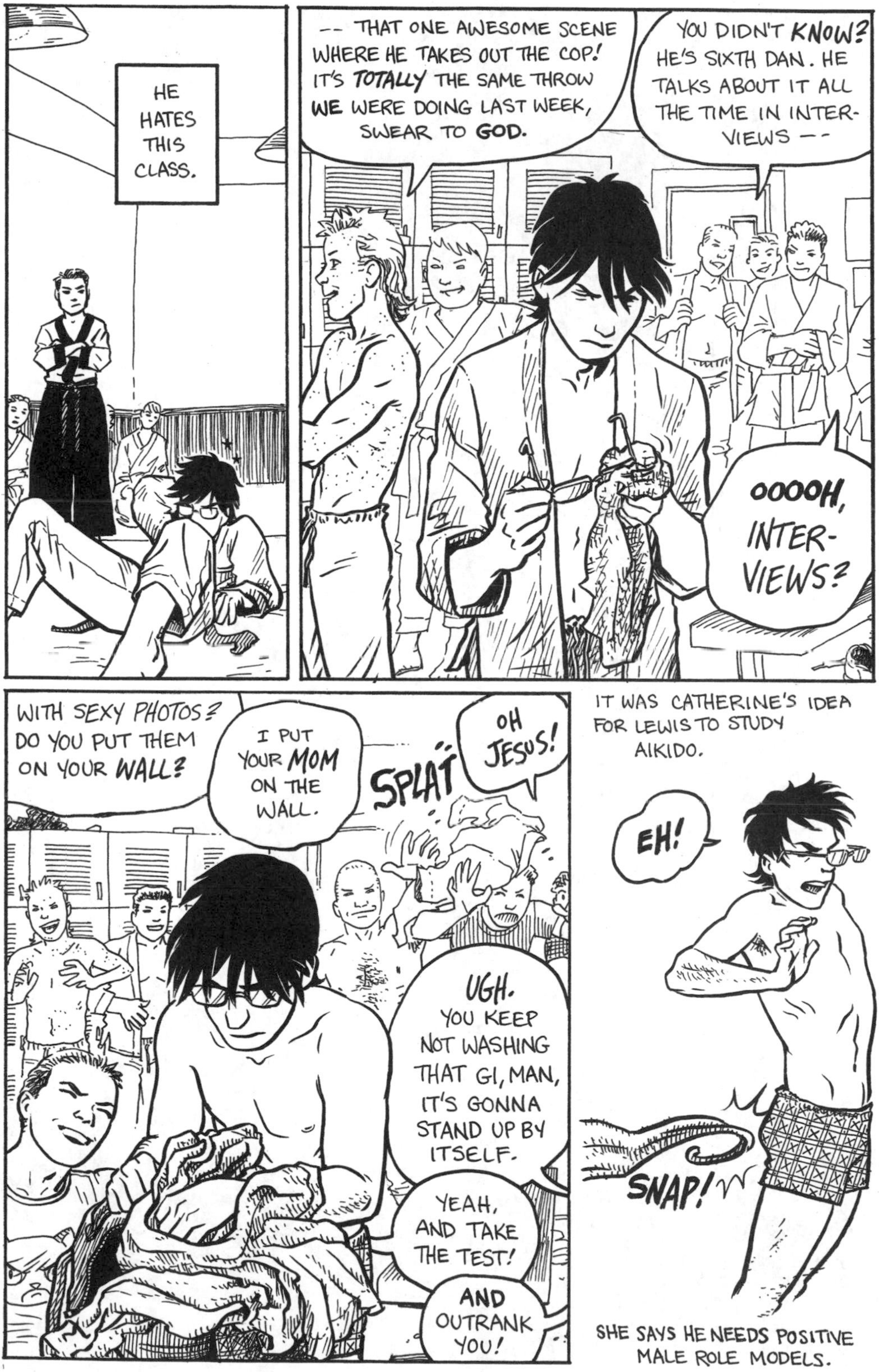
HE HATES THIS CLASS.
-- THAT ONE AWESOME SCENE WHERE HE TAKES OUT THE COP! IT'S TOTALLY THE SAME THROW WE WERE DOING LAST WEEK, SWEAR TO GOD.
YOU DIDN'T KNOW? HE'S SIXTH DAN. HE TALKS ABOUT IT ALL THE TIME IN INTER-VIEWS --
OOOOH, INTER-VIEWS?
WITH SEXY PHOTOS? DO YOU PUT THEM ON YOUR WALL?
I PUT YOUR MOM ON THE WALL.
SPLAT
OH JESUS!
UGH. YOU KEEP NOT WASHING THAT GI, MAN, IT'S GONNA STAND UP BY ITSELF.
YEAH, AND TAKE THE TEST!
AND OUTRANK YOU!
IT WAS CATHERINE'S IDEA FOR LEWIS TO STUDY AIKIDO.
EH!
SNAP!
SHE SAYS HE NEEDS POSITIVE MALE ROLE MODELS.

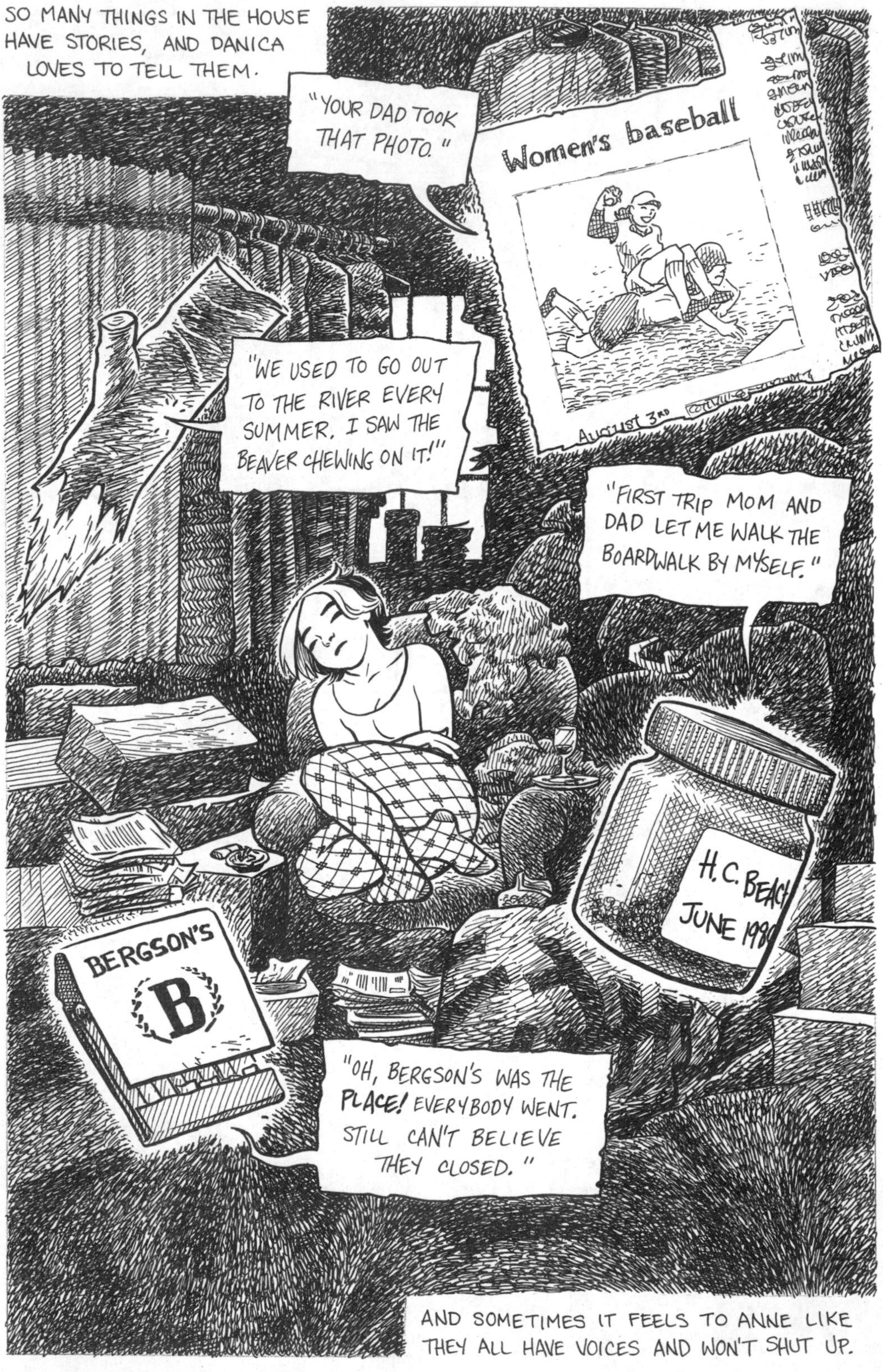

SO MANY THINGS IN THE HOUSE HAVE STORIES, AND DANICA LOVES TO TELL THEM.
"YOUR DAD TOOK THAT PHOTO."
Women's baseball
AUGUST 3RD
"WE USED TO GO OUT TO THE RIVER EVERY SUMMER. I SAW THE BEAVER CHEWING ON IT!"
"FIRST TRIP MOM AND DAD LET ME WALK THE BOARDWALK BY MYSELF."
H.C. BEACH
JUNE 198
BERGSON'S
B
"OH, BERGSON'S WAS THE PLACE! EVERYBODY WENT. STILL CAN'T BELIEVE THEY CLOSED."
AND SOMETIMES IT FEELS TO ANNE LIKE THEY ALL HAVE VOICES AND WON'T SHUT UP.

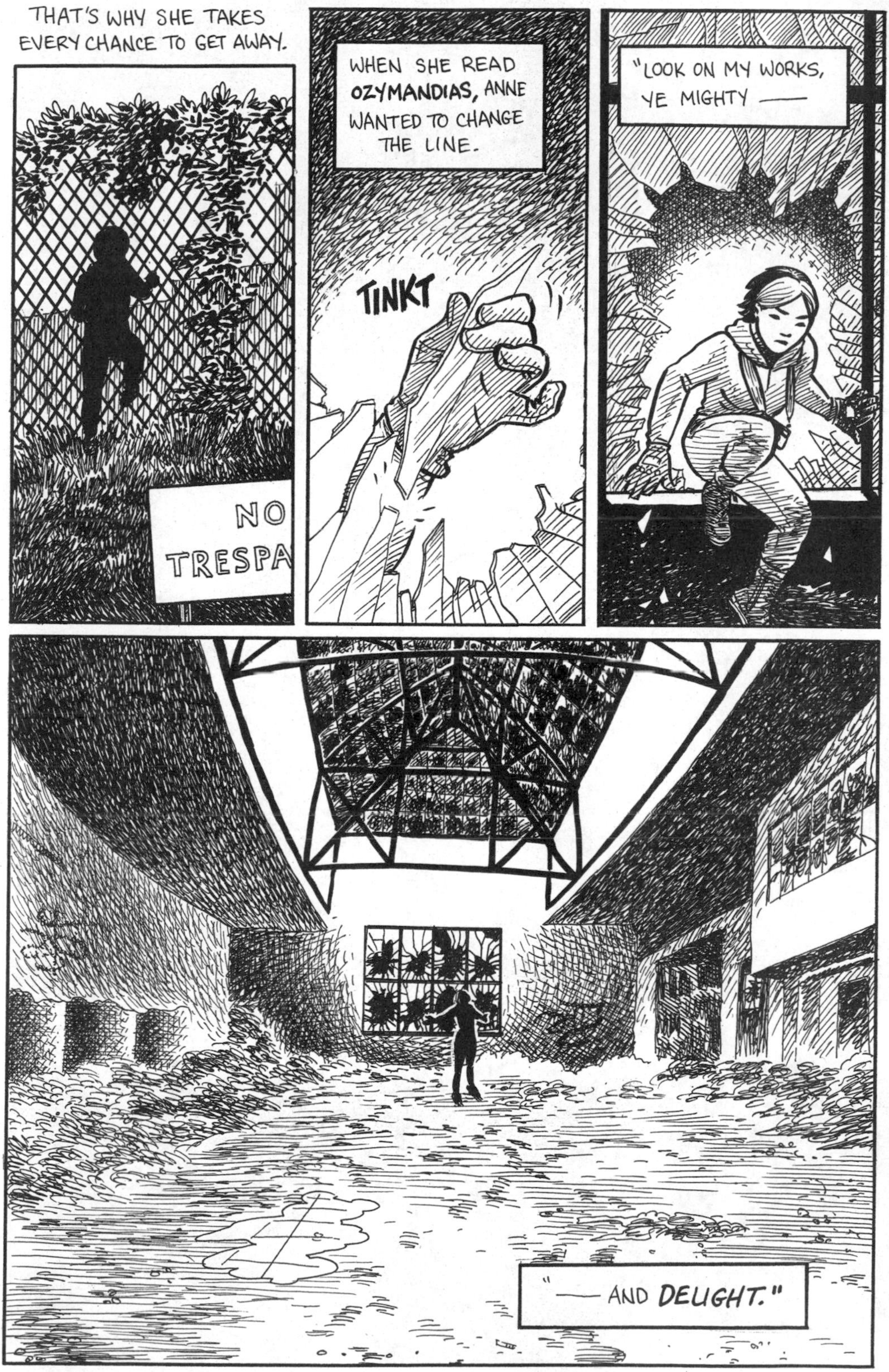
THAT'S WHY SHE TAKES EVERY CHANCE TO GET AWAY.
NO TRESPA
WHEN SHE READ OZYMANDIAS, ANNE WANTED TO CHANGE THE LINE.
TINKT
"LOOK ON MY WORKS, YE MIGHTY ——
"—— AND DELIGHT."

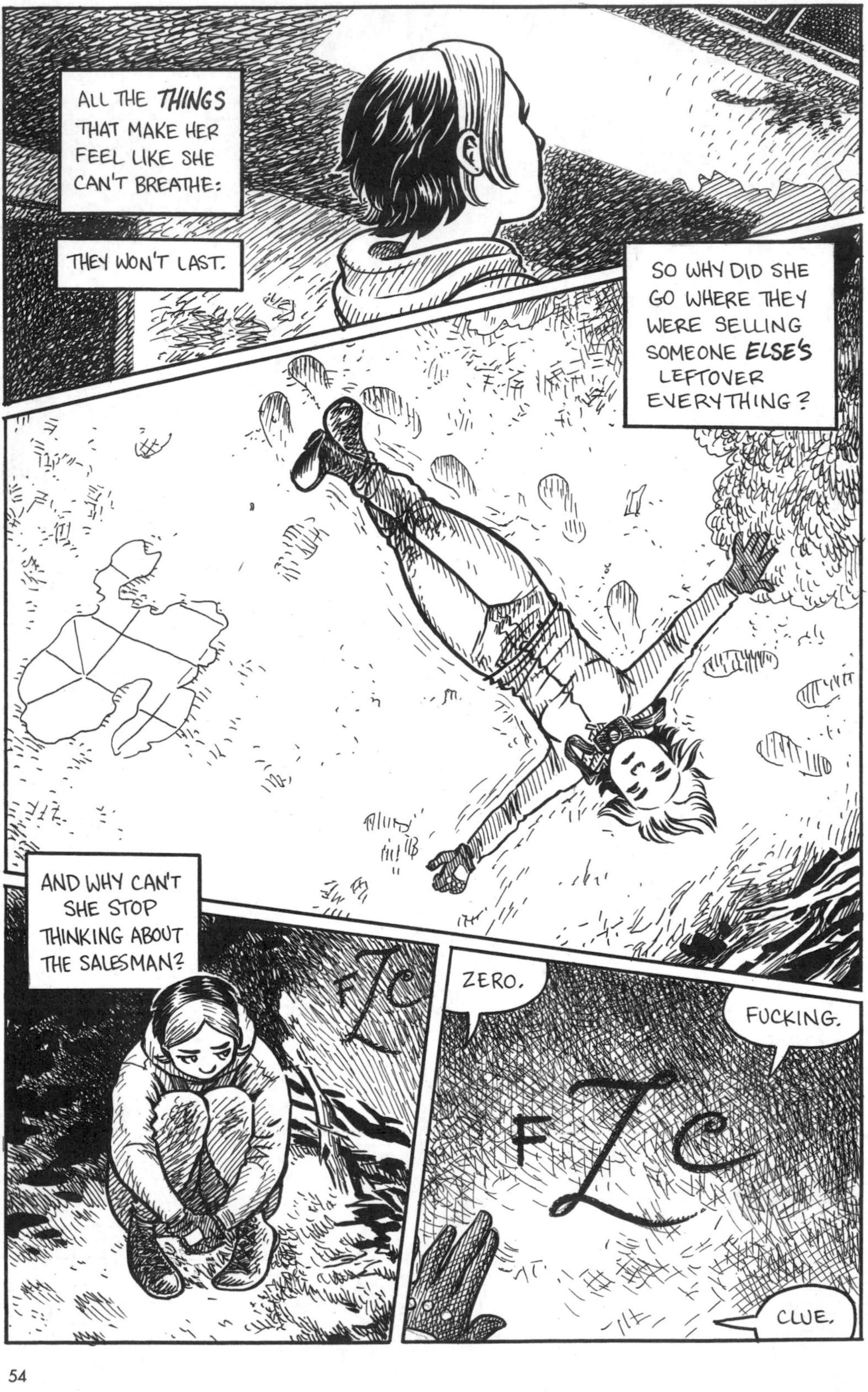
ALL THE THINGS THAT MAKE HER FEEL LIKE SHE CAN'T BREATHE:
THEY WON'T LAST.
SO WHY DID SHE GO WHERE THEY WERE SELLING SOMEONE ELSE'S LEFTOVER EVERYTHING?
AND WHY CAN'T SHE STOP THINKING ABOUT THE SALESMAN?
FZC
ZERO.
FUCKING.
FZC
CLUE.

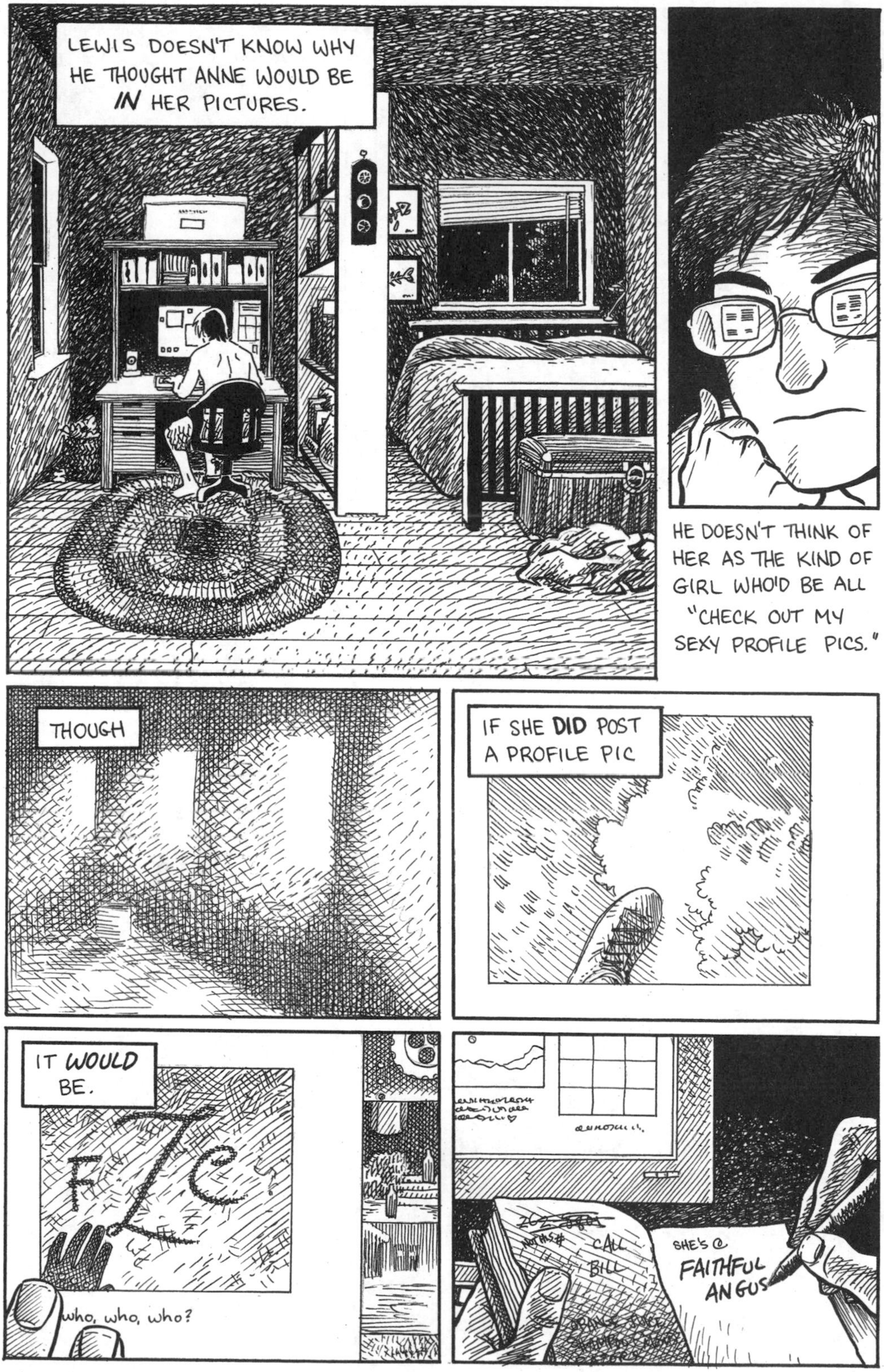
LEWIS DOESN'T KNOW WHY HE THOUGHT ANNE WOULD BE ***IN*** HER PICTURES.
HE DOESN'T THINK OF HER AS THE KIND OF GIRL WHO'D BE ALL "CHECK OUT MY SEXY PROFILE PICS."
THOUGH
IF SHE **DID** POST A PROFILE PIC
IT ***WOULD*** BE.
who, who, who?
CALL BILL
SHE'S @ FAITHFUL ANGUS

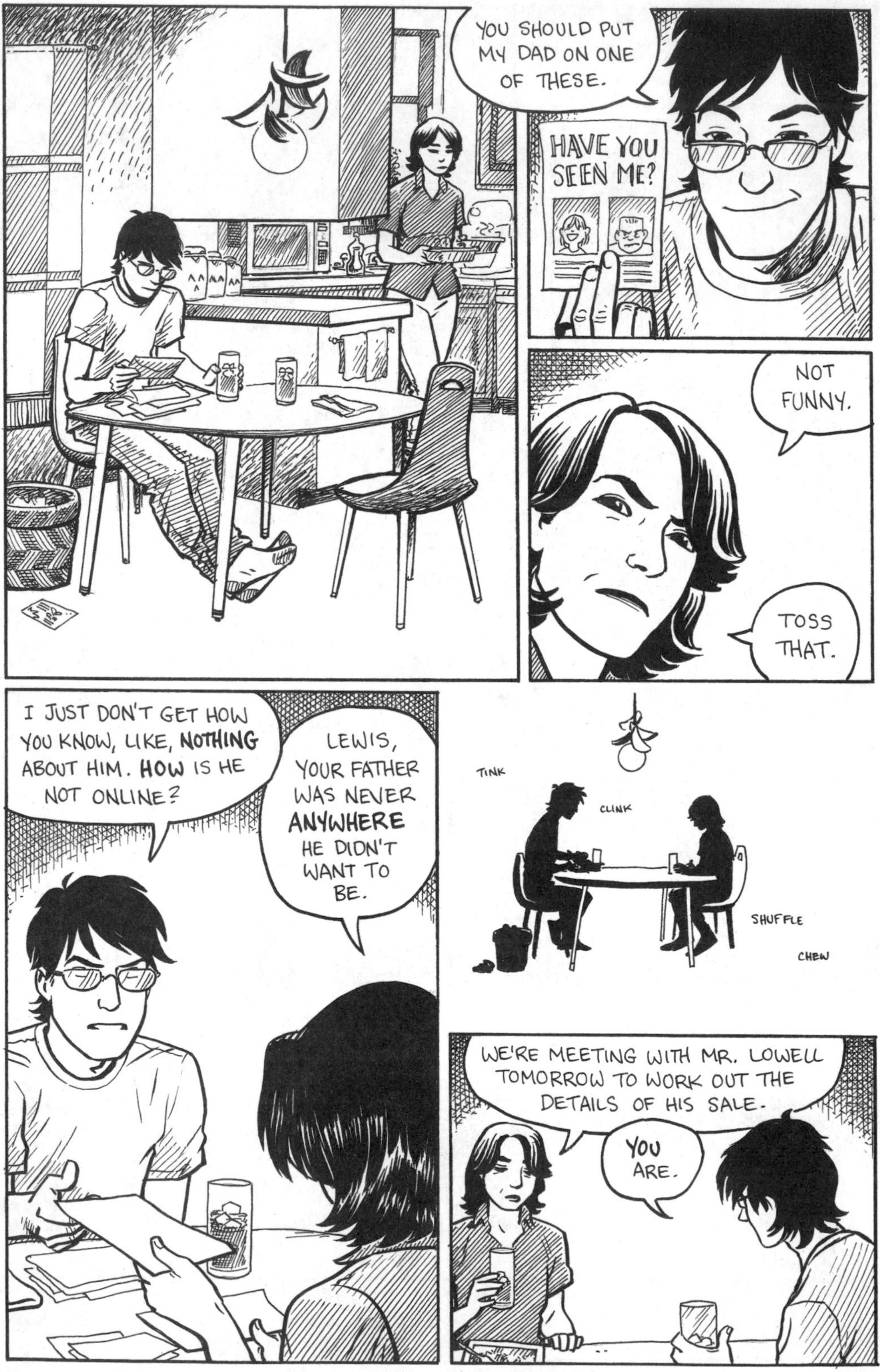
YOU SHOULD PUT MY DAD ON ONE OF THESE.
HAVE YOU SEEN ME?
NOT FUNNY.
TOSS THAT.
I JUST DON'T GET HOW YOU KNOW, LIKE, NOTHING ABOUT HIM. HOW IS HE NOT ONLINE?
LEWIS, YOUR FATHER WAS NEVER ANYWHERE HE DIDN'T WANT TO BE.
TINK
CLINK
SHUFFLE
CHEW
WE'RE MEETING WITH MR. LOWELL TOMORROW TO WORK OUT THE DETAILS OF HIS SALE.
YOU ARE.

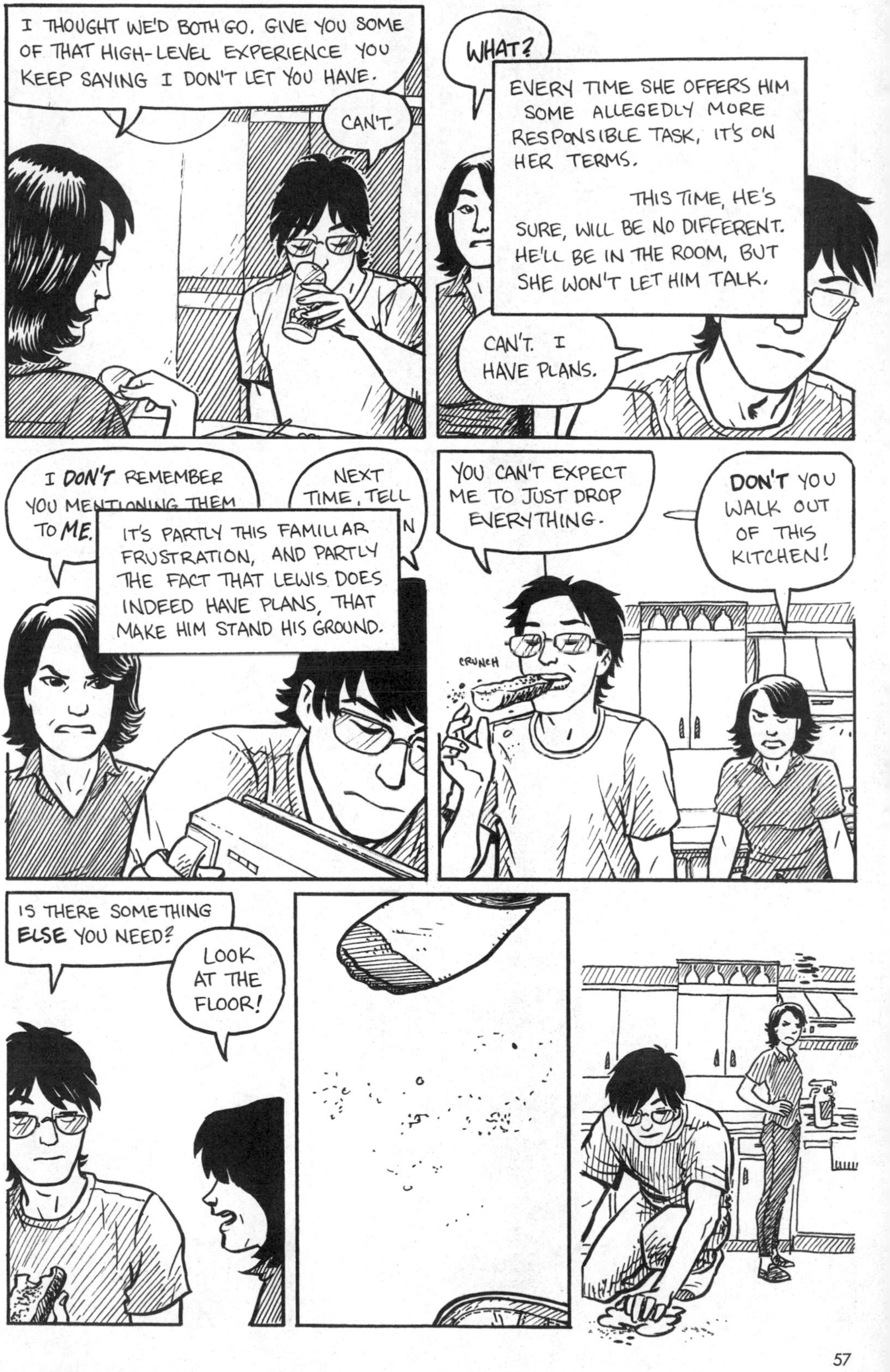

I THOUGHT WE'D BOTH GO. GIVE YOU SOME OF THAT HIGH-LEVEL EXPERIENCE YOU KEEP SAYING I DON'T LET YOU HAVE.
CAN'T.
WHAT?
EVERY TIME SHE OFFERS HIM SOME ALLEGEDLY MORE RESPONSIBLE TASK, IT'S ON HER TERMS.
THIS TIME, HE'S SURE, WILL BE NO DIFFERENT. HE'LL BE IN THE ROOM, BUT SHE WON'T LET HIM TALK.
CAN'T. I HAVE PLANS.
I DON'T REMEMBER YOU MENTIONING THEM TO ME.
NEXT TIME, TELL
IT'S PARTLY THIS FAMILIAR FRUSTRATION, AND PARTLY THE FACT THAT LEWIS DOES INDEED HAVE PLANS, THAT MAKE HIM STAND HIS GROUND.
YOU CAN'T EXPECT ME TO JUST DROP EVERYTHING.
CRUNCH
DON'T YOU WALK OUT OF THIS KITCHEN!
IS THERE SOMETHING ELSE YOU NEED?
LOOK AT THE FLOOR!

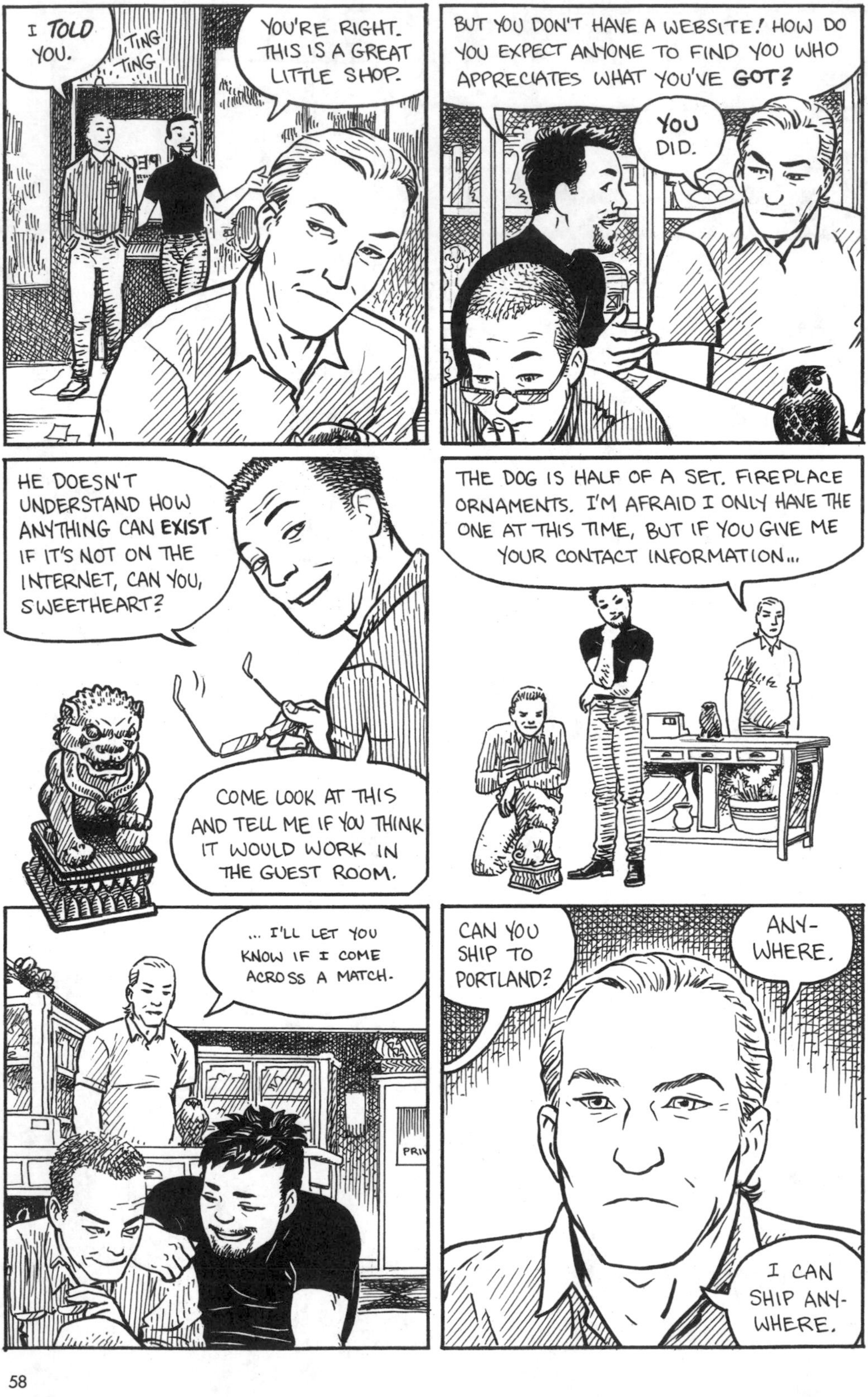
I TOLD YOU.
TING TING
YOU'RE RIGHT. THIS IS A GREAT LITTLE SHOP.
BUT YOU DON'T HAVE A WEBSITE! HOW DO YOU EXPECT ANYONE TO FIND YOU WHO APPRECIATES WHAT YOU'VE GOT?
YOU DID.
HE DOESN'T UNDERSTAND HOW ANYTHING CAN EXIST IF IT'S NOT ON THE INTERNET, CAN YOU, SWEETHEART?
COME LOOK AT THIS AND TELL ME IF YOU THINK IT WOULD WORK IN THE GUEST ROOM.
THE DOG IS HALF OF A SET. FIREPLACE ORNAMENTS. I'M AFRAID I ONLY HAVE THE ONE AT THIS TIME, BUT IF YOU GIVE ME YOUR CONTACT INFORMATION...
... I'LL LET YOU KNOW IF I COME ACROSS A MATCH.
CAN YOU SHIP TO PORTLAND?
ANY-WHERE.
I CAN SHIP ANY-WHERE.

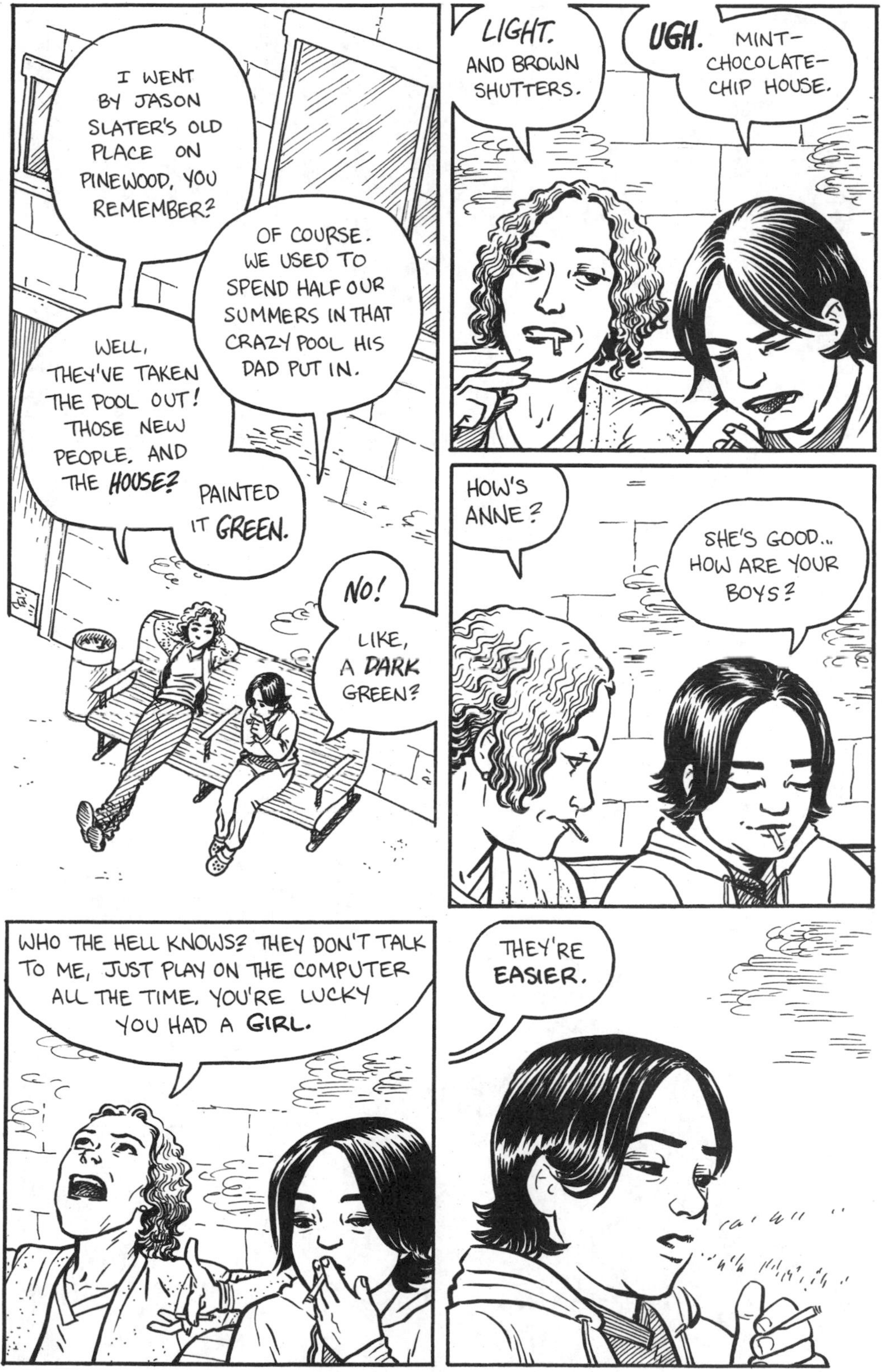
I WENT BY JASON SLATER'S OLD PLACE ON PINEWOOD, YOU REMEMBER?
OF COURSE. WE USED TO SPEND HALF OUR SUMMERS IN THAT CRAZY POOL HIS DAD PUT IN.
WELL, THEY'VE TAKEN THE POOL OUT! THOSE NEW PEOPLE. AND THE HOUSE?
PAINTED IT GREEN.
NO!
LIKE, A DARK GREEN?
LIGHT. AND BROWN SHUTTERS.
UGH. MINT-CHOCOLATE-CHIP HOUSE.
HOW'S ANNE?
SHE'S GOOD... HOW ARE YOUR BOYS?
WHO THE HELL KNOWS? THEY DON'T TALK TO ME, JUST PLAY ON THE COMPUTER ALL THE TIME. YOU'RE LUCKY YOU HAD A GIRL.
THEY'RE EASIER.

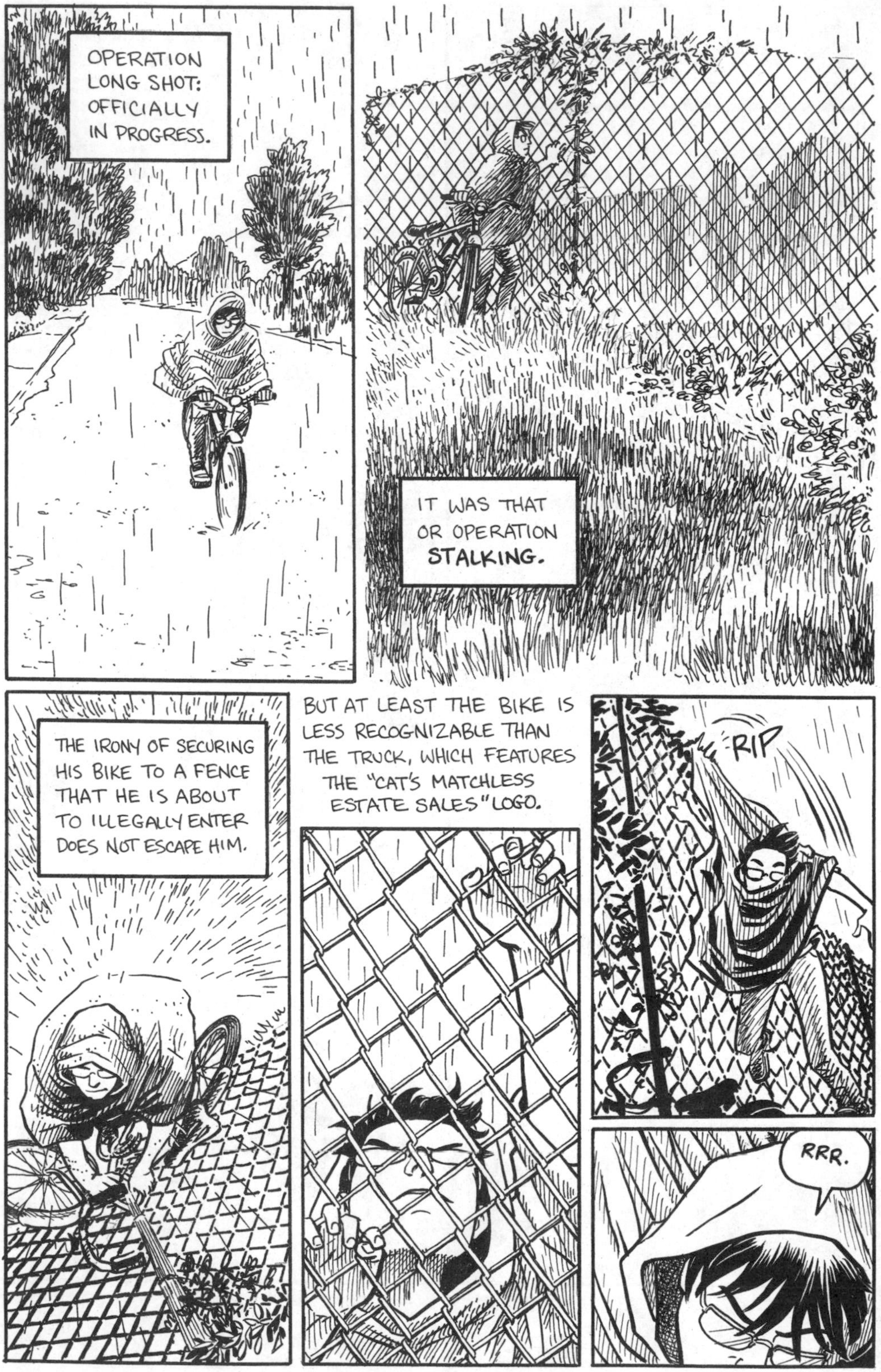

OPERATION LONG SHOT: OFFICIALLY IN PROGRESS.
IT WAS THAT OR OPERATION **STALKING.**
THE IRONY OF SECURING HIS BIKE TO A FENCE THAT HE IS ABOUT TO ILLEGALLY ENTER DOES NOT ESCAPE HIM.
BUT AT LEAST THE BIKE IS LESS RECOGNIZABLE THAN THE TRUCK, WHICH FEATURES THE "CAT'S MATCHLESS ESTATE SALES" LOGO.
RIP
RRR.

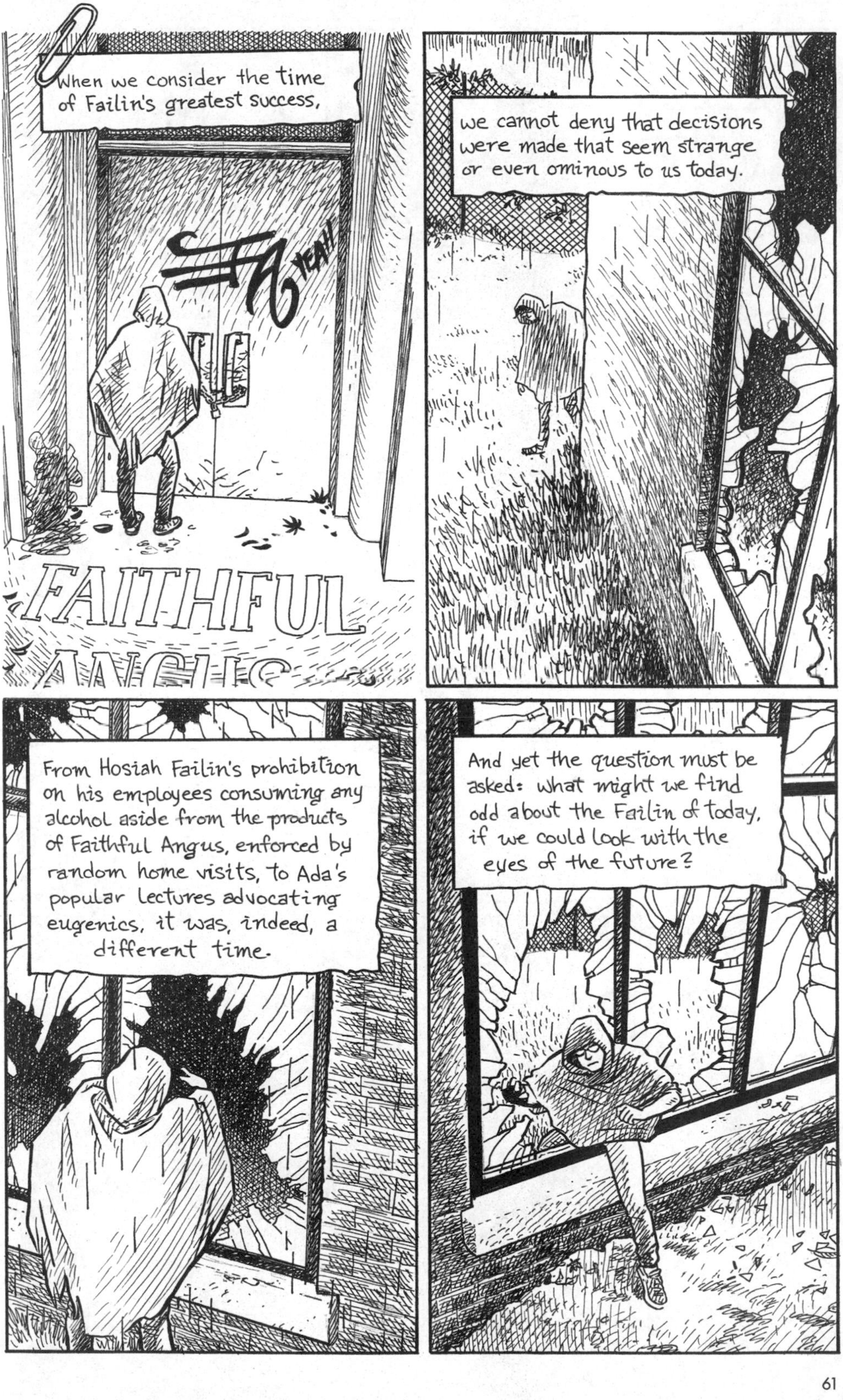
When we consider the time of Failin's greatest success,
YEAH!
FAITHFUL
we cannot deny that decisions were made that seem strange or even ominous to us today.
From Hosiah Failin's prohibition on his employees consuming any alcohol aside from the products of Faithful Angus, enforced by random home visits, to Ada's popular lectures advocating eugenics, it was, indeed, a different time.
And yet the question must be asked: what might we find odd about the Failin of today, if we could look with the eyes of the future?

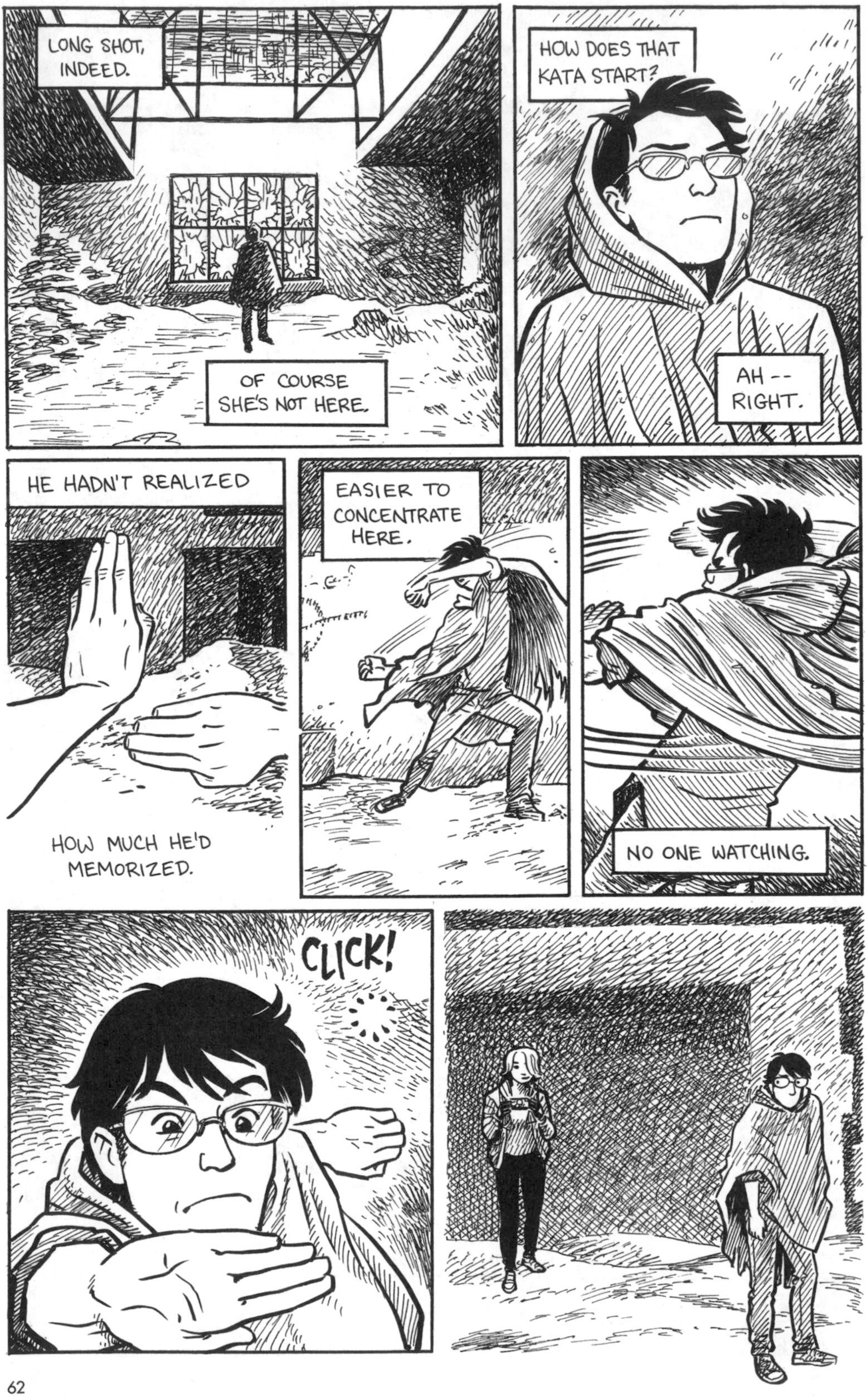
LONG SHOT, INDEED.
OF COURSE SHE'S NOT HERE.
HOW DOES THAT KATA START?
AH -- RIGHT.
HE HADN'T REALIZED
HOW MUCH HE'D MEMORIZED.
EASIER TO CONCENTRATE HERE.
NO ONE WATCHING.
CLICK!

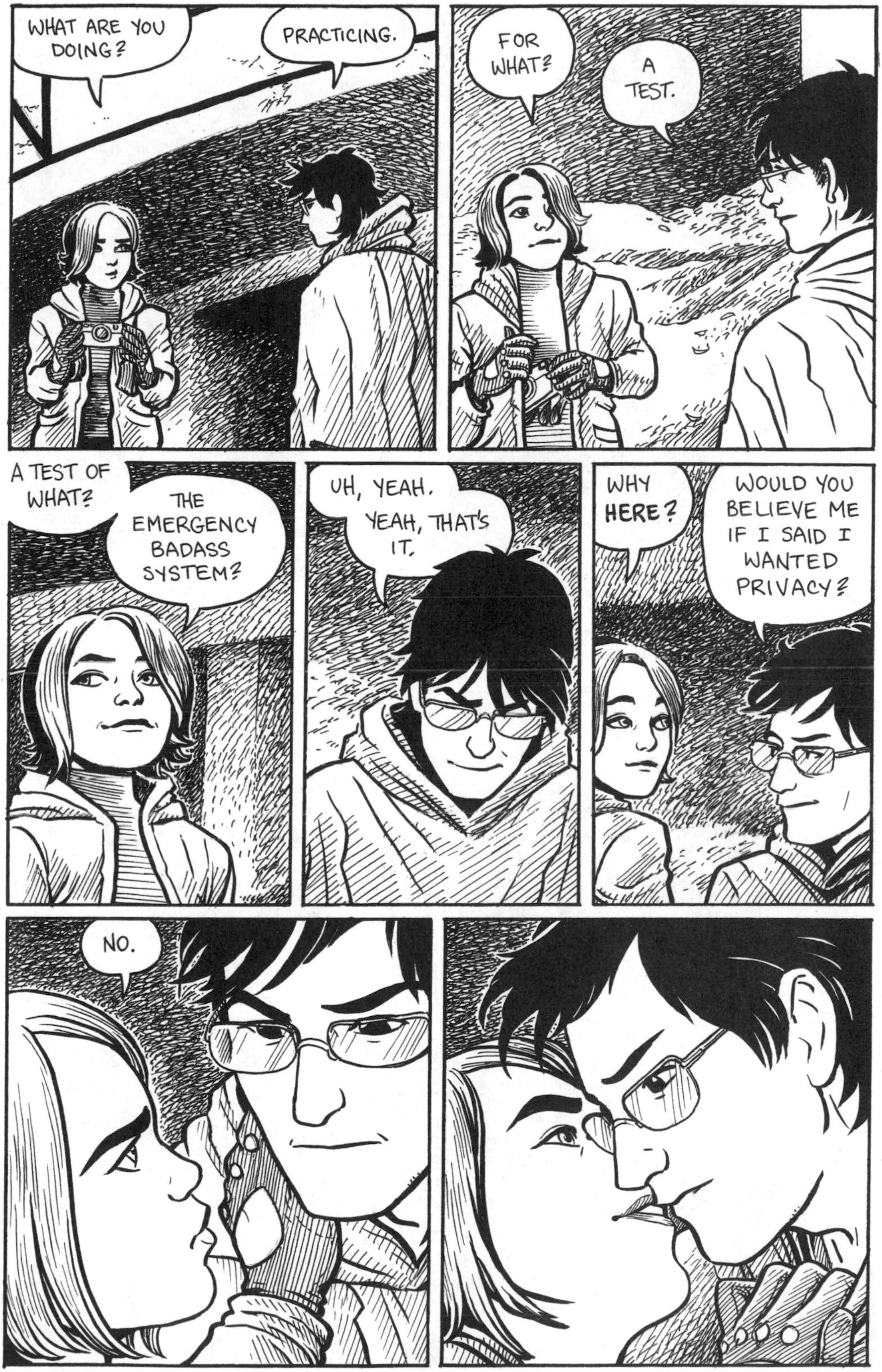
WHAT ARE YOU DOING?
PRACTICING.
FOR WHAT?
A TEST.
A TEST OF WHAT?
THE EMERGENCY BADASS SYSTEM?
UH, YEAH.
YEAH, THAT'S IT.
WHY HERE?
WOULD YOU BELIEVE ME IF I SAID I WANTED PRIVACY?
NO.

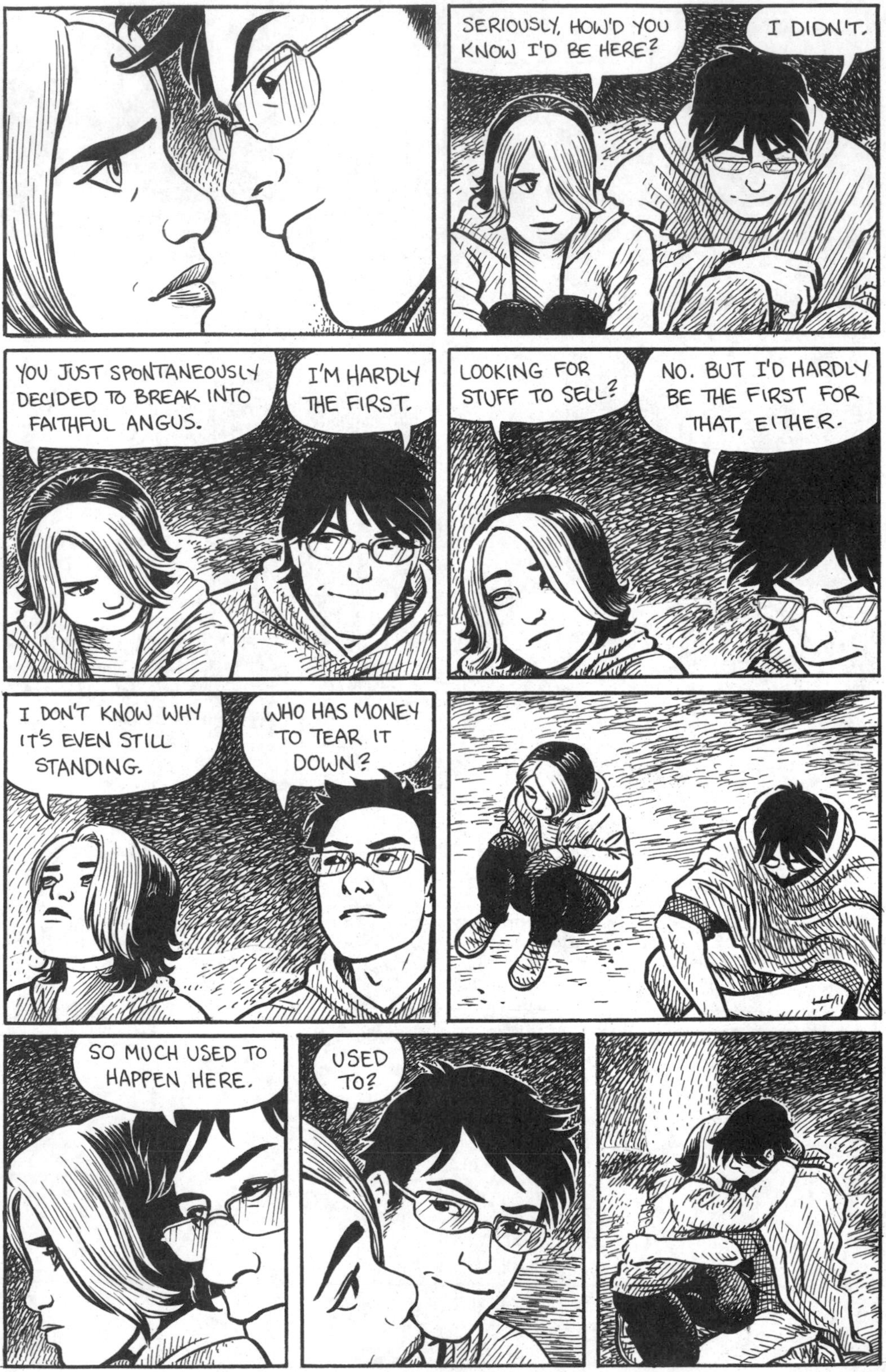
SERIOUSLY, HOW'D YOU KNOW I'D BE HERE?
I DIDN'T.
YOU JUST SPONTANEOUSLY DECIDED TO BREAK INTO FAITHFUL ANGUS.
I'M HARDLY THE FIRST.
LOOKING FOR STUFF TO SELL?
NO. BUT I'D HARDLY BE THE FIRST FOR THAT, EITHER.
I DON'T KNOW WHY IT'S EVEN STILL STANDING.
WHO HAS MONEY TO TEAR IT DOWN?
SO MUCH USED TO HAPPEN HERE.
USED TO?

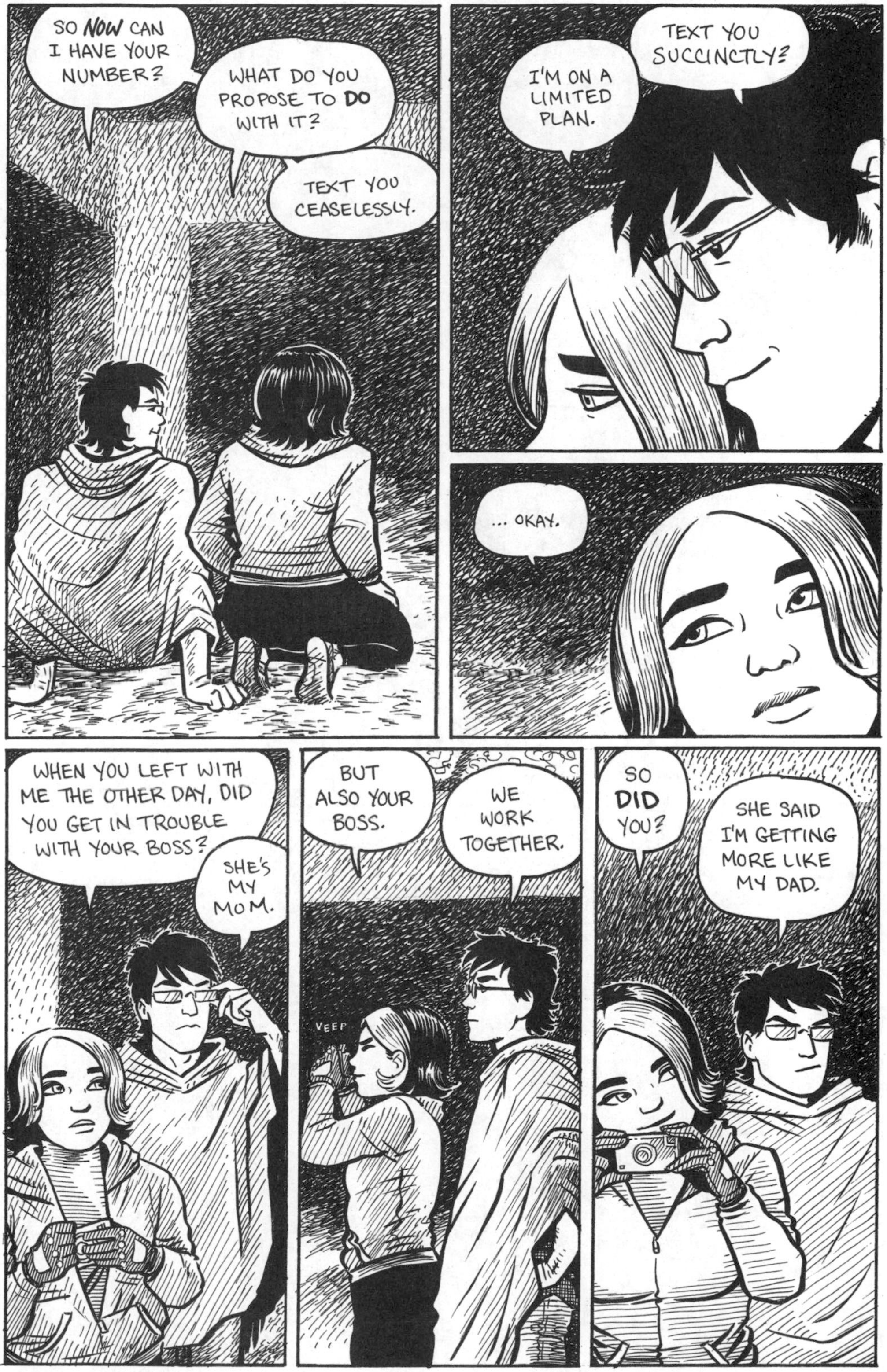
SO NOW CAN I HAVE YOUR NUMBER?
WHAT DO YOU PROPOSE TO DO WITH IT?
TEXT YOU CEASELESSLY.
I'M ON A LIMITED PLAN.
TEXT YOU SUCCINCTLY?
... OKAY.
WHEN YOU LEFT WITH ME THE OTHER DAY, DID YOU GET IN TROUBLE WITH YOUR BOSS?
SHE'S MY MOM.
BUT ALSO YOUR BOSS.
WE WORK TOGETHER.
VEEP
SO DID YOU?
SHE SAID I'M GETTING MORE LIKE MY DAD.

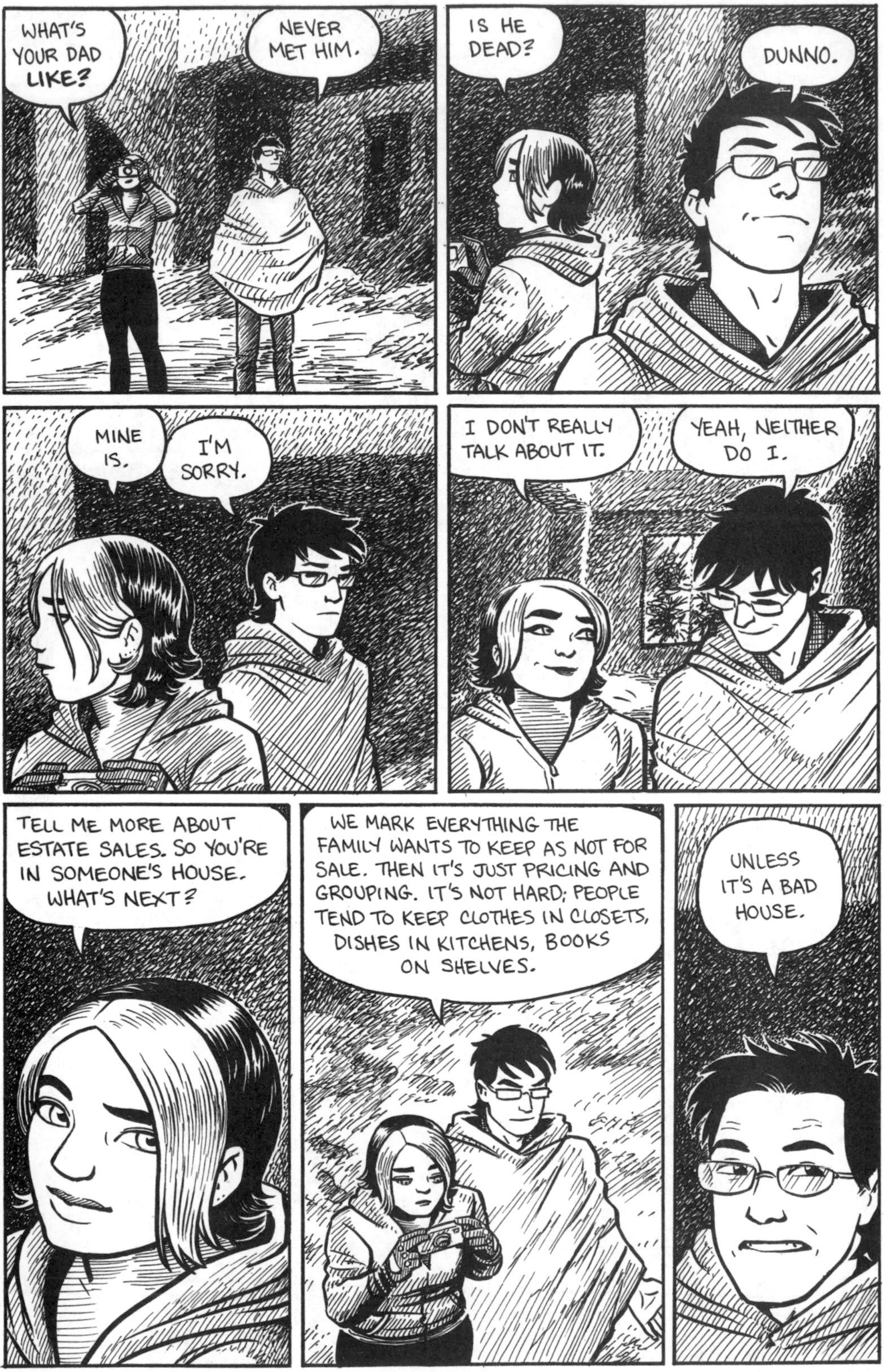
WHAT'S YOUR DAD LIKE?
NEVER MET HIM.
IS HE DEAD?
DUNNO.
MINE IS.
I'M SORRY.
I DON'T REALLY TALK ABOUT IT.
YEAH, NEITHER DO I.
TELL ME MORE ABOUT ESTATE SALES. SO YOU'RE IN SOMEONE'S HOUSE. WHAT'S NEXT?
WE MARK EVERYTHING THE FAMILY WANTS TO KEEP AS NOT FOR SALE. THEN IT'S JUST PRICING AND GROUPING. IT'S NOT HARD; PEOPLE TEND TO KEEP CLOTHES IN CLOSETS, DISHES IN KITCHENS, BOOKS ON SHELVES.
UNLESS IT'S A BAD HOUSE.

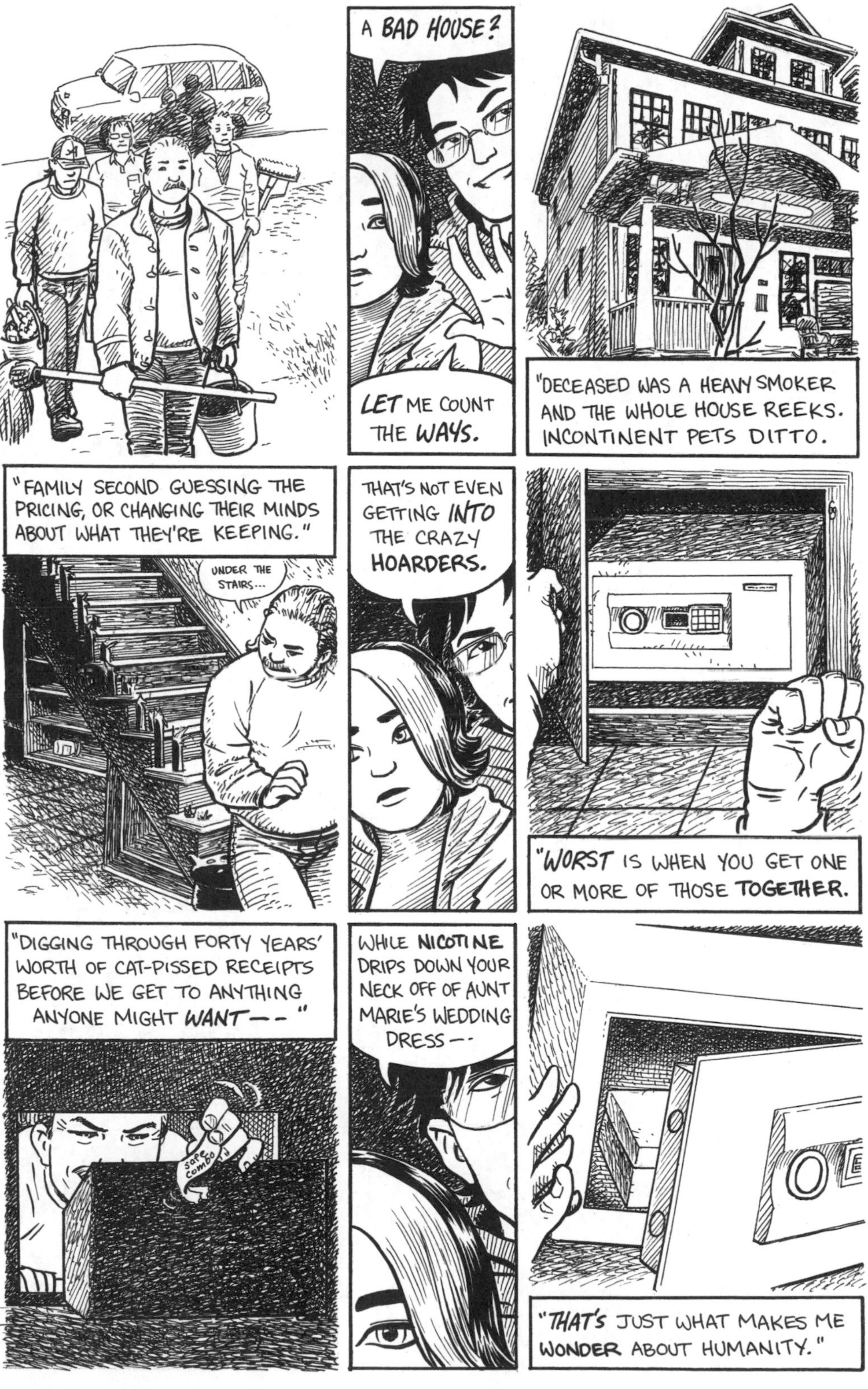
A BAD HOUSE?
LET ME COUNT THE WAYS.
"DECEASED WAS A HEAVY SMOKER AND THE WHOLE HOUSE REEKS. INCONTINENT PETS DITTO.
"FAMILY SECOND GUESSING THE PRICING, OR CHANGING THEIR MINDS ABOUT WHAT THEY'RE KEEPING."
UNDER THE STAIRS...
THAT'S NOT EVEN GETTING INTO THE CRAZY HOARDERS.
"WORST IS WHEN YOU GET ONE OR MORE OF THOSE TOGETHER.
"DIGGING THROUGH FORTY YEARS' WORTH OF CAT-PISSED RECEIPTS BEFORE WE GET TO ANYTHING ANYONE MIGHT WANT-- "
safe combo
WHILE NICOTINE DRIPS DOWN YOUR NECK OFF OF AUNT MARIE'S WEDDING DRESS--
"THAT'S JUST WHAT MAKES ME WONDER ABOUT HUMANITY."

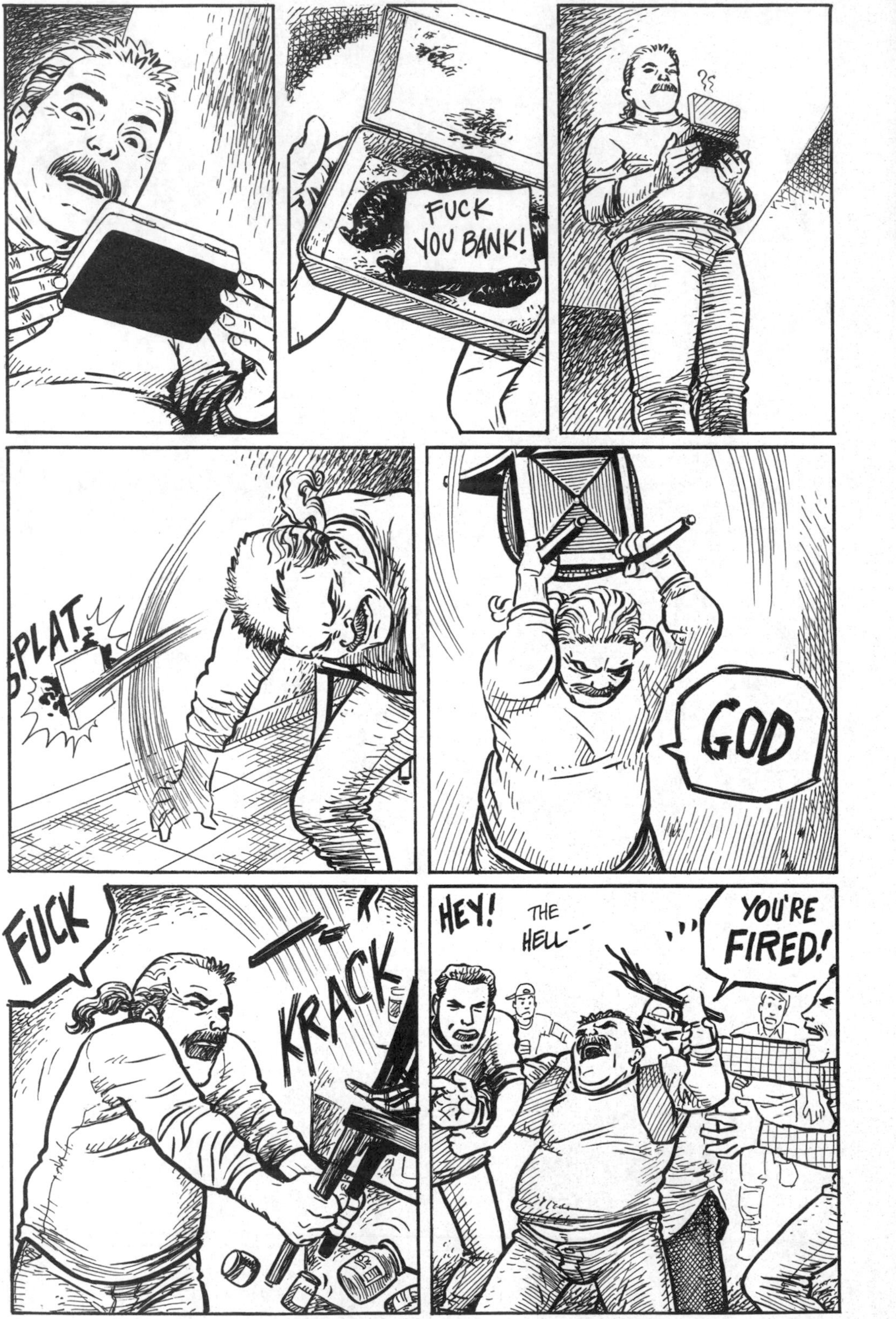
FUCK YOU BANK!
SPLAT
GOD
FUCK
KRACK
HEY!
THE HELL--
YOU'RE FIRED!

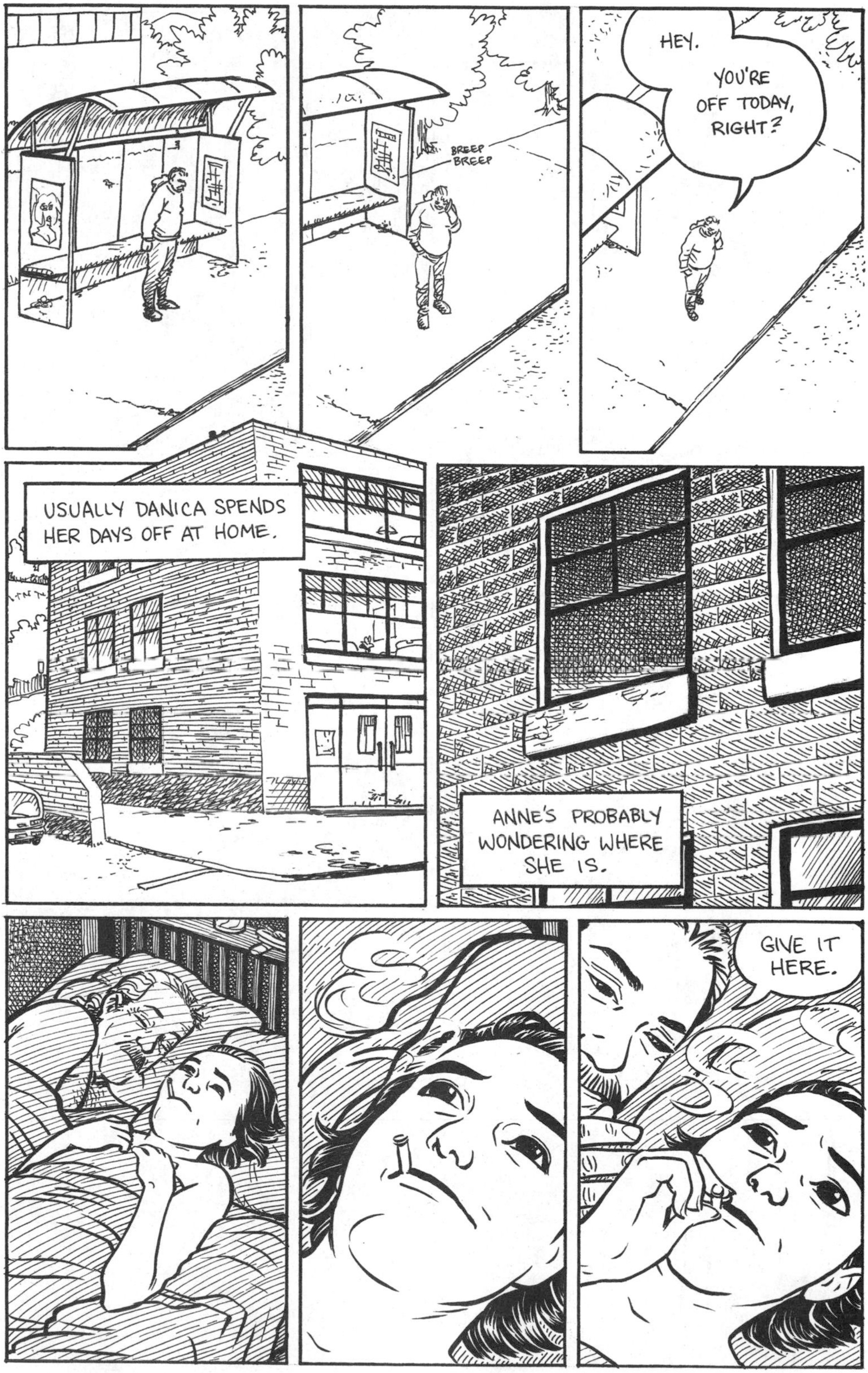
BREEP
BREEP
HEY.
YOU'RE OFF TODAY, RIGHT?
USUALLY DANICA SPENDS HER DAYS OFF AT HOME.
ANNE'S PROBABLY WONDERING WHERE SHE IS.
GIVE IT HERE.

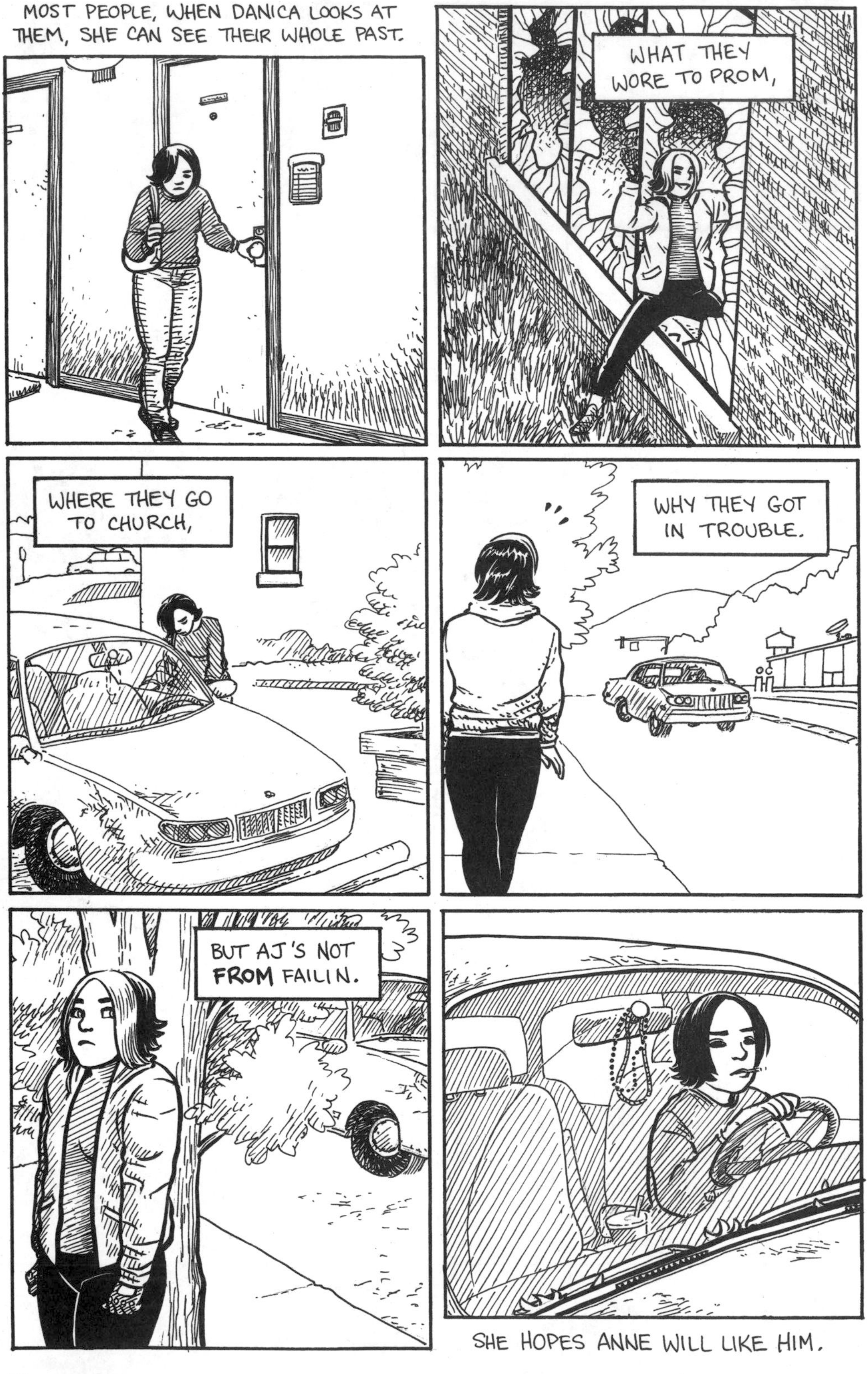
MOST PEOPLE, WHEN DANICA LOOKS AT THEM, SHE CAN SEE THEIR WHOLE PAST.
WHAT THEY WORE TO PROM,
WHERE THEY GO TO CHURCH,
WHY THEY GOT IN TROUBLE.
BUT AJ'S NOT FROM FAILIN.
SHE HOPES ANNE WILL LIKE HIM.

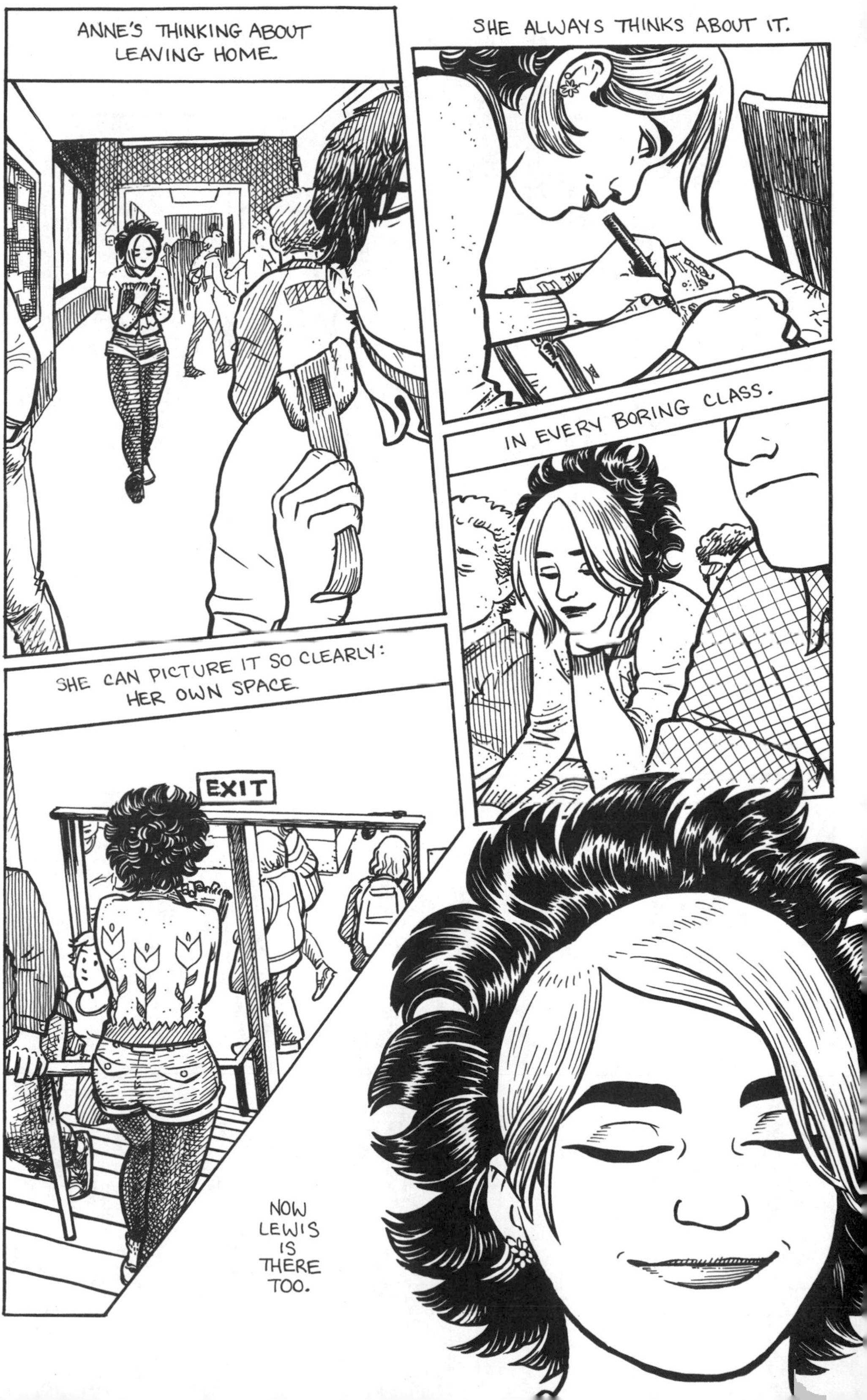
ANNE'S THINKING ABOUT LEAVING HOME.
SHE ALWAYS THINKS ABOUT IT.
IN EVERY BORING CLASS.
SHE CAN PICTURE IT SO CLEARLY: HER OWN SPACE.
EXIT
NOW LEWIS IS THERE TOO.

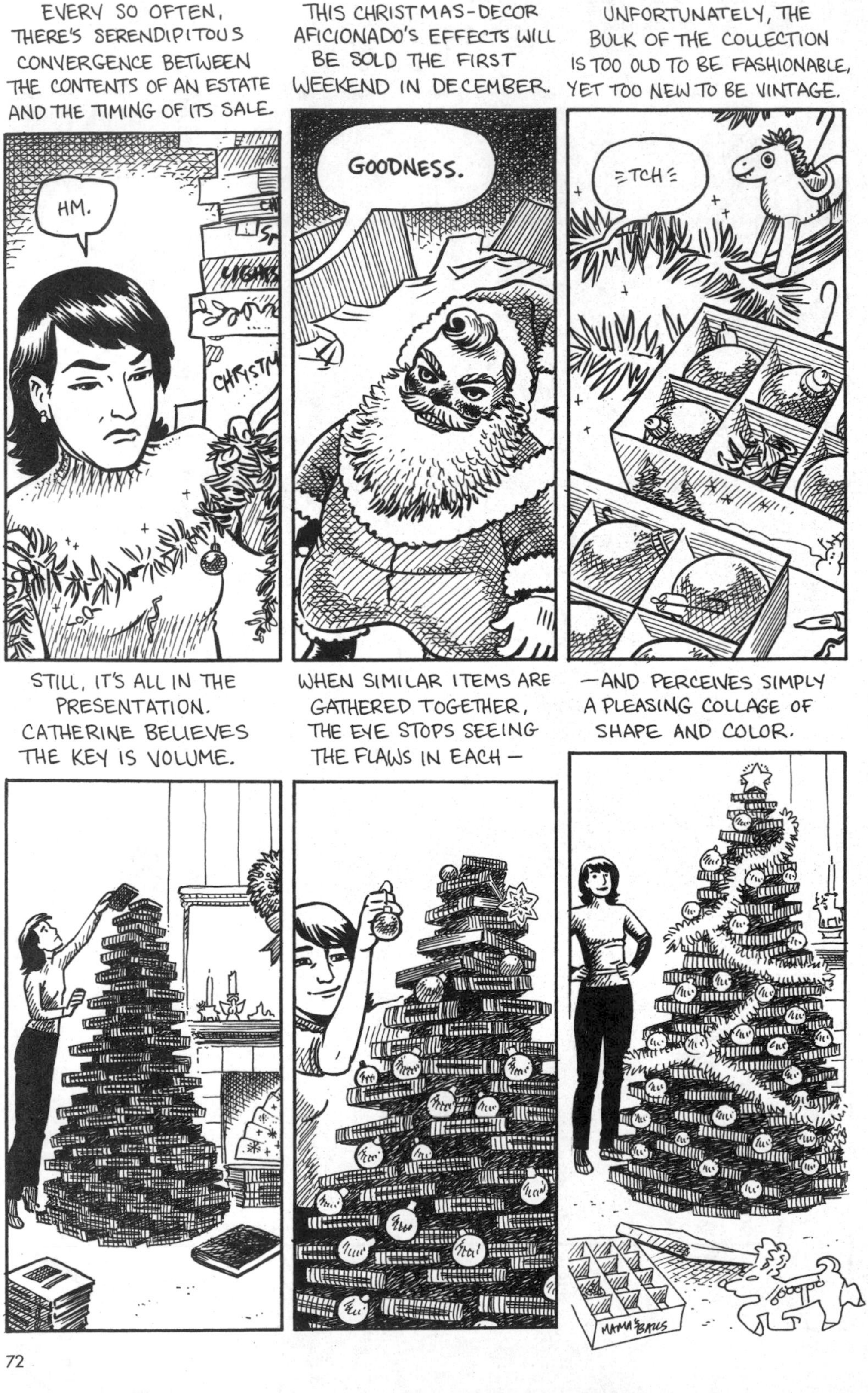
EVERY SO OFTEN, THERE'S SERENDIPITOUS CONVERGENCE BETWEEN THE CONTENTS OF AN ESTATE AND THE TIMING OF ITS SALE.
HM.
THIS CHRISTMAS-DECOR AFICIONADO'S EFFECTS WILL BE SOLD THE FIRST WEEKEND IN DECEMBER.
GOODNESS.
UNFORTUNATELY, THE BULK OF THE COLLECTION IS TOO OLD TO BE FASHIONABLE, YET TOO NEW TO BE VINTAGE.
TCH
STILL, IT'S ALL IN THE PRESENTATION. CATHERINE BELIEVES THE KEY IS VOLUME.
WHEN SIMILAR ITEMS ARE GATHERED TOGETHER, THE EYE STOPS SEEING THE FLAWS IN EACH —
— AND PERCEIVES SIMPLY A PLEASING COLLAGE OF SHAPE AND COLOR.
MAMA'S BALLS

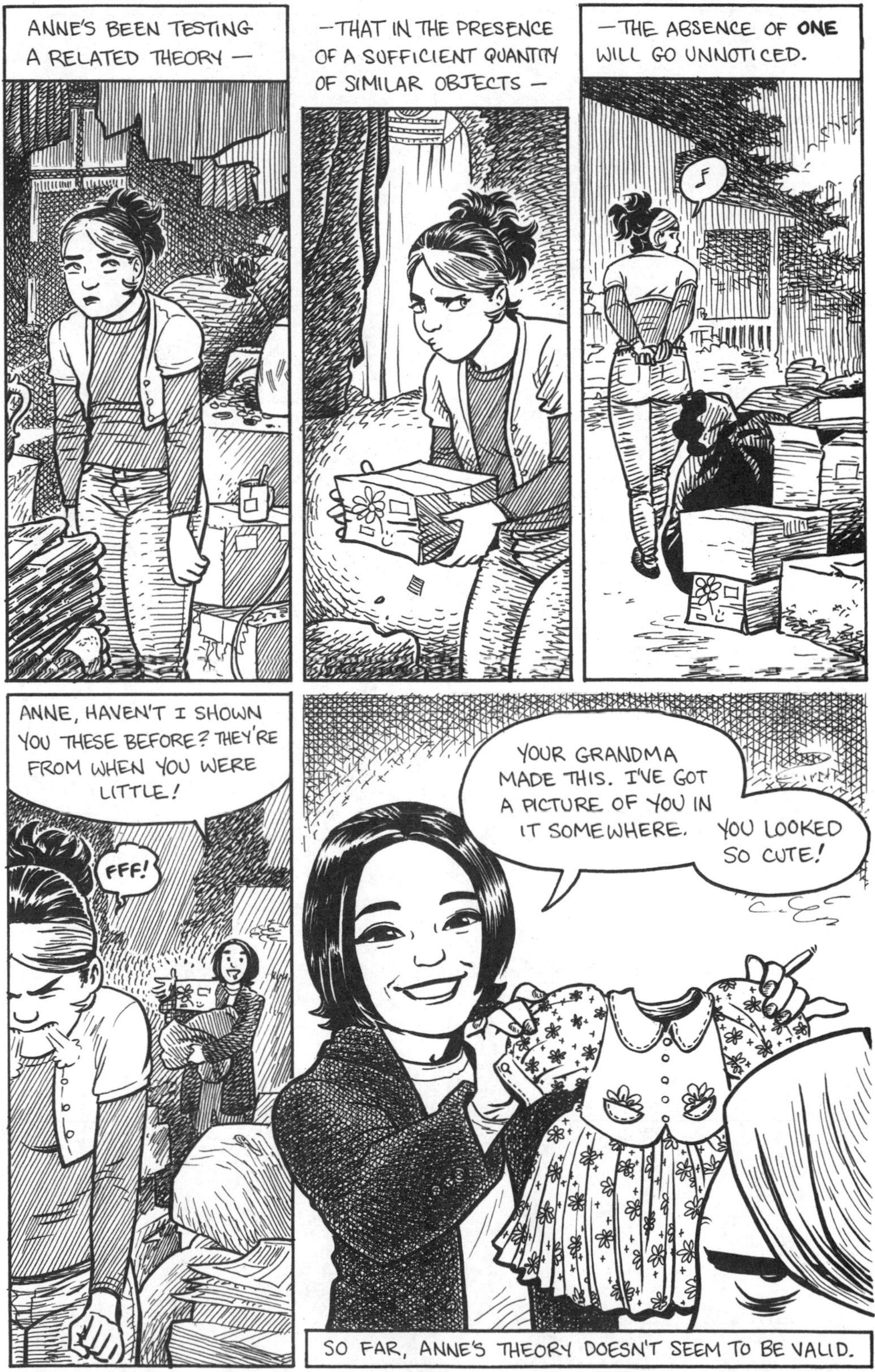
ANNE'S BEEN TESTING A RELATED THEORY —
—THAT IN THE PRESENCE OF A SUFFICIENT QUANTITY OF SIMILAR OBJECTS —
—THE ABSENCE OF **ONE** WILL GO UNNOTICED.
ANNE, HAVEN'T I SHOWN YOU THESE BEFORE? THEY'RE FROM WHEN YOU WERE LITTLE!
FFF!
YOUR GRANDMA MADE THIS. I'VE GOT A PICTURE OF YOU IN IT SOMEWHERE.
YOU LOOKED SO CUTE!
SO FAR, ANNE'S THEORY DOESN'T SEEM TO BE VALID.

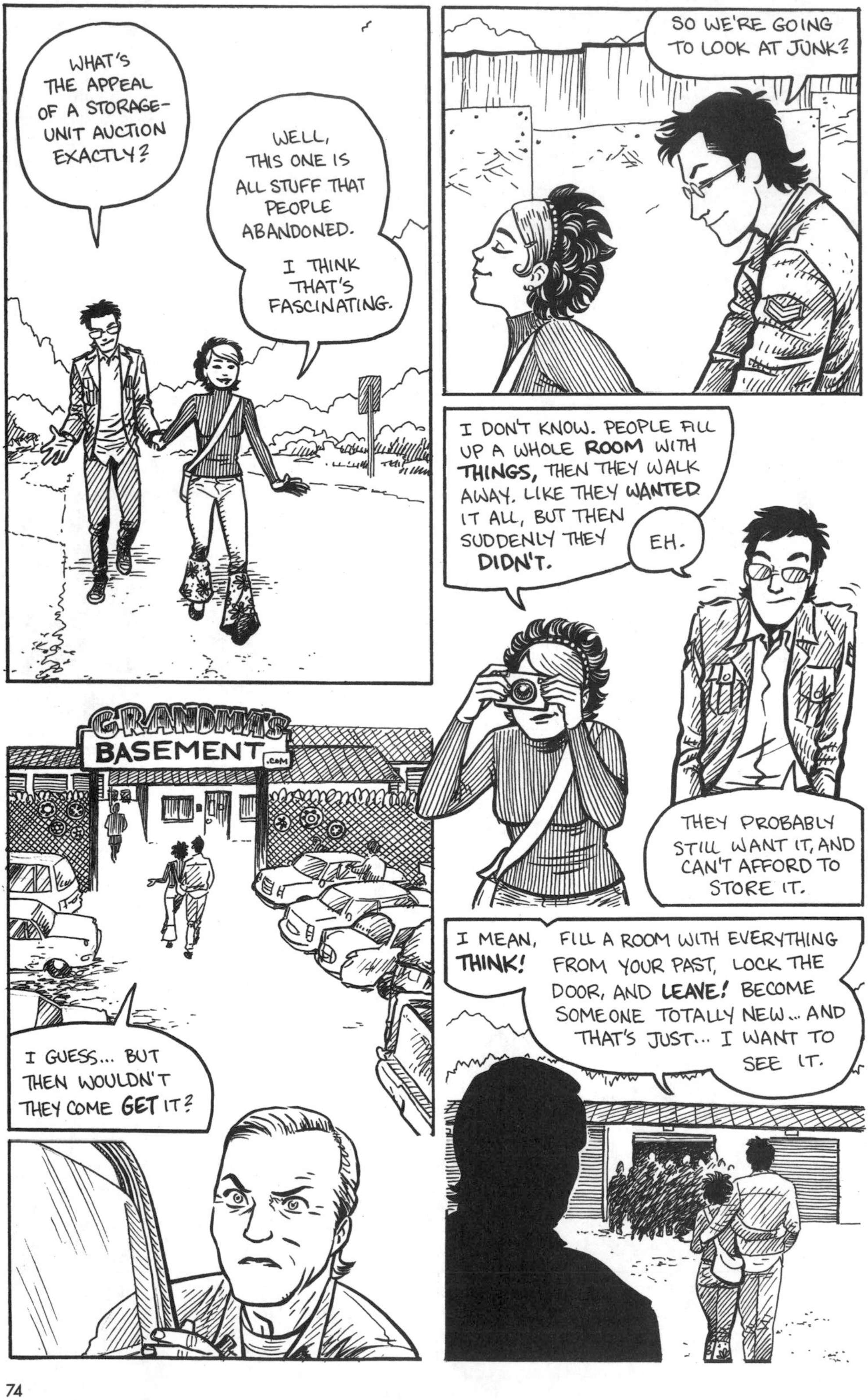
WHAT'S THE APPEAL OF A STORAGE-UNIT AUCTION EXACTLY?
WELL, THIS ONE IS ALL STUFF THAT PEOPLE ABANDONED.
I THINK THAT'S FASCINATING.
SO WE'RE GOING TO LOOK AT JUNK?
I DON'T KNOW. PEOPLE FILL UP A WHOLE ROOM WITH THINGS, THEN THEY WALK AWAY. LIKE THEY WANTED IT ALL, BUT THEN SUDDENLY THEY DIDN'T.
EH.
THEY PROBABLY STILL WANT IT, AND CAN'T AFFORD TO STORE IT.
GRANDMA'S BASEMENT .com
I GUESS... BUT THEN WOULDN'T THEY COME GET IT?
I MEAN, THINK!
FILL A ROOM WITH EVERYTHING FROM YOUR PAST, LOCK THE DOOR, AND LEAVE! BECOME SOMEONE TOTALLY NEW... AND THAT'S JUST... I WANT TO SEE IT.

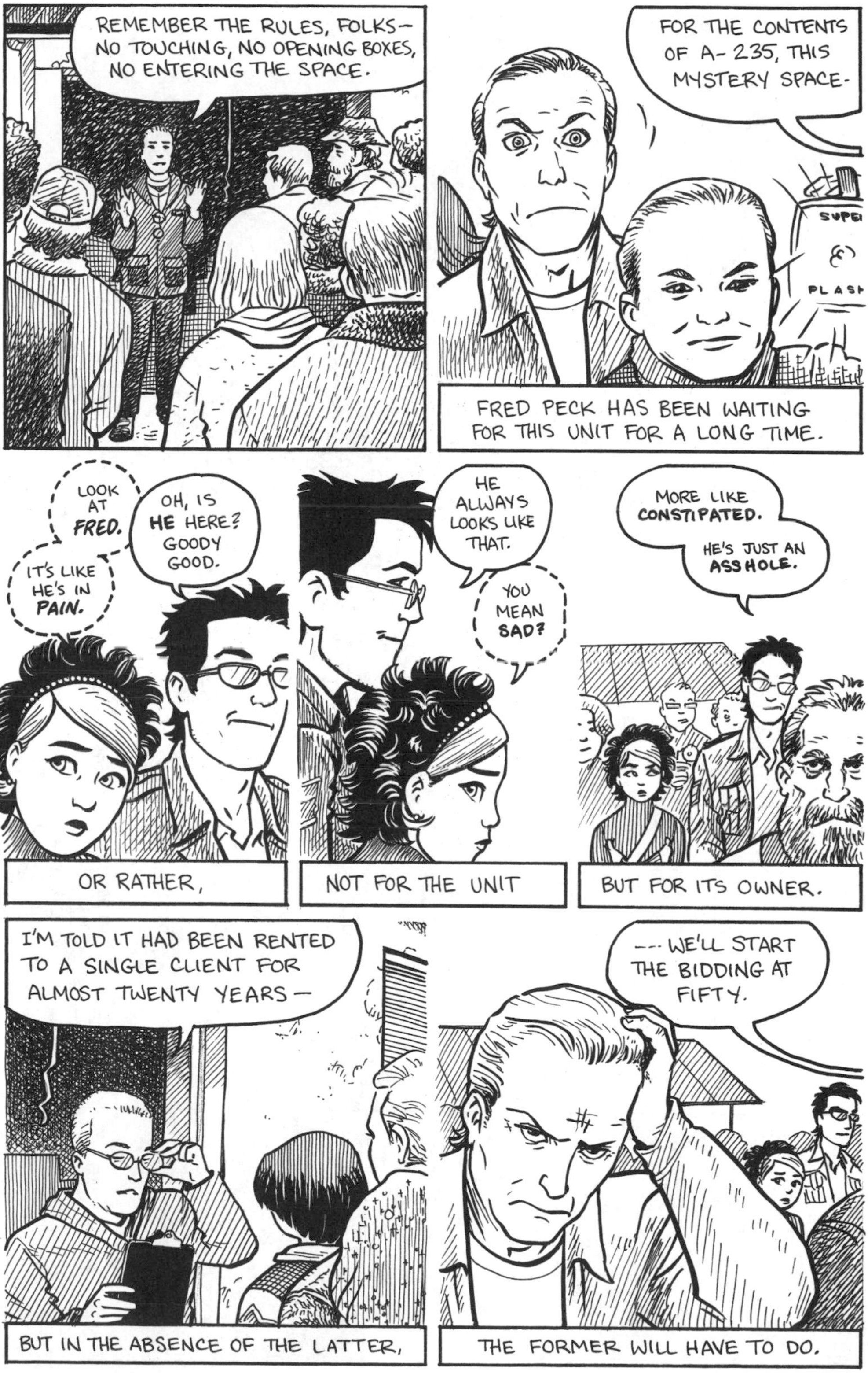

REMEMBER THE RULES, FOLKS— NO TOUCHING, NO OPENING BOXES, NO ENTERING THE SPACE.
FOR THE CONTENTS OF A-235, THIS MYSTERY SPACE-
FRED PECK HAS BEEN WAITING FOR THIS UNIT FOR A LONG TIME.
LOOK AT FRED.
IT'S LIKE HE'S IN PAIN.
OH, IS HE HERE? GOODY GOOD.
OR RATHER,
HE ALWAYS LOOKS LIKE THAT.
YOU MEAN SAD?
NOT FOR THE UNIT
MORE LIKE CONSTIPATED.
HE'S JUST AN ASSHOLE.
BUT FOR ITS OWNER.
I'M TOLD IT HAD BEEN RENTED TO A SINGLE CLIENT FOR ALMOST TWENTY YEARS—
BUT IN THE ABSENCE OF THE LATTER,
---WE'LL START THE BIDDING AT FIFTY.
THE FORMER WILL HAVE TO DO.

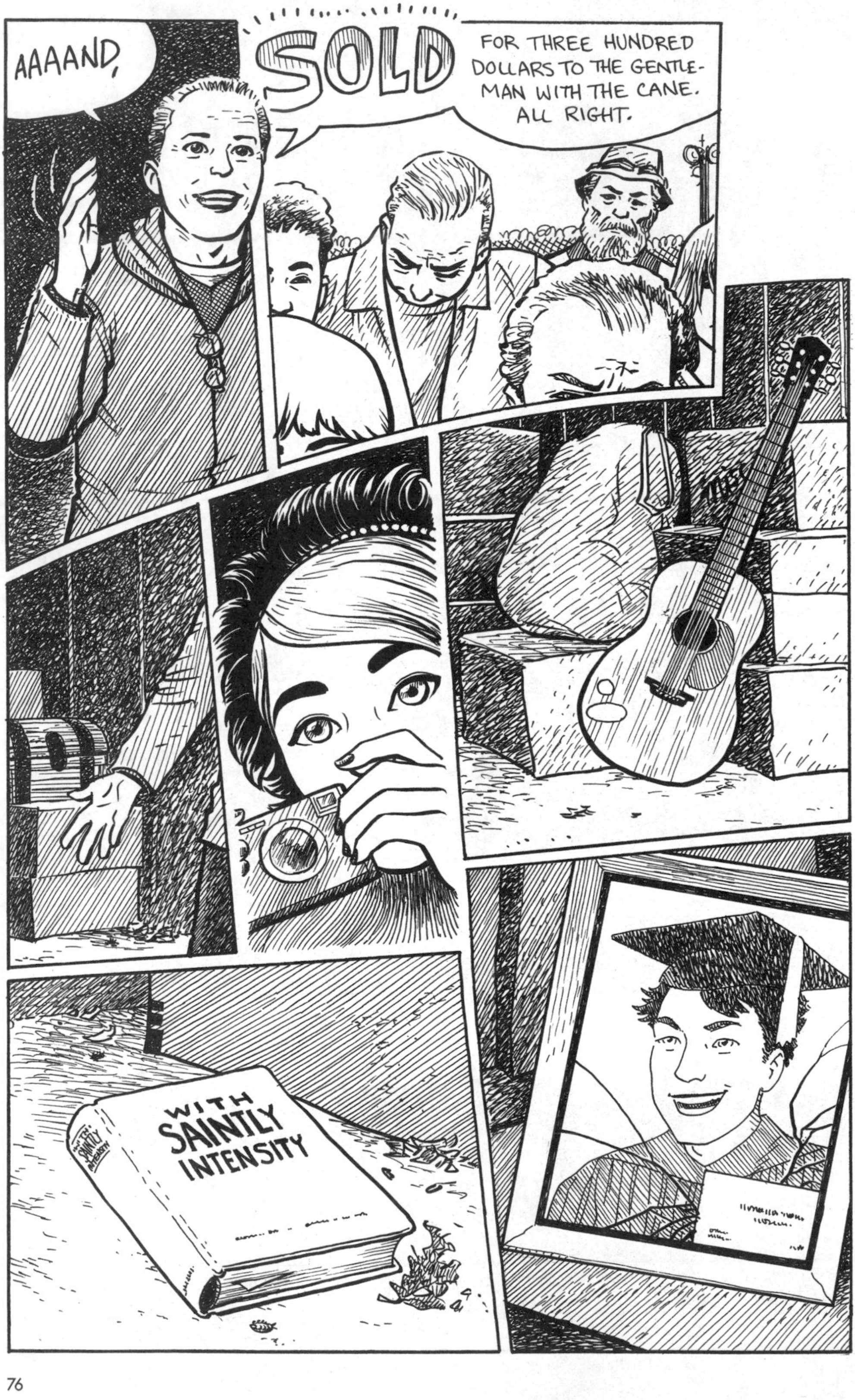
AAAAND,
SOLD
FOR THREE HUNDRED DOLLARS TO THE GENTLEMAN WITH THE CANE. ALL RIGHT.
WITH SAINTLY INTENSITY

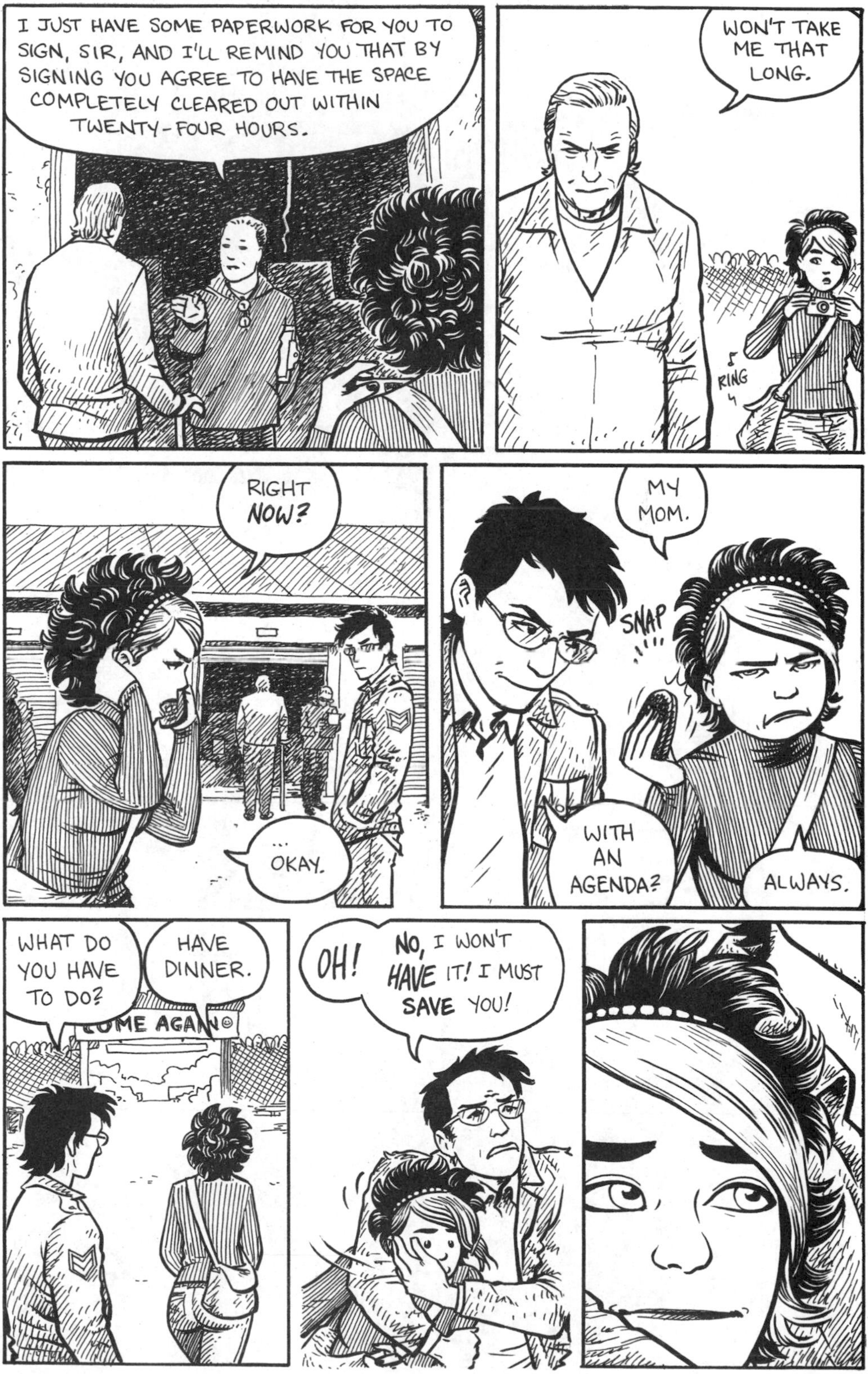
I JUST HAVE SOME PAPERWORK FOR YOU TO SIGN, SIR, AND I'LL REMIND YOU THAT BY SIGNING YOU AGREE TO HAVE THE SPACE COMPLETELY CLEARED OUT WITHIN TWENTY-FOUR HOURS.
WON'T TAKE ME THAT LONG.
RING
RIGHT NOW?
... OKAY.
MY MOM.
SNAP
WITH AN AGENDA?
ALWAYS.
WHAT DO YOU HAVE TO DO?
HAVE DINNER.
COME AGAIN
OH!
NO, I WON'T HAVE IT! I MUST SAVE YOU!

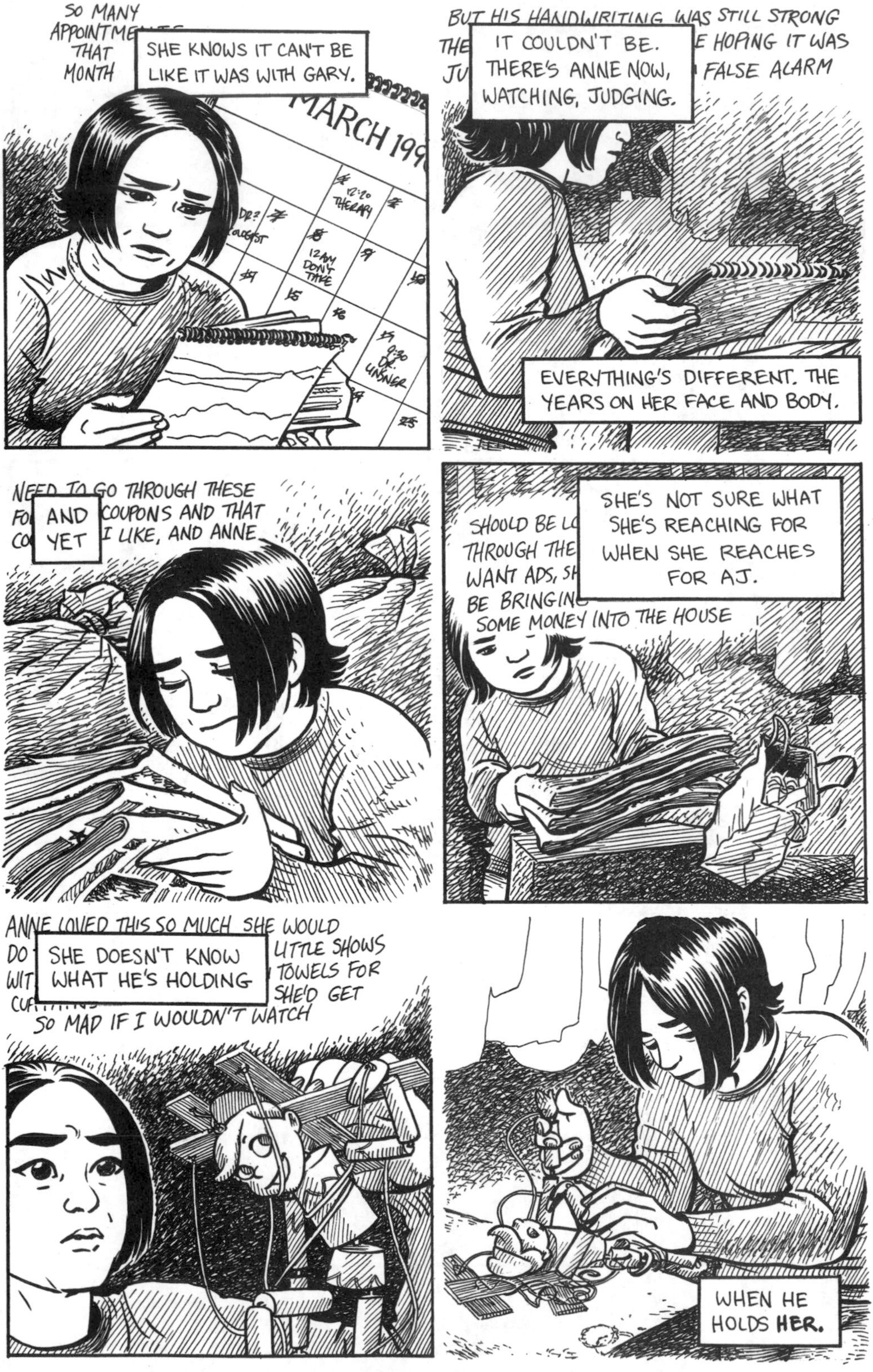

SO MANY APPOINTME THAT MONTH
SHE KNOWS IT CAN'T BE LIKE IT WAS WITH GARY.
MARCH 199
12:20 THERAPY
12AM DON'T TAKE
9:30 DR. UNSNER
BUT HIS HANDWRITING WAS STILL STRONG THE E HOPING IT WAS JU FALSE ALARM
IT COULDN'T BE. THERE'S ANNE NOW, WATCHING, JUDGING.
EVERYTHING'S DIFFERENT. THE YEARS ON HER FACE AND BODY.
NEED TO GO THROUGH THESE FO COUPONS AND THAT CO I LIKE, AND ANNE
AND YET
SHOULD BE LO THROUGH THE WANT ADS, SH BE BRINGIN SOME MONEY INTO THE HOUSE
SHE'S NOT SURE WHAT SHE'S REACHING FOR WHEN SHE REACHES FOR AJ.
ANNE LOVED THIS SO MUCH SHE WOULD DO LITTLE SHOWS WIT TOWELS FOR SHE'D GET SO MAD IF I WOULDN'T WATCH
SHE DOESN'T KNOW WHAT HE'S HOLDING
WHEN HE HOLDS **HER.**

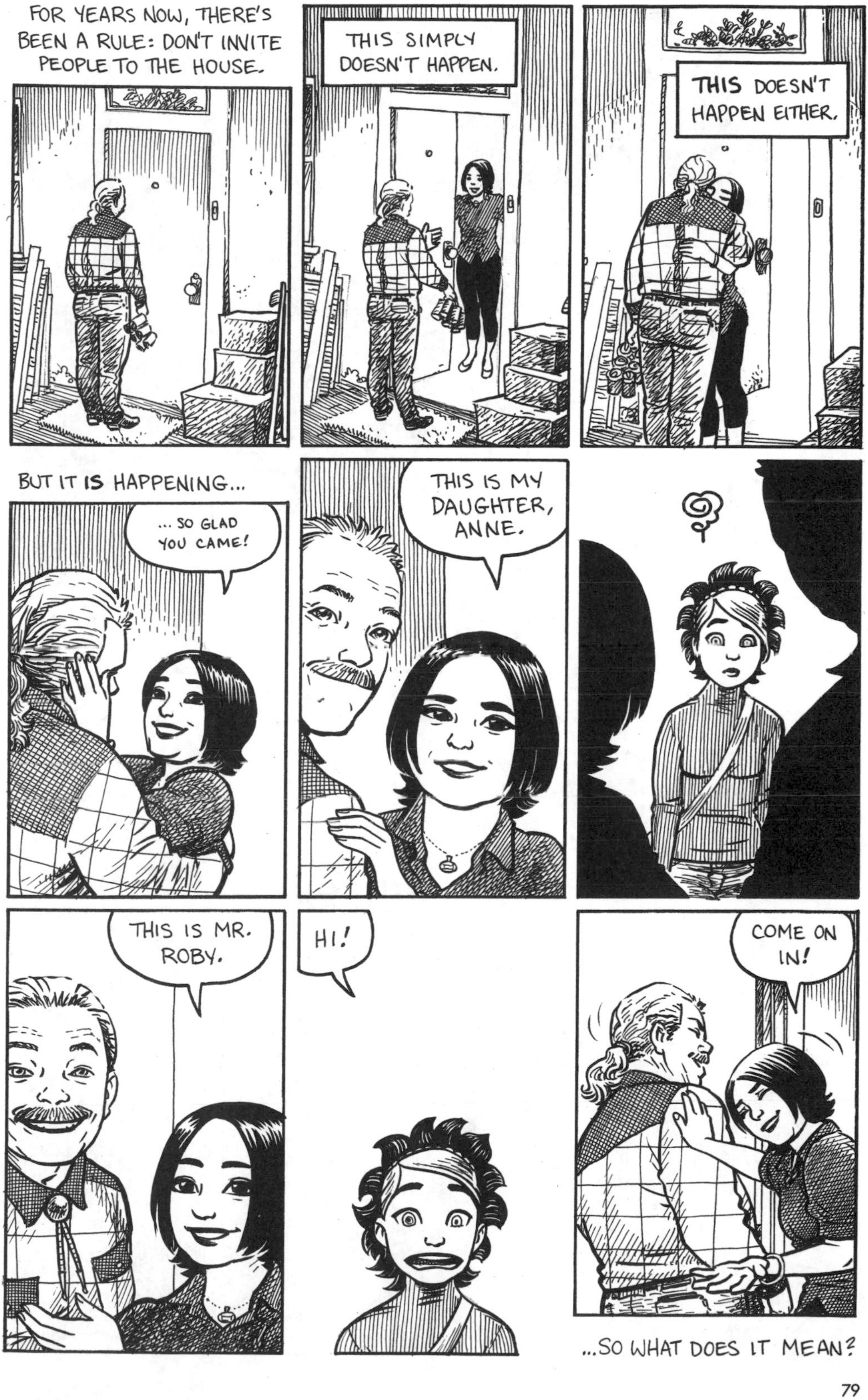
FOR YEARS NOW, THERE'S BEEN A RULE: DON'T INVITE PEOPLE TO THE HOUSE.
THIS SIMPLY DOESN'T HAPPEN.
THIS DOESN'T HAPPEN EITHER.
BUT IT IS HAPPENING...
...SO GLAD YOU CAME!
THIS IS MY DAUGHTER, ANNE.
THIS IS MR. ROBY.
HI!
COME ON IN!
...SO WHAT DOES IT MEAN?

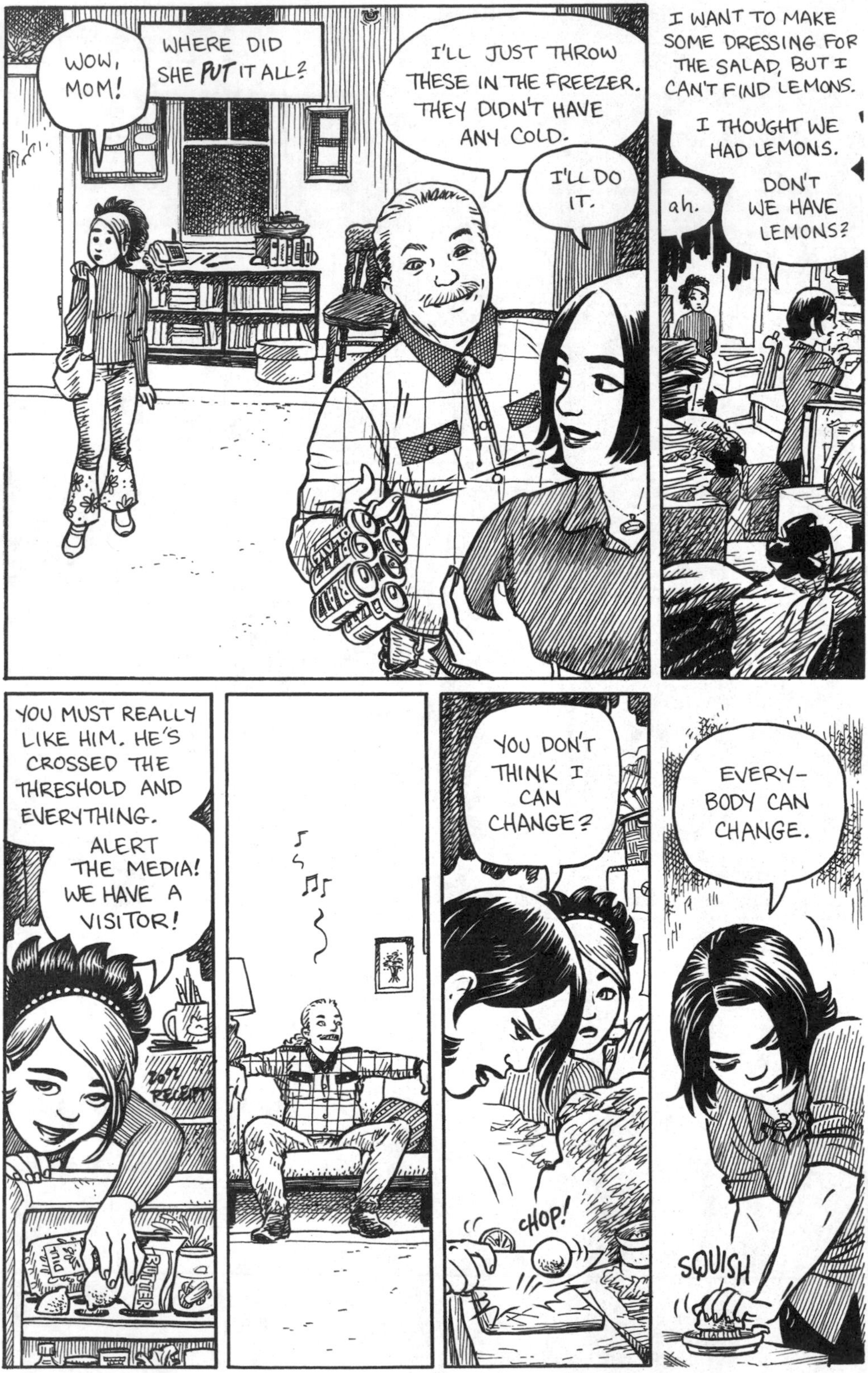
WOW, MOM!
WHERE DID SHE PUT IT ALL?
I'LL JUST THROW THESE IN THE FREEZER. THEY DIDN'T HAVE ANY COLD.
I'LL DO IT.
I WANT TO MAKE SOME DRESSING FOR THE SALAD, BUT I CAN'T FIND LEMONS.
I THOUGHT WE HAD LEMONS.
ah.
DON'T WE HAVE LEMONS?
YOU MUST REALLY LIKE HIM. HE'S CROSSED THE THRESHOLD AND EVERYTHING.
ALERT THE MEDIA! WE HAVE A VISITOR!
YOU DON'T THINK I CAN CHANGE?
CHOP!
EVERY-BODY CAN CHANGE.
SQUISH

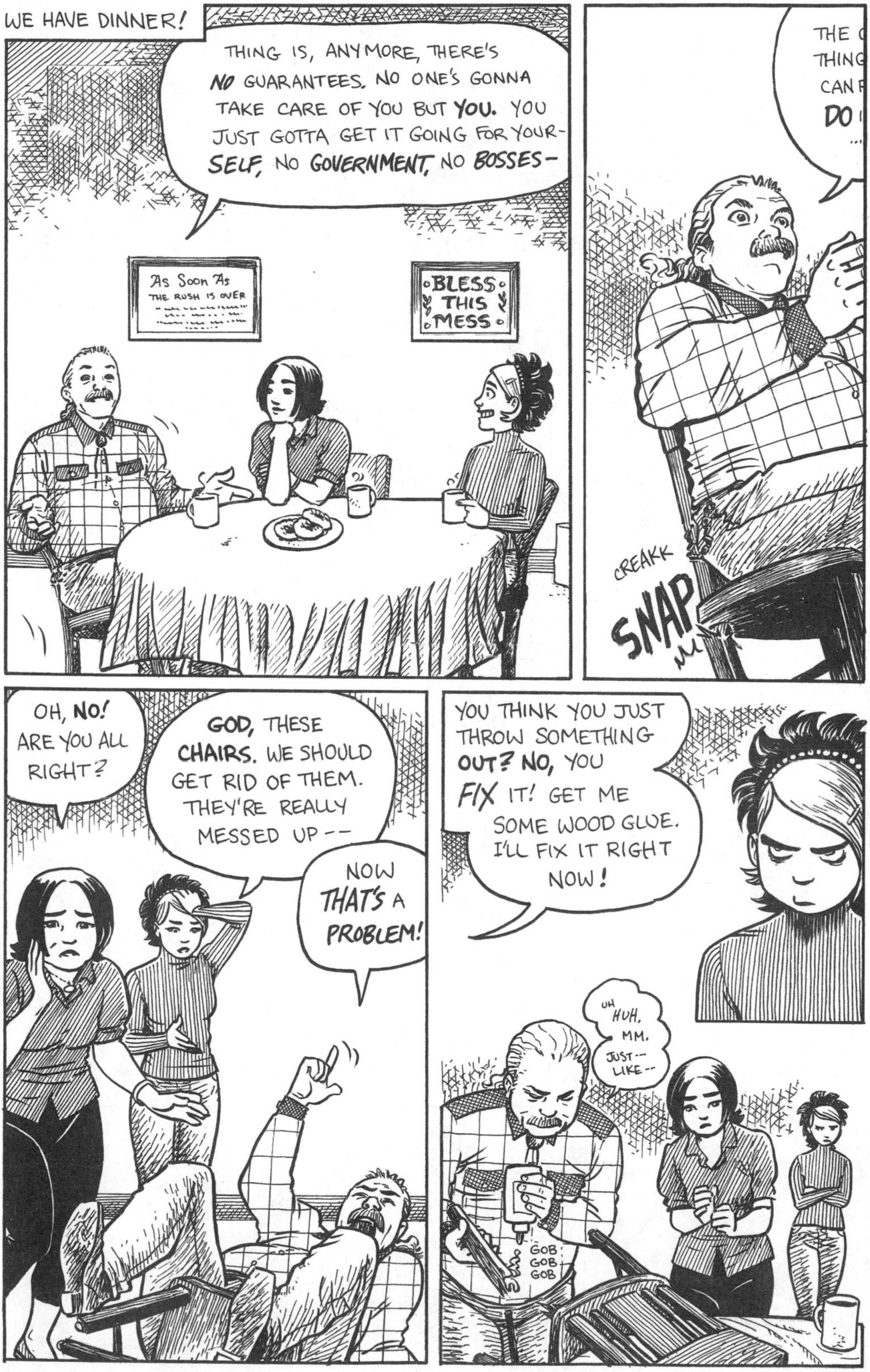

WE HAVE DINNER!
THING IS, ANYMORE, THERE'S NO GUARANTEES. NO ONE'S GONNA TAKE CARE OF YOU BUT YOU. YOU JUST GOTTA GET IT GOING FOR YOURSELF, NO GOVERNMENT, NO BOSSES-
As Soon As THE RUSH IS OVER
BLESS THIS MESS
CREAKK
SNAP
OH, NO! ARE YOU ALL RIGHT?
GOD, THESE CHAIRS. WE SHOULD GET RID OF THEM. THEY'RE REALLY MESSED UP --
NOW THAT'S A PROBLEM!
YOU THINK YOU JUST THROW SOMETHING OUT? NO, YOU FIX IT! GET ME SOME WOOD GLUE. I'LL FIX IT RIGHT NOW!
UH HUH. MM. JUST -- LIKE --
GOB GOB GOB

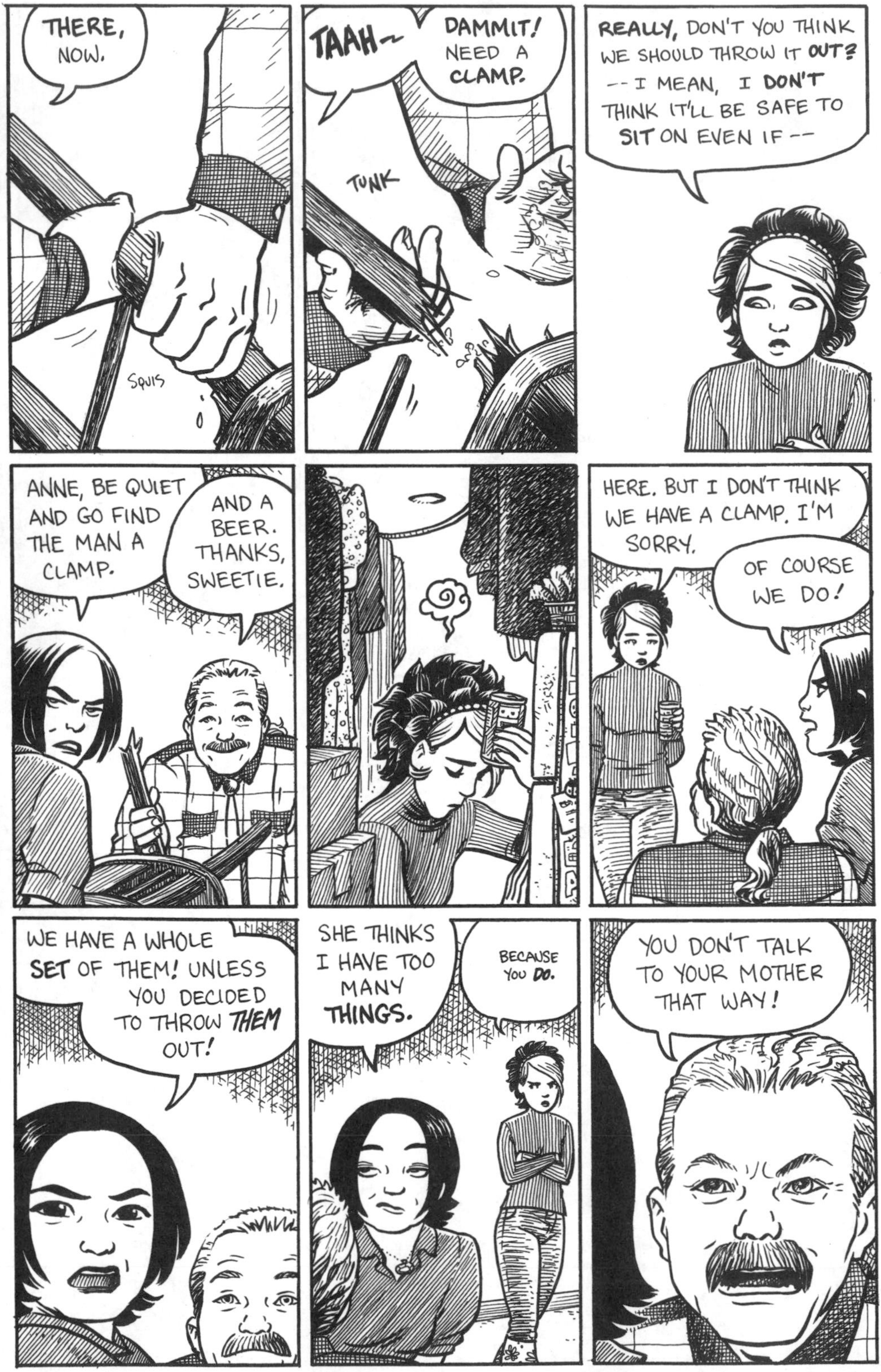
THERE, NOW.
SQUIS
TAAH~
DAMMIT! NEED A CLAMP.
TUNK
REALLY, DON'T YOU THINK WE SHOULD THROW IT OUT? -- I MEAN, I DON'T THINK IT'LL BE SAFE TO SIT ON EVEN IF --
ANNE, BE QUIET AND GO FIND THE MAN A CLAMP.
AND A BEER. THANKS, SWEETIE.
HERE. BUT I DON'T THINK WE HAVE A CLAMP. I'M SORRY.
OF COURSE WE DO!
WE HAVE A WHOLE SET OF THEM! UNLESS YOU DECIDED TO THROW THEM OUT!
SHE THINKS I HAVE TOO MANY THINGS.
BECAUSE YOU DO.
YOU DON'T TALK TO YOUR MOTHER THAT WAY!

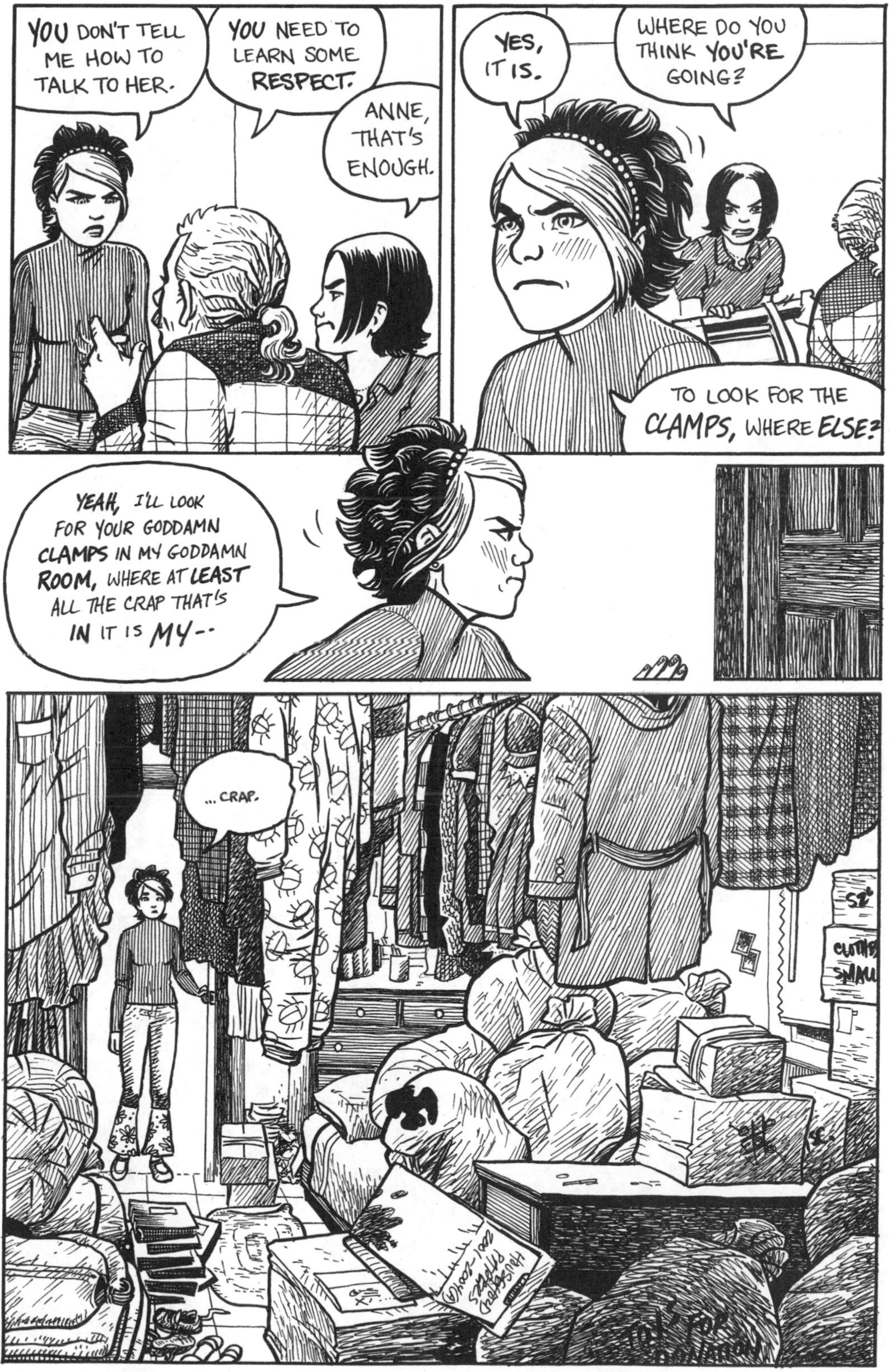
YOU DON'T TELL ME HOW TO TALK TO HER.
YOU NEED TO LEARN SOME RESPECT.
ANNE, THAT'S ENOUGH.
YES, IT IS.
WHERE DO YOU THINK YOU'RE GOING?
TO LOOK FOR THE CLAMPS, WHERE ELSE?
YEAH, I'LL LOOK FOR YOUR GODDAMN CLAMPS IN MY GODDAMN ROOM, WHERE AT LEAST ALL THE CRAP THAT'S IN IT IS MY--
...CRAP.

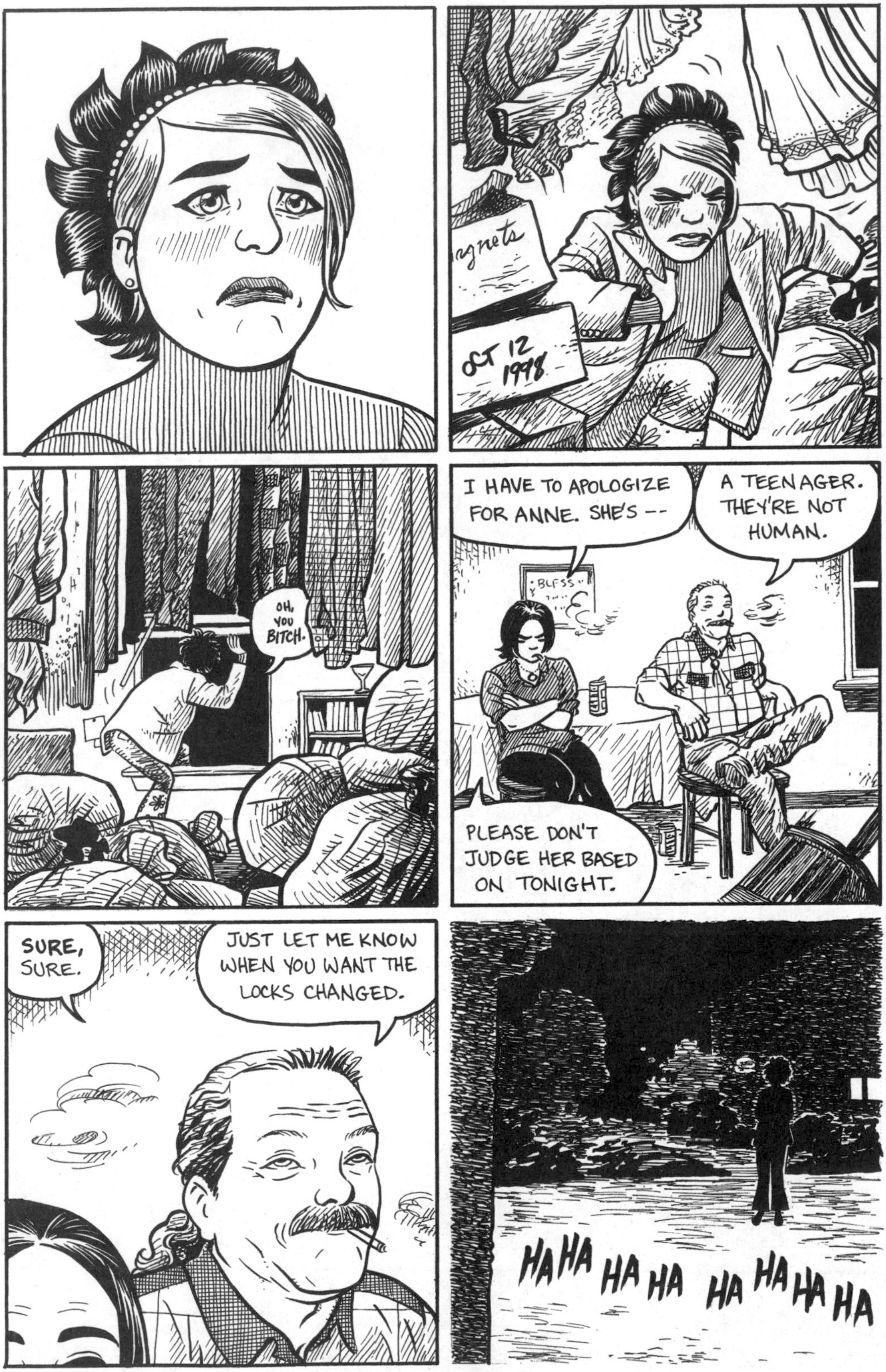
OCT 12 1998
OH, YOU BITCH.
I HAVE TO APOLOGIZE FOR ANNE. SHE'S --
A TEENAGER. THEY'RE NOT HUMAN.
PLEASE DON'T JUDGE HER BASED ON TONIGHT.
SURE, SURE.
JUST LET ME KNOW WHEN YOU WANT THE LOCKS CHANGED.
HA HA HA HA HA HA HA HA HA

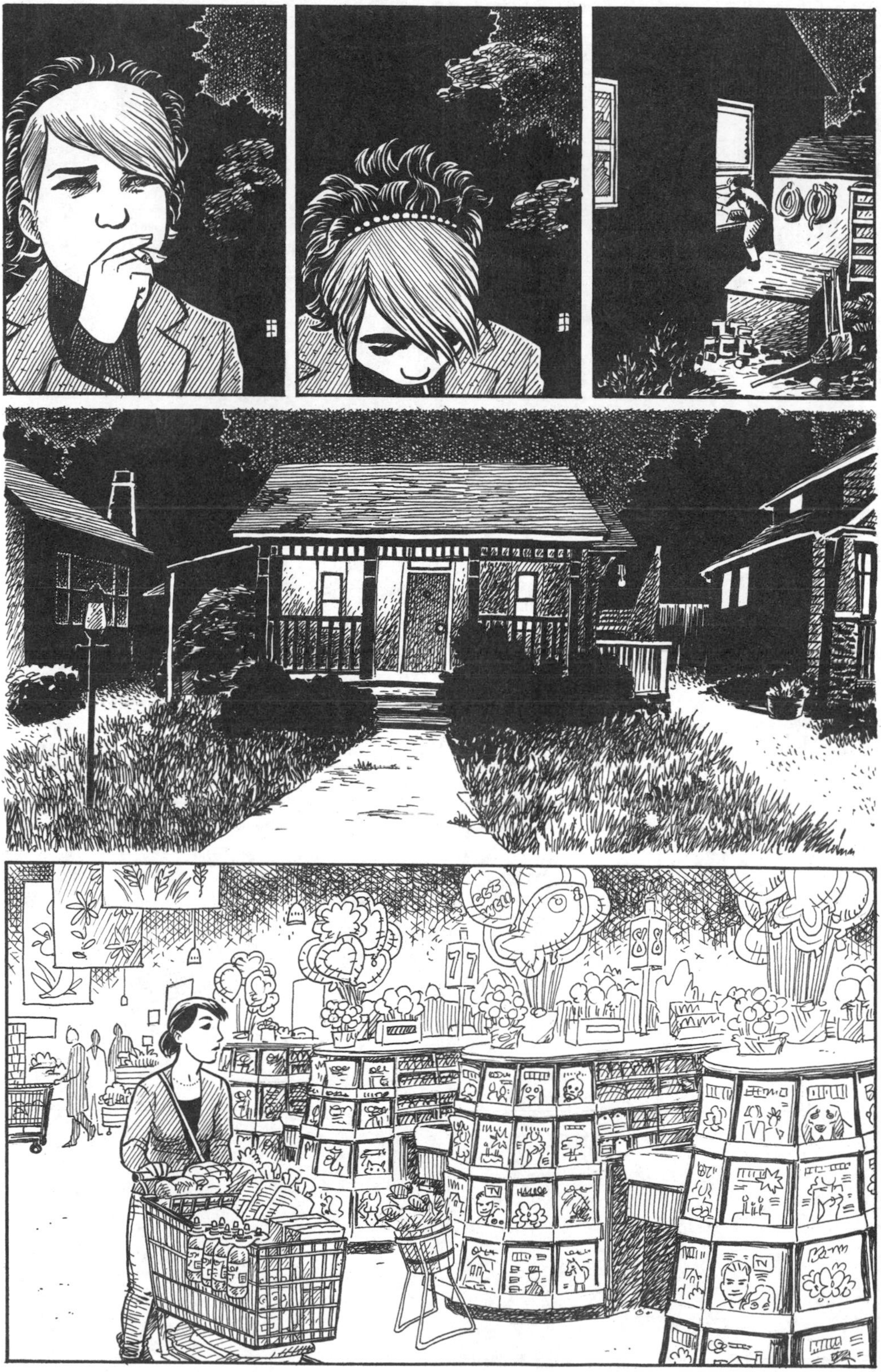
77
88

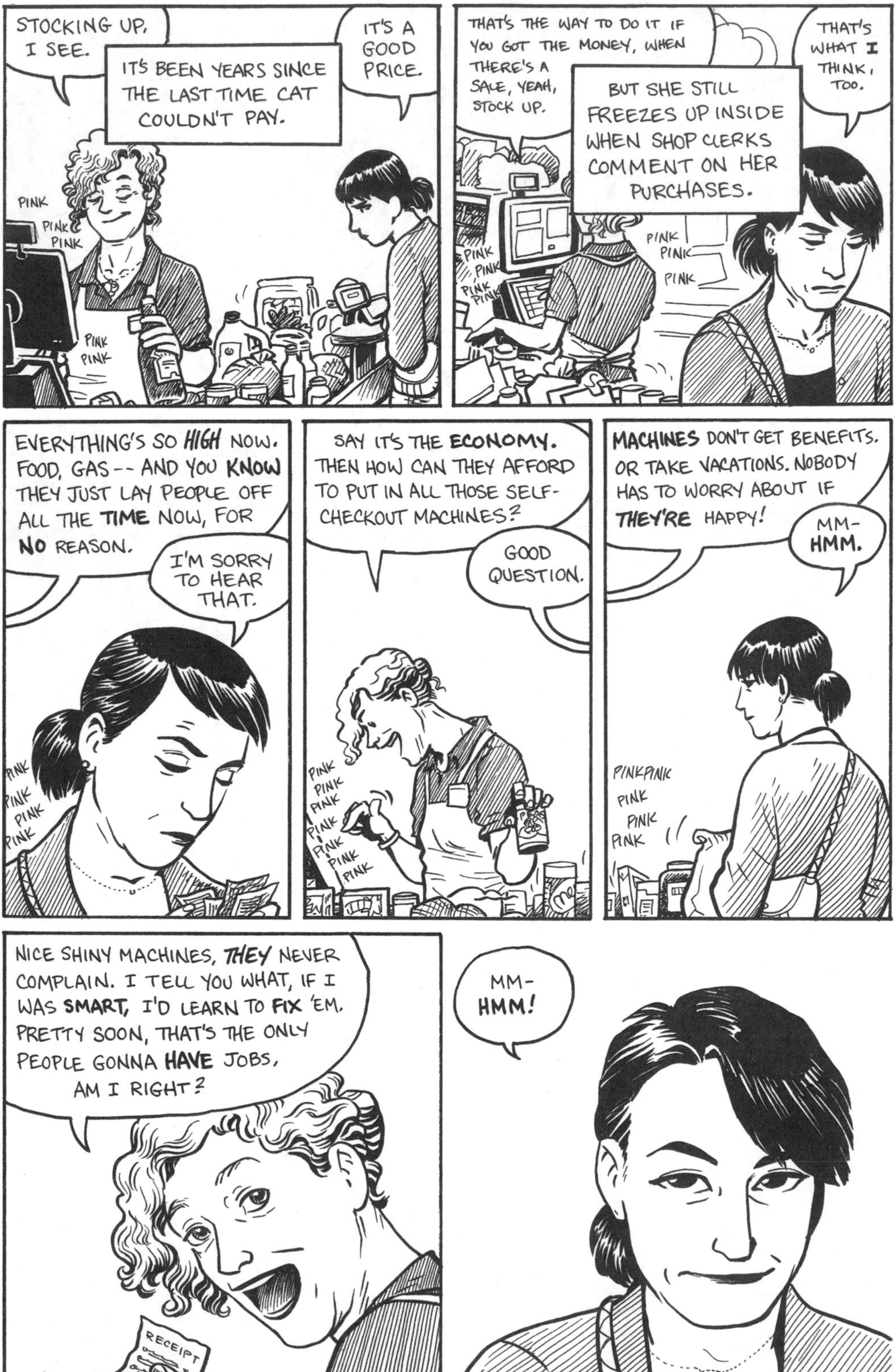
STOCKING UP, I SEE.
IT'S BEEN YEARS SINCE THE LAST TIME CAT COULDN'T PAY.
IT'S A GOOD PRICE.
PINK PINK PINK
PINK PINK
THAT'S THE WAY TO DO IT IF YOU GOT THE MONEY, WHEN THERE'S A SALE, YEAH, STOCK UP.
BUT SHE STILL FREEZES UP INSIDE WHEN SHOP CLERKS COMMENT ON HER PURCHASES.
THAT'S WHAT I THINK, TOO.
PINK PINK PINK PINK
PINK PINK PINK
EVERYTHING'S SO HIGH NOW. FOOD, GAS-- AND YOU KNOW THEY JUST LAY PEOPLE OFF ALL THE TIME NOW, FOR NO REASON.
I'M SORRY TO HEAR THAT.
PINK PINK PINK PINK
SAY IT'S THE ECONOMY. THEN HOW CAN THEY AFFORD TO PUT IN ALL THOSE SELF-CHECKOUT MACHINES?
GOOD QUESTION.
PINK PINK PINK PINK PINK PINK PINK
MACHINES DON'T GET BENEFITS. OR TAKE VACATIONS. NOBODY HAS TO WORRY ABOUT IF THEY'RE HAPPY!
MM-HMM.
PINKPINK PINK PINK PINK
NICE SHINY MACHINES, THEY NEVER COMPLAIN. I TELL YOU WHAT, IF I WAS SMART, I'D LEARN TO FIX 'EM. PRETTY SOON, THAT'S THE ONLY PEOPLE GONNA HAVE JOBS, AM I RIGHT?
MM-HMM!
RECEIPT

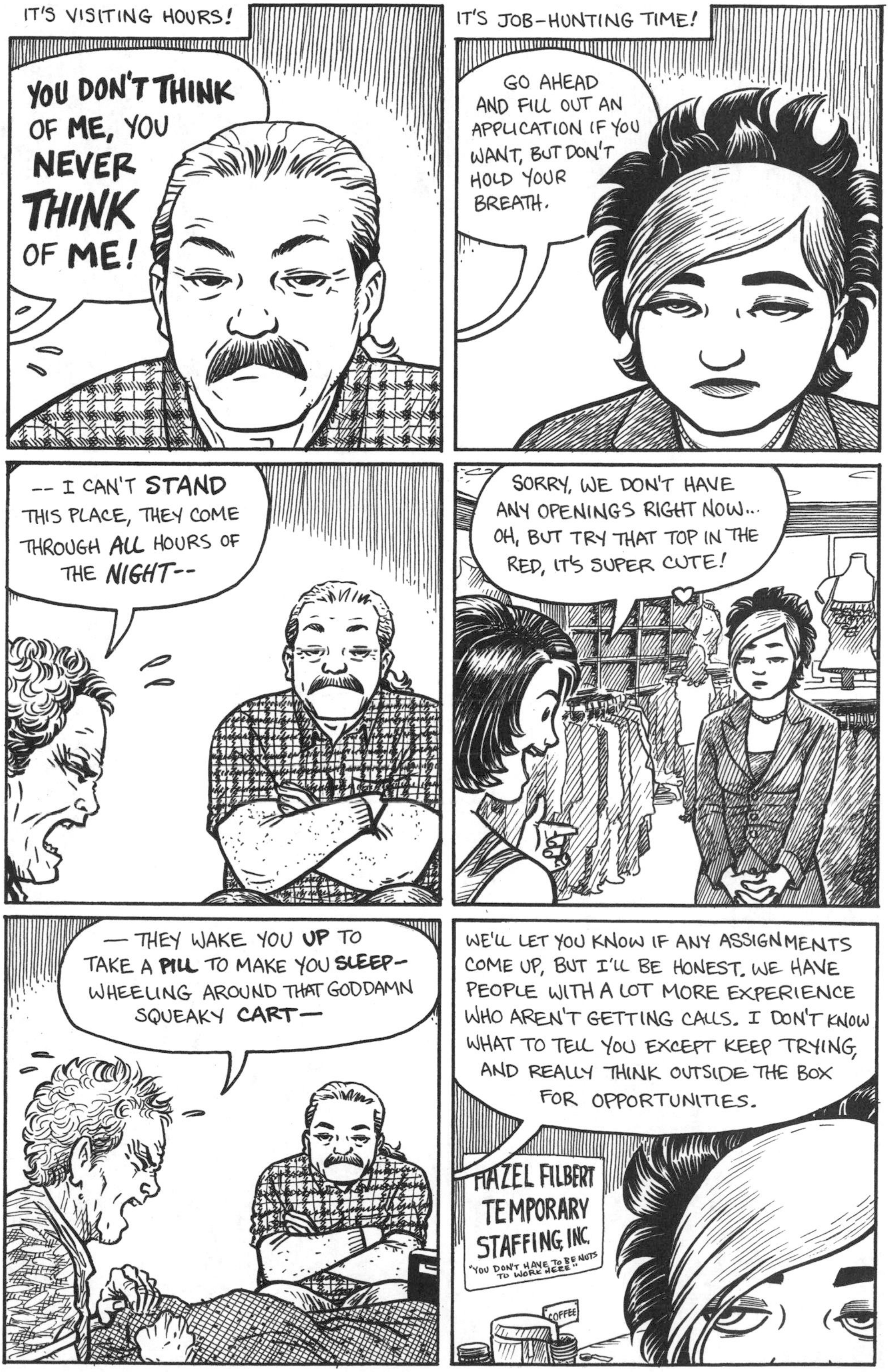
IT'S VISITING HOURS!
YOU DON'T THINK OF ME, YOU NEVER THINK OF ME!
IT'S JOB-HUNTING TIME!
GO AHEAD AND FILL OUT AN APPLICATION IF YOU WANT, BUT DON'T HOLD YOUR BREATH.
-- I CAN'T STAND THIS PLACE, THEY COME THROUGH ALL HOURS OF THE NIGHT--
SORRY, WE DON'T HAVE ANY OPENINGS RIGHT NOW... OH, BUT TRY THAT TOP IN THE RED, IT'S SUPER CUTE!
— THEY WAKE YOU UP TO TAKE A PILL TO MAKE YOU SLEEP- WHEELING AROUND THAT GODDAMN SQUEAKY CART—
WE'LL LET YOU KNOW IF ANY ASSIGNMENTS COME UP, BUT I'LL BE HONEST. WE HAVE PEOPLE WITH A LOT MORE EXPERIENCE WHO AREN'T GETTING CALLS. I DON'T KNOW WHAT TO TELL YOU EXCEPT KEEP TRYING, AND REALLY THINK OUTSIDE THE BOX FOR OPPORTUNITIES.
HAZEL FILBERT TEMPORARY STAFFING, INC.
"YOU DON'T HAVE TO BE NUTS TO WORK HERE"
COFFEE

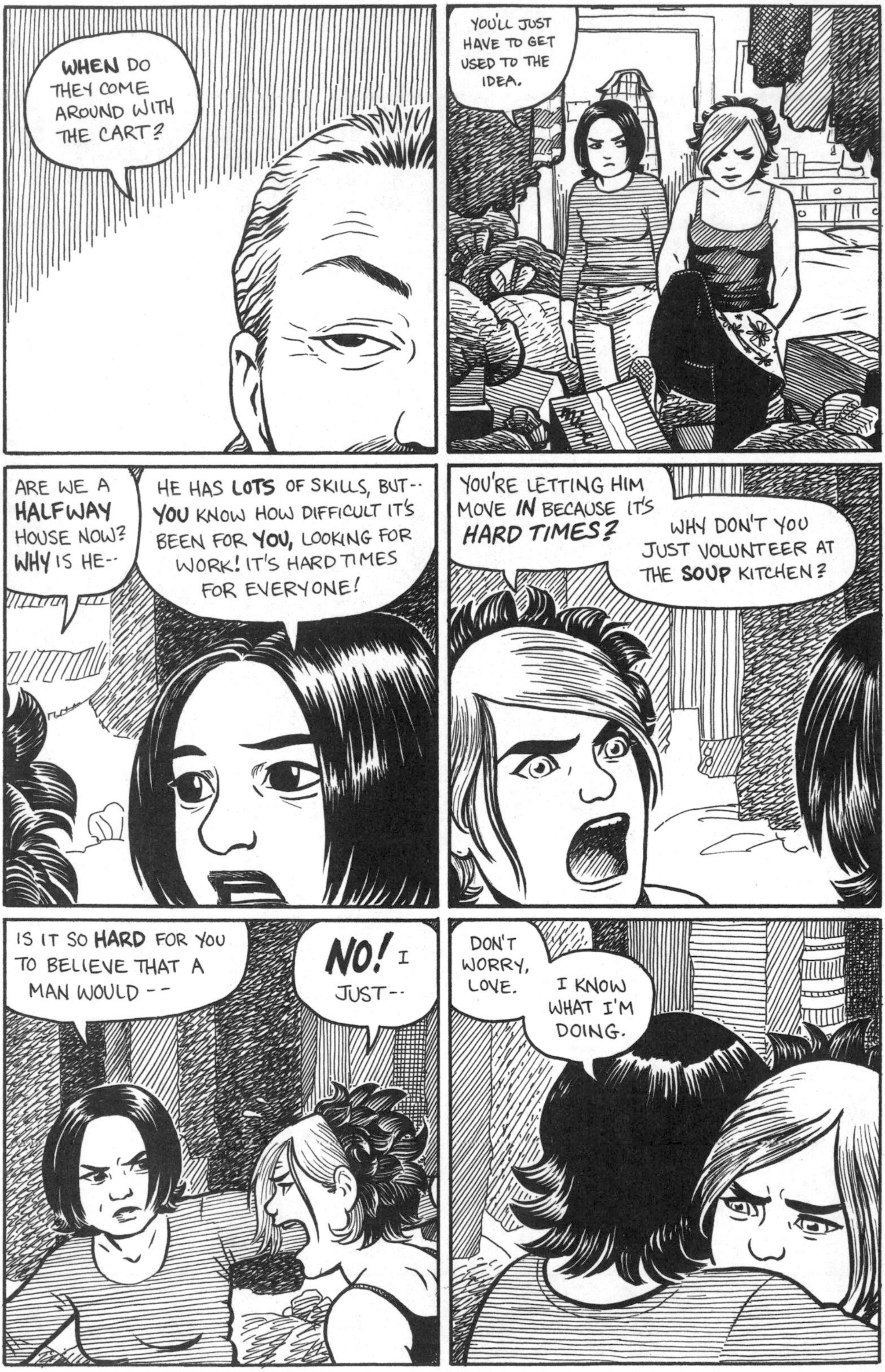
WHEN DO THEY COME AROUND WITH THE CART?
YOU'LL JUST HAVE TO GET USED TO THE IDEA.
ARE WE A HALFWAY HOUSE NOW? WHY IS HE--
HE HAS LOTS OF SKILLS, BUT-- YOU KNOW HOW DIFFICULT IT'S BEEN FOR YOU, LOOKING FOR WORK! IT'S HARD TIMES FOR EVERYONE!
YOU'RE LETTING HIM MOVE IN BECAUSE IT'S HARD TIMES?
WHY DON'T YOU JUST VOLUNTEER AT THE SOUP KITCHEN?
IS IT SO HARD FOR YOU TO BELIEVE THAT A MAN WOULD --
NO! I JUST--
DON'T WORRY, LOVE.
I KNOW WHAT I'M DOING.

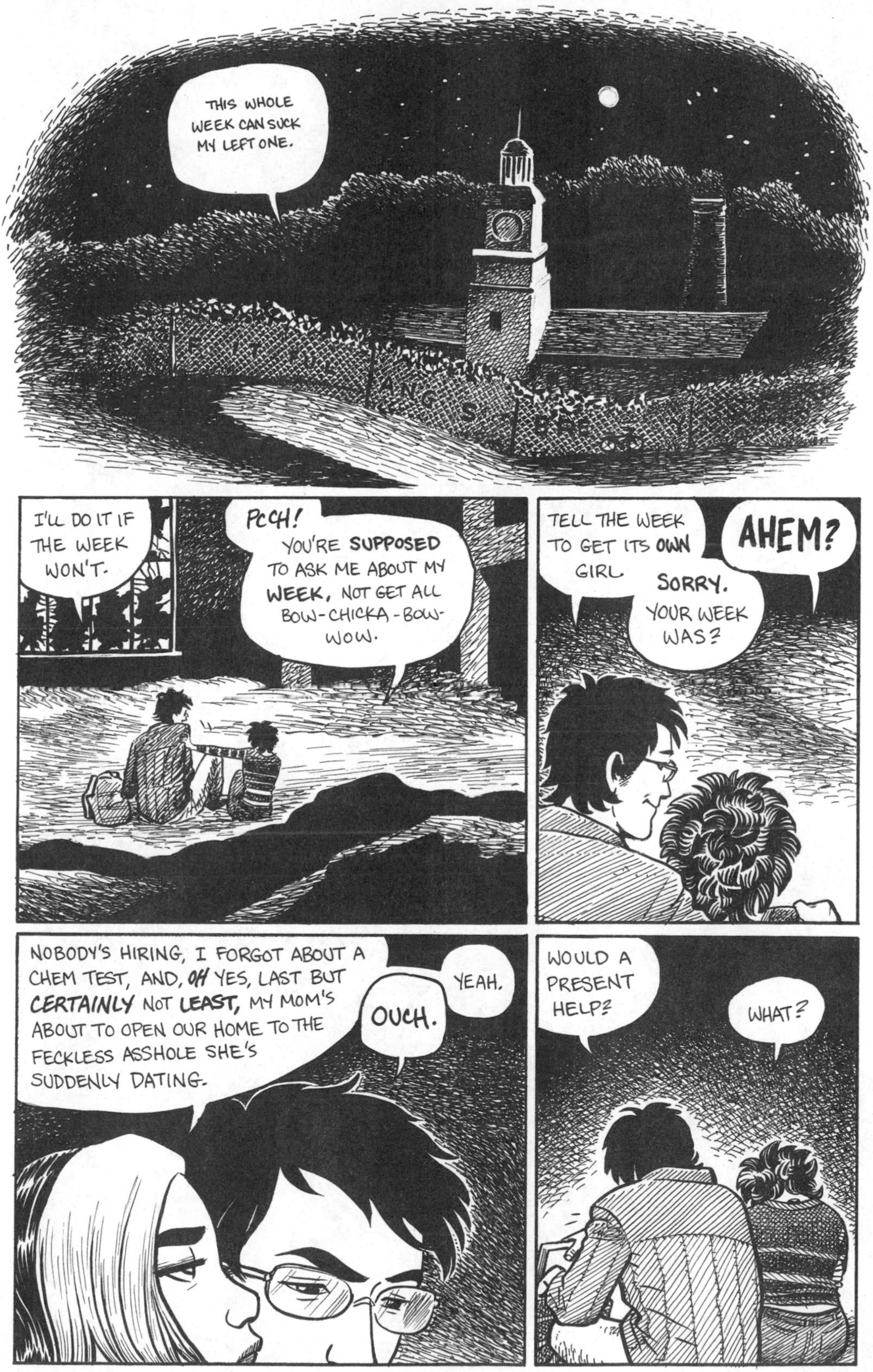
THIS WHOLE WEEK CAN SUCK MY LEFT ONE.
I'LL DO IT IF THE WEEK WON'T.
PCCH! YOU'RE **SUPPOSED** TO ASK ME ABOUT MY **WEEK**, NOT GET ALL BOW-CHICKA-BOW-WOW.
TELL THE WEEK TO GET ITS **OWN** GIRL.
AHEM?
SORRY. YOUR WEEK WAS?
NOBODY'S HIRING, I FORGOT ABOUT A CHEM TEST, AND, *OH* YES, LAST BUT **CERTAINLY** NOT **LEAST**, MY MOM'S ABOUT TO OPEN OUR HOME TO THE FECKLESS ASSHOLE SHE'S SUDDENLY DATING.
OUCH.
YEAH.
WOULD A PRESENT HELP?
WHAT?

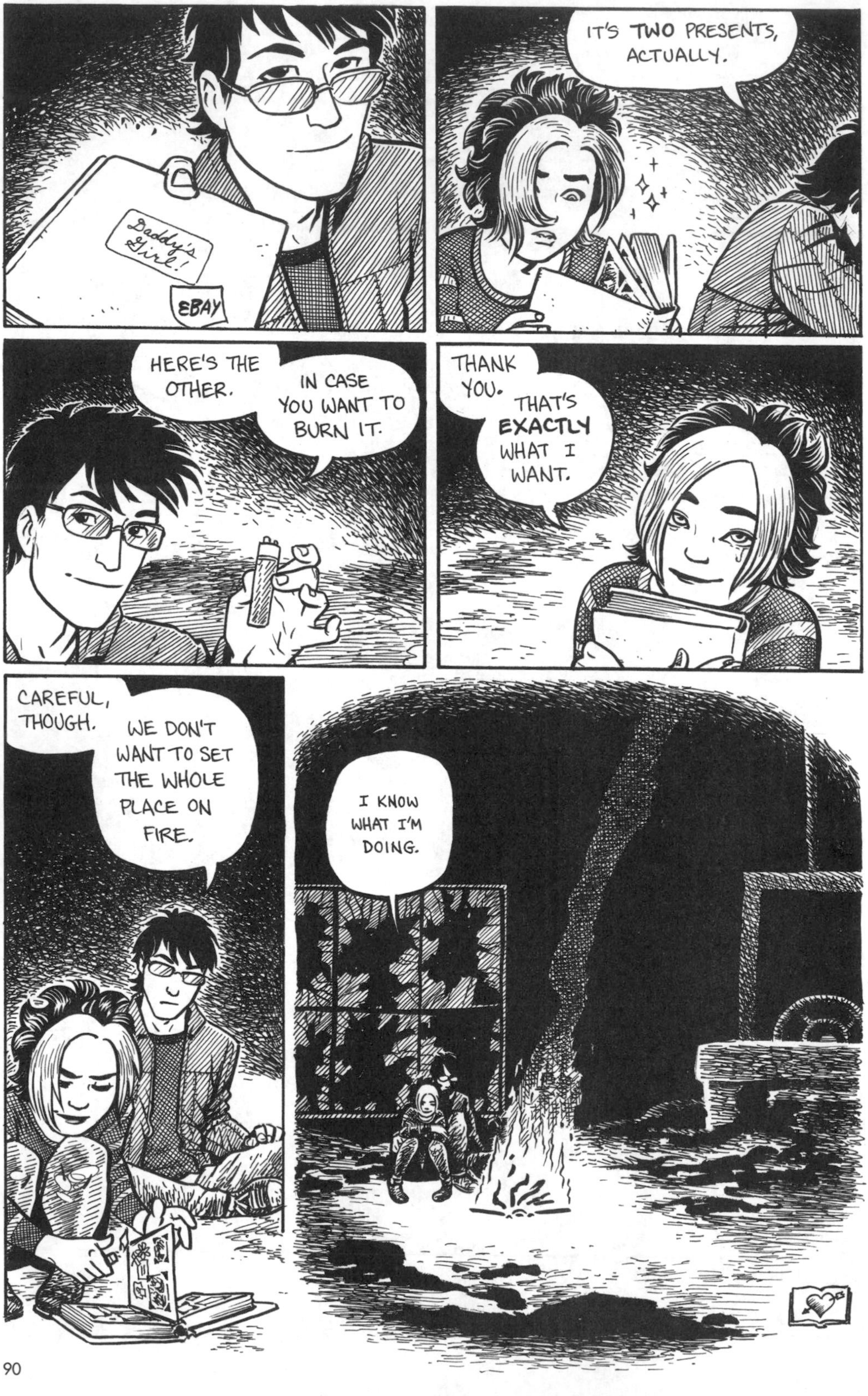
Daddy's Girl!
EBAY
IT'S TWO PRESENTS, ACTUALLY.
HERE'S THE OTHER.
IN CASE YOU WANT TO BURN IT.
THANK YOU.
THAT'S EXACTLY WHAT I WANT.
CAREFUL, THOUGH.
WE DON'T WANT TO SET THE WHOLE PLACE ON FIRE.
I KNOW WHAT I'M DOING.

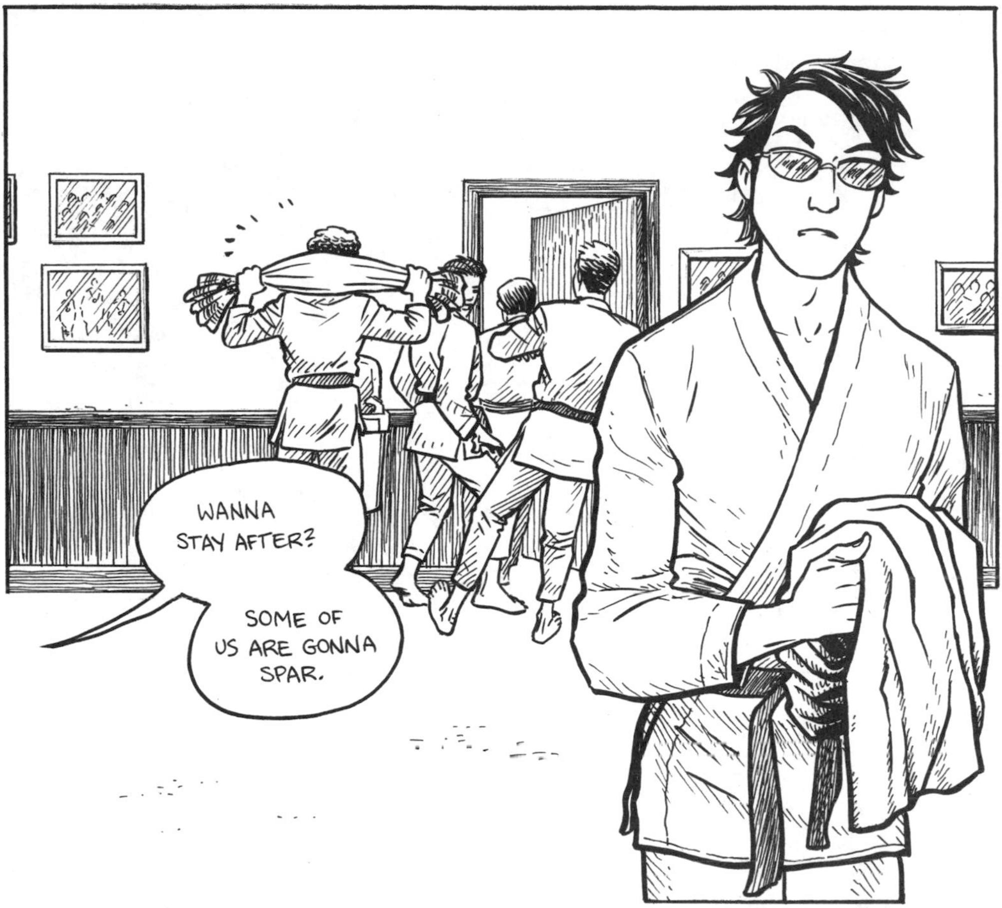
WANNA STAY AFTER?
SOME OF US ARE GONNA SPAR.

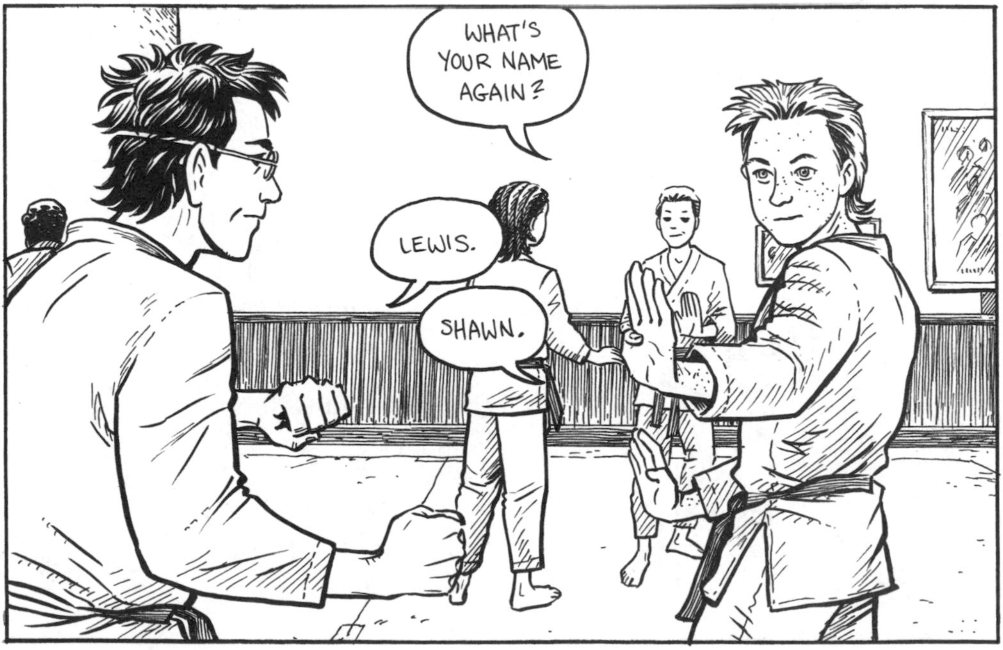
WHAT'S YOUR NAME AGAIN?
LEWIS.
SHAWN.

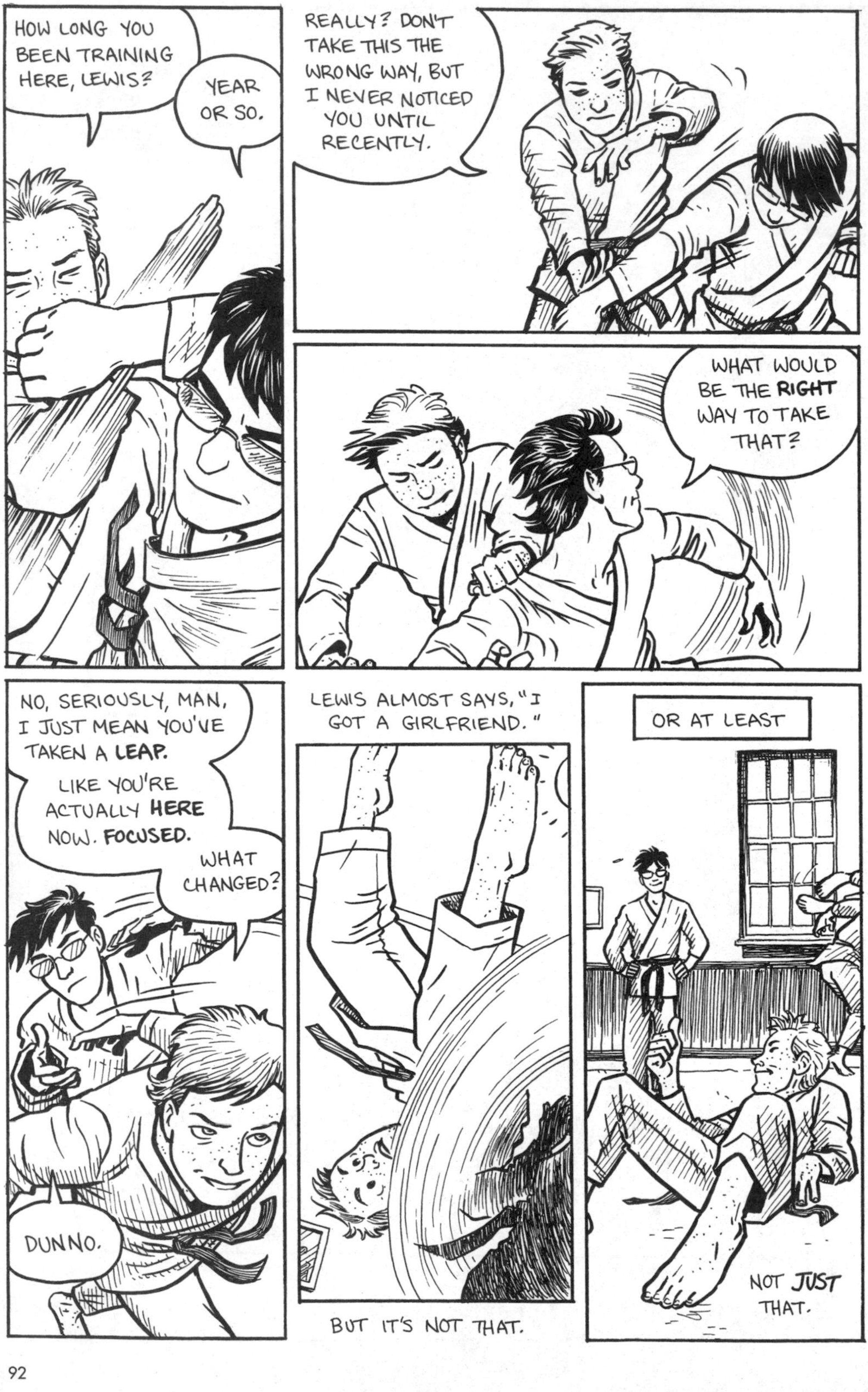
HOW LONG YOU BEEN TRAINING HERE, LEWIS?
YEAR OR SO.
REALLY? DON'T TAKE THIS THE WRONG WAY, BUT I NEVER NOTICED YOU UNTIL RECENTLY.
WHAT WOULD BE THE **RIGHT** WAY TO TAKE THAT?
NO, SERIOUSLY, MAN, I JUST MEAN YOU'VE TAKEN A **LEAP.**
LIKE YOU'RE ACTUALLY **HERE** NOW. **FOCUSED.**
WHAT CHANGED?
DUNNO.
LEWIS ALMOST SAYS, "I GOT A GIRLFRIEND."
BUT IT'S NOT THAT.
OR AT LEAST
NOT **JUST** THAT.

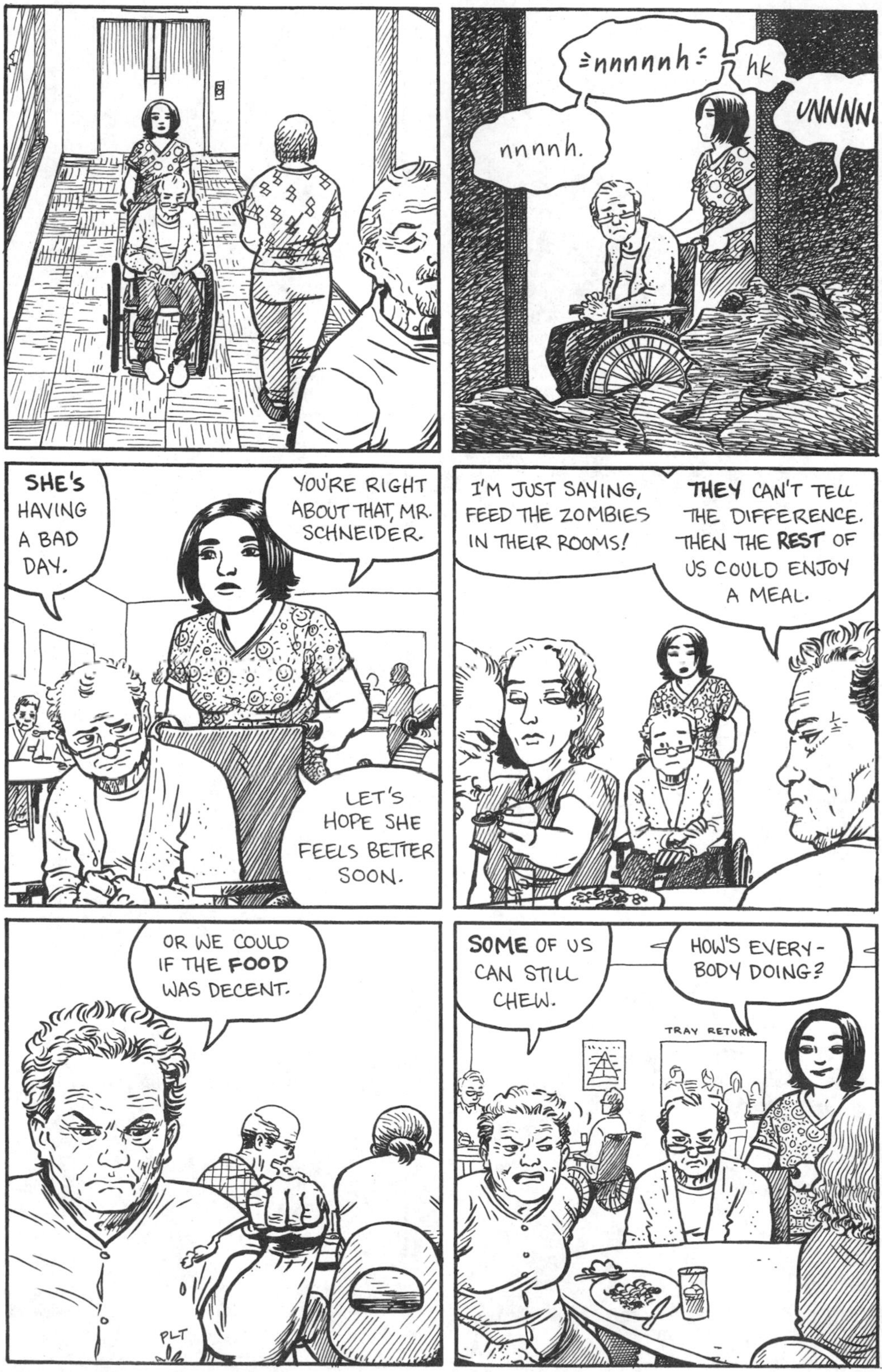
nnnnh.
nnnnnh
hk
UNNNN
SHE'S HAVING A BAD DAY.
YOU'RE RIGHT ABOUT THAT, MR. SCHNEIDER.
LET'S HOPE SHE FEELS BETTER SOON.
I'M JUST SAYING, FEED THE ZOMBIES IN THEIR ROOMS!
THEY CAN'T TELL THE DIFFERENCE. THEN THE REST OF US COULD ENJOY A MEAL.
OR WE COULD IF THE FOOD WAS DECENT.
PLT
SOME OF US CAN STILL CHEW.
HOW'S EVERY-BODY DOING?
TRAY RETURN

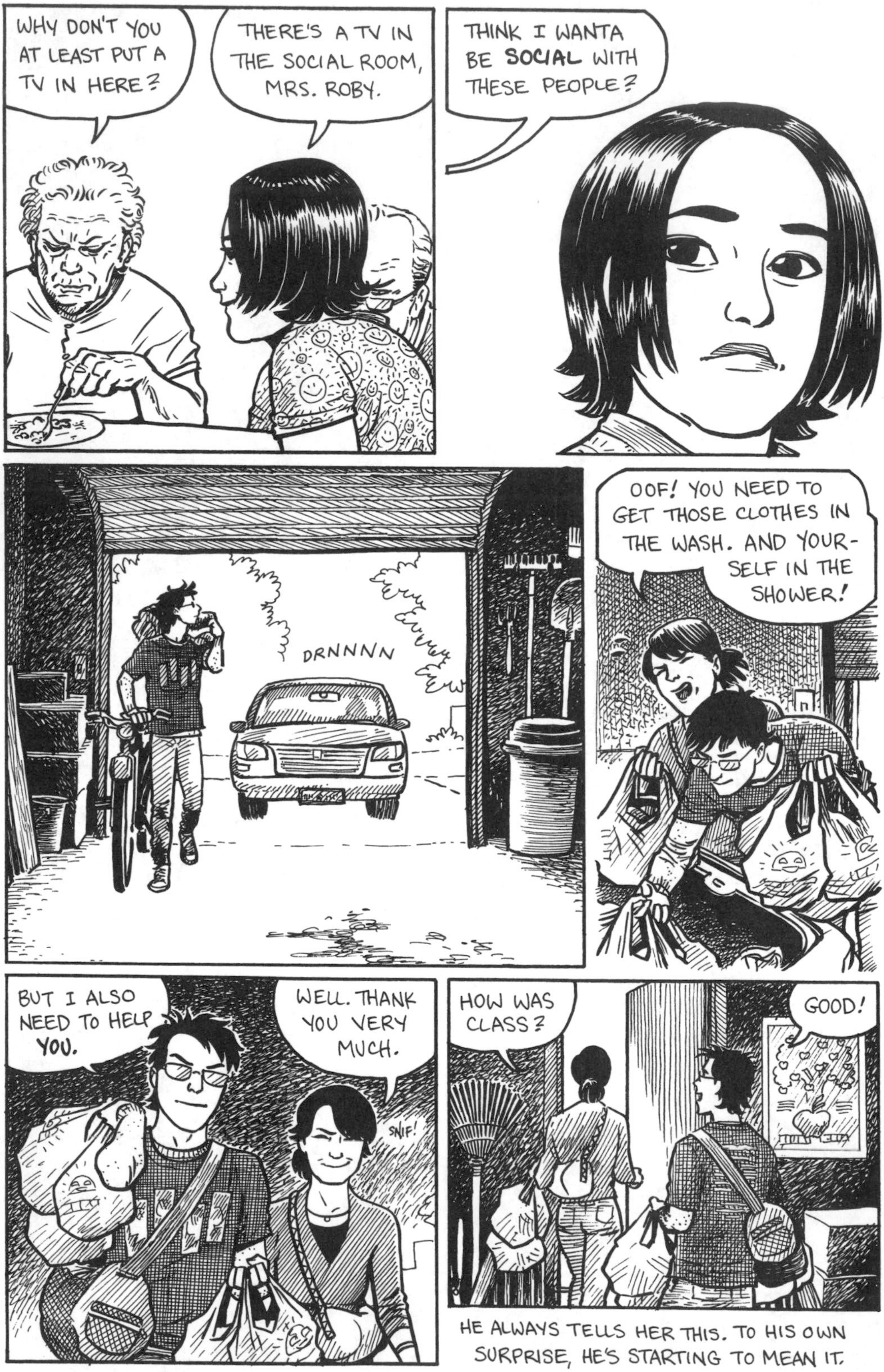
WHY DON'T YOU AT LEAST PUT A TV IN HERE?
THERE'S A TV IN THE SOCIAL ROOM, MRS. ROBY.
THINK I WANTA BE **SOCIAL** WITH THESE PEOPLE?
DRNNNN
OOF! YOU NEED TO GET THOSE CLOTHES IN THE WASH. AND YOURSELF IN THE SHOWER!
BUT I ALSO NEED TO HELP **YOU**.
WELL. THANK YOU VERY MUCH.
SNIF!
HOW WAS CLASS?
GOOD!
HE ALWAYS TELLS HER THIS. TO HIS OWN SURPRISE, HE'S STARTING TO MEAN IT.

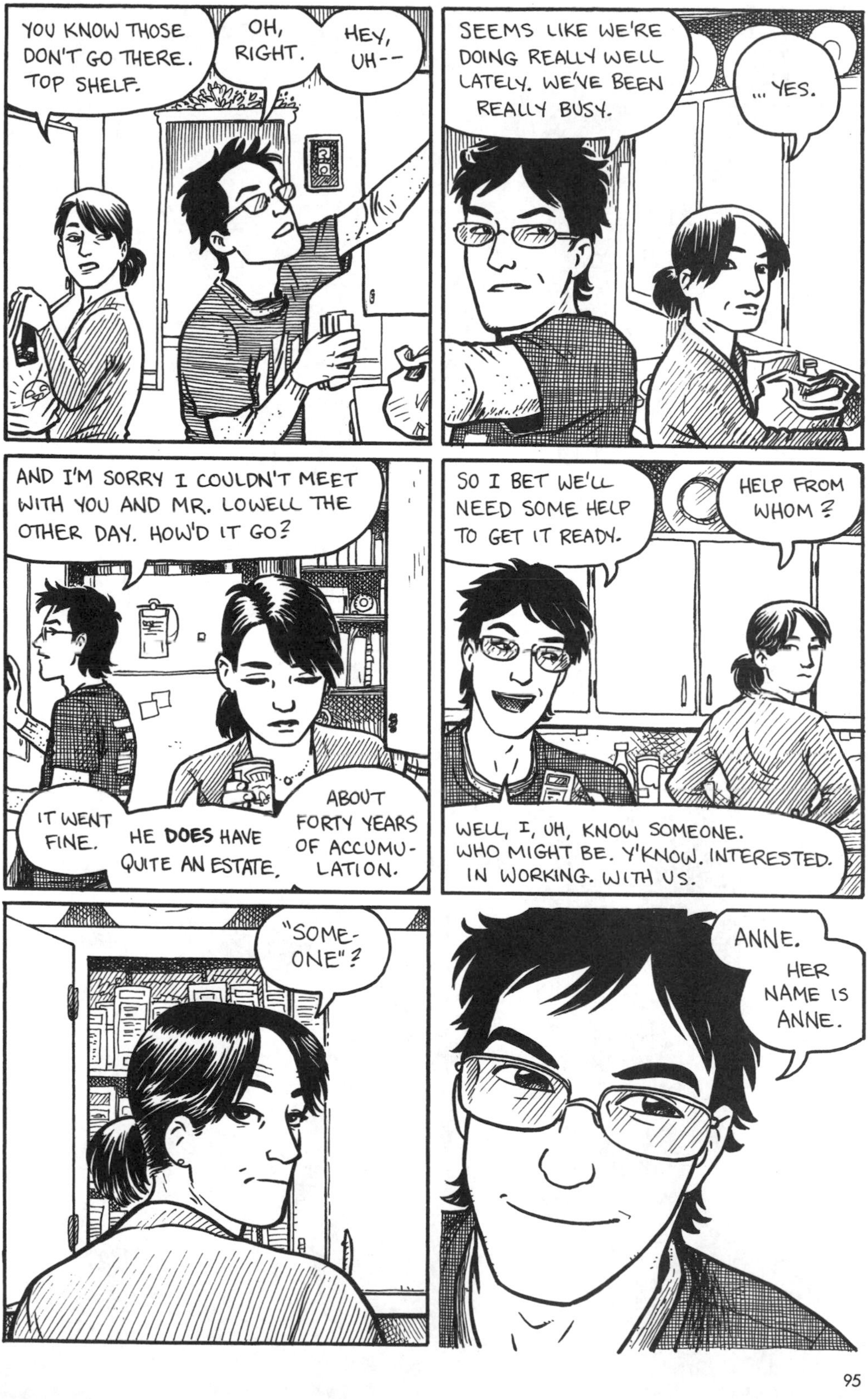
YOU KNOW THOSE DON'T GO THERE. TOP SHELF.
OH, RIGHT.
HEY, UH--
SEEMS LIKE WE'RE DOING REALLY WELL LATELY. WE'VE BEEN REALLY BUSY.
... YES.
AND I'M SORRY I COULDN'T MEET WITH YOU AND MR. LOWELL THE OTHER DAY. HOW'D IT GO?
IT WENT FINE.
HE **DOES** HAVE QUITE AN ESTATE.
ABOUT FORTY YEARS OF ACCUMU-LATION.
SO I BET WE'LL NEED SOME HELP TO GET IT READY.
HELP FROM WHOM?
WELL, I, UH, KNOW SOMEONE. WHO MIGHT BE. Y'KNOW. INTERESTED. IN WORKING. WITH US.
"SOME-ONE"?
ANNE.
HER NAME IS ANNE.

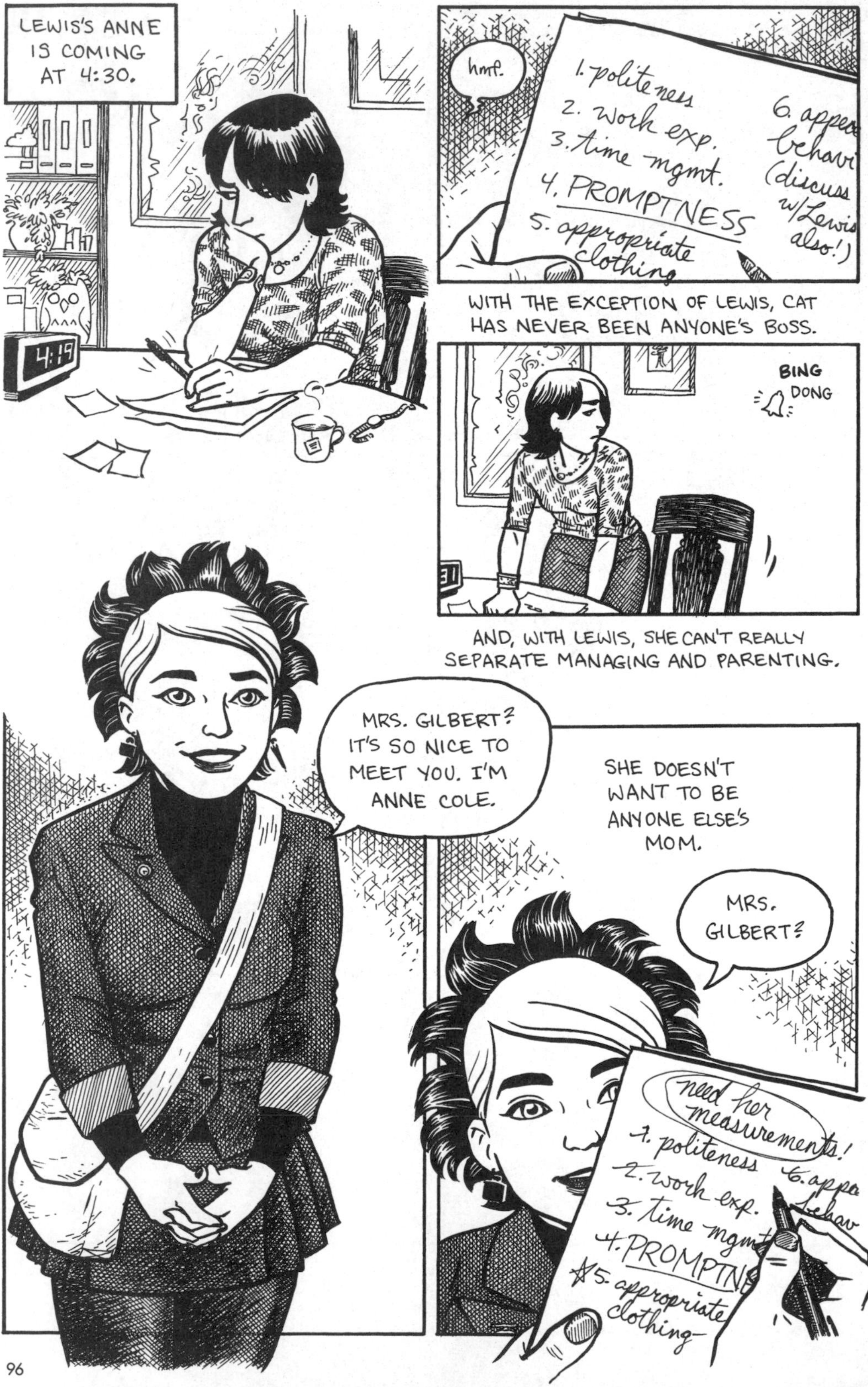
LEWIS'S ANNE IS COMING AT 4:30.
4:19
hmf.
1. politeness
2. work exp.
3. time mgmt.
4. PROMPTNESS
5. appropriate clothing
6. appea behavi (discuss w/Lewis also!)
WITH THE EXCEPTION OF LEWIS, CAT HAS NEVER BEEN ANYONE'S BOSS.
BING DONG
AND, WITH LEWIS, SHE CAN'T REALLY SEPARATE MANAGING AND PARENTING.
MRS. GILBERT? IT'S SO NICE TO MEET YOU. I'M ANNE COLE.
SHE DOESN'T WANT TO BE ANYONE ELSE'S MOM.
MRS. GILBERT?
need her measurements!
1. politeness
2. work exp.
3. time mgmt.
4. PROMPTN
5. appropriate clothing
6. appa behav

WOULD YOU MIND TELLING ME A LITTLE ABOUT HOW YOU STARTED THE BUSINESS?

I... IT BEGAN AS A FAVOR. FOR A FRIEND. HIS GRANDMOTHER'S ESTATE.

ZACH COULDN'T DO IT.

IN LOVING MEMORY

MARIAN MIHAIL

BUT HE HAD TO. WHICH MEANT **SHE** HAD TO.

AND THAT'S HOW YOU REALIZED YOU HAD A TALENT FOR IT?

"YOU'RE GOOD AT THIS," ZACH SAID.

SHE NEVER KNEW IF HE MEANT THE ORGANIZING AND PRICING OR THE SEX.

IT WAS... A START. IT GAVE ME A START. AND I JUST KEPT GOING FROM THERE.

STATE OF OREG(
CERTIFICATE OF S

HE SPENT MOST OF HIS HALF OF THE MONEY ON A CAR. COULDN'T WAIT TO GET OUT OF FAILIN.

THAT'S REALLY COOL. IT'S AWE-SOME WHEN WOMEN RUN THEIR OWN BUSINESSES AND DON'T HAVE TO BE DEPENDENT ON A MAN.

WELL, I DO THINK DEVELOPING SELF-SUFFICIENCY IS IMPORTANT FOR EVERYONE.

0 PREGNANCY

IF SHE'D TOLD HIM SHE WAS PREGNANT, WOULD HE HAVE STAYED?

SHE WAS SO SURE HE WOULDN'T THAT SHE NEVER DID.

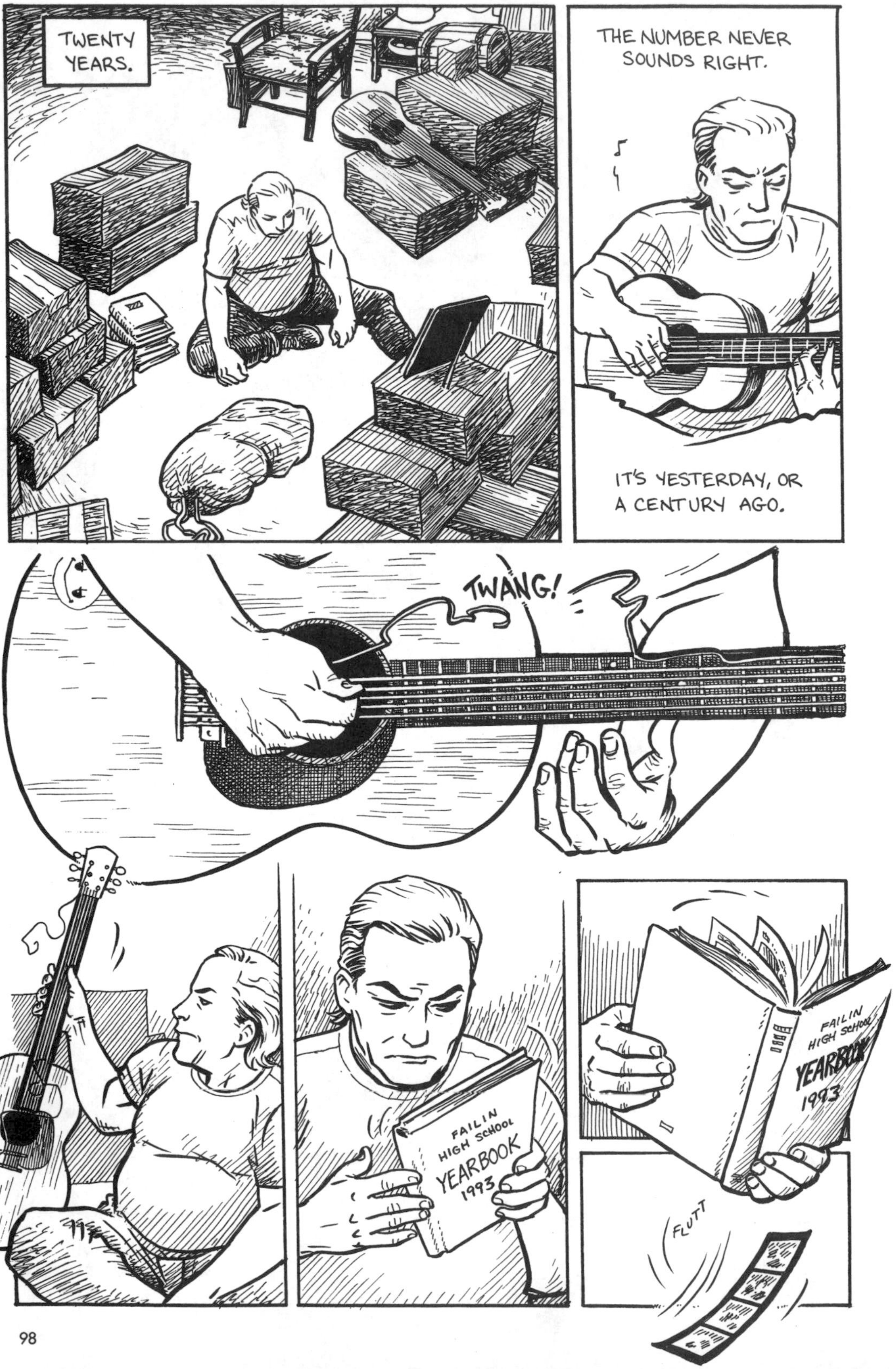

TWENTY YEARS.
THE NUMBER NEVER SOUNDS RIGHT.
IT'S YESTERDAY, OR A CENTURY AGO.
TWANG!
FAILIN HIGH SCHOOL YEARBOOK 1993
FAILIN HIGH SCHOOL YEARBOOK 1993
FLUTT

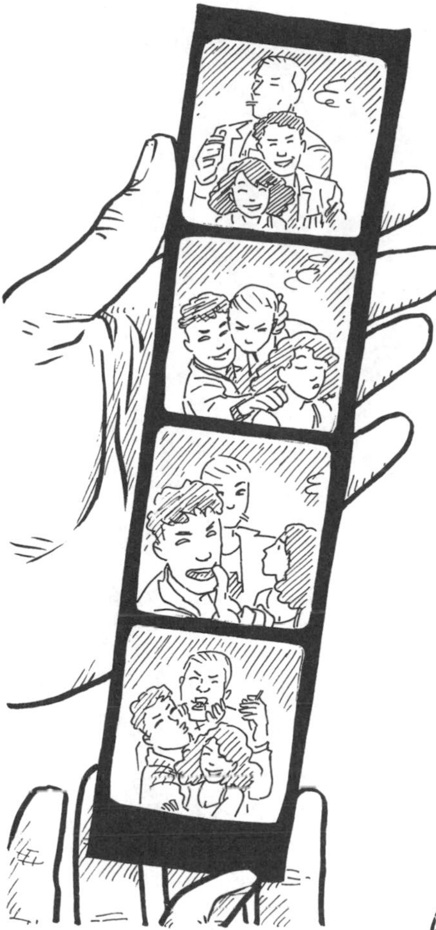

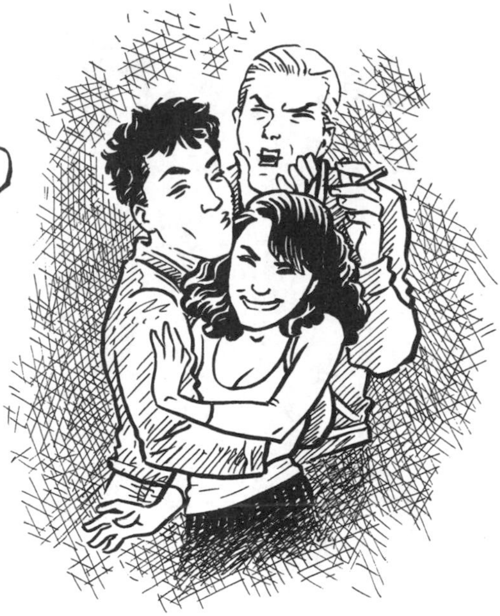

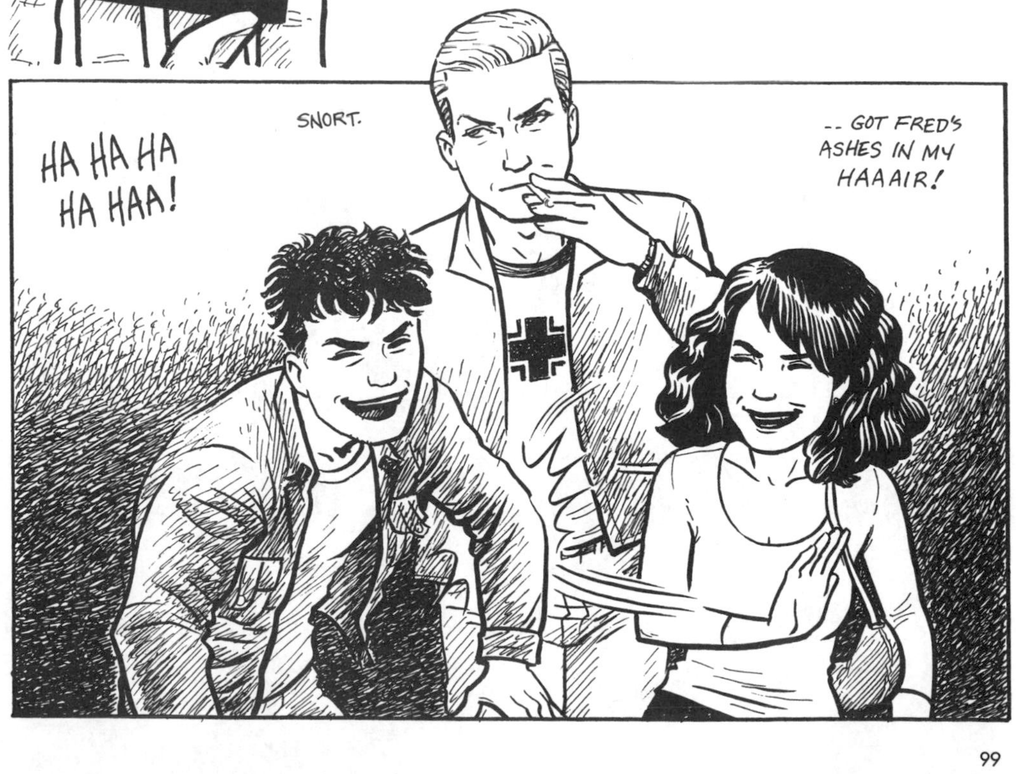
HA HA HA
HA HAA!
SNORT.
-- GOT FRED'S
ASHES IN MY
HAAAIR!

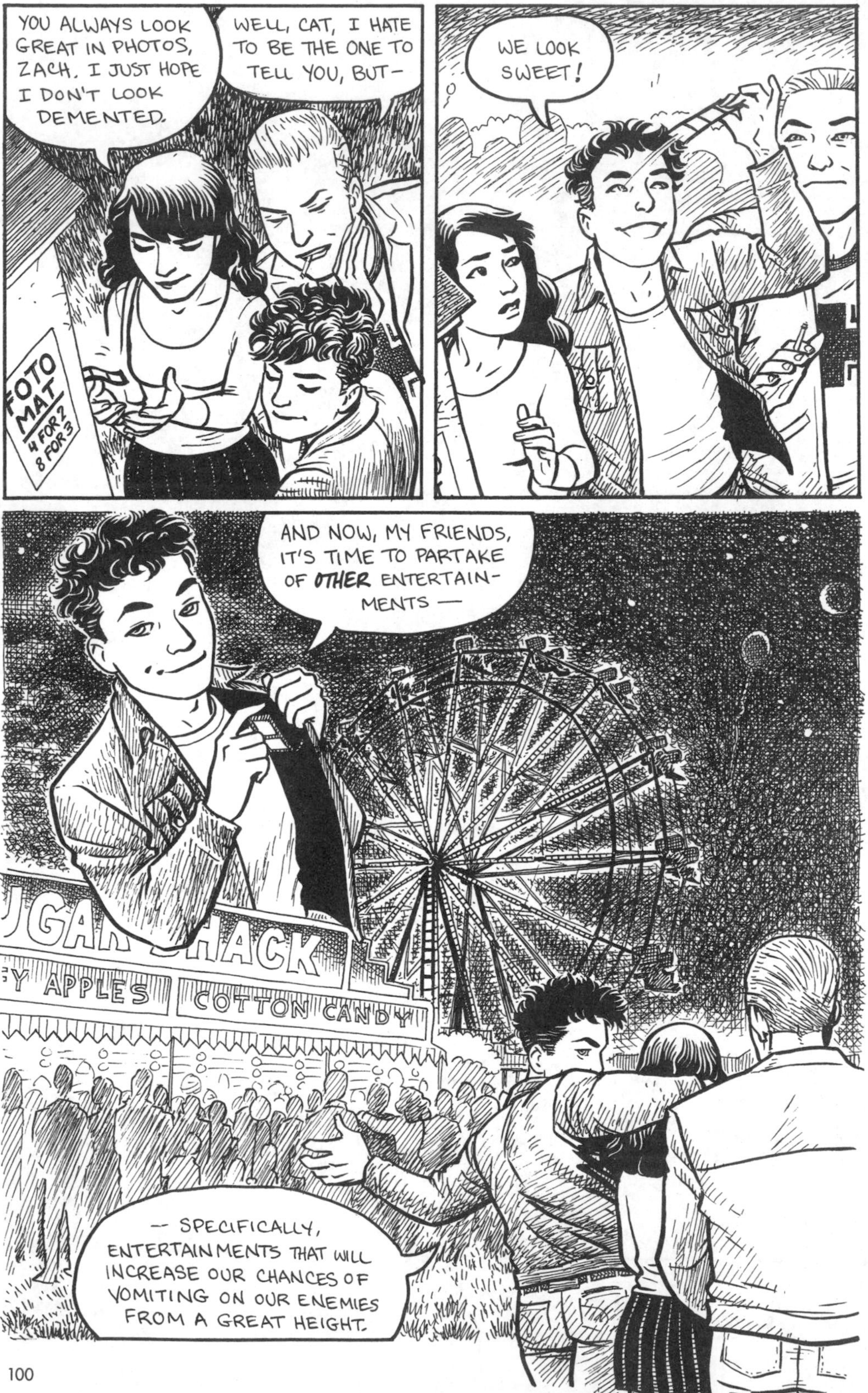
YOU ALWAYS LOOK GREAT IN PHOTOS, ZACH. I JUST HOPE I DON'T LOOK DEMENTED.
WELL, CAT, I HATE TO BE THE ONE TO TELL YOU, BUT-
FOTO MAT
4 FOR 2
8 FOR 3
WE LOOK SWEET!
AND NOW, MY FRIENDS, IT'S TIME TO PARTAKE OF **OTHER** ENTERTAIN-MENTS —
UGAR SHACK
Y APPLES
COTTON CANDY
— SPECIFICALLY, ENTERTAINMENTS THAT WILL INCREASE OUR CHANCES OF VOMITING ON OUR ENEMIES FROM A GREAT HEIGHT.

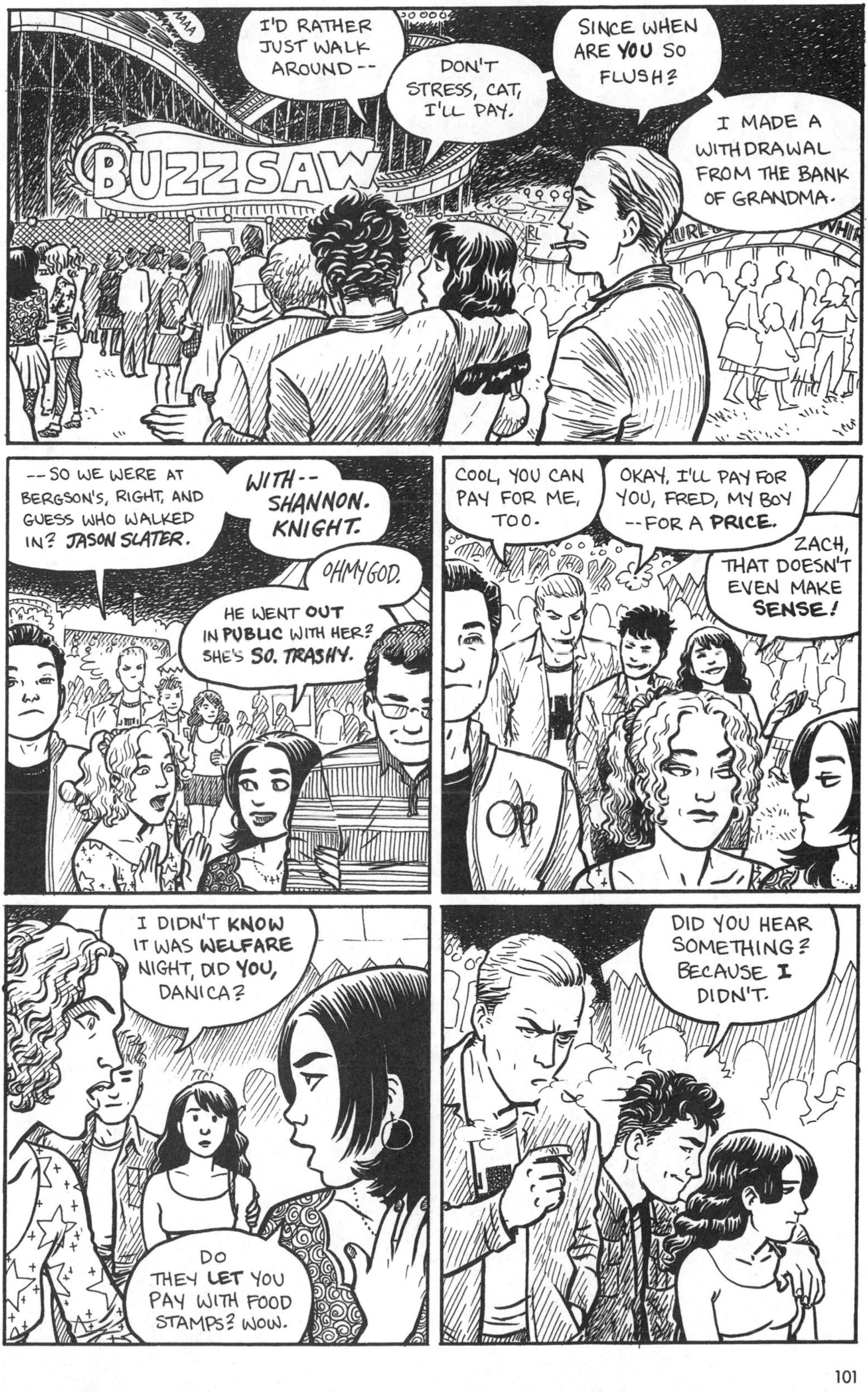
AAAA
I'D RATHER JUST WALK AROUND --
DON'T STRESS, CAT, I'LL PAY.
SINCE WHEN ARE YOU SO FLUSH?
I MADE A WITHDRAWAL FROM THE BANK OF GRANDMA.
BUZZSAW
-- SO WE WERE AT BERGSON'S, RIGHT, AND GUESS WHO WALKED IN? JASON SLATER.
WITH -- SHANNON. KNIGHT.
OHMYGOD.
HE WENT OUT IN PUBLIC WITH HER? SHE'S SO. TRASHY.
COOL, YOU CAN PAY FOR ME, TOO.
OKAY, I'LL PAY FOR YOU, FRED, MY BOY -- FOR A PRICE.
ZACH, THAT DOESN'T EVEN MAKE SENSE!
I DIDN'T KNOW IT WAS WELFARE NIGHT, DID YOU, DANICA?
DO THEY LET YOU PAY WITH FOOD STAMPS? WOW.
DID YOU HEAR SOMETHING? BECAUSE I DIDN'T.

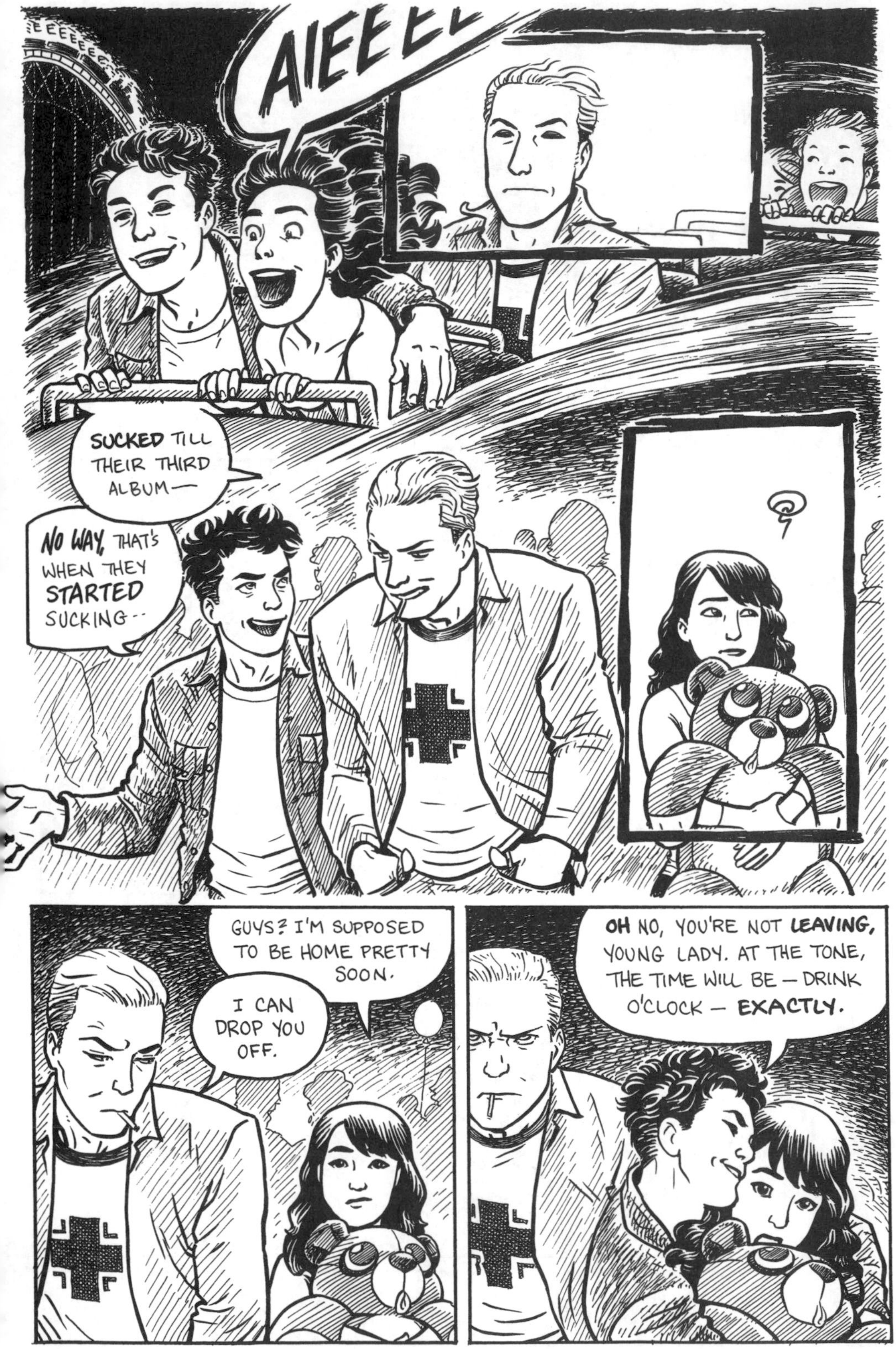
AIEEEE
EEEEEEEE
SUCKED TILL THEIR THIRD ALBUM—
NO WAY, THAT'S WHEN THEY STARTED SUCKING--
GUYS? I'M SUPPOSED TO BE HOME PRETTY SOON.
I CAN DROP YOU OFF.
OH NO, YOU'RE NOT LEAVING, YOUNG LADY. AT THE TONE, THE TIME WILL BE — DRINK O'CLOCK — EXACTLY.

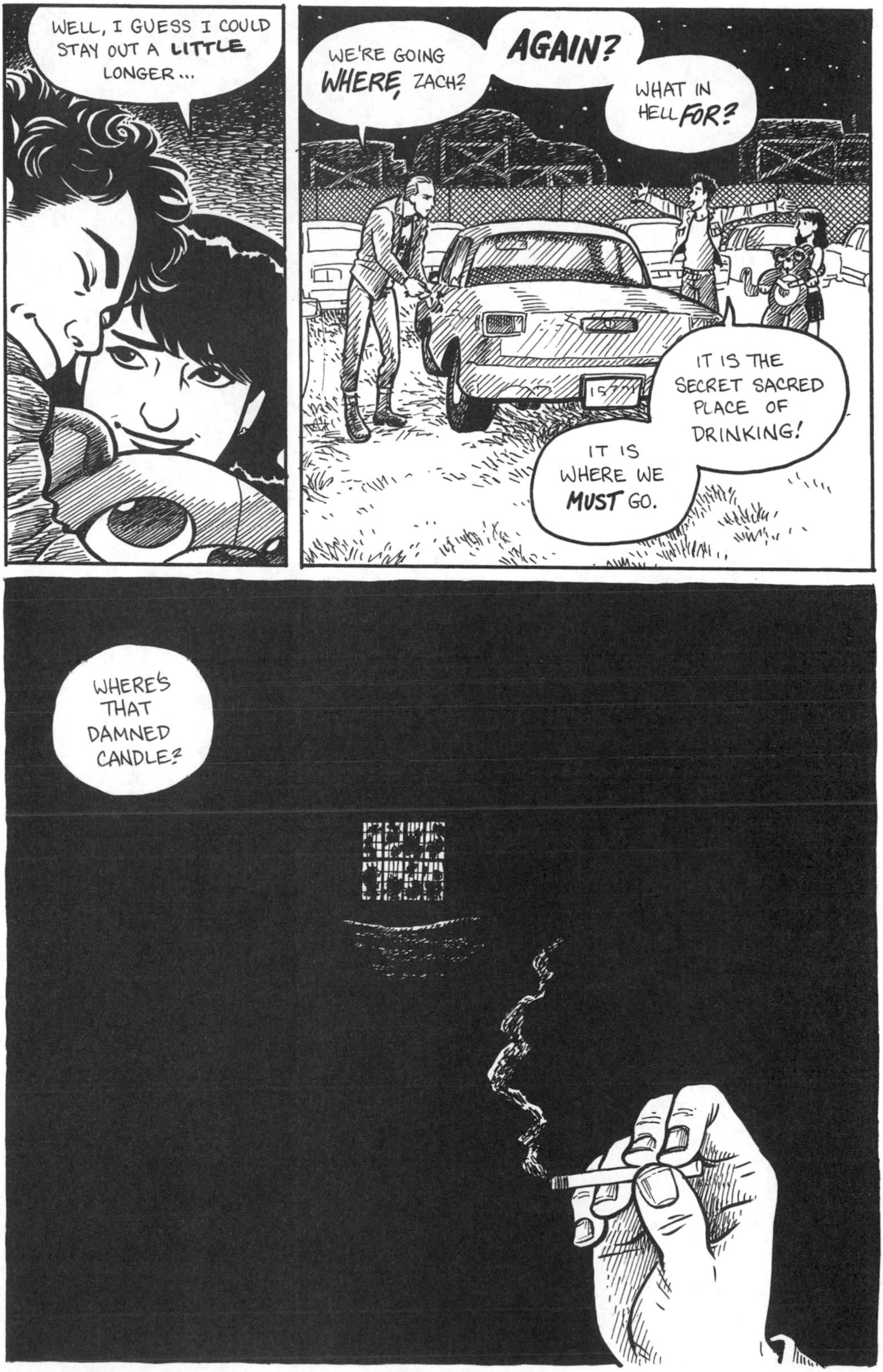
WELL, I GUESS I COULD STAY OUT A LITTLE LONGER...
WE'RE GOING WHERE, ZACH?
AGAIN?
WHAT IN HELL FOR?
IT IS THE SECRET SACRED PLACE OF DRINKING!
IT IS WHERE WE MUST GO.
WHERE'S THAT DAMNED CANDLE?

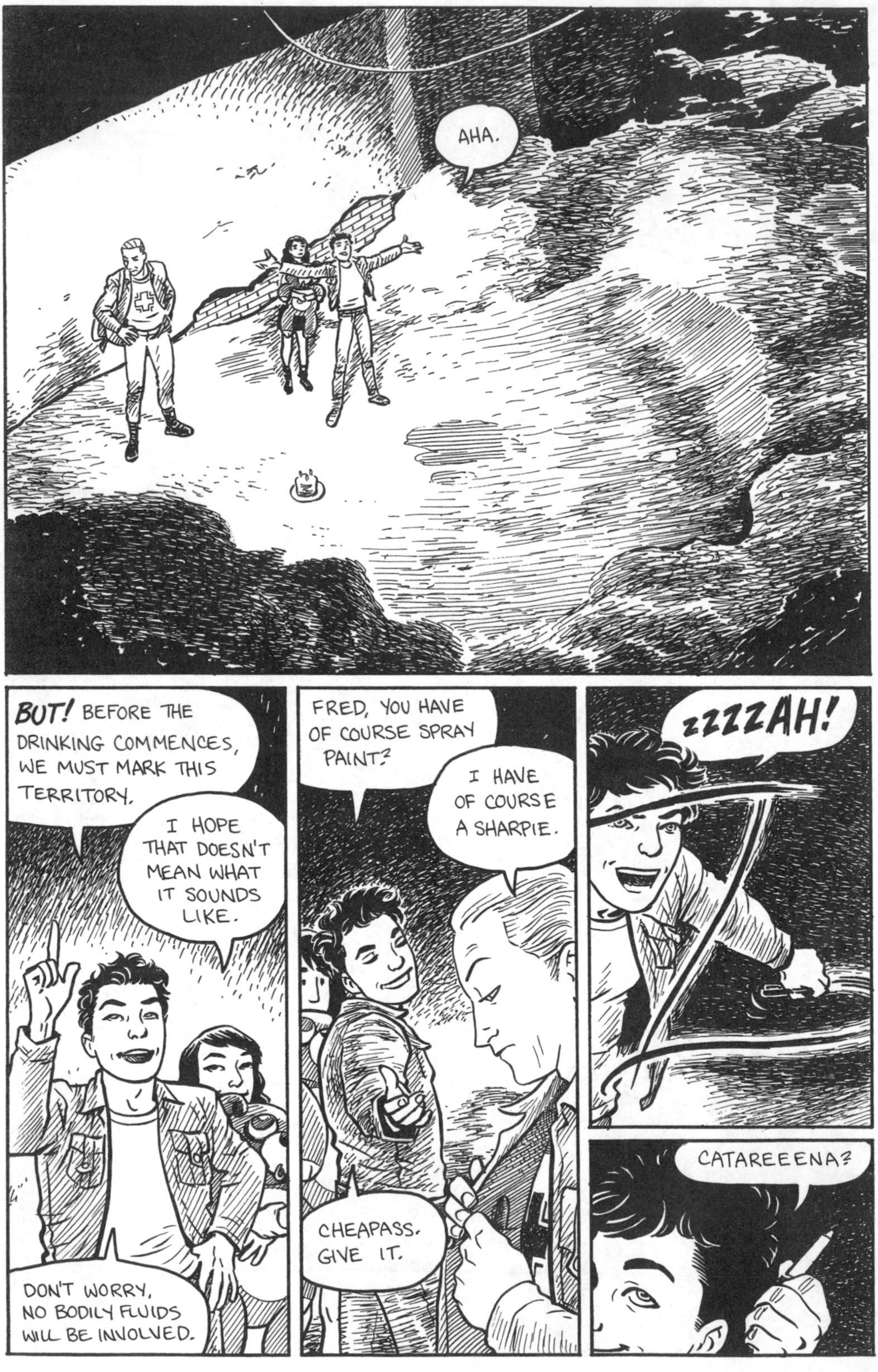
AHA.
BUT! BEFORE THE DRINKING COMMENCES, WE MUST MARK THIS TERRITORY.
I HOPE THAT DOESN'T MEAN WHAT IT SOUNDS LIKE.
DON'T WORRY, NO BODILY FLUIDS WILL BE INVOLVED.
FRED, YOU HAVE OF COURSE SPRAY PAINT?
I HAVE OF COURSE A SHARPIE.
CHEAPASS. GIVE IT.
ZZZZAH!
CATAREEENA?

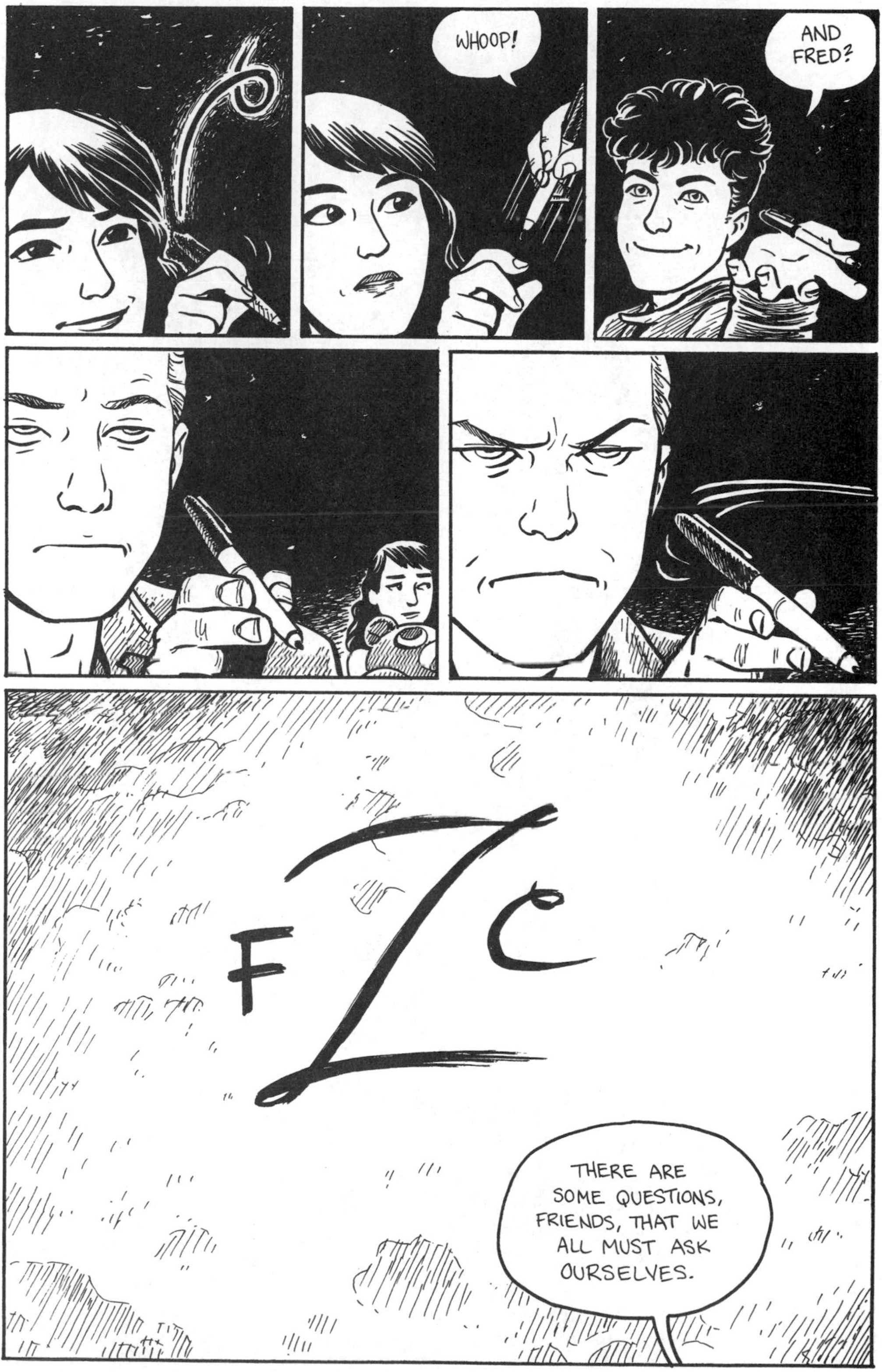

WHOOP!
AND FRED?
F
Z
C
THERE ARE SOME QUESTIONS, FRIENDS, THAT WE ALL MUST ASK OURSELVES.

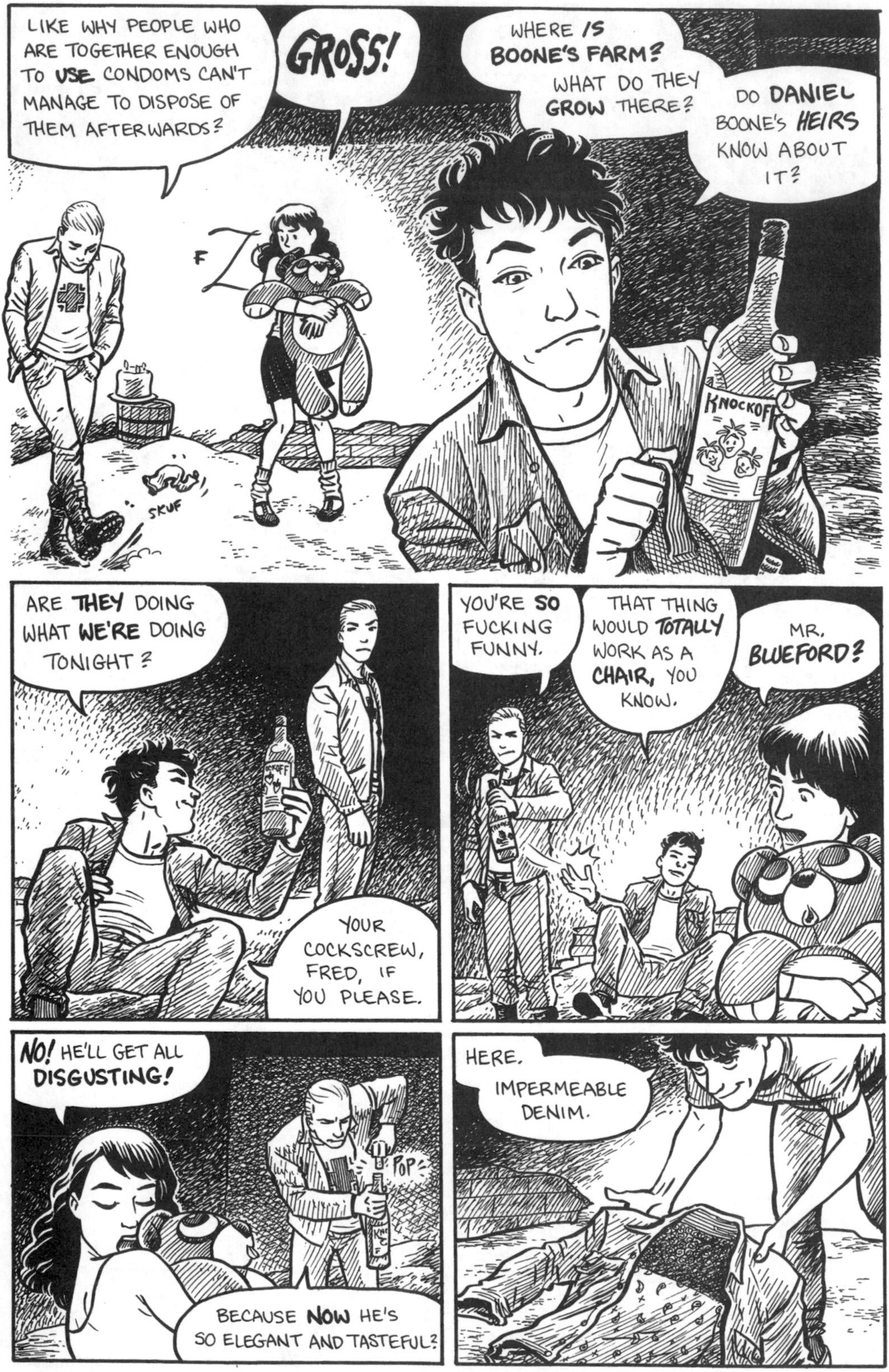
LIKE WHY PEOPLE WHO ARE TOGETHER ENOUGH TO USE CONDOMS CAN'T MANAGE TO DISPOSE OF THEM AFTERWARDS?
GROSS!
F
Z
SKUF
WHERE IS BOONE'S FARM?
WHAT DO THEY GROW THERE?
DO DANIEL BOONE'S HEIRS KNOW ABOUT IT?
KNOCKOFF
ARE THEY DOING WHAT WE'RE DOING TONIGHT?
YOUR COCKSCREW, FRED, IF YOU PLEASE.
YOU'RE SO FUCKING FUNNY.
THAT THING WOULD TOTALLY WORK AS A CHAIR, YOU KNOW.
MR. BLUEFORD?
NO! HE'LL GET ALL DISGUSTING!
POP
BECAUSE NOW HE'S SO ELEGANT AND TASTEFUL?
HERE.
IMPERMEABLE DENIM.

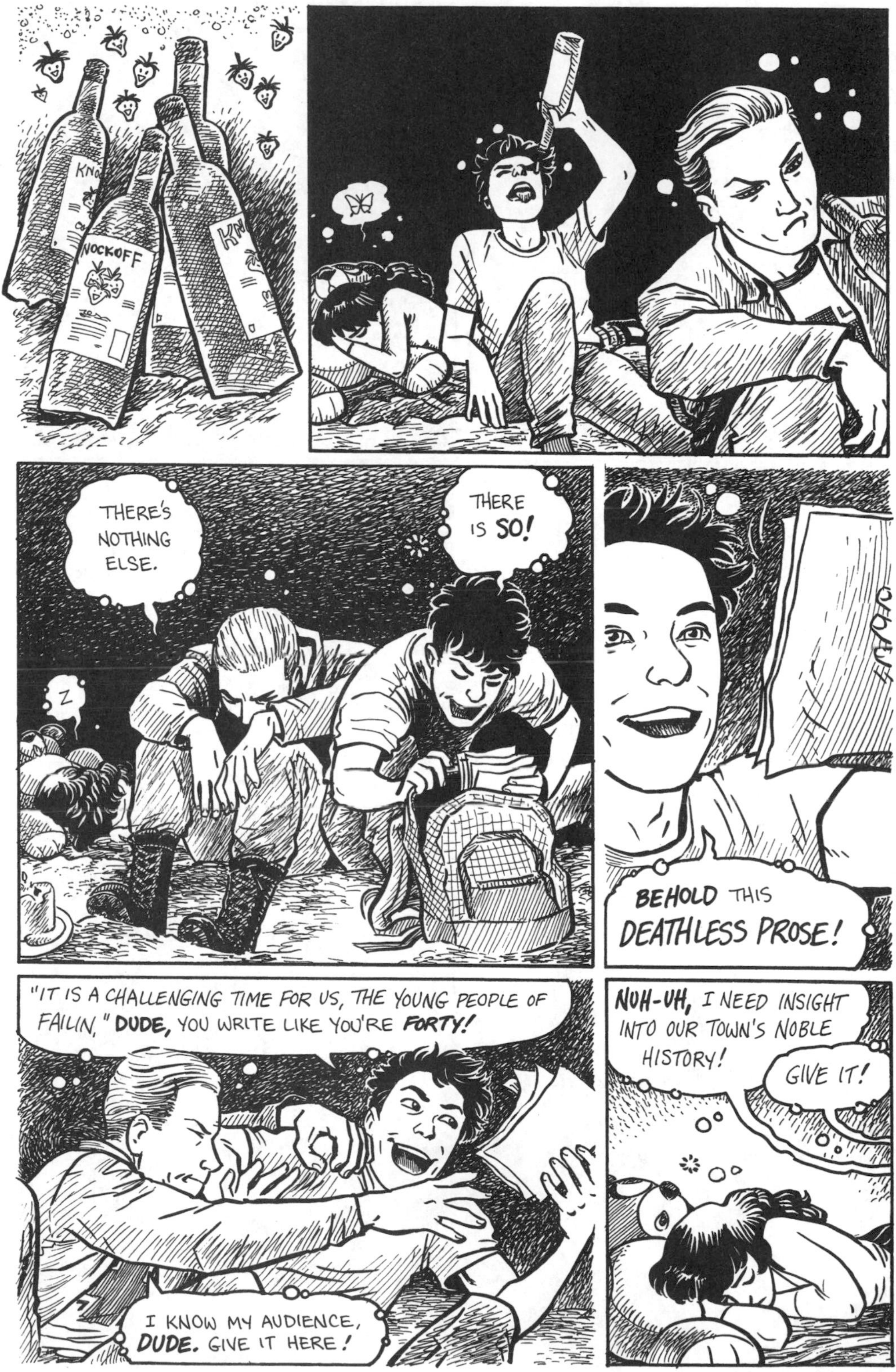
NOCKOFF
THERE'S NOTHING ELSE.
THERE IS SO!
BEHOLD THIS DEATHLESS PROSE!
"IT IS A CHALLENGING TIME FOR US, THE YOUNG PEOPLE OF FAILIN." DUDE, YOU WRITE LIKE YOU'RE FORTY!
I KNOW MY AUDIENCE, DUDE. GIVE IT HERE!
NUH-UH, I NEED INSIGHT INTO OUR TOWN'S NOBLE HISTORY!
GIVE IT!

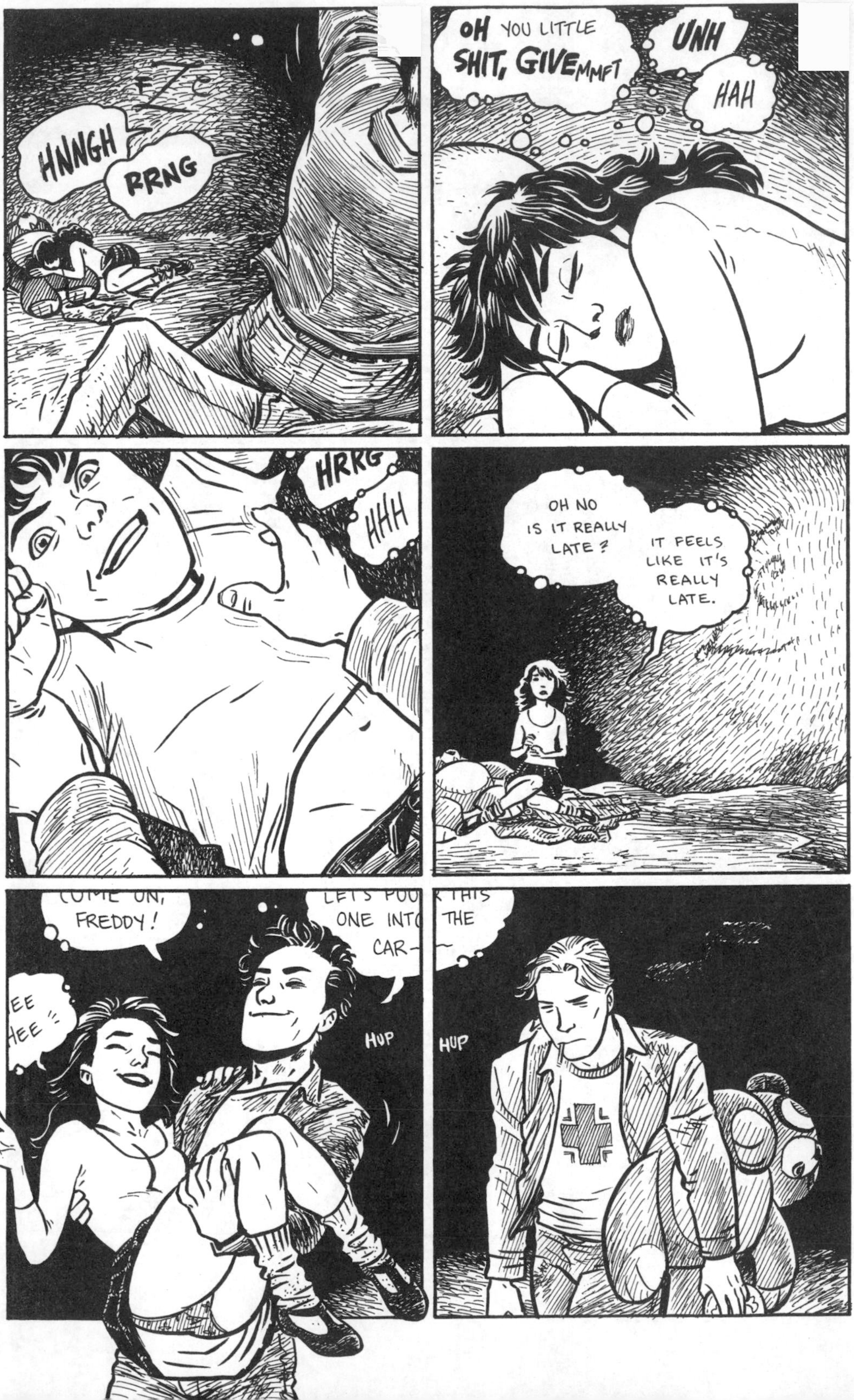
HNNGH
RRNG
OH YOU LITTLE SHIT, GIVE MMFT
UNH
HAH
HRRG
HHH
OH NO IS IT REALLY LATE?
IT FEELS LIKE IT'S REALLY LATE.
COME ON, FREDDY!
LET'S POUR THIS ONE INTO THE CAR—
HEE HEE!!
HUP
HUP

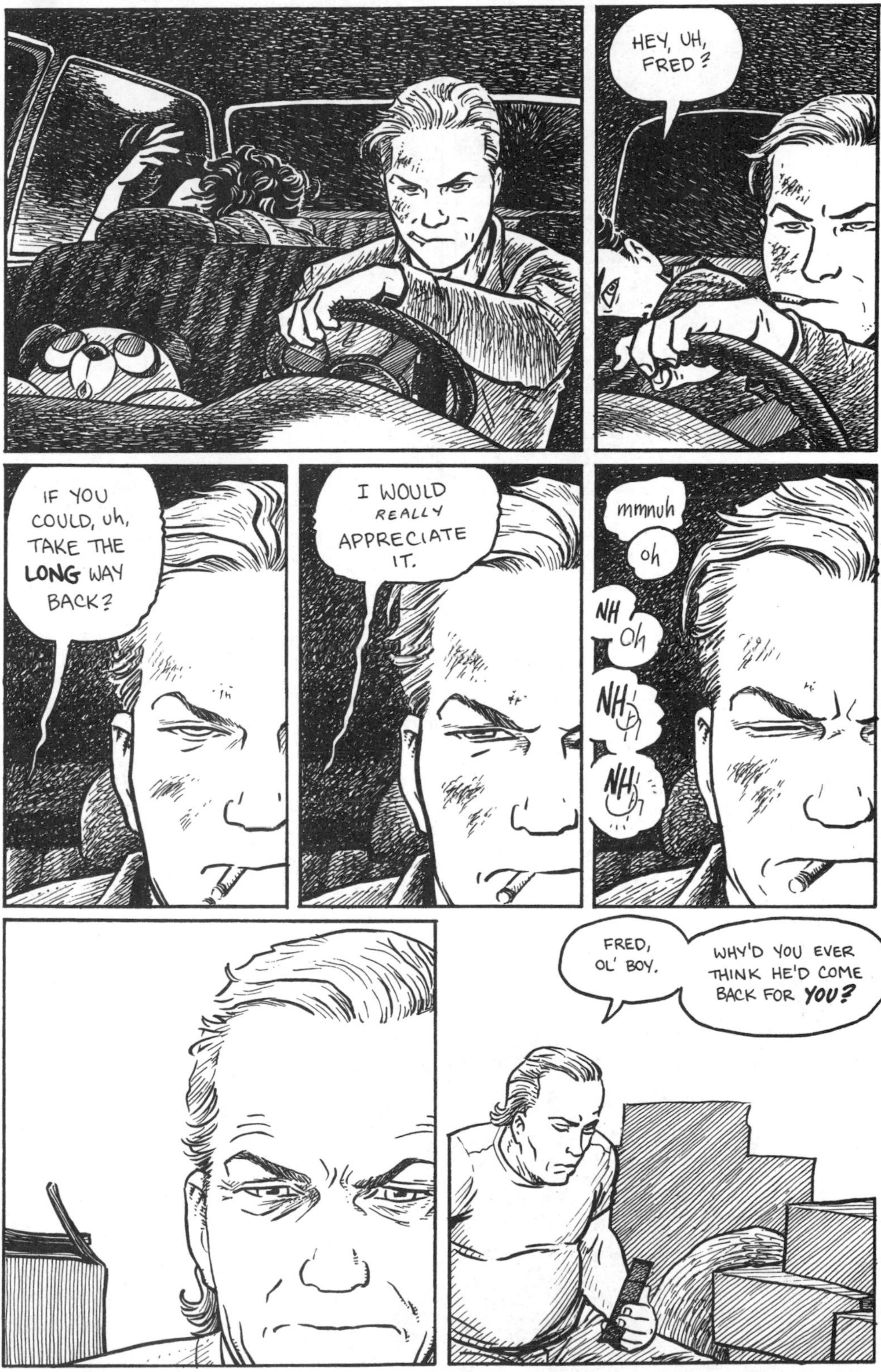
HEY, UH, FRED?
IF YOU COULD, uh, TAKE THE LONG WAY BACK?
I WOULD REALLY APPRECIATE IT.
mmnuh
oh
NH
Oh
NH
NH
FRED, OL' BOY.
WHY'D YOU EVER THINK HE'D COME BACK FOR YOU?

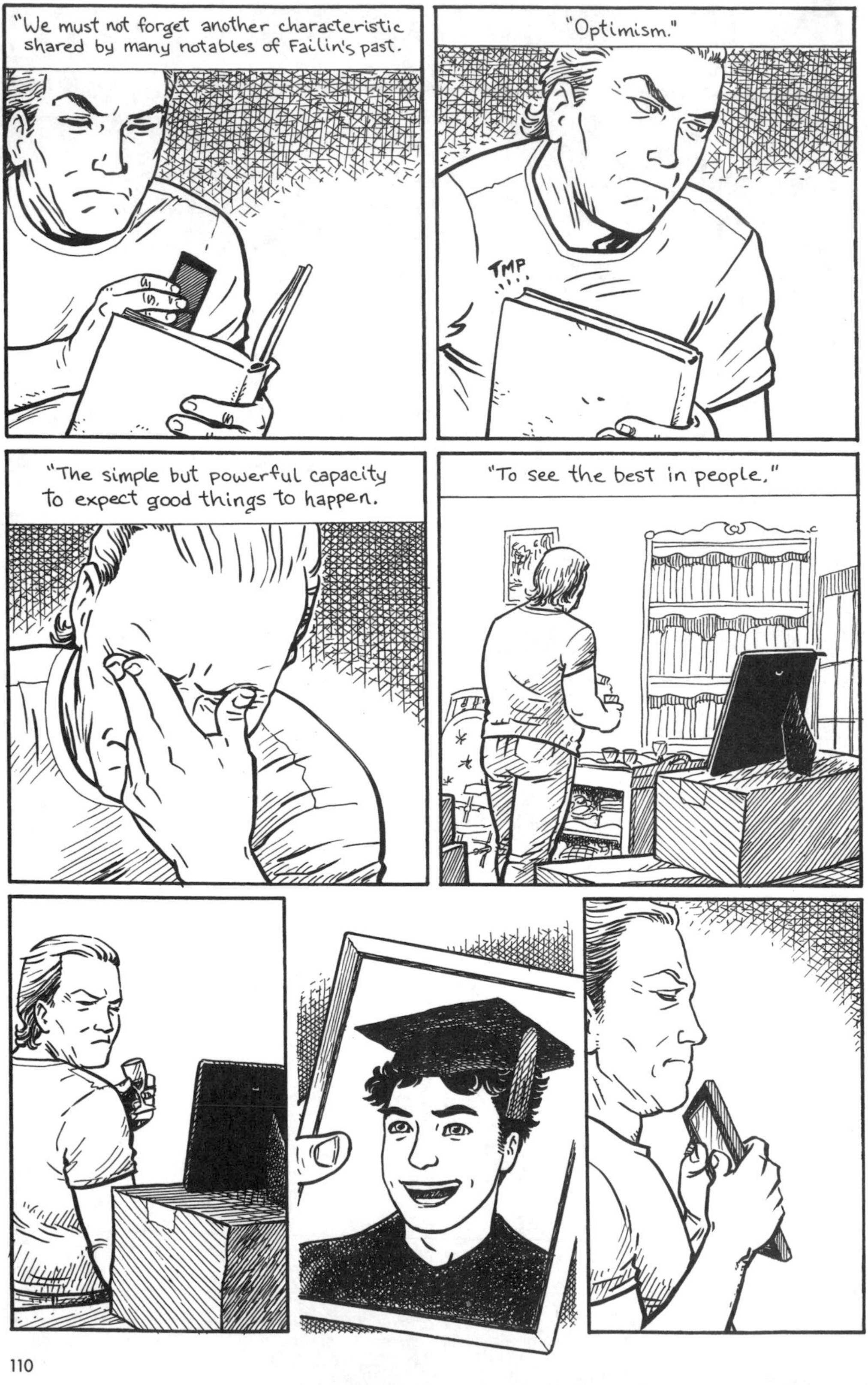
"We must not forget another characteristic shared by many notables of Failin's past.
"Optimism."
TMP
"The simple but powerful capacity to expect good things to happen.
"To see the best in people."

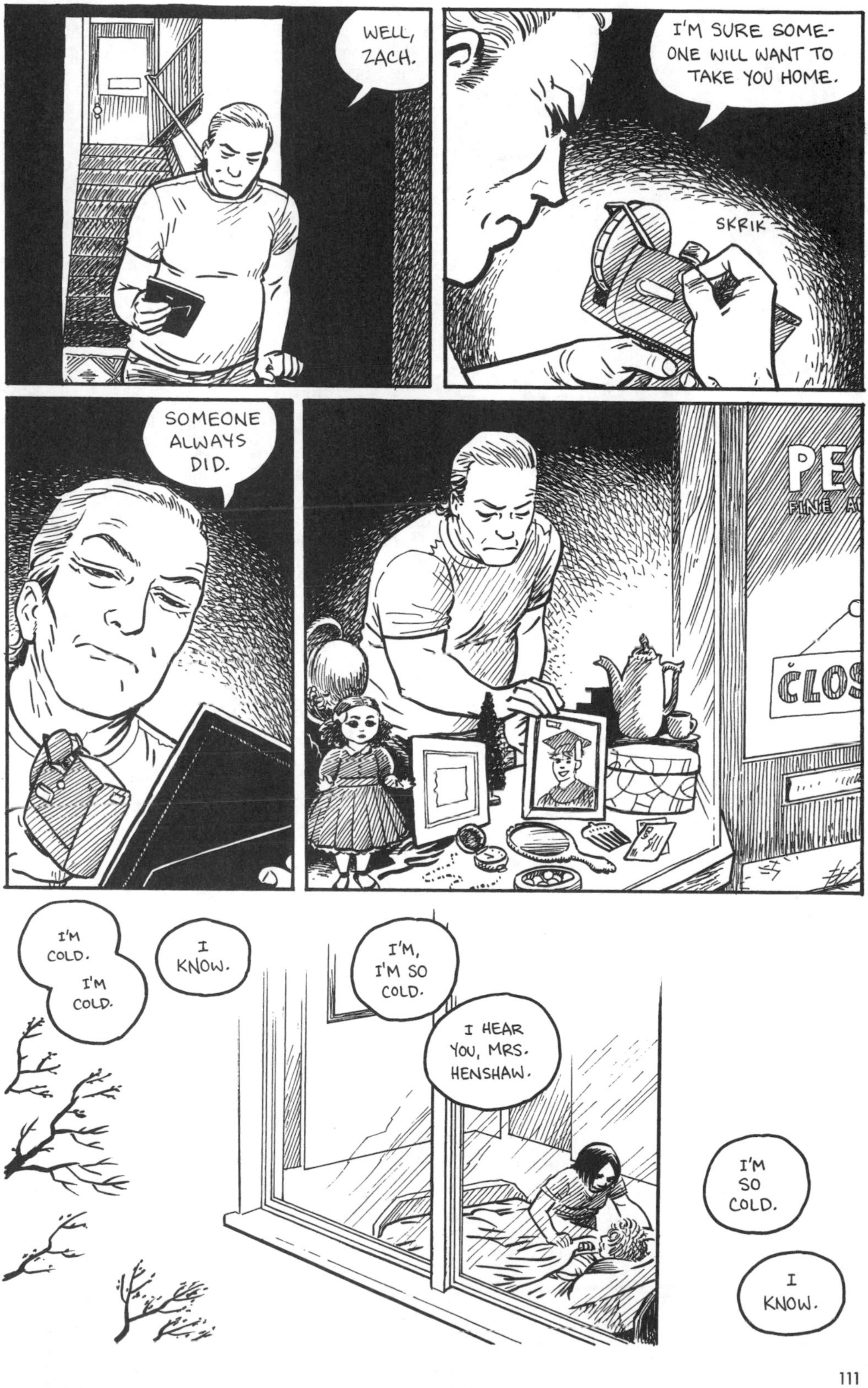
WELL, ZACH.
I'M SURE SOME-ONE WILL WANT TO TAKE YOU HOME.
SKRIK
SOMEONE ALWAYS DID.
PE
FINE A
CLOS
I'M COLD. I'M COLD.
I KNOW.
I'M, I'M SO COLD.
I HEAR YOU, MRS. HENSHAW.
I'M SO COLD.
I KNOW.

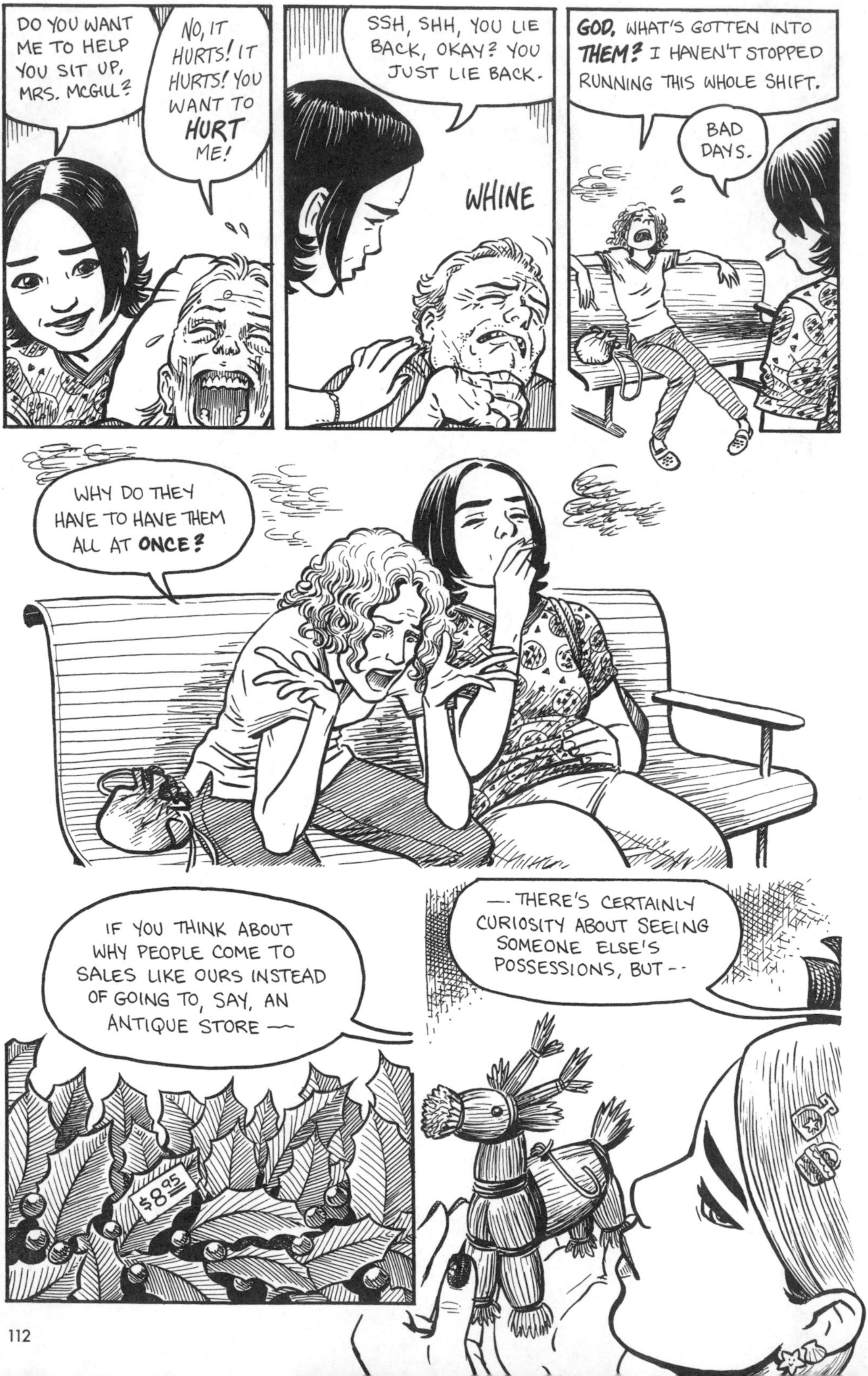
DO YOU WANT ME TO HELP YOU SIT UP, MRS. MCGILL?
NO, IT HURTS! IT HURTS! YOU WANT TO HURT ME!
SSH, SHH, YOU LIE BACK, OKAY? YOU JUST LIE BACK.
WHINE
GOD, WHAT'S GOTTEN INTO THEM? I HAVEN'T STOPPED RUNNING THIS WHOLE SHIFT.
BAD DAYS.
WHY DO THEY HAVE TO HAVE THEM ALL AT ONCE?
IF YOU THINK ABOUT WHY PEOPLE COME TO SALES LIKE OURS INSTEAD OF GOING TO, SAY, AN ANTIQUE STORE —
— THERE'S CERTAINLY CURIOSITY ABOUT SEEING SOMEONE ELSE'S POSSESSIONS, BUT --
$8.95

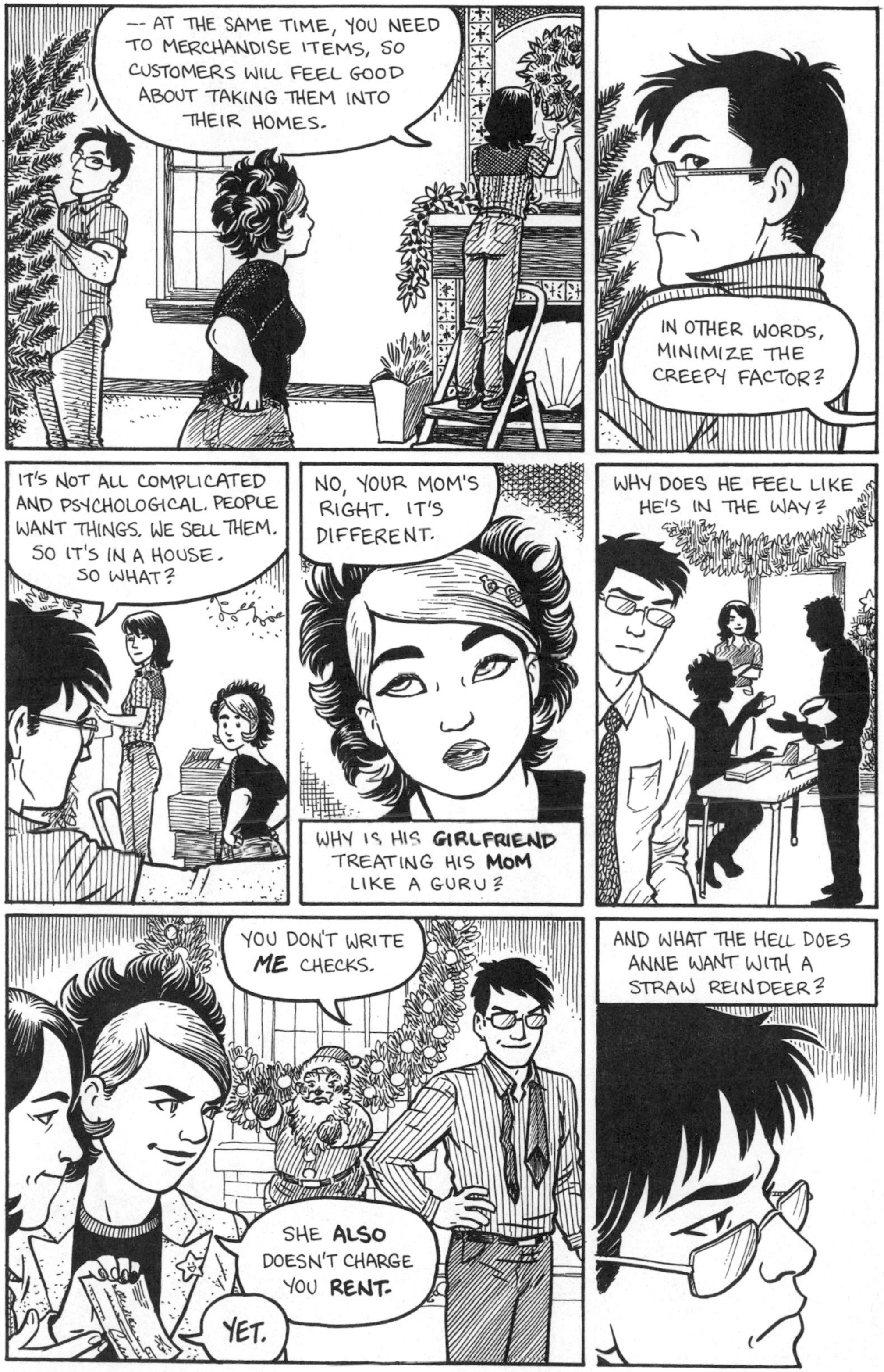

-- AT THE SAME TIME, YOU NEED TO MERCHANDISE ITEMS, SO CUSTOMERS WILL FEEL GOOD ABOUT TAKING THEM INTO THEIR HOMES.
IN OTHER WORDS, MINIMIZE THE CREEPY FACTOR?
IT'S NOT ALL COMPLICATED AND PSYCHOLOGICAL. PEOPLE WANT THINGS. WE SELL THEM. SO IT'S IN A HOUSE. SO WHAT?
NO, YOUR MOM'S RIGHT. IT'S DIFFERENT.
WHY IS HIS GIRLFRIEND TREATING HIS MOM LIKE A GURU?
WHY DOES HE FEEL LIKE HE'S IN THE WAY?
YOU DON'T WRITE ME CHECKS.
SHE ALSO DOESN'T CHARGE YOU RENT.
YET.
AND WHAT THE HELL DOES ANNE WANT WITH A STRAW REINDEER?

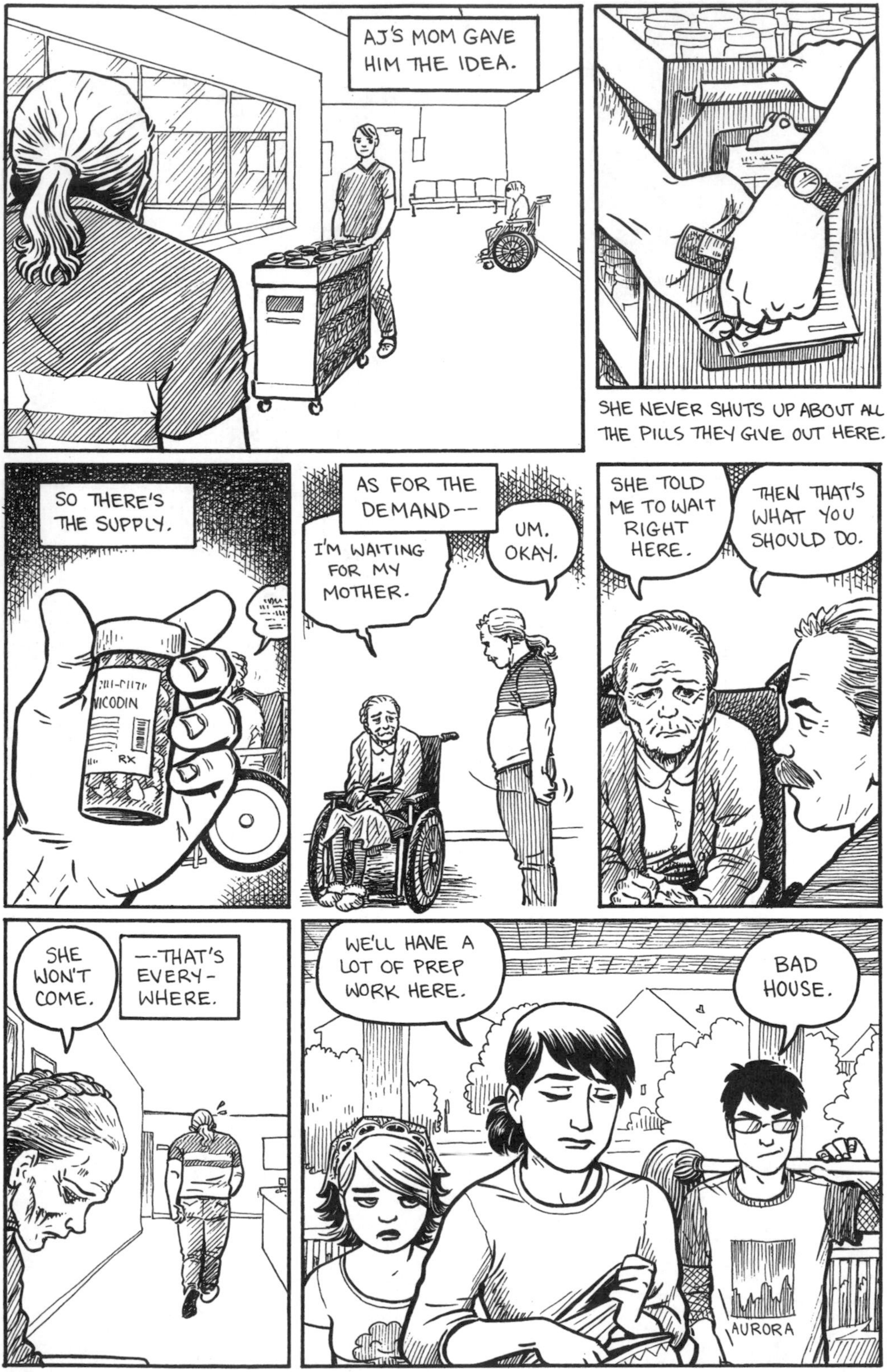
AJ'S MOM GAVE HIM THE IDEA.
SHE NEVER SHUTS UP ABOUT ALL THE PILLS THEY GIVE OUT HERE.
SO THERE'S THE SUPPLY.
NICODIN
RX
AS FOR THE DEMAND--
I'M WAITING FOR MY MOTHER.
UM. OKAY.
SHE TOLD ME TO WAIT RIGHT HERE.
THEN THAT'S WHAT YOU SHOULD DO.
SHE WON'T COME.
--THAT'S EVERY-WHERE.
WE'LL HAVE A LOT OF PREP WORK HERE.
BAD HOUSE.
AURORA

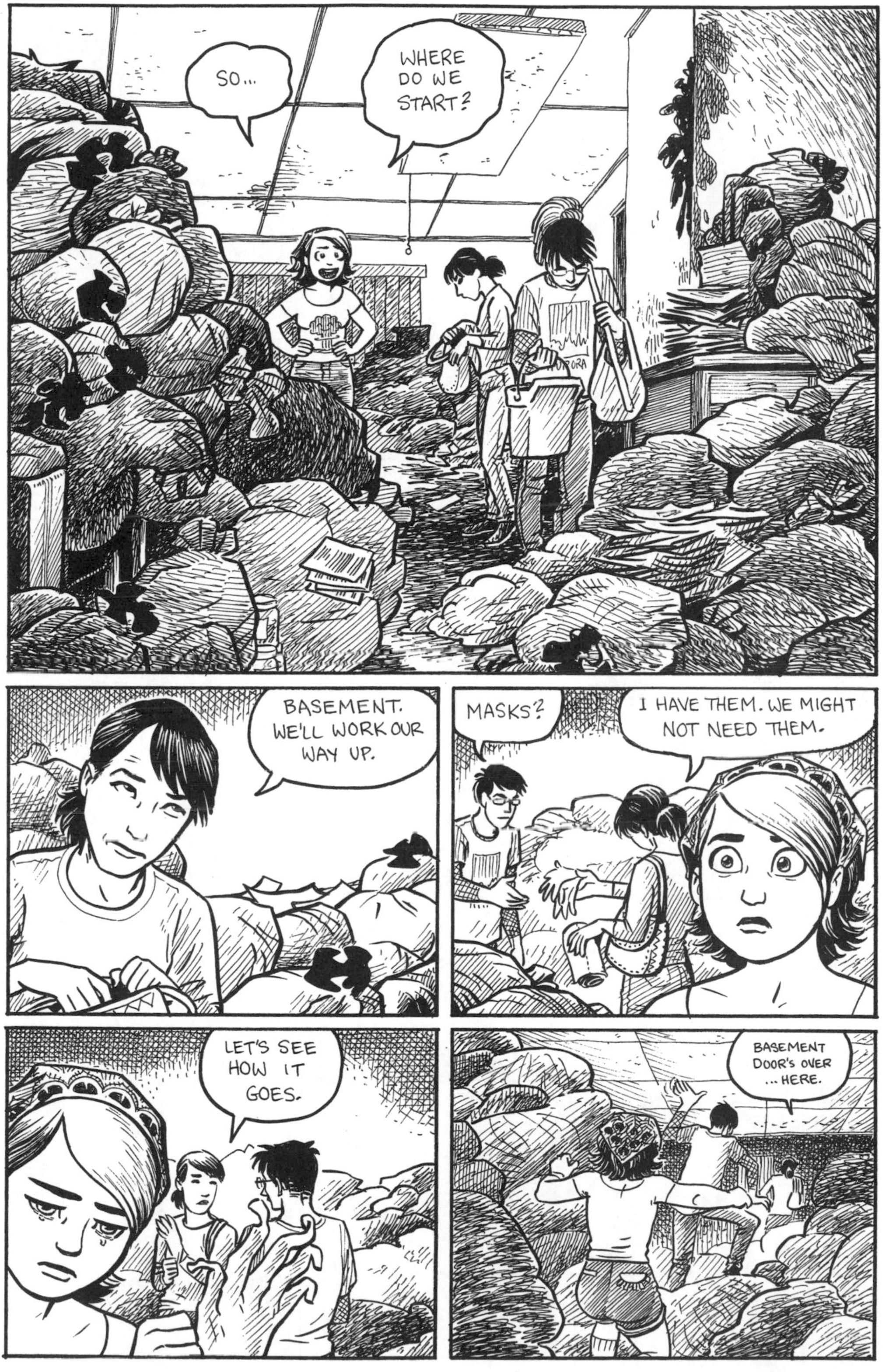

SO...
WHERE DO WE START?
BASEMENT. WE'LL WORK OUR WAY UP.
MASKS?
I HAVE THEM. WE MIGHT NOT NEED THEM.
LET'S SEE HOW IT GOES.
BASEMENT DOOR'S OVER ...HERE.

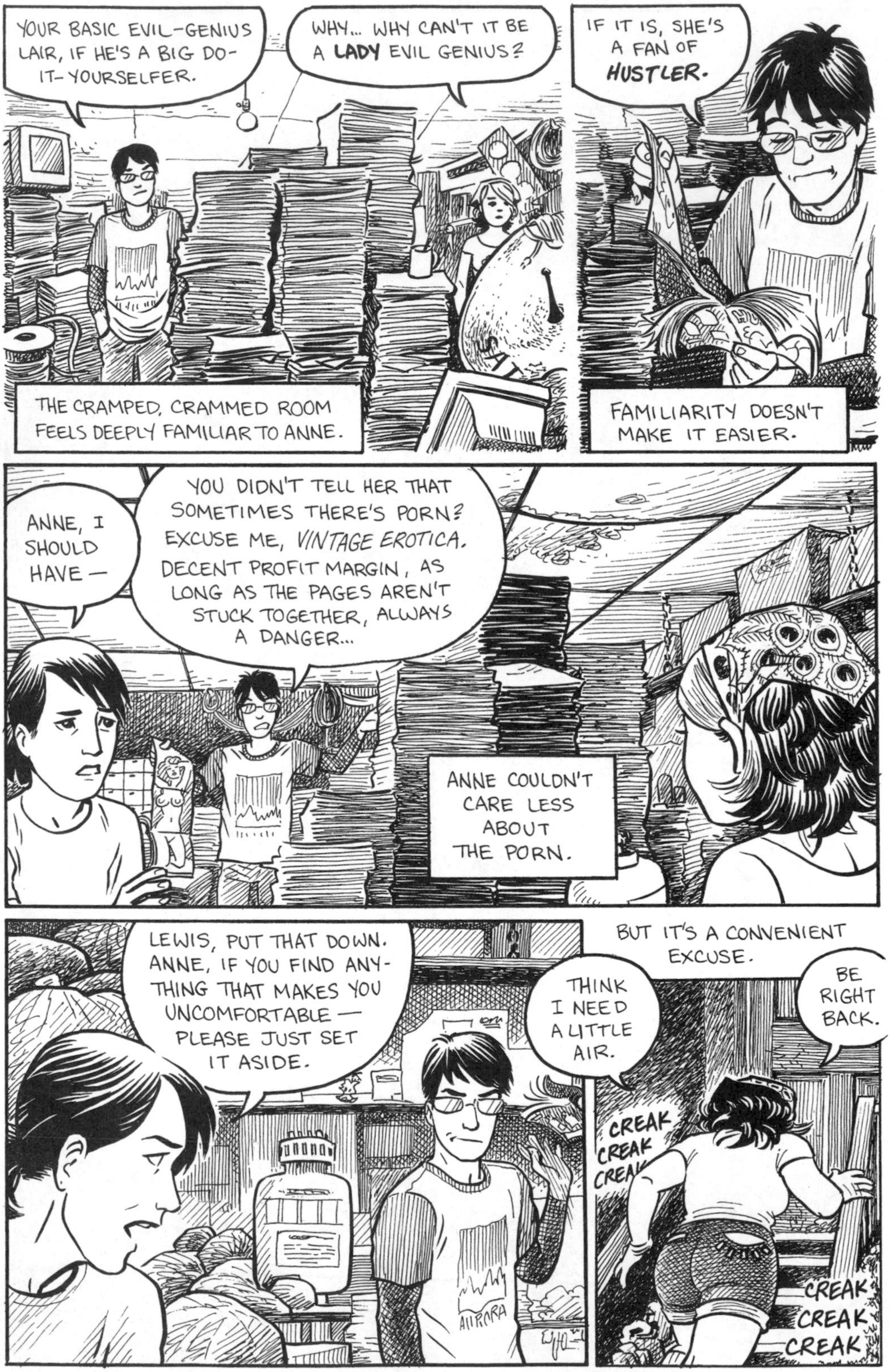
YOUR BASIC EVIL-GENIUS LAIR, IF HE'S A BIG DO-IT-YOURSELFER.
WHY... WHY CAN'T IT BE A **LADY** EVIL GENIUS?
THE CRAMPED, CRAMMED ROOM FEELS DEEPLY FAMILIAR TO ANNE.
IF IT IS, SHE'S A FAN OF **HUSTLER**.
FAMILIARITY DOESN'T MAKE IT EASIER.
ANNE, I SHOULD HAVE—
YOU DIDN'T TELL HER THAT SOMETIMES THERE'S PORN? EXCUSE ME, *VINTAGE EROTICA*. DECENT PROFIT MARGIN, AS LONG AS THE PAGES AREN'T STUCK TOGETHER, ALWAYS A DANGER...
ANNE COULDN'T CARE LESS ABOUT THE PORN.
LEWIS, PUT THAT DOWN. ANNE, IF YOU FIND ANYTHING THAT MAKES YOU UNCOMFORTABLE— PLEASE JUST SET IT ASIDE.
BUT IT'S A CONVENIENT EXCUSE.
THINK I NEED A LITTLE AIR.
BE RIGHT BACK.
CREAK CREAK CREAK
CREAK CREAK CREAK

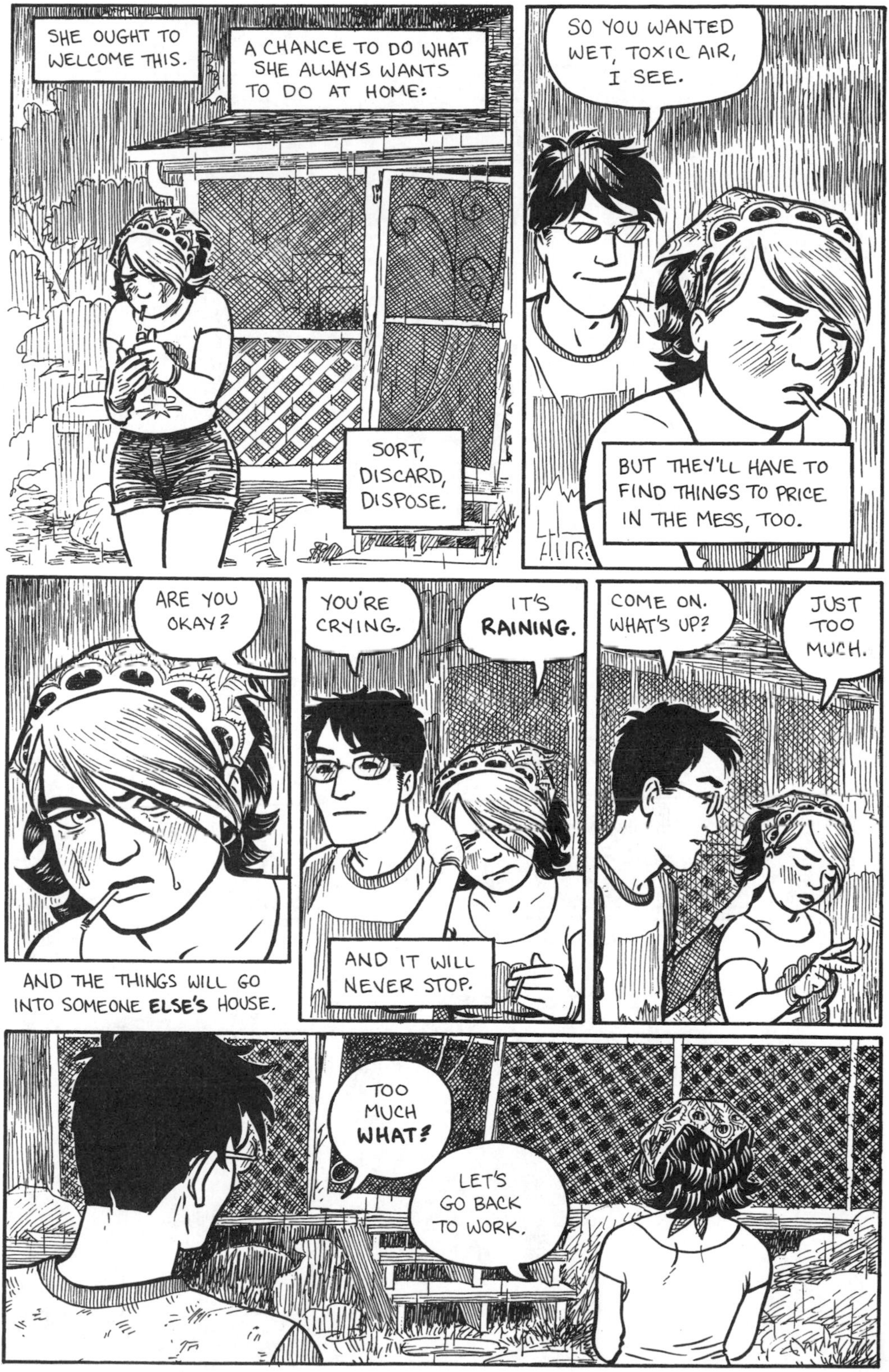
SHE OUGHT TO WELCOME THIS.
A CHANCE TO DO WHAT SHE ALWAYS WANTS TO DO AT HOME:
SORT, DISCARD, DISPOSE.
SO YOU WANTED WET, TOXIC AIR, I SEE.
BUT THEY'LL HAVE TO FIND THINGS TO PRICE IN THE MESS, TOO.
ARE YOU OKAY?
AND THE THINGS WILL GO INTO SOMEONE **ELSE'S** HOUSE.
YOU'RE CRYING.
IT'S **RAINING.**
AND IT WILL NEVER STOP.
COME ON. WHAT'S UP?
JUST TOO MUCH.
TOO MUCH **WHAT?**
LET'S GO BACK TO WORK.

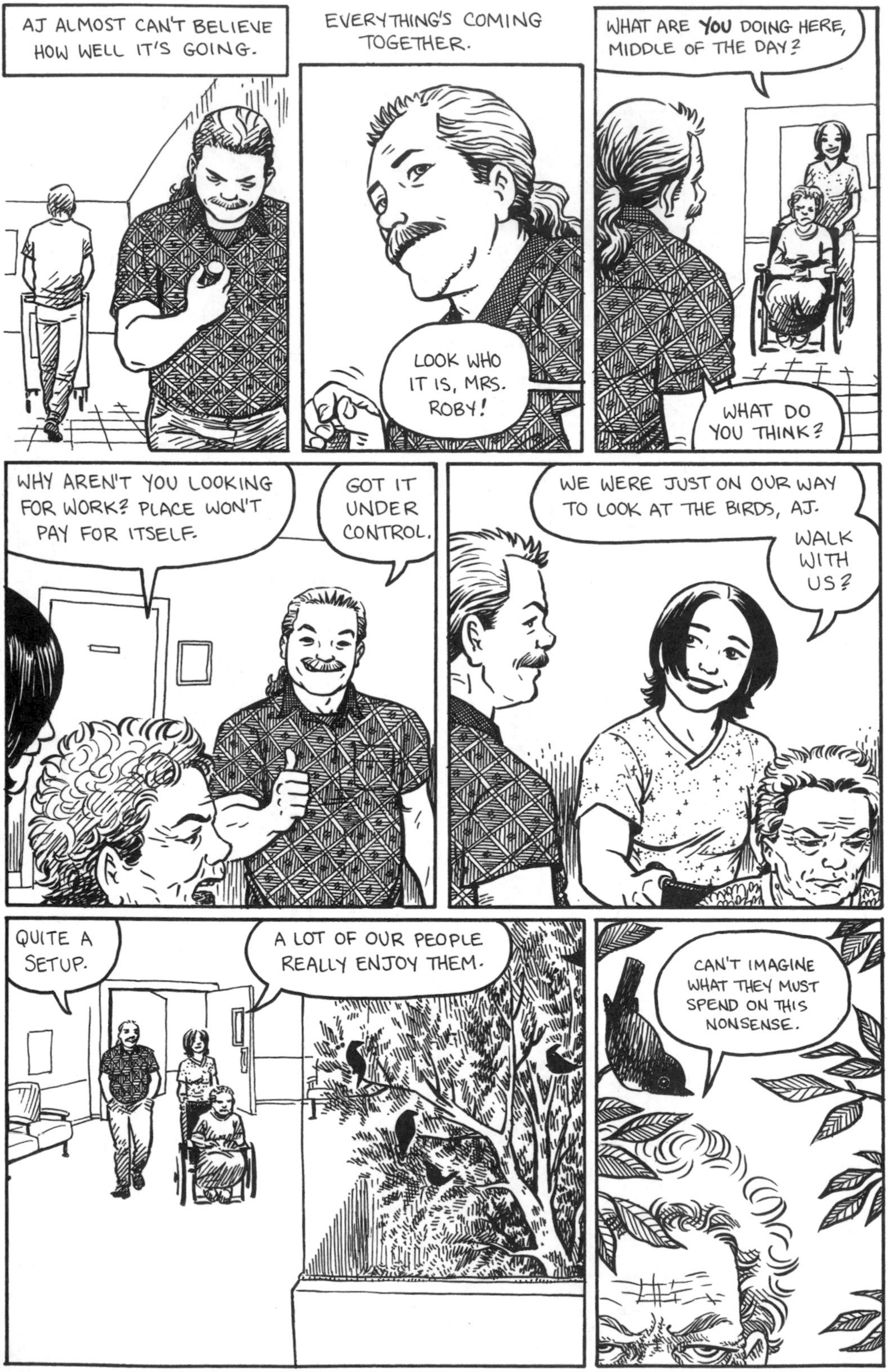
AJ ALMOST CAN'T BELIEVE HOW WELL IT'S GOING.
EVERYTHING'S COMING TOGETHER.
LOOK WHO IT IS, MRS. ROBY!
WHAT ARE YOU DOING HERE, MIDDLE OF THE DAY?
WHAT DO YOU THINK?
WHY AREN'T YOU LOOKING FOR WORK? PLACE WON'T PAY FOR ITSELF.
GOT IT UNDER CONTROL.
WE WERE JUST ON OUR WAY TO LOOK AT THE BIRDS, AJ.
WALK WITH US?
QUITE A SETUP.
A LOT OF OUR PEOPLE REALLY ENJOY THEM.
CAN'T IMAGINE WHAT THEY MUST SPEND ON THIS NONSENSE.

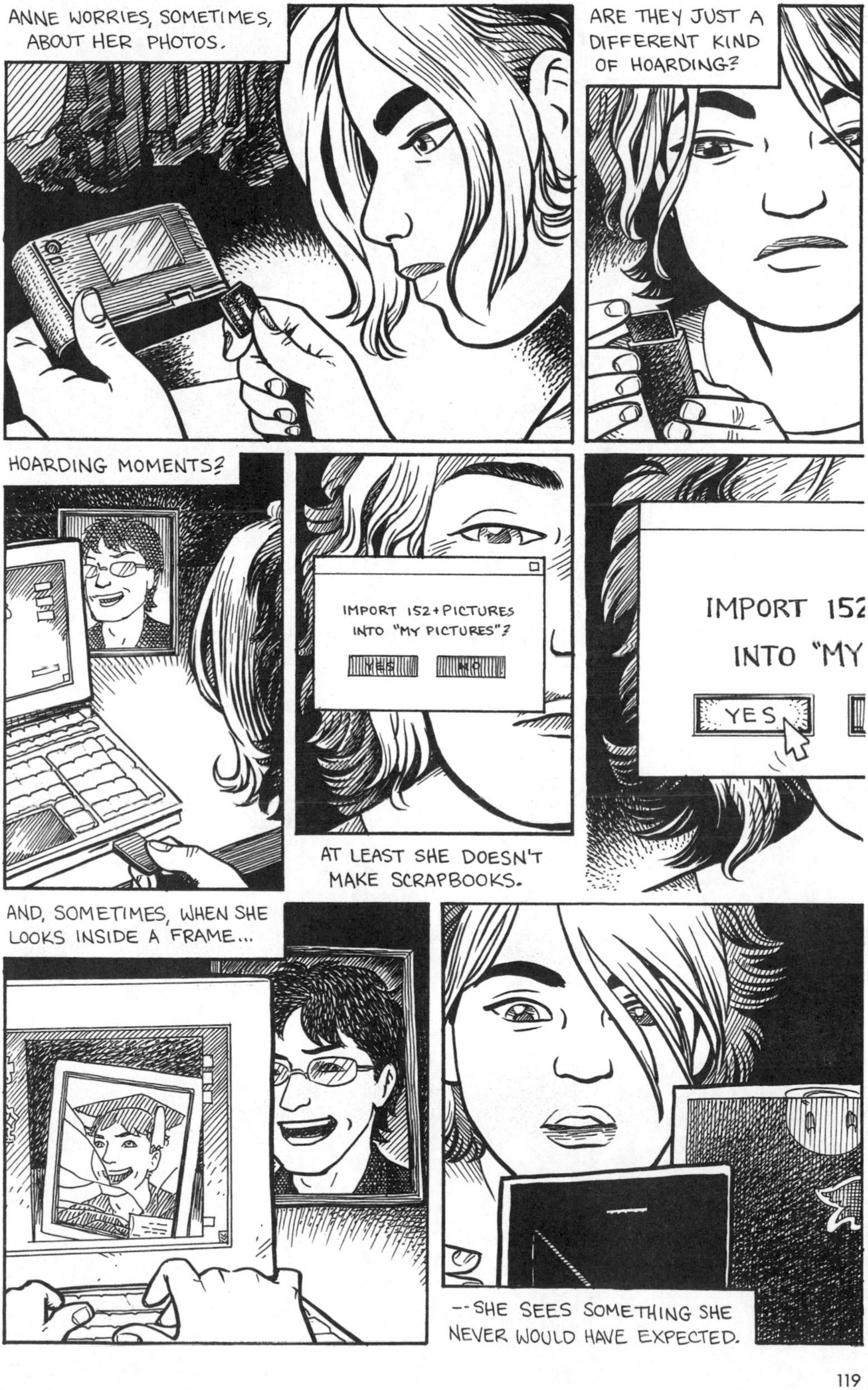
ANNE WORRIES, SOMETIMES, ABOUT HER PHOTOS.
ARE THEY JUST A DIFFERENT KIND OF HOARDING?
HOARDING MOMENTS?
IMPORT 152+PICTURES INTO "MY PICTURES"?
YES
NO
IMPORT 152
INTO "MY
YES
AT LEAST SHE DOESN'T MAKE SCRAPBOOKS.
AND, SOMETIMES, WHEN SHE LOOKS INSIDE A FRAME...
--SHE SEES SOMETHING SHE NEVER WOULD HAVE EXPECTED.

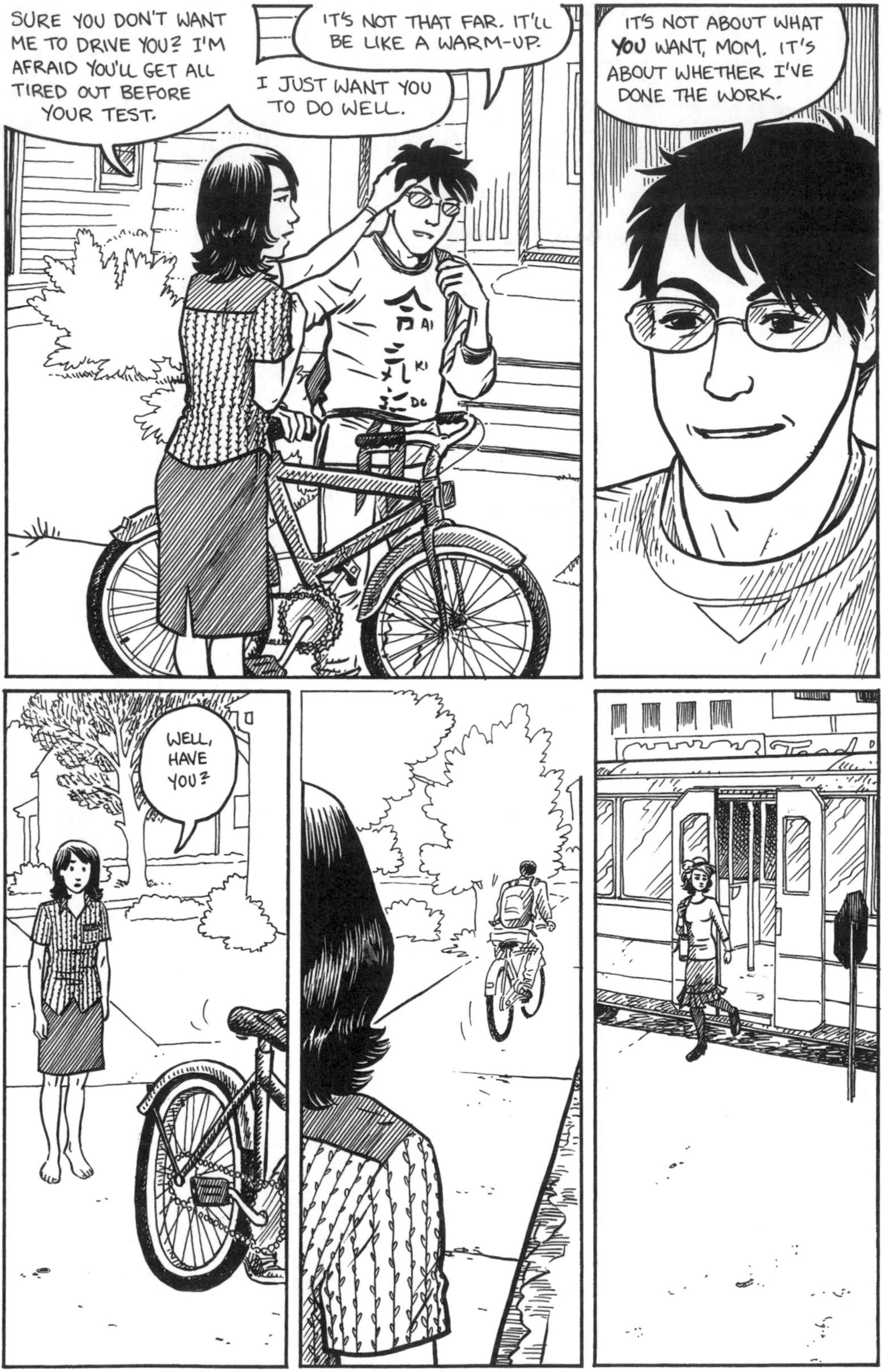
SURE YOU DON'T WANT ME TO DRIVE YOU? I'M AFRAID YOU'LL GET ALL TIRED OUT BEFORE YOUR TEST.
IT'S NOT THAT FAR. IT'LL BE LIKE A WARM-UP.
I JUST WANT YOU TO DO WELL.
AI
KI
DO
IT'S NOT ABOUT WHAT YOU WANT, MOM. IT'S ABOUT WHETHER I'VE DONE THE WORK.
WELL, HAVE YOU?

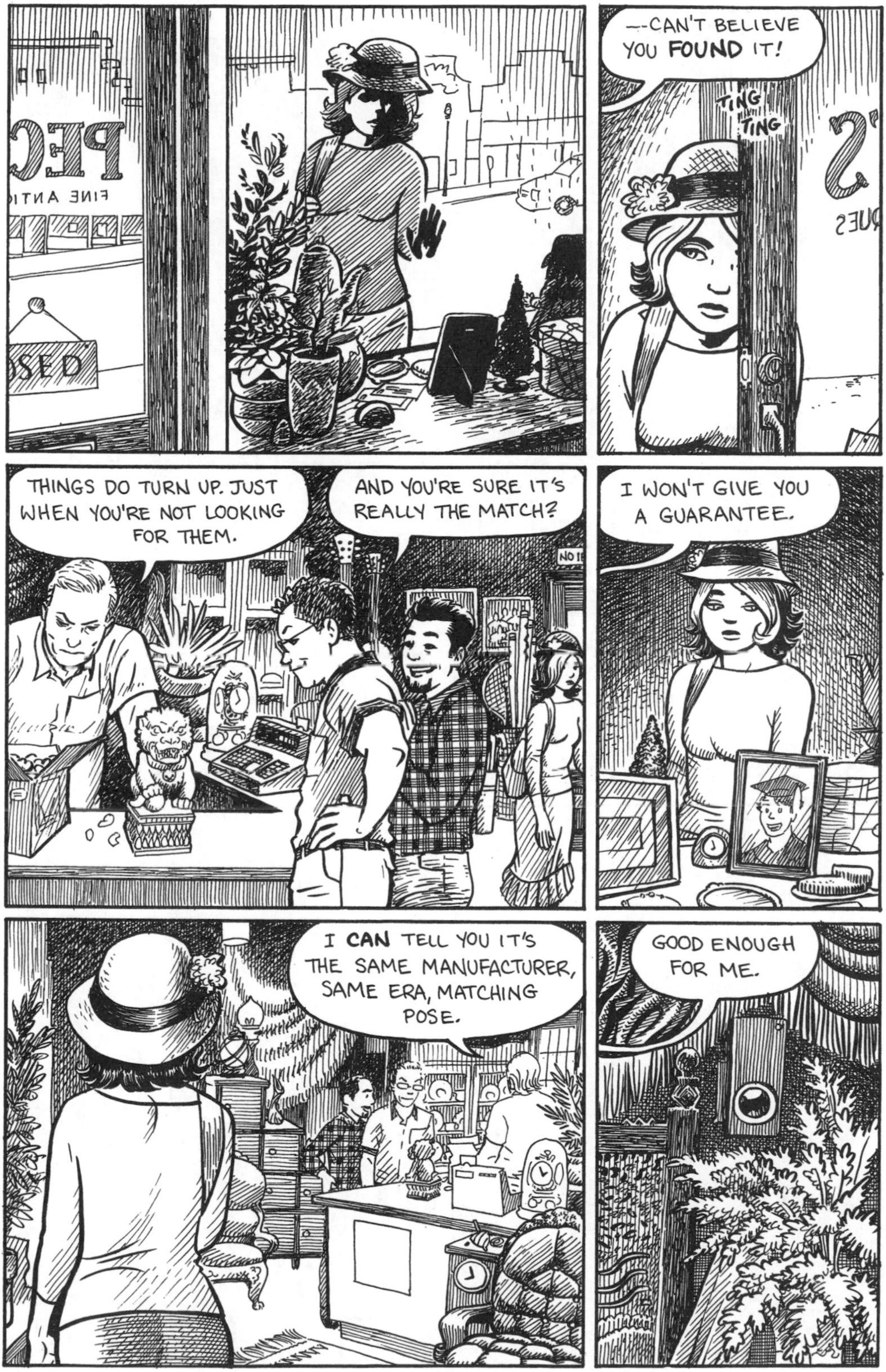
FINE ANTI
SED
--CAN'T BELIEVE YOU FOUND IT!
TING TING
THINGS DO TURN UP. JUST WHEN YOU'RE NOT LOOKING FOR THEM.
AND YOU'RE SURE IT'S REALLY THE MATCH?
I WON'T GIVE YOU A GUARANTEE.
I CAN TELL YOU IT'S THE SAME MANUFACTURER, SAME ERA, MATCHING POSE.
GOOD ENOUGH FOR ME.

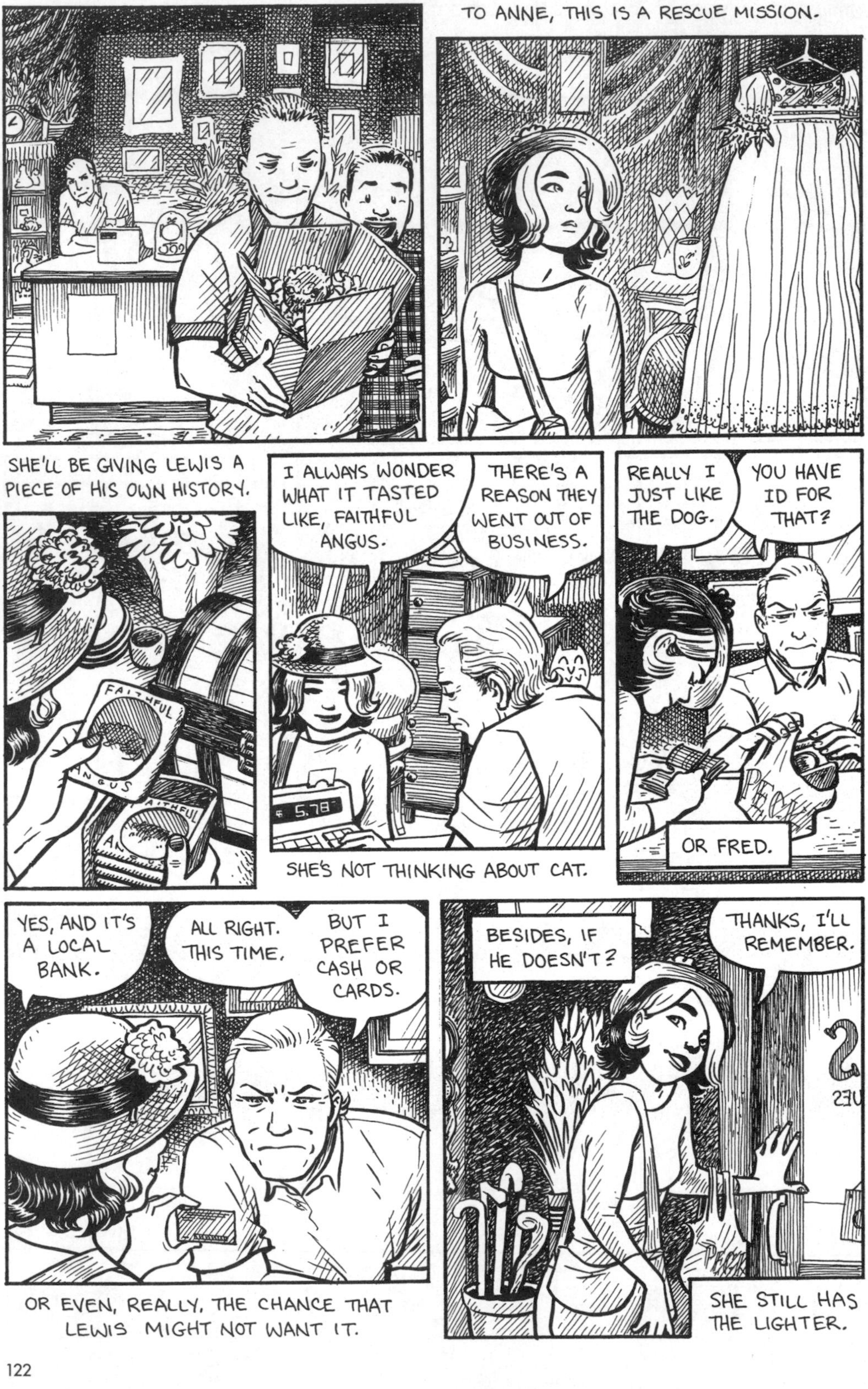
TO ANNE, THIS IS A RESCUE MISSION.
SHE'LL BE GIVING LEWIS A PIECE OF HIS OWN HISTORY.
FAITHFUL ANGUS
I ALWAYS WONDER WHAT IT TASTED LIKE, FAITHFUL ANGUS.
THERE'S A REASON THEY WENT OUT OF BUSINESS.
5.78
SHE'S NOT THINKING ABOUT CAT.
REALLY I JUST LIKE THE DOG.
YOU HAVE ID FOR THAT?
OR FRED.
YES, AND IT'S A LOCAL BANK.
ALL RIGHT. THIS TIME.
BUT I PREFER CASH OR CARDS.
OR EVEN, REALLY, THE CHANCE THAT LEWIS MIGHT NOT WANT IT.
BESIDES, IF HE DOESN'T?
THANKS, I'LL REMEMBER.
SHE STILL HAS THE LIGHTER.

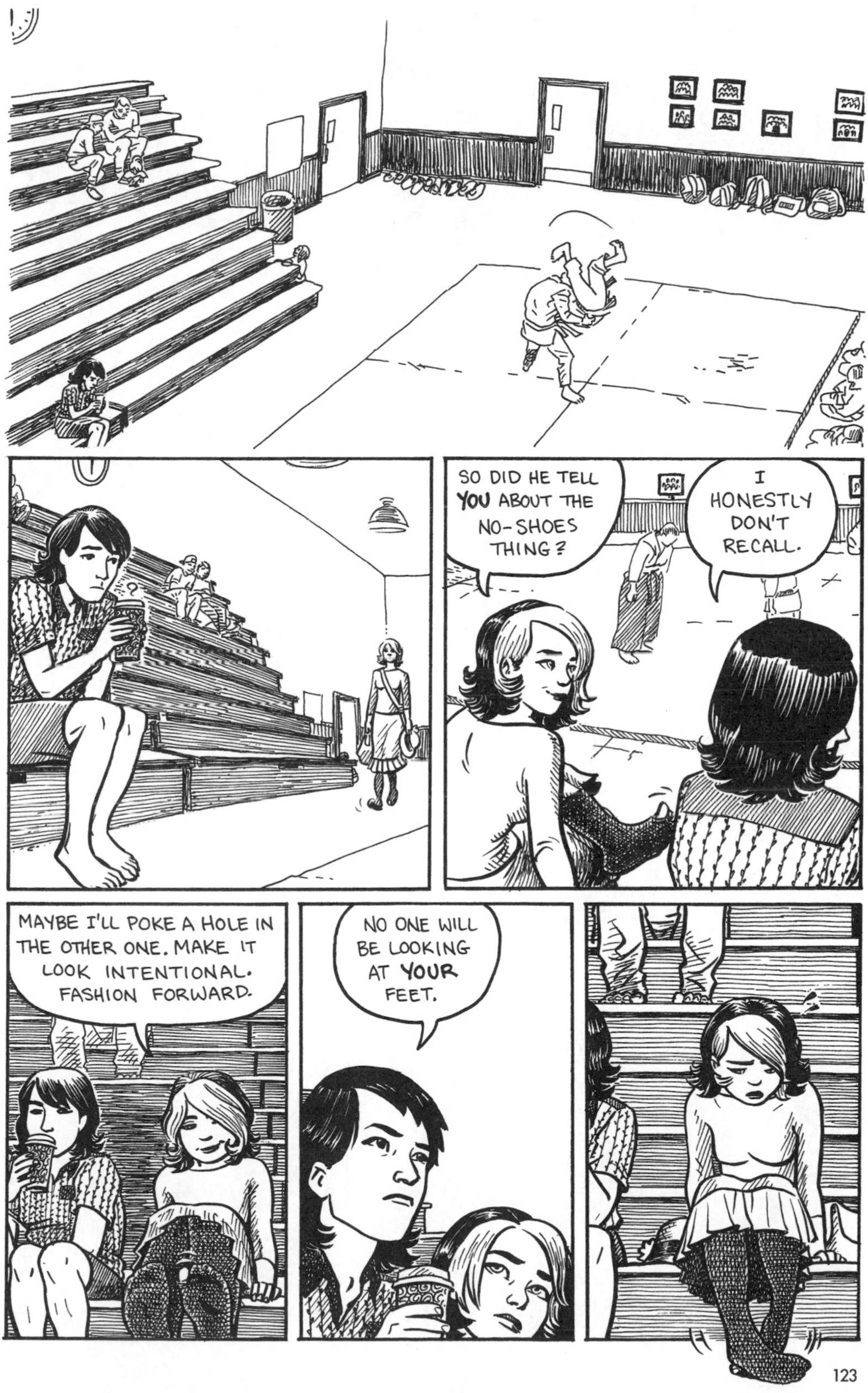
SO DID HE TELL YOU ABOUT THE NO-SHOES THING?
I HONESTLY DON'T RECALL.
MAYBE I'LL POKE A HOLE IN THE OTHER ONE. MAKE IT LOOK INTENTIONAL. FASHION FORWARD.
NO ONE WILL BE LOOKING AT YOUR FEET.

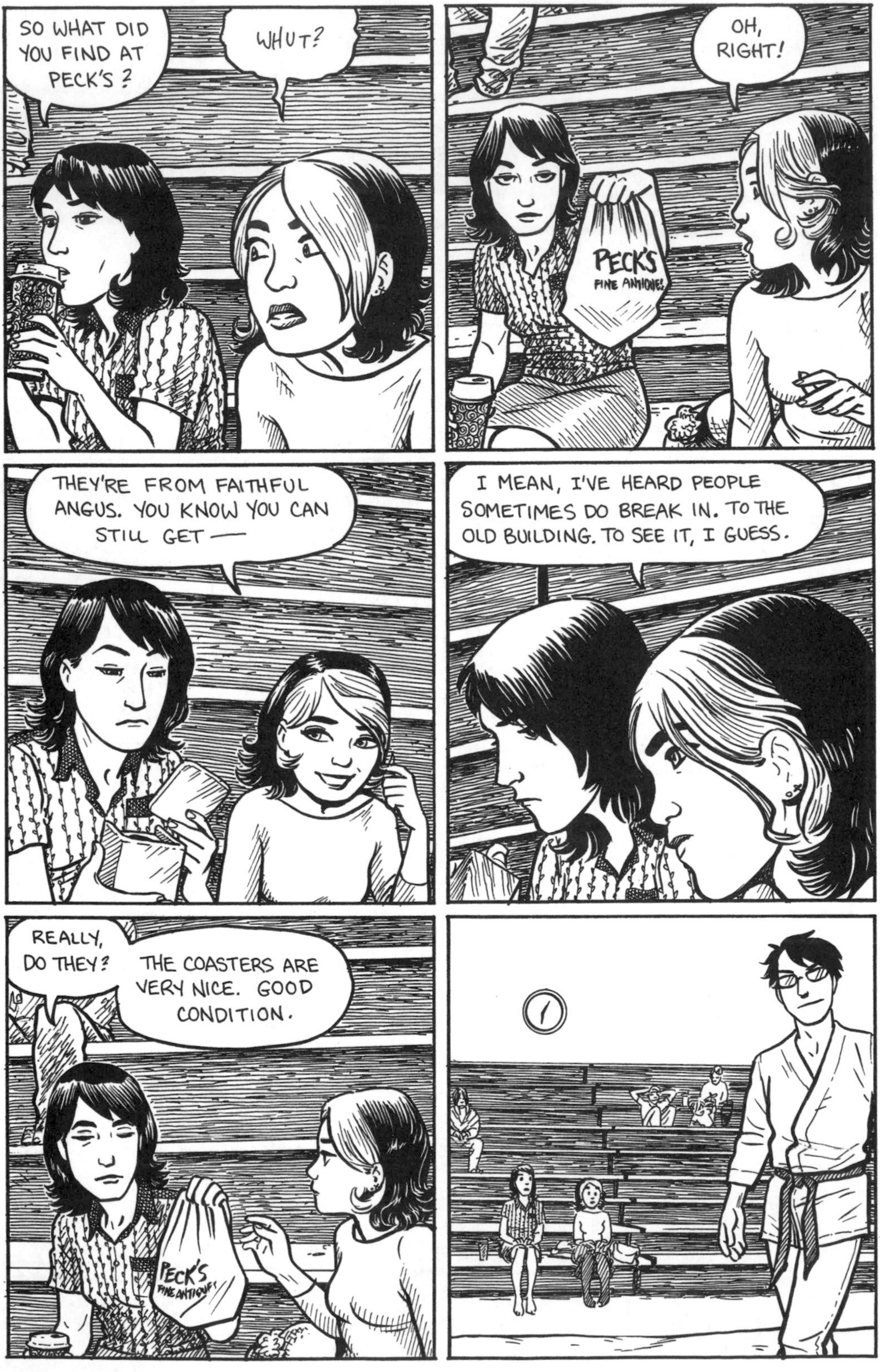
SO WHAT DID YOU FIND AT PECK'S?
WHUT?
OH, RIGHT!
PECK'S FINE ANTIQUES
THEY'RE FROM FAITHFUL ANGUS. YOU KNOW YOU CAN STILL GET—
I MEAN, I'VE HEARD PEOPLE SOMETIMES DO BREAK IN. TO THE OLD BUILDING. TO SEE IT, I GUESS.
REALLY, DO THEY?
THE COASTERS ARE VERY NICE. GOOD CONDITION.
PECK'S FINE ANTIQUES

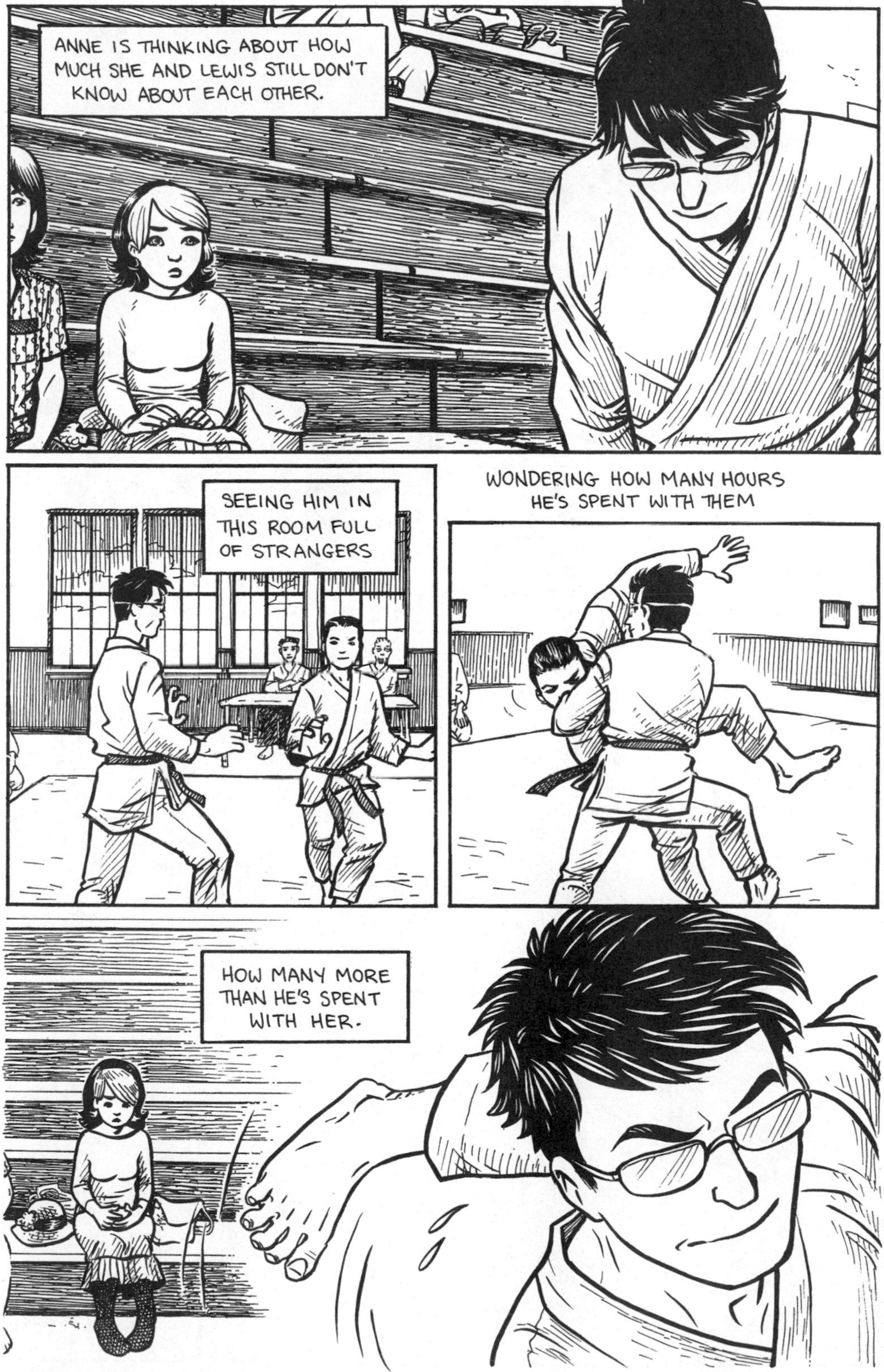
ANNE IS THINKING ABOUT HOW MUCH SHE AND LEWIS STILL DON'T KNOW ABOUT EACH OTHER.
SEEING HIM IN THIS ROOM FULL OF STRANGERS
WONDERING HOW MANY HOURS HE'S SPENT WITH THEM
HOW MANY MORE THAN HE'S SPENT WITH HER.

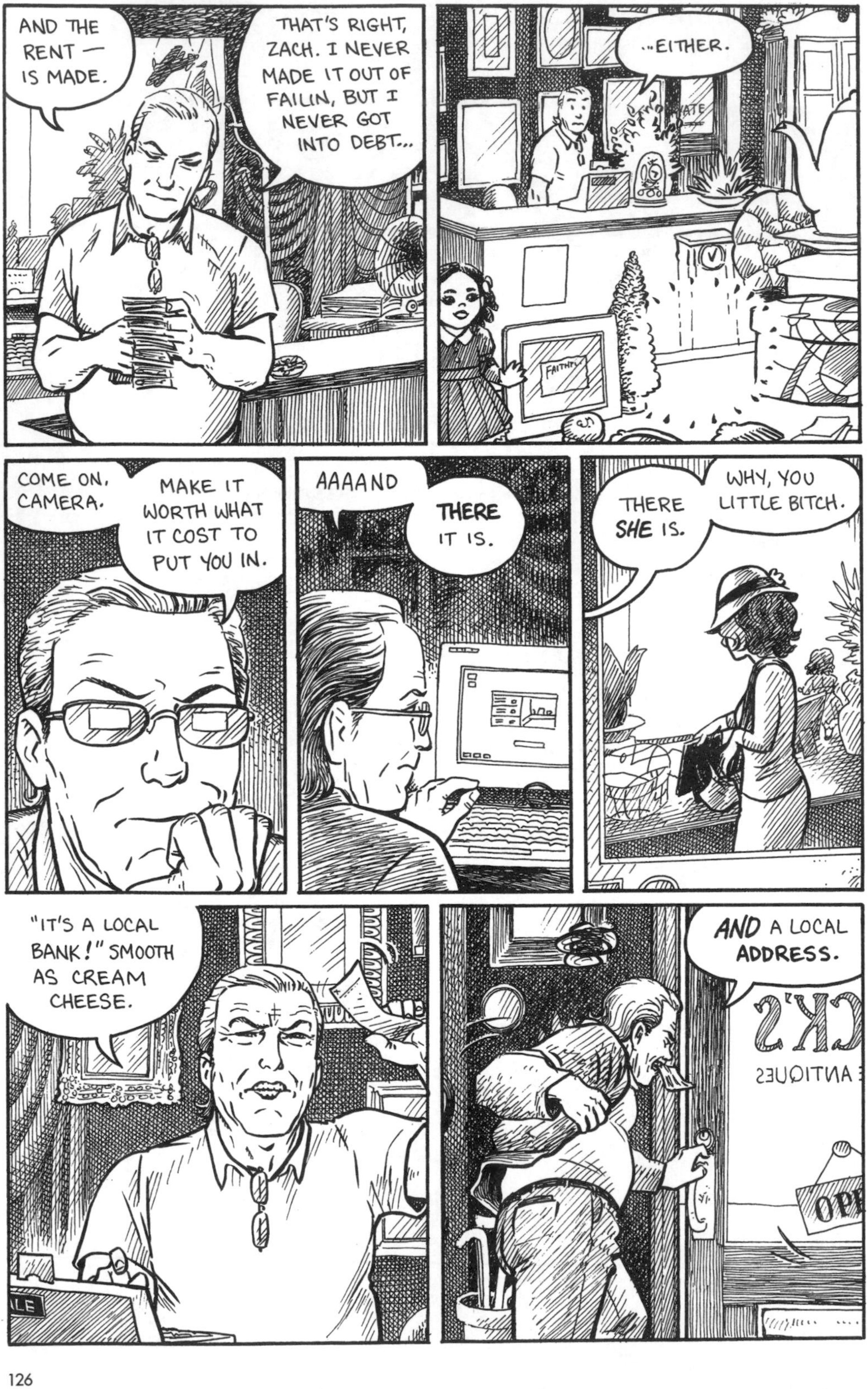
AND THE RENT — IS MADE.
THAT'S RIGHT, ZACH. I NEVER MADE IT OUT OF FAILIN, BUT I NEVER GOT INTO DEBT...
...EITHER.
COME ON, CAMERA.
MAKE IT WORTH WHAT IT COST TO PUT YOU IN.
AAAAND
THERE IT IS.
THERE SHE IS.
WHY, YOU LITTLE BITCH.
"IT'S A LOCAL BANK!" SMOOTH AS CREAM CHEESE.
AND A LOCAL ADDRESS.

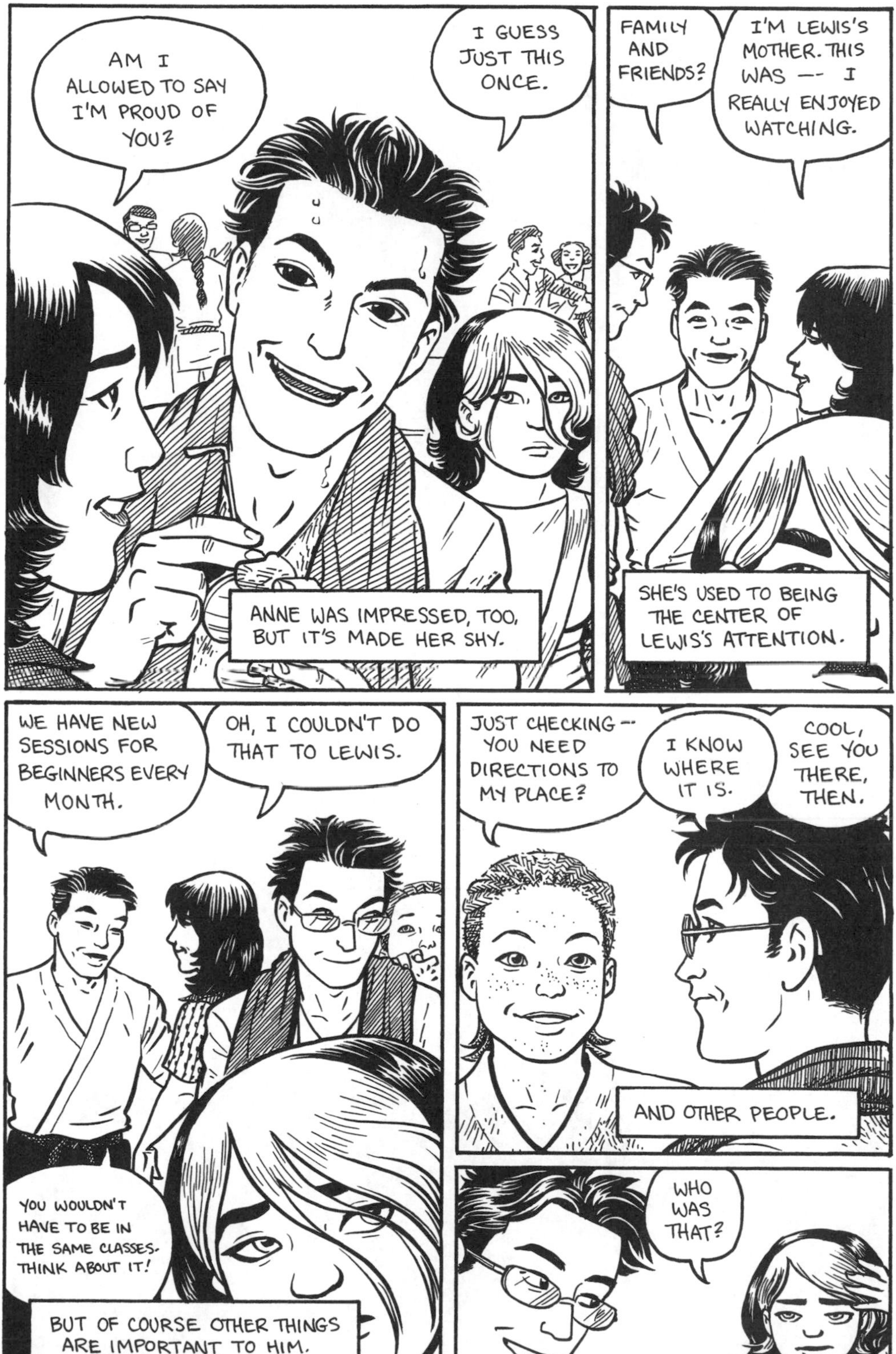
AM I ALLOWED TO SAY I'M PROUD OF YOU?
I GUESS JUST THIS ONCE.
ANNE WAS IMPRESSED, TOO, BUT IT'S MADE HER SHY.
FAMILY AND FRIENDS?
I'M LEWIS'S MOTHER. THIS WAS -- I REALLY ENJOYED WATCHING.
SHE'S USED TO BEING THE CENTER OF LEWIS'S ATTENTION.
WE HAVE NEW SESSIONS FOR BEGINNERS EVERY MONTH.
OH, I COULDN'T DO THAT TO LEWIS.
YOU WOULDN'T HAVE TO BE IN THE SAME CLASSES. THINK ABOUT IT!
BUT OF COURSE OTHER THINGS ARE IMPORTANT TO HIM.
JUST CHECKING -- YOU NEED DIRECTIONS TO MY PLACE?
I KNOW WHERE IT IS.
COOL, SEE YOU THERE, THEN.
AND OTHER PEOPLE.
WHO WAS THAT?

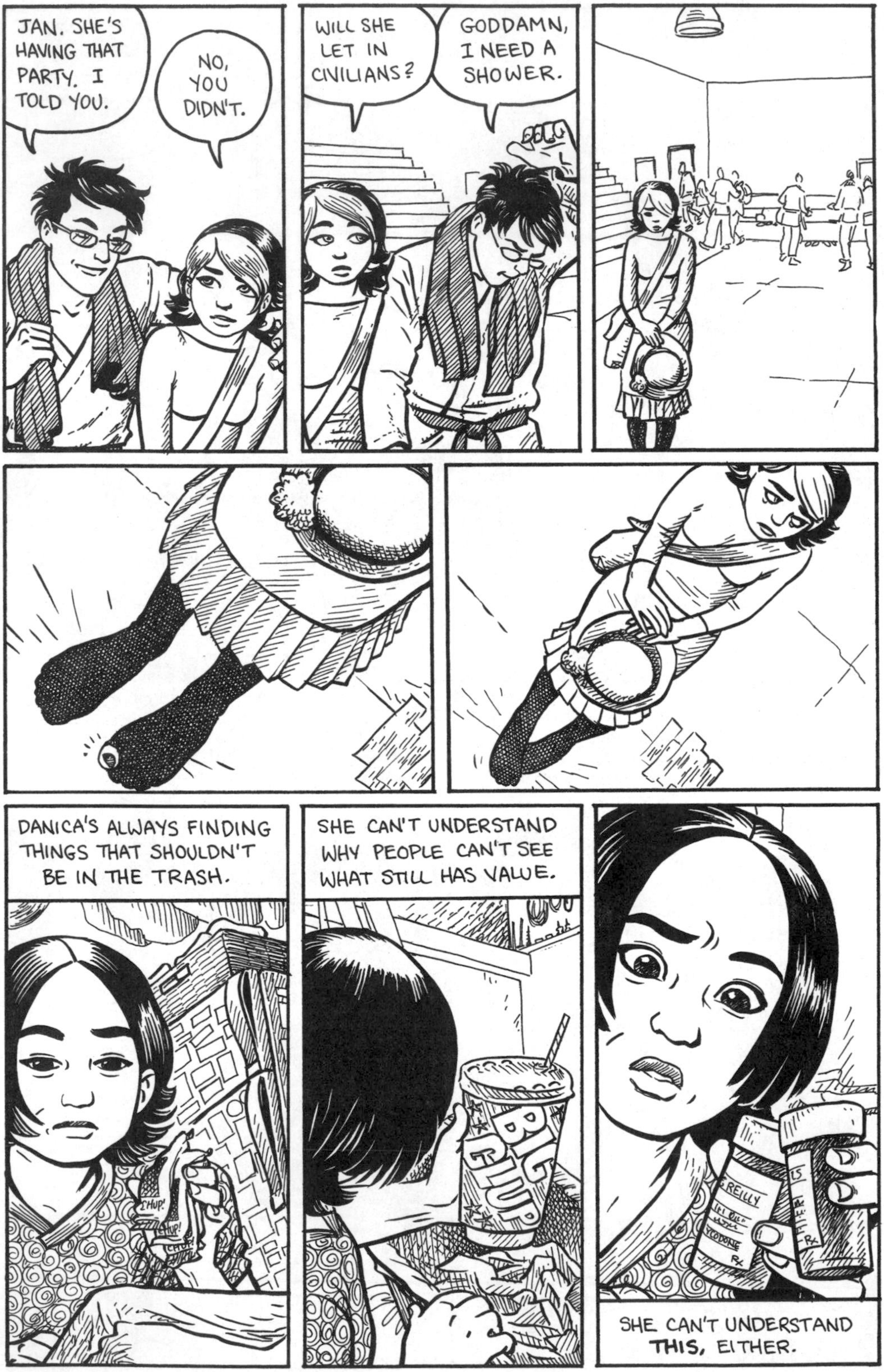
JAN. SHE'S HAVING THAT PARTY. I TOLD YOU.
NO, YOU DIDN'T.
WILL SHE LET IN CIVILIANS?
GODDAMN, I NEED A SHOWER.
DANICA'S ALWAYS FINDING THINGS THAT SHOULDN'T BE IN THE TRASH.
SHE CAN'T UNDERSTAND WHY PEOPLE CAN'T SEE WHAT STILL HAS VALUE.
SHE CAN'T UNDERSTAND **THIS,** EITHER.

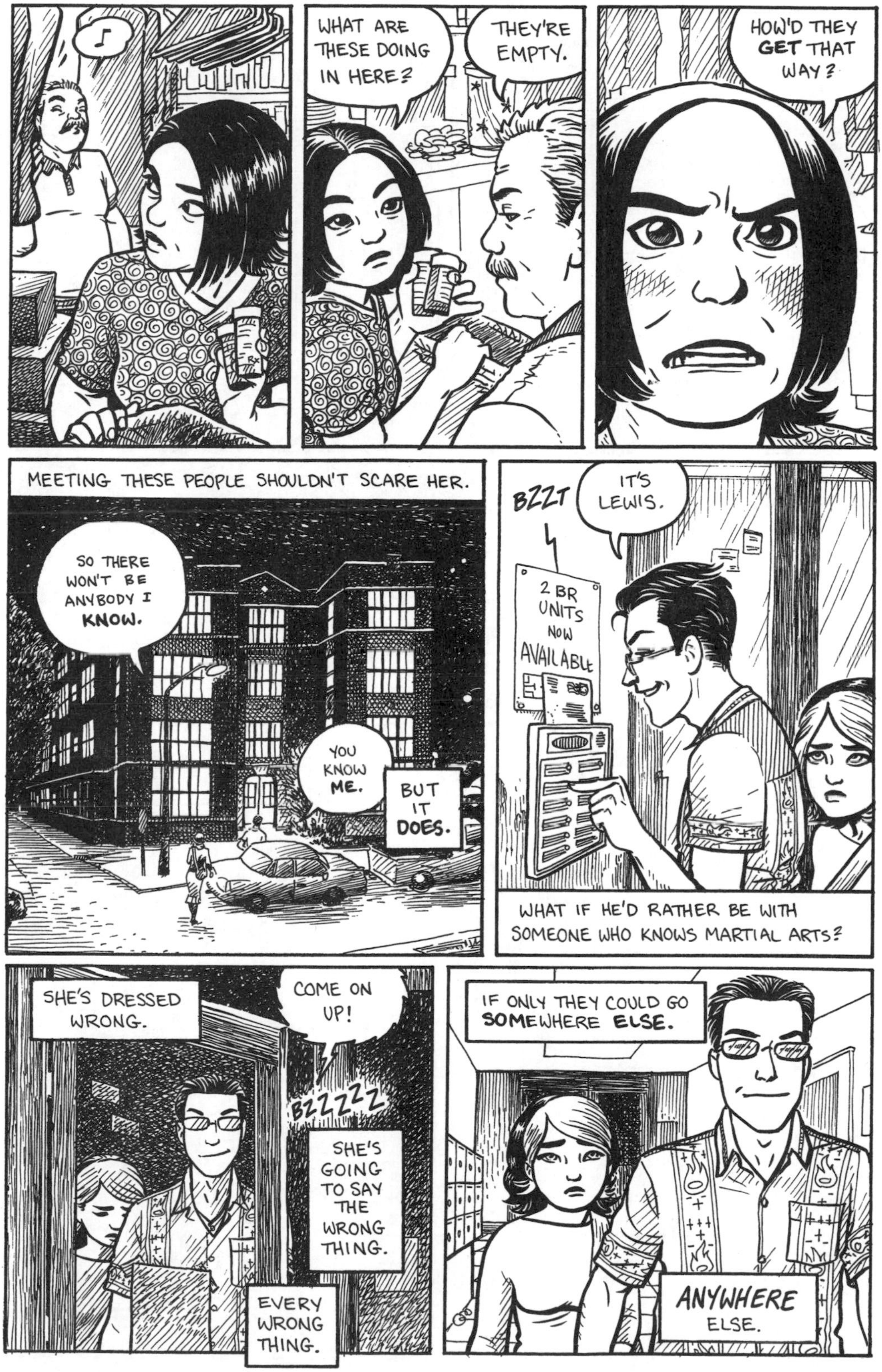
WHAT ARE THESE DOING IN HERE?
THEY'RE EMPTY.
HOW'D THEY GET THAT WAY?
MEETING THESE PEOPLE SHOULDN'T SCARE HER.
SO THERE WON'T BE ANYBODY I KNOW.
YOU KNOW ME.
BUT IT DOES.
BZZT
IT'S LEWIS.
2 BR UNITS NOW AVAILABLE
WHAT IF HE'D RATHER BE WITH SOMEONE WHO KNOWS MARTIAL ARTS?
SHE'S DRESSED WRONG.
COME ON UP!
BZZZZZ
SHE'S GOING TO SAY THE WRONG THING.
EVERY WRONG THING.
IF ONLY THEY COULD GO SOMEWHERE ELSE.
ANYWHERE ELSE.

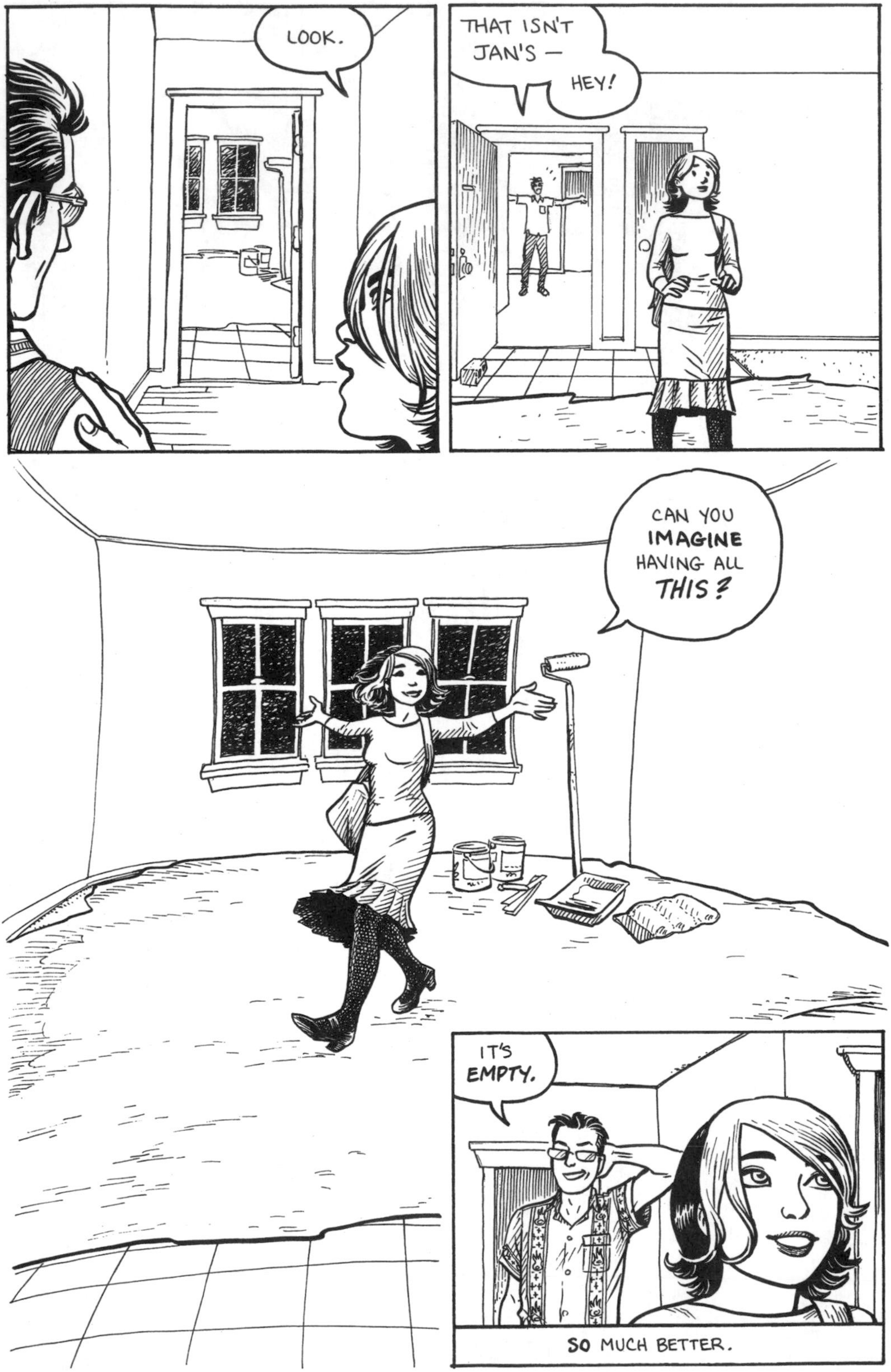
LOOK.
THAT ISN'T JAN'S —
HEY!
CAN YOU IMAGINE HAVING ALL THIS?
IT'S EMPTY.
SO MUCH BETTER.

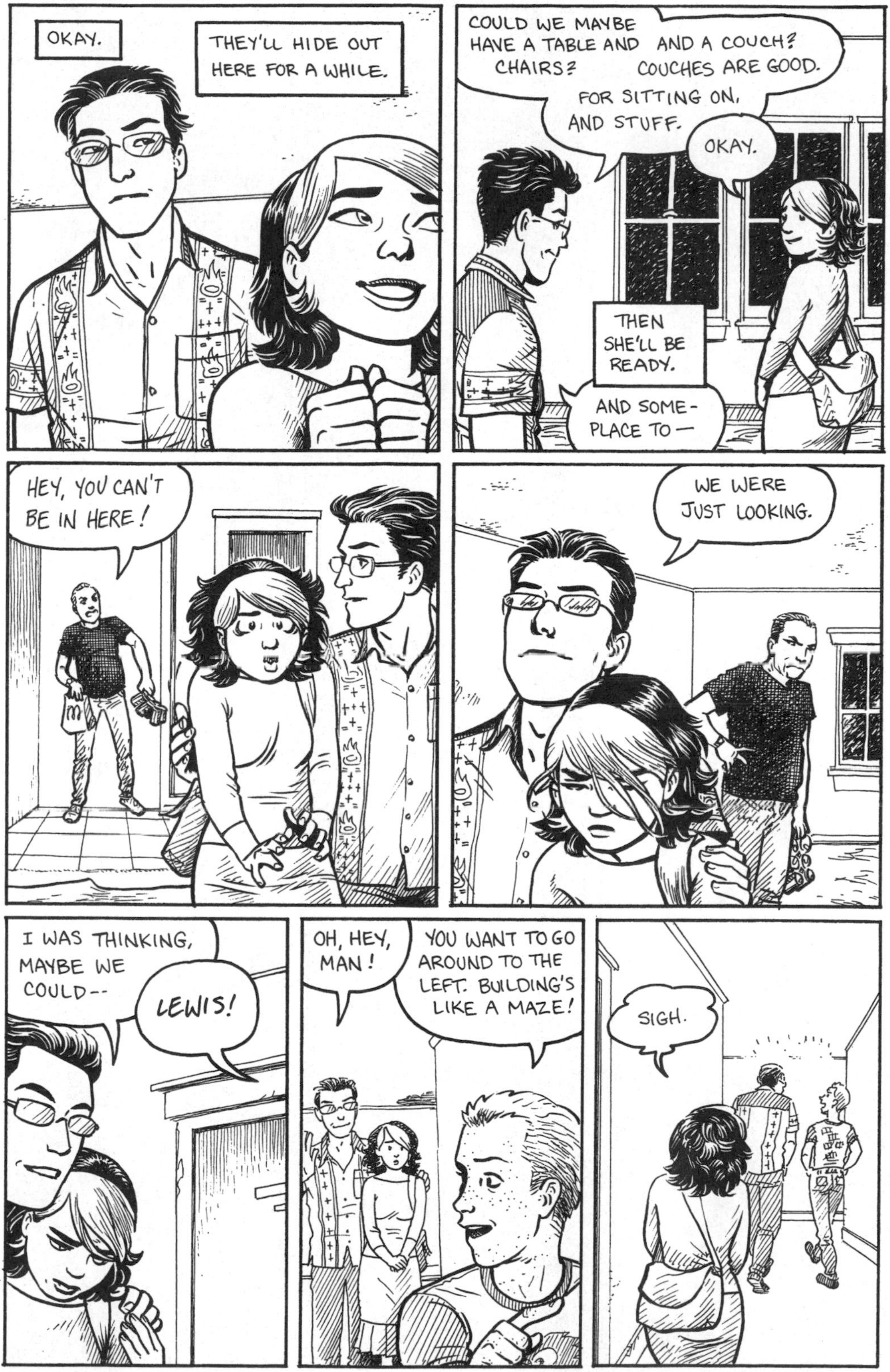
OKAY.
THEY'LL HIDE OUT HERE FOR A WHILE.
COULD WE MAYBE HAVE A TABLE AND CHAIRS?
AND A COUCH? COUCHES ARE GOOD.
FOR SITTING ON, AND STUFF.
OKAY.
THEN SHE'LL BE READY.
AND SOME-PLACE TO—
HEY, YOU CAN'T BE IN HERE!
WE WERE JUST LOOKING.
I WAS THINKING, MAYBE WE COULD--
LEWIS!
OH, HEY, MAN!
YOU WANT TO GO AROUND TO THE LEFT. BUILDING'S LIKE A MAZE!
SIGH.

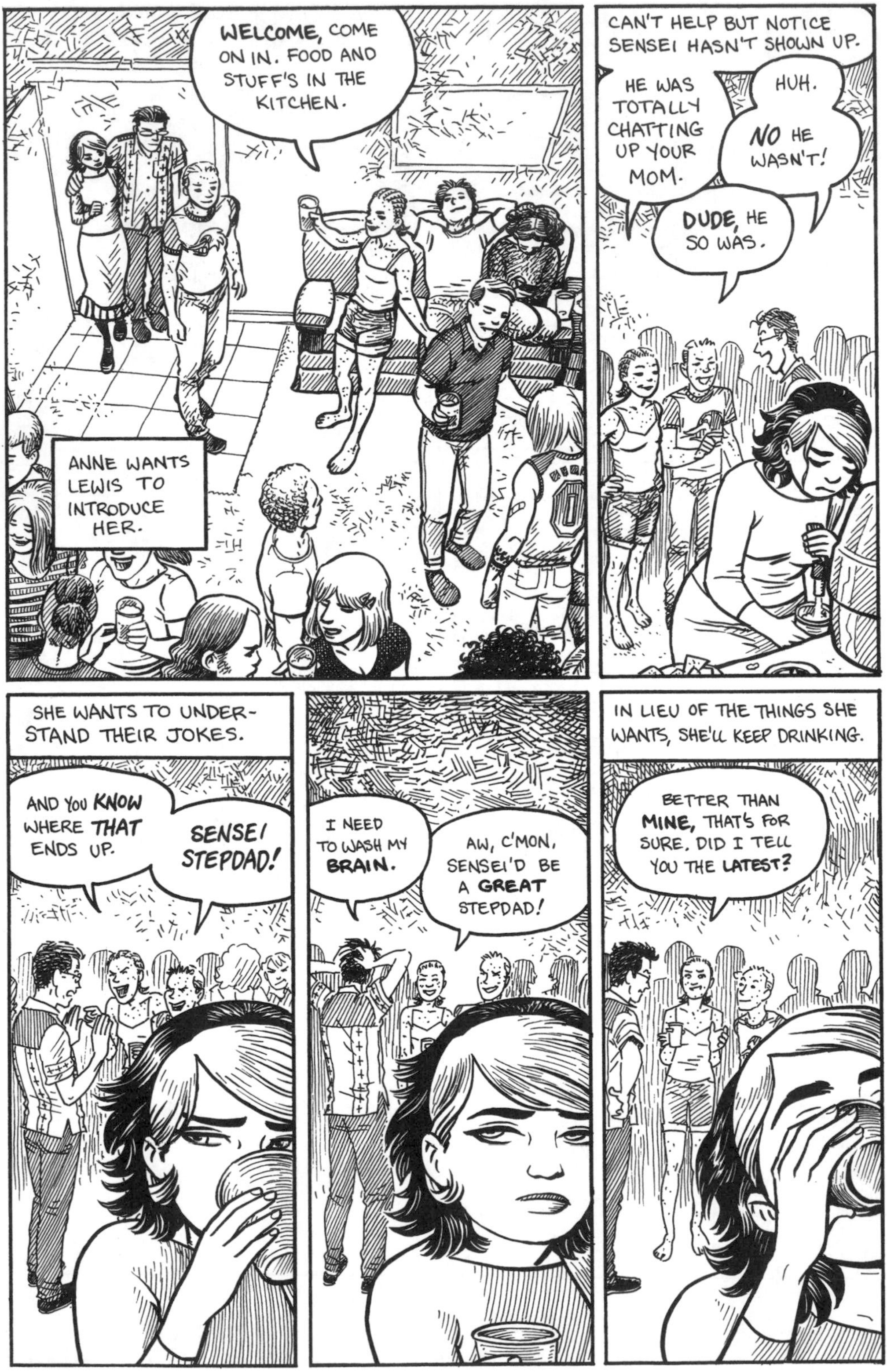
WELCOME, COME ON IN. FOOD AND STUFF'S IN THE KITCHEN.
ANNE WANTS LEWIS TO INTRODUCE HER.
CAN'T HELP BUT NOTICE SENSEI HASN'T SHOWN UP.
HE WAS TOTALLY CHATTING UP YOUR MOM.
HUH.
NO HE WASN'T!
DUDE, HE SO WAS.
SHE WANTS TO UNDER-STAND THEIR JOKES.
AND YOU KNOW WHERE THAT ENDS UP.
SENSEI STEPDAD!
I NEED TO WASH MY BRAIN.
AW, C'MON, SENSEI'D BE A GREAT STEPDAD!
IN LIEU OF THE THINGS SHE WANTS, SHE'LL KEEP DRINKING.
BETTER THAN MINE, THAT'S FOR SURE. DID I TELL YOU THE LATEST?

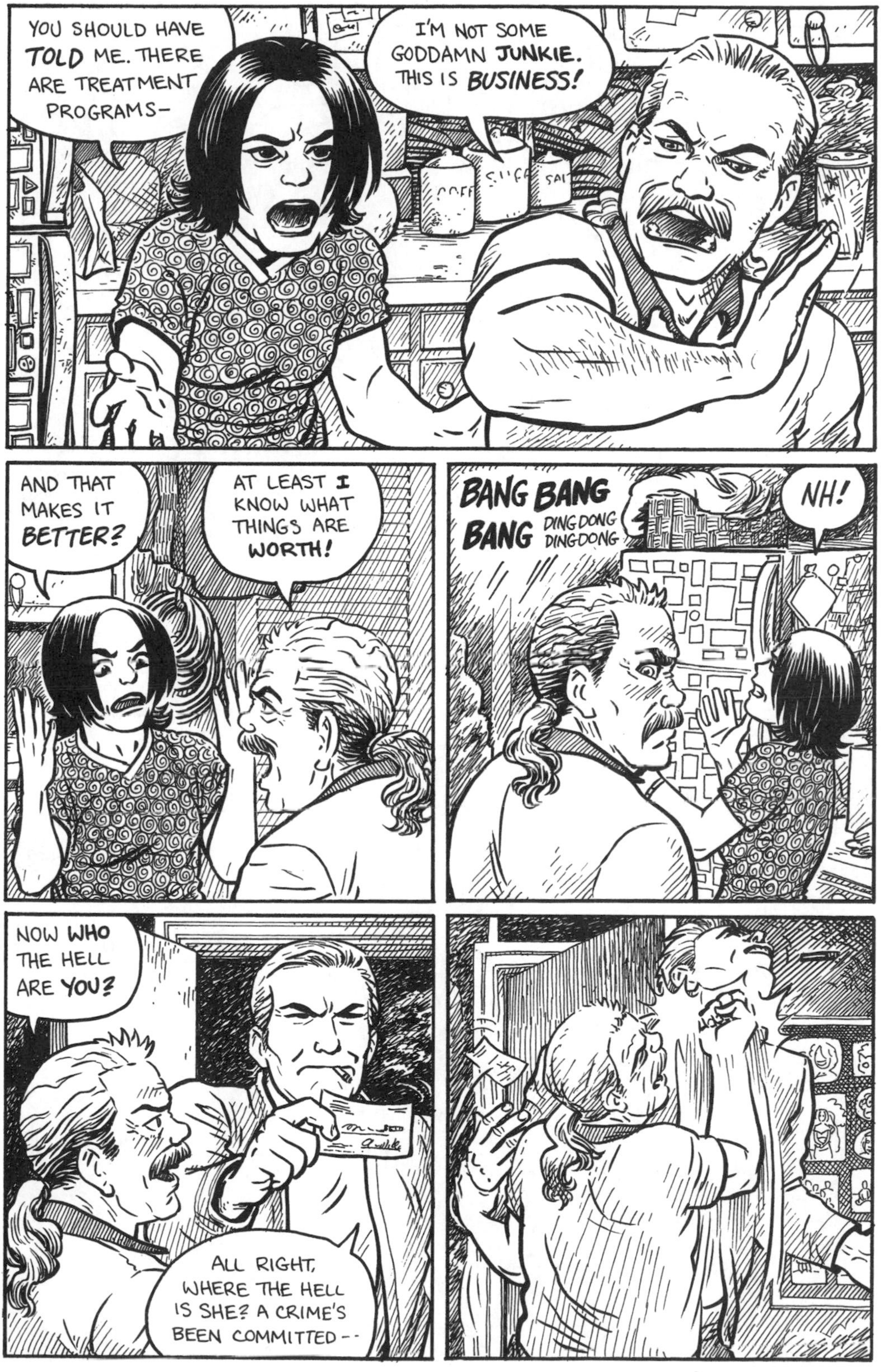

YOU SHOULD HAVE TOLD ME. THERE ARE TREATMENT PROGRAMS-
I'M NOT SOME GODDAMN JUNKIE. THIS IS BUSINESS!
AND THAT MAKES IT BETTER?
AT LEAST I KNOW WHAT THINGS ARE WORTH!
BANG BANG BANG
DING DONG DING DONG
NH!
NOW WHO THE HELL ARE YOU?
ALL RIGHT, WHERE THE HELL IS SHE? A CRIME'S BEEN COMMITTED--

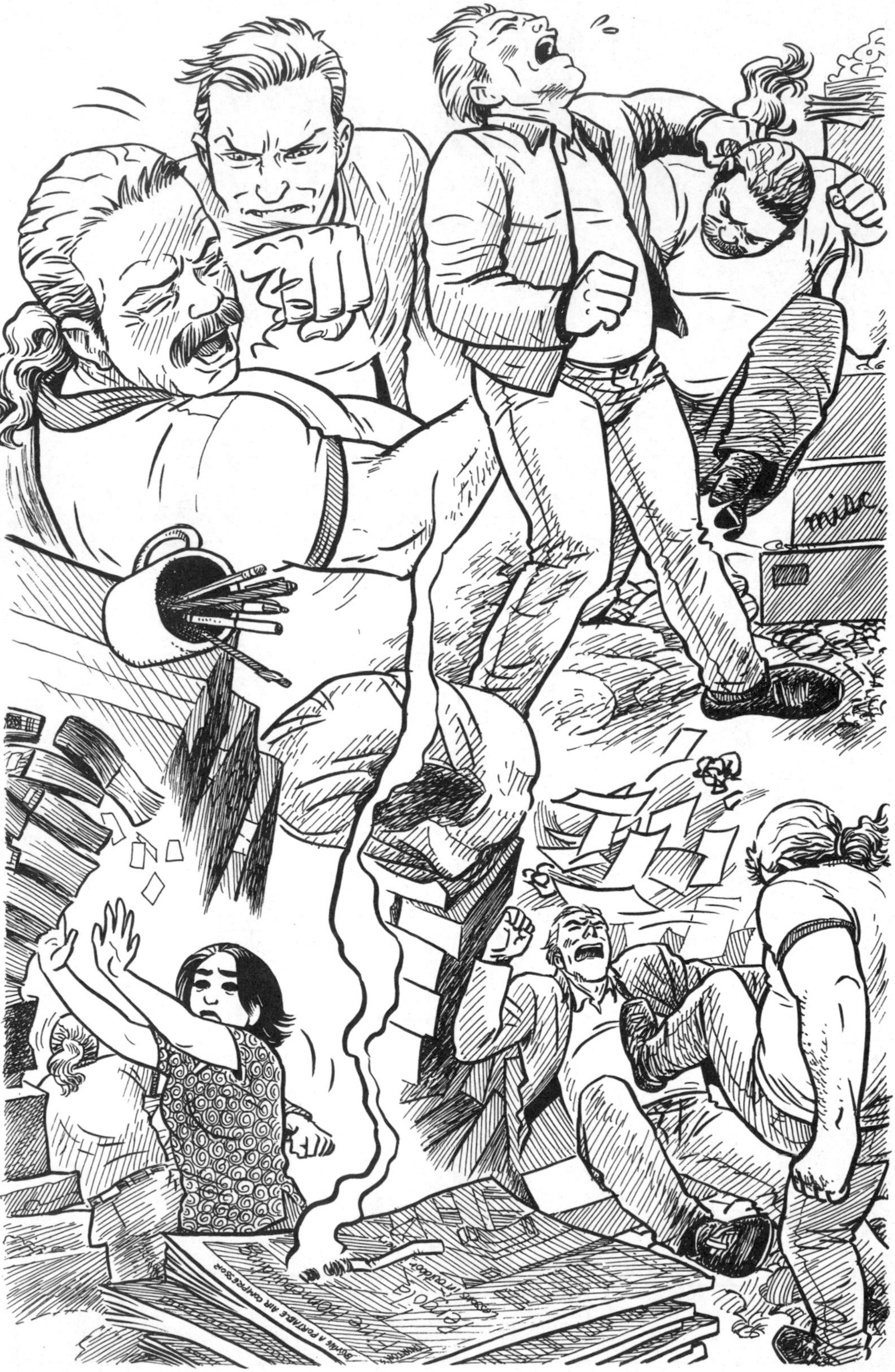
misc.
BUYING A PORTABLE AIR COMPRESSOR

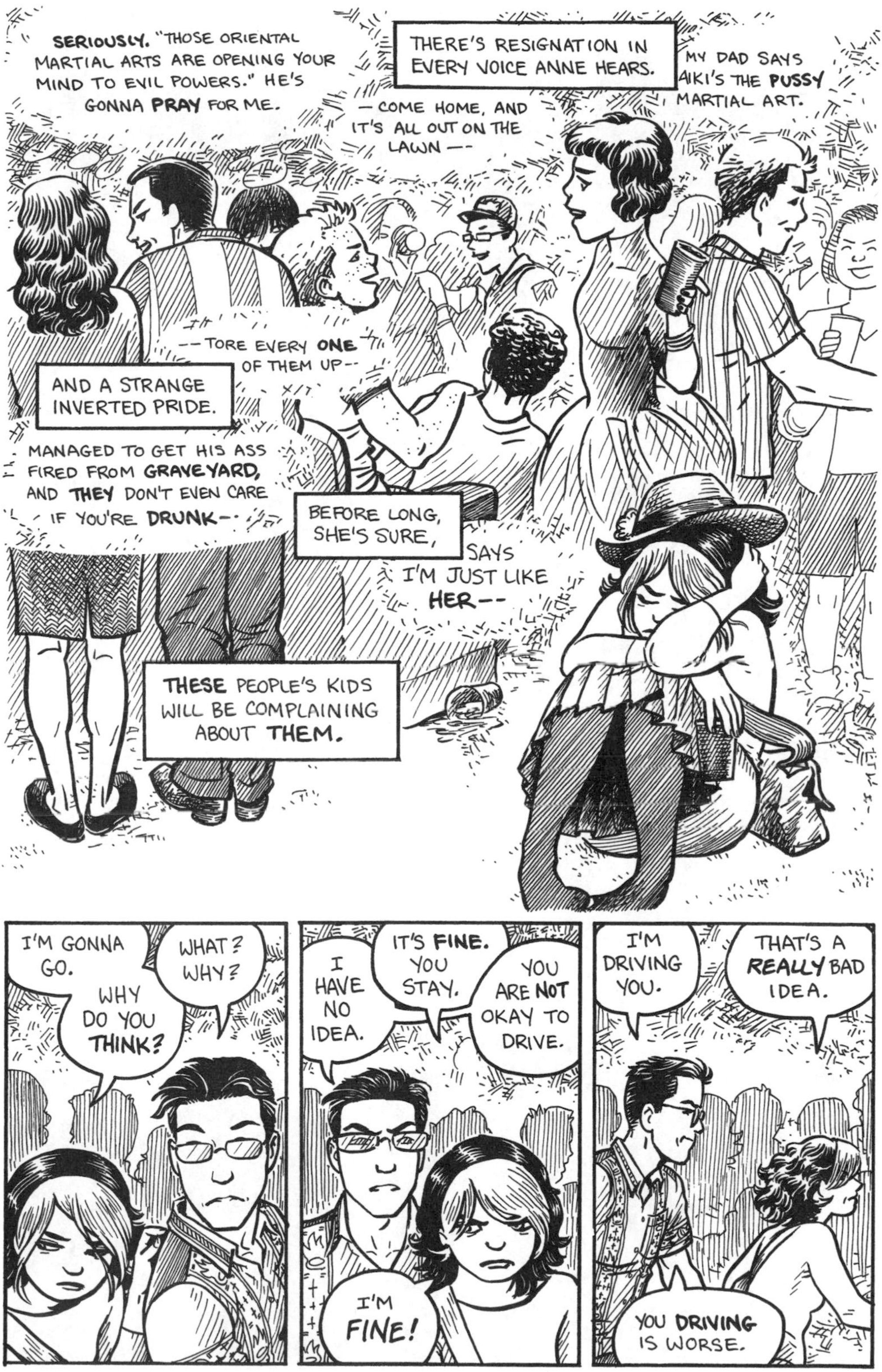
SERIOUSLY. "THOSE ORIENTAL MARTIAL ARTS ARE OPENING YOUR MIND TO EVIL POWERS." HE'S GONNA PRAY FOR ME.
THERE'S RESIGNATION IN EVERY VOICE ANNE HEARS.
— COME HOME, AND IT'S ALL OUT ON THE LAWN --
MY DAD SAYS AIKI'S THE PUSSY MARTIAL ART.
-- TORE EVERY ONE OF THEM UP--
AND A STRANGE INVERTED PRIDE.
MANAGED TO GET HIS ASS FIRED FROM GRAVEYARD, AND THEY DON'T EVEN CARE IF YOU'RE DRUNK--
BEFORE LONG, SHE'S SURE,
SAYS I'M JUST LIKE HER--
THESE PEOPLE'S KIDS WILL BE COMPLAINING ABOUT THEM.
I'M GONNA GO.
WHAT? WHY?
WHY DO YOU THINK?
I HAVE NO IDEA.
IT'S FINE. YOU STAY.
YOU ARE NOT OKAY TO DRIVE.
I'M FINE!
I'M DRIVING YOU.
THAT'S A REALLY BAD IDEA.
YOU DRIVING IS WORSE.

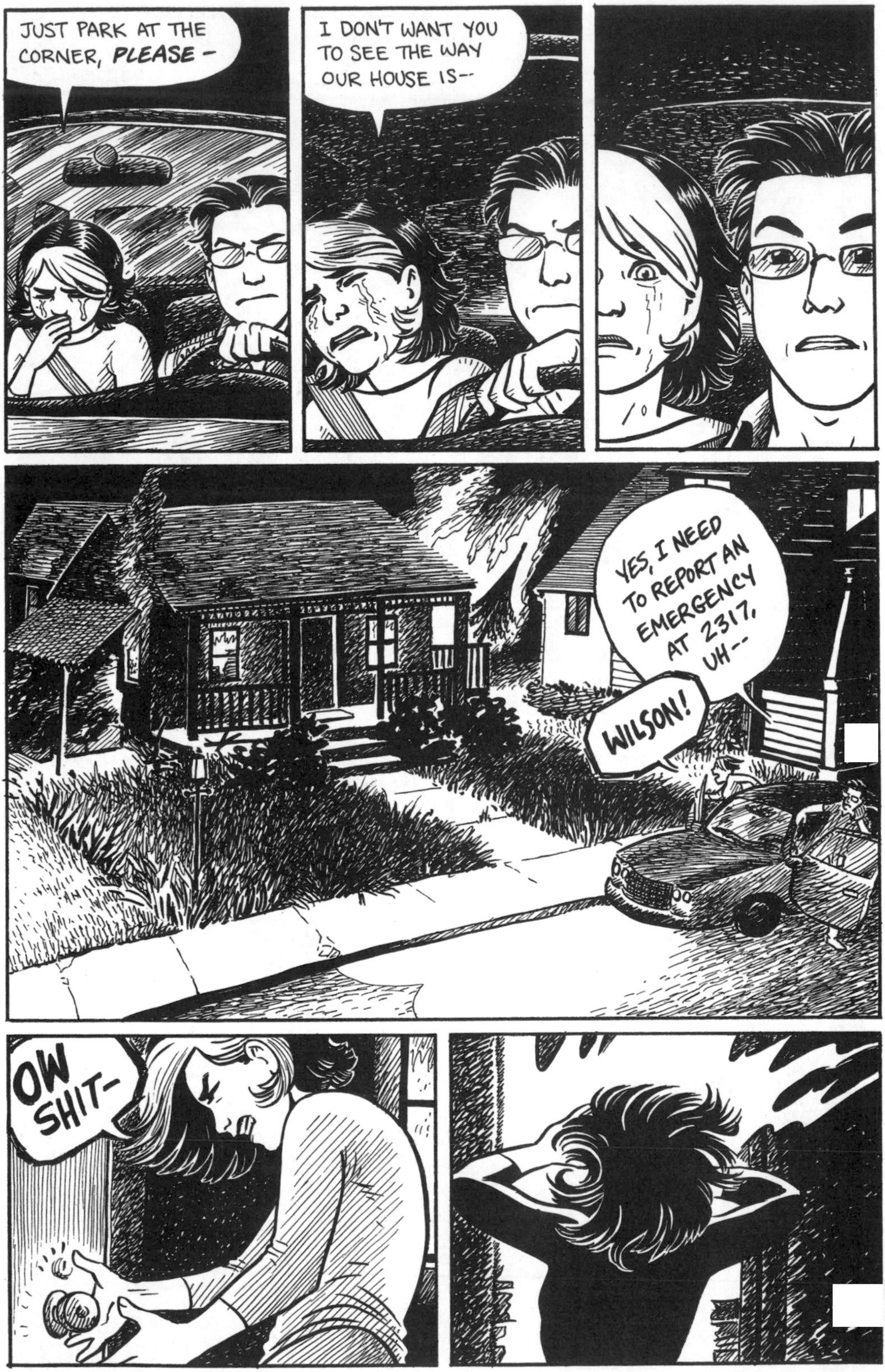

JUST PARK AT THE CORNER, PLEASE -
I DON'T WANT YOU TO SEE THE WAY OUR HOUSE IS--
YES, I NEED TO REPORT AN EMERGENCY AT 2317, UH--
WILSON!
OW SHIT-

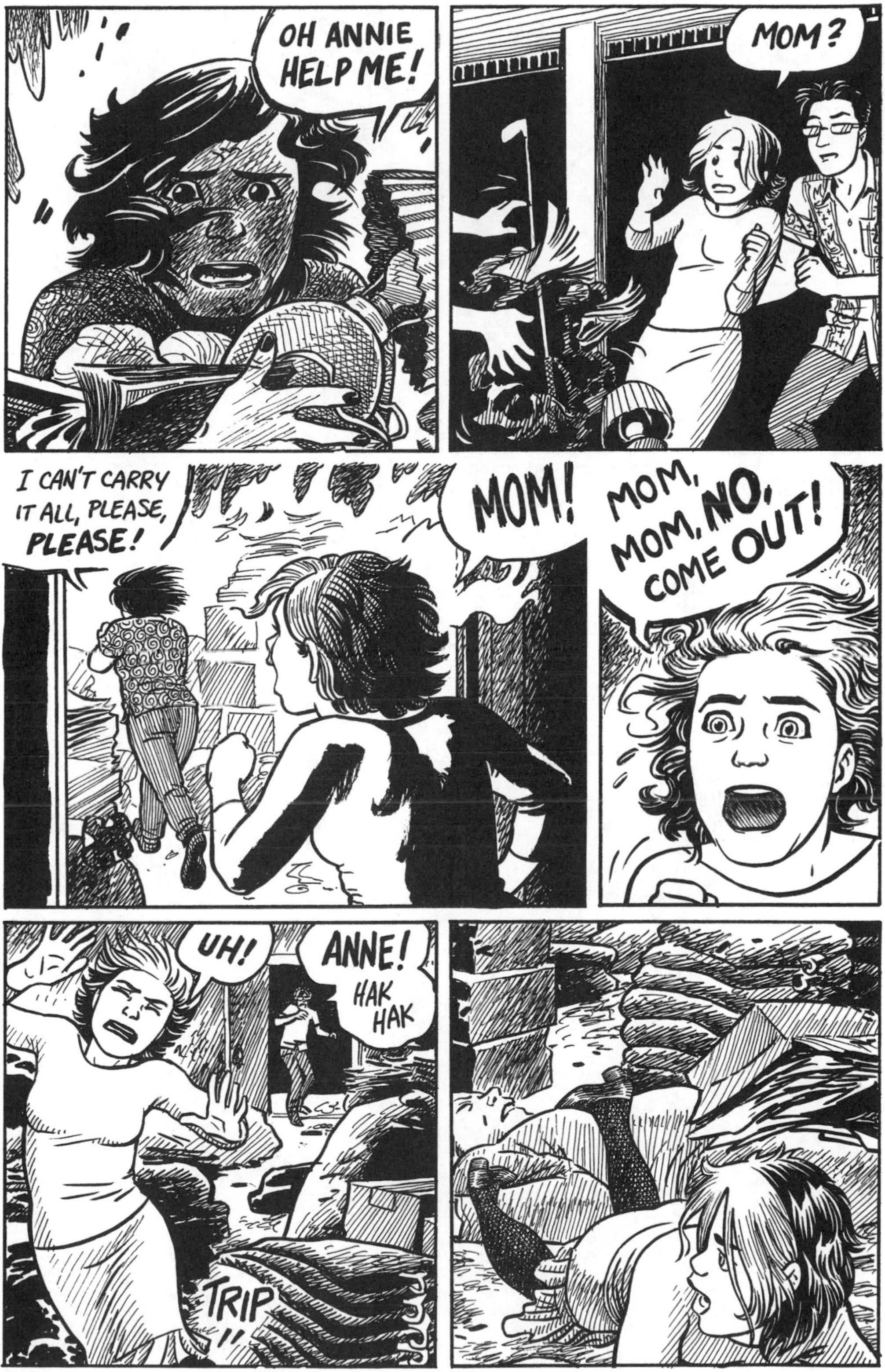
OH ANNIE HELP ME!
MOM?
I CAN'T CARRY IT ALL, PLEASE, PLEASE!
MOM!
MOM, MOM, NO, COME OUT!
UH!
ANNE! HAK HAK
TRIP

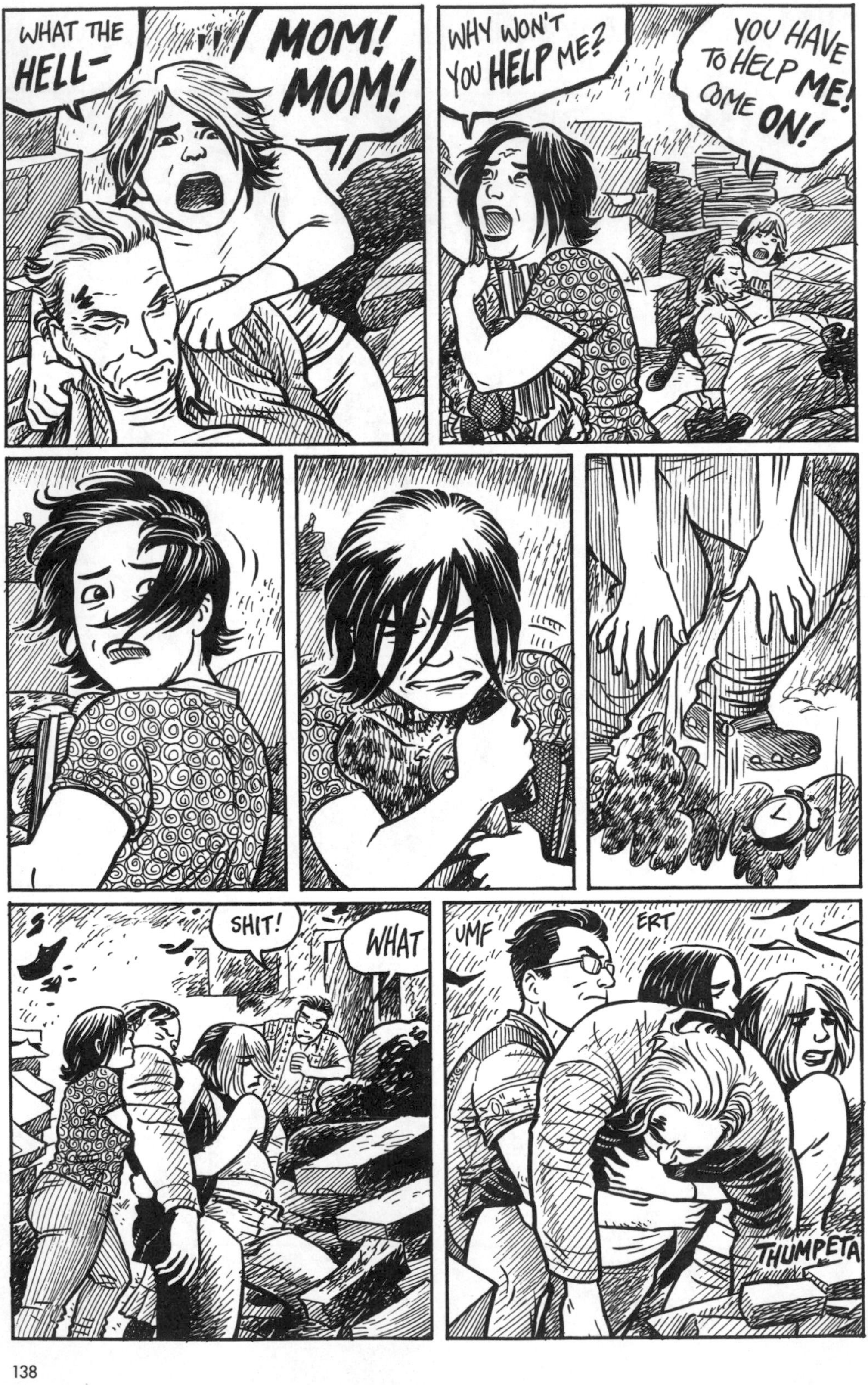
WHAT THE HELL-
MOM! MOM!
WHY WON'T YOU HELP ME?
YOU HAVE TO HELP ME! COME ON!
SHIT!
WHAT
UMF
ERT
THUMPETA

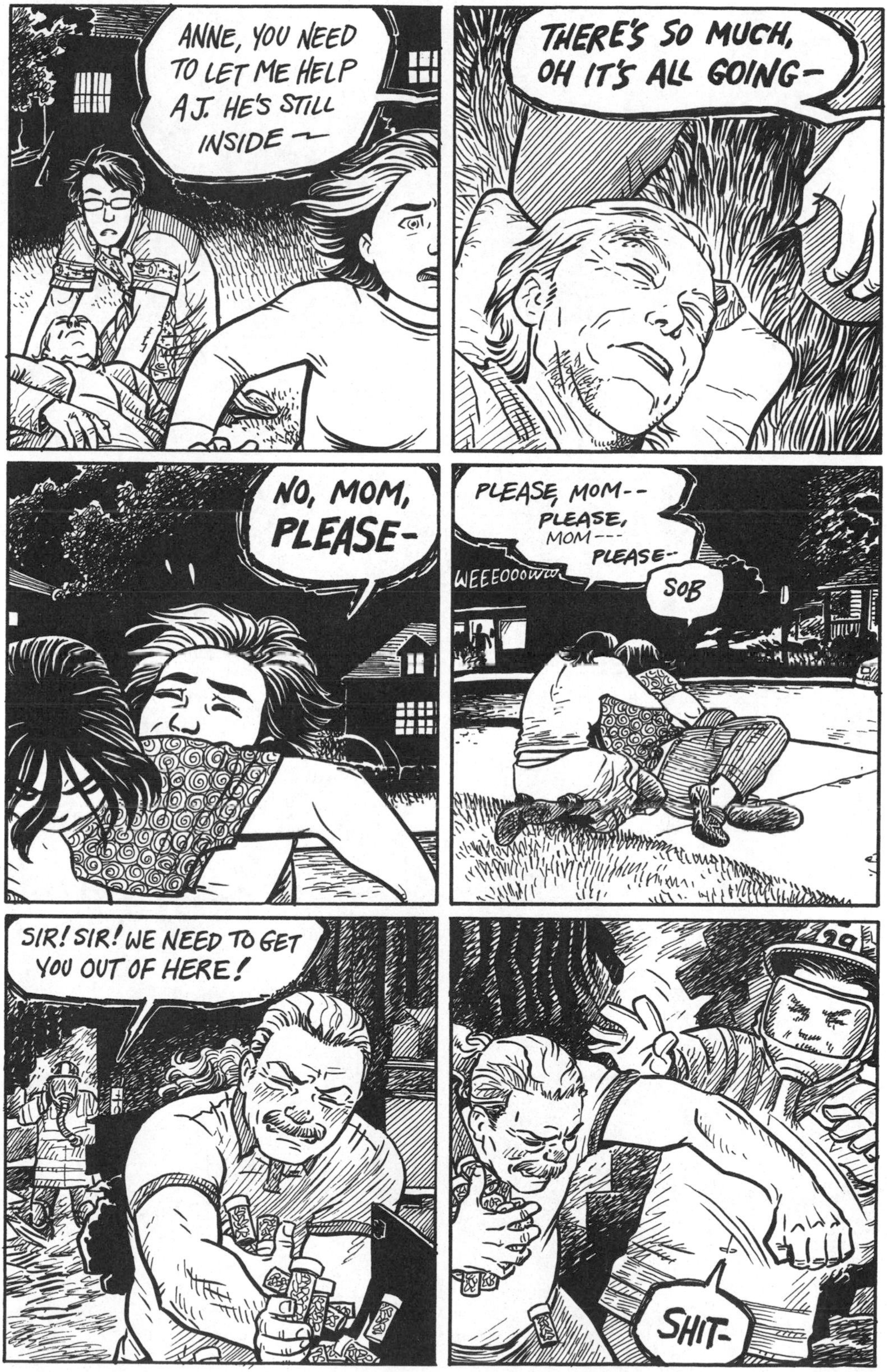
ANNE, YOU NEED TO LET ME HELP A.J. HE'S STILL INSIDE ~
THERE'S SO MUCH, OH IT'S ALL GOING-
NO, MOM, PLEASE-
PLEASE, MOM-- PLEASE, MOM--- PLEASE--
WEEEOOOWW
SOB
SIR! SIR! WE NEED TO GET YOU OUT OF HERE!
SHIT-

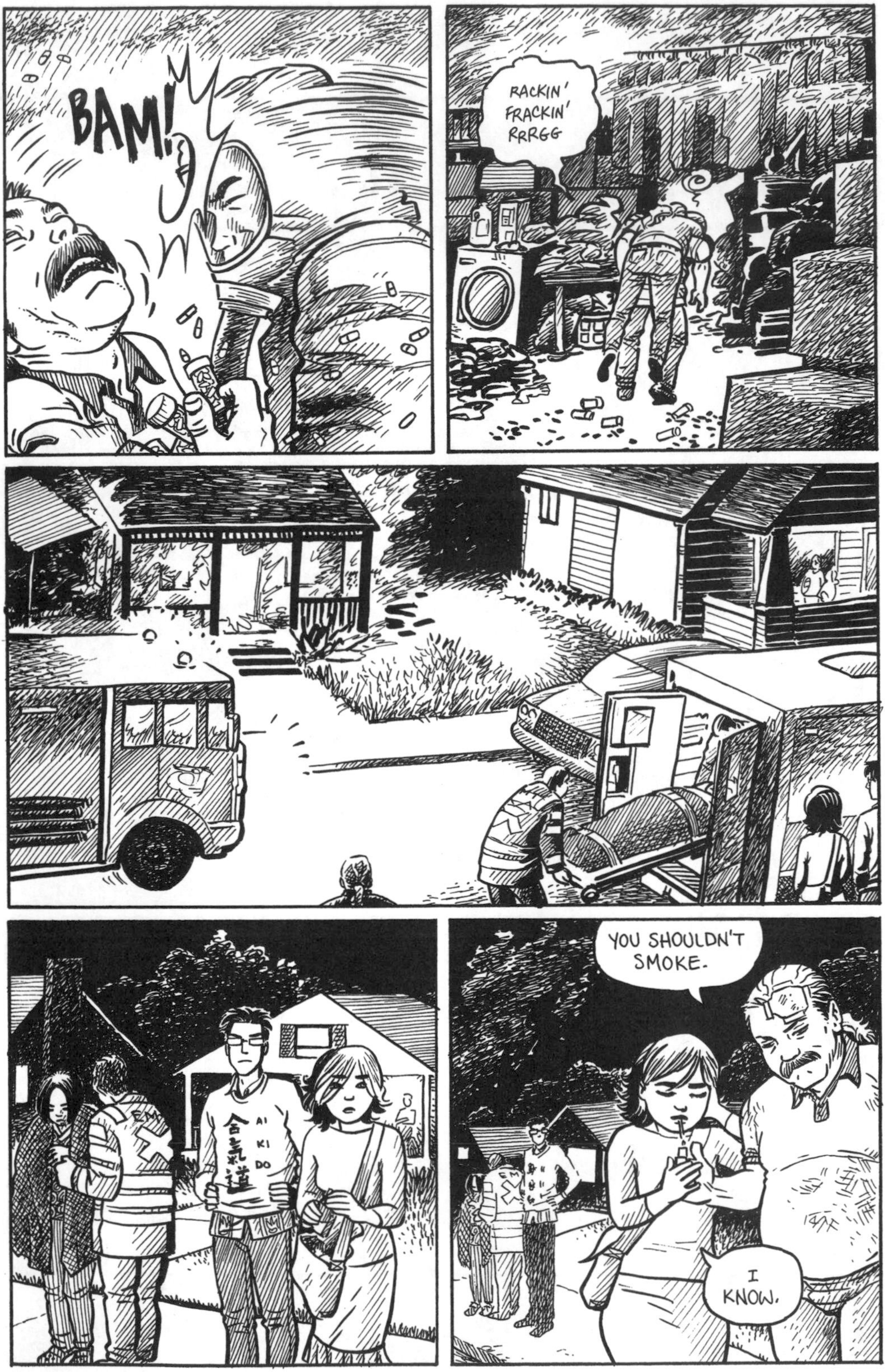
BAM!
RACKIN' FRACKIN' RRRGG
YOU SHOULDN'T SMOKE.
I KNOW.

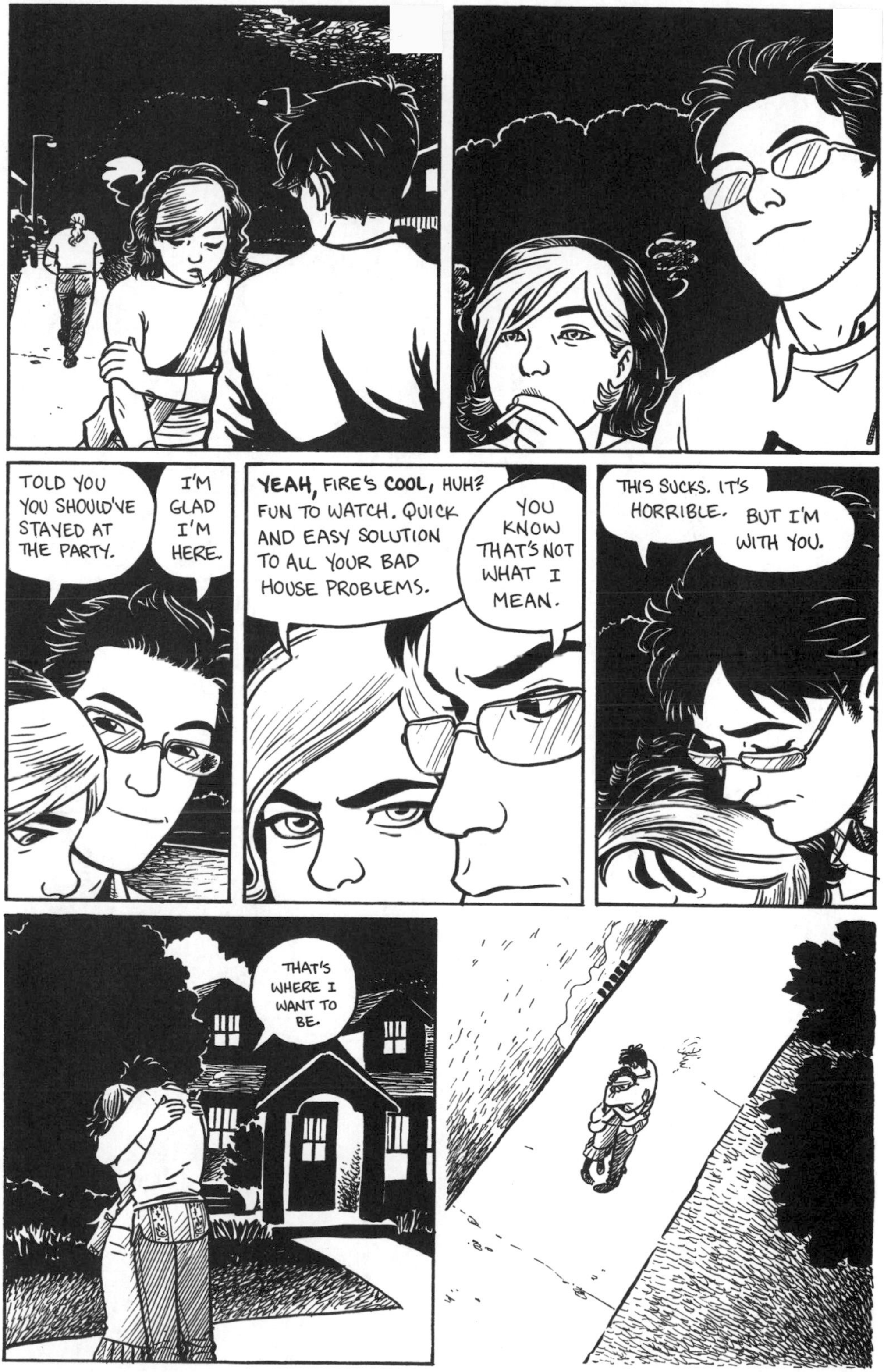
TOLD YOU YOU SHOULD'VE STAYED AT THE PARTY.
I'M GLAD I'M HERE.
YEAH, FIRE'S COOL, HUH? FUN TO WATCH. QUICK AND EASY SOLUTION TO ALL YOUR BAD HOUSE PROBLEMS.
YOU KNOW THAT'S NOT WHAT I MEAN.
THIS SUCKS. IT'S HORRIBLE.
BUT I'M WITH YOU.
THAT'S WHERE I WANT TO BE.

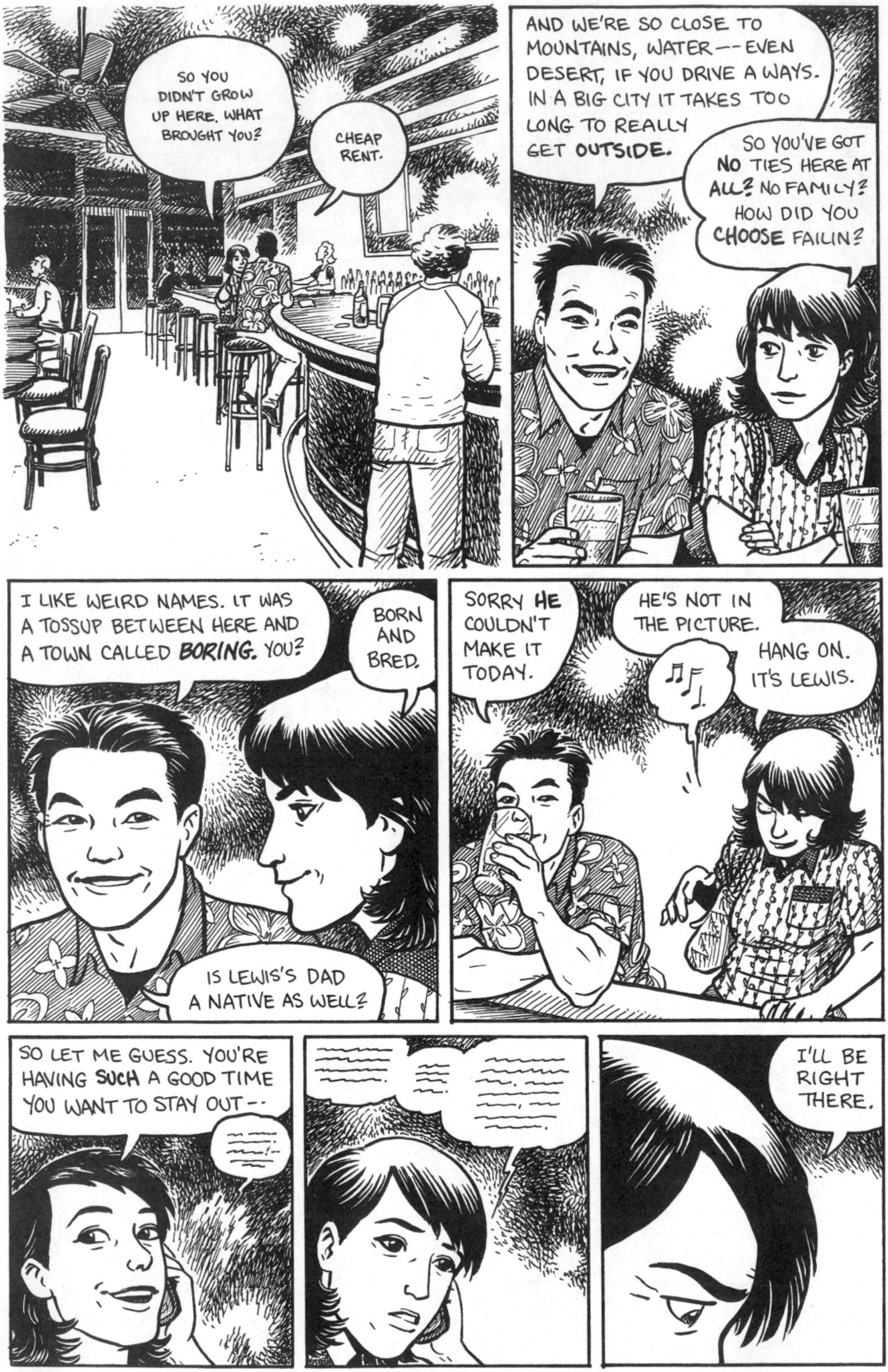
SO YOU DIDN'T GROW UP HERE. WHAT BROUGHT YOU?
CHEAP RENT.
AND WE'RE SO CLOSE TO MOUNTAINS, WATER -- EVEN DESERT, IF YOU DRIVE A WAYS. IN A BIG CITY IT TAKES TOO LONG TO REALLY GET OUTSIDE.
SO YOU'VE GOT NO TIES HERE AT ALL? NO FAMILY? HOW DID YOU CHOOSE FAILIN?
I LIKE WEIRD NAMES. IT WAS A TOSSUP BETWEEN HERE AND A TOWN CALLED BORING. YOU?
BORN AND BRED.
IS LEWIS'S DAD A NATIVE AS WELL?
SORRY HE COULDN'T MAKE IT TODAY.
HE'S NOT IN THE PICTURE.
HANG ON. IT'S LEWIS.
SO LET ME GUESS. YOU'RE HAVING SUCH A GOOD TIME YOU WANT TO STAY OUT --
I'LL BE RIGHT THERE.

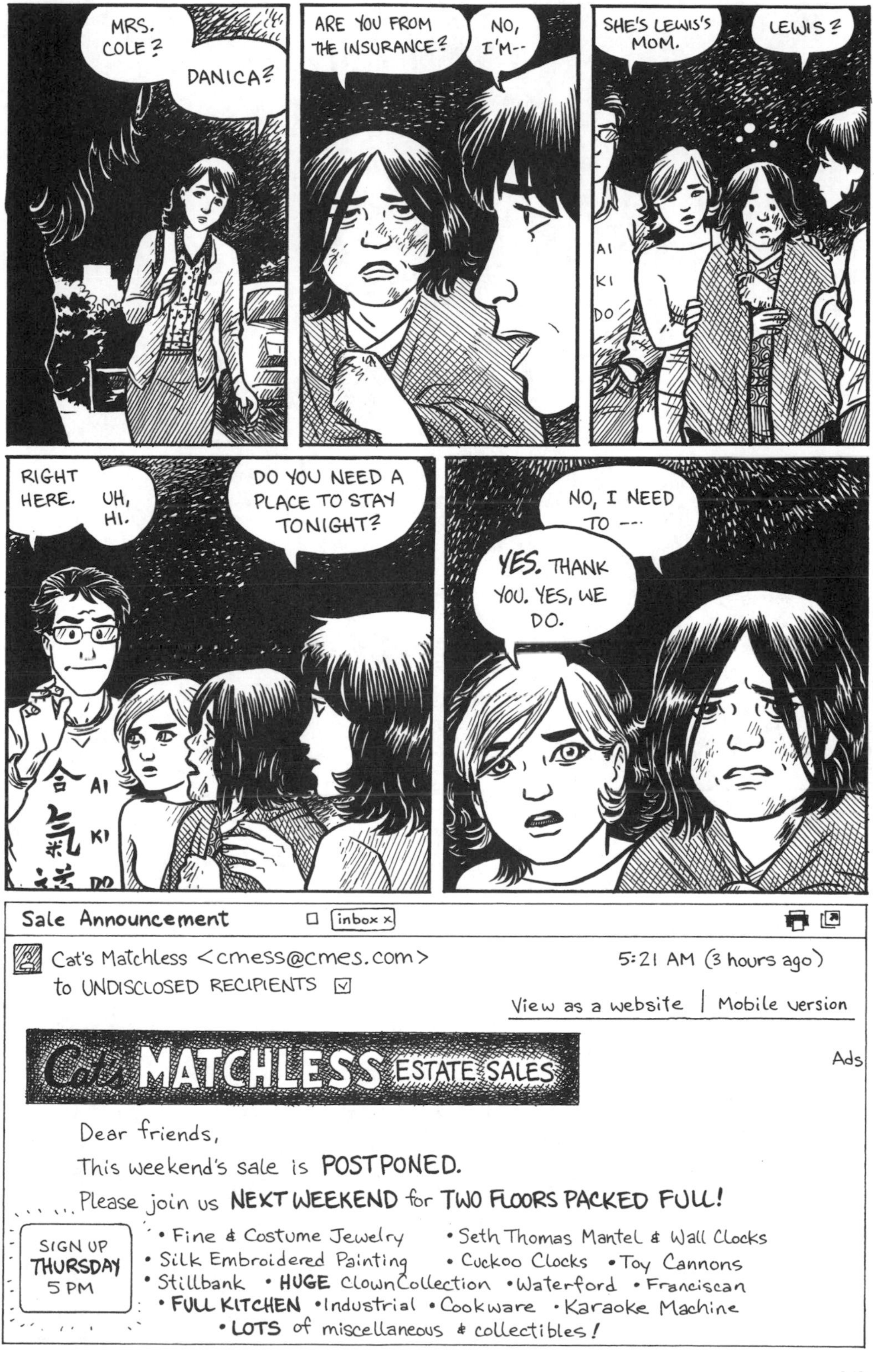
MRS. COLE?
DANICA?
ARE YOU FROM THE INSURANCE?
NO, I'M--
SHE'S LEWIS'S MOM.
LEWIS?
AI KI DO
RIGHT HERE.
UH, HI.
DO YOU NEED A PLACE TO STAY TONIGHT?
AI KI DO
NO, I NEED TO --
YES. THANK YOU. YES, WE DO.
Sale Announcement
inbox x
Cat's Matchless <cmess@cmes.com>
5:21 AM (3 hours ago)
to UNDISCLOSED RECIPIENTS
View as a website | Mobile version
Cat's MATCHLESS ESTATE SALES
Ads
Dear friends,
This weekend's sale is POSTPONED.
Please join us NEXT WEEKEND for TWO FLOORS PACKED FULL!
SIGN UP THURSDAY 5 PM
• Fine & Costume Jewelry • Seth Thomas Mantel & Wall Clocks
• Silk Embroidered Painting • Cuckoo Clocks • Toy Cannons
• Stillbank • HUGE Clown Collection • Waterford • Franciscan
• FULL KITCHEN • Industrial • Cookware • Karaoke Machine
• LOTS of miscellaneous & collectibles!

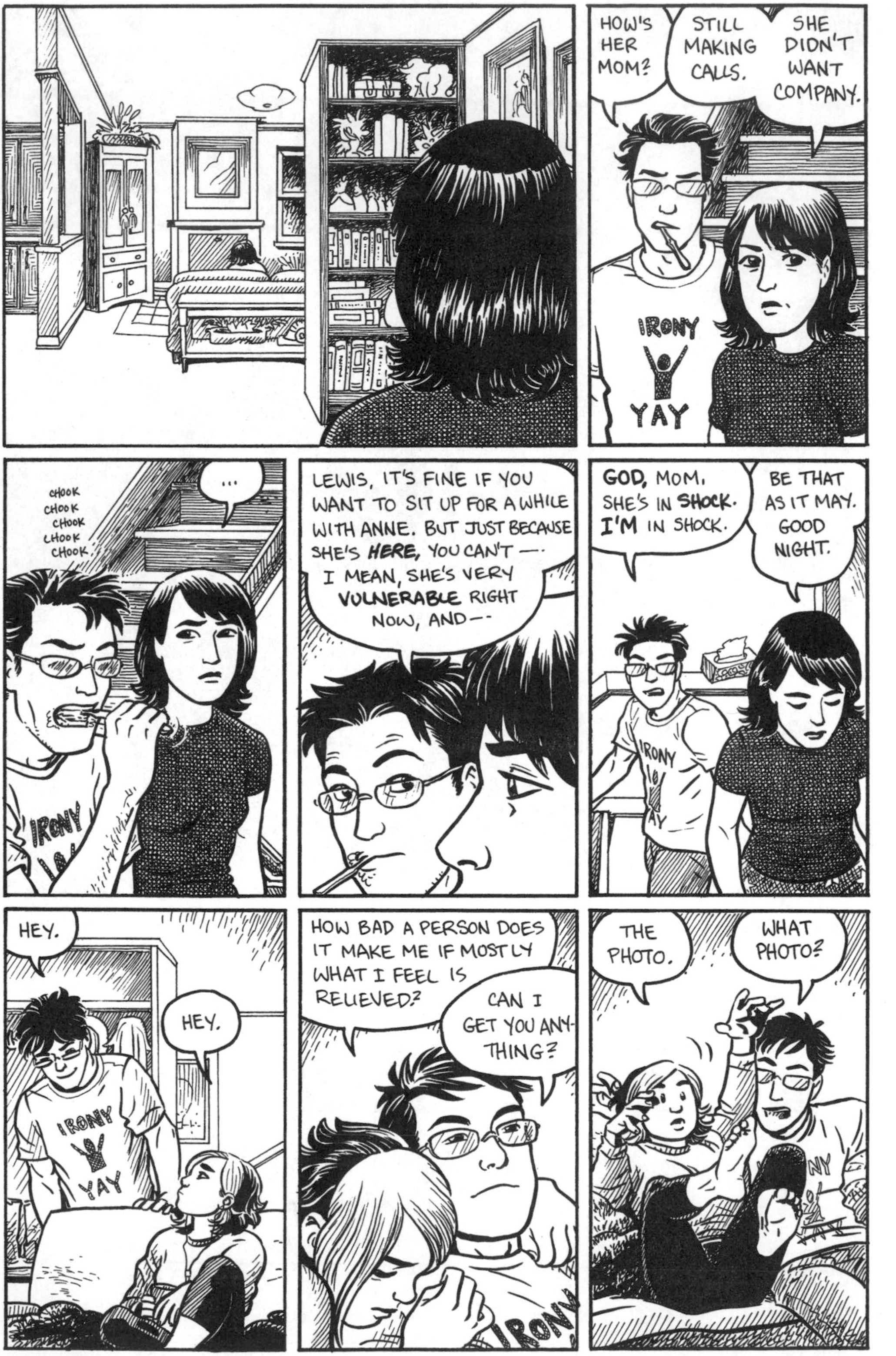

HOW'S HER MOM?
STILL MAKING CALLS.
SHE DIDN'T WANT COMPANY.
CHOOK CHOOK CHOOK CHOOK CHOOK
...
LEWIS, IT'S FINE IF YOU WANT TO SIT UP FOR A WHILE WITH ANNE. BUT JUST BECAUSE SHE'S **HERE**, YOU CAN'T —. I MEAN, SHE'S VERY **VULNERABLE** RIGHT NOW, AND—-
GOD, MOM, SHE'S IN **SHOCK**. **I'M** IN SHOCK.
BE THAT AS IT MAY. GOOD NIGHT.
IRONY
YAY
HEY.
HEY.
HOW BAD A PERSON DOES IT MAKE ME IF MOSTLY WHAT I FEEL IS RELIEVED?
CAN I GET YOU ANYTHING?
THE PHOTO.
WHAT PHOTO?

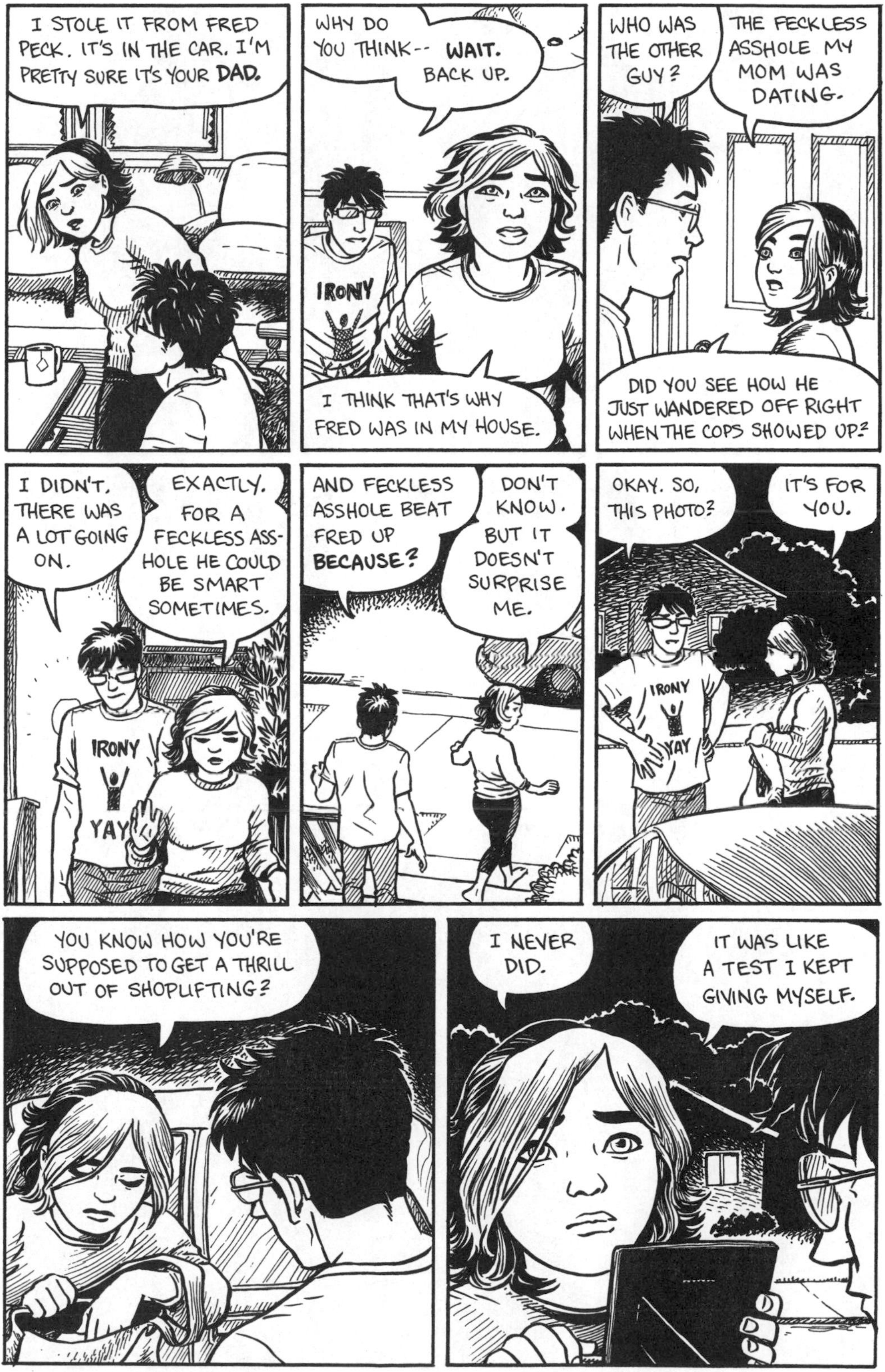
I STOLE IT FROM FRED PECK. IT'S IN THE CAR. I'M PRETTY SURE IT'S YOUR **DAD.**
WHY DO YOU THINK-- **WAIT.** BACK UP.
I THINK THAT'S WHY FRED WAS IN MY HOUSE.
WHO WAS THE OTHER GUY?
THE FECKLESS ASSHOLE MY MOM WAS DATING.
DID YOU SEE HOW HE JUST WANDERED OFF RIGHT WHEN THE COPS SHOWED UP?
I DIDN'T. THERE WAS A LOT GOING ON.
EXACTLY. FOR A FECKLESS ASS-HOLE HE COULD BE SMART SOMETIMES.
IRONY YAY
AND FECKLESS ASSHOLE BEAT FRED UP **BECAUSE?**
DON'T KNOW. BUT IT DOESN'T SURPRISE ME.
OKAY. SO, THIS PHOTO?
IT'S FOR YOU.
YOU KNOW HOW YOU'RE SUPPOSED TO GET A THRILL OUT OF SHOPLIFTING?
I NEVER DID.
IT WAS LIKE A TEST I KEPT GIVING MYSELF.

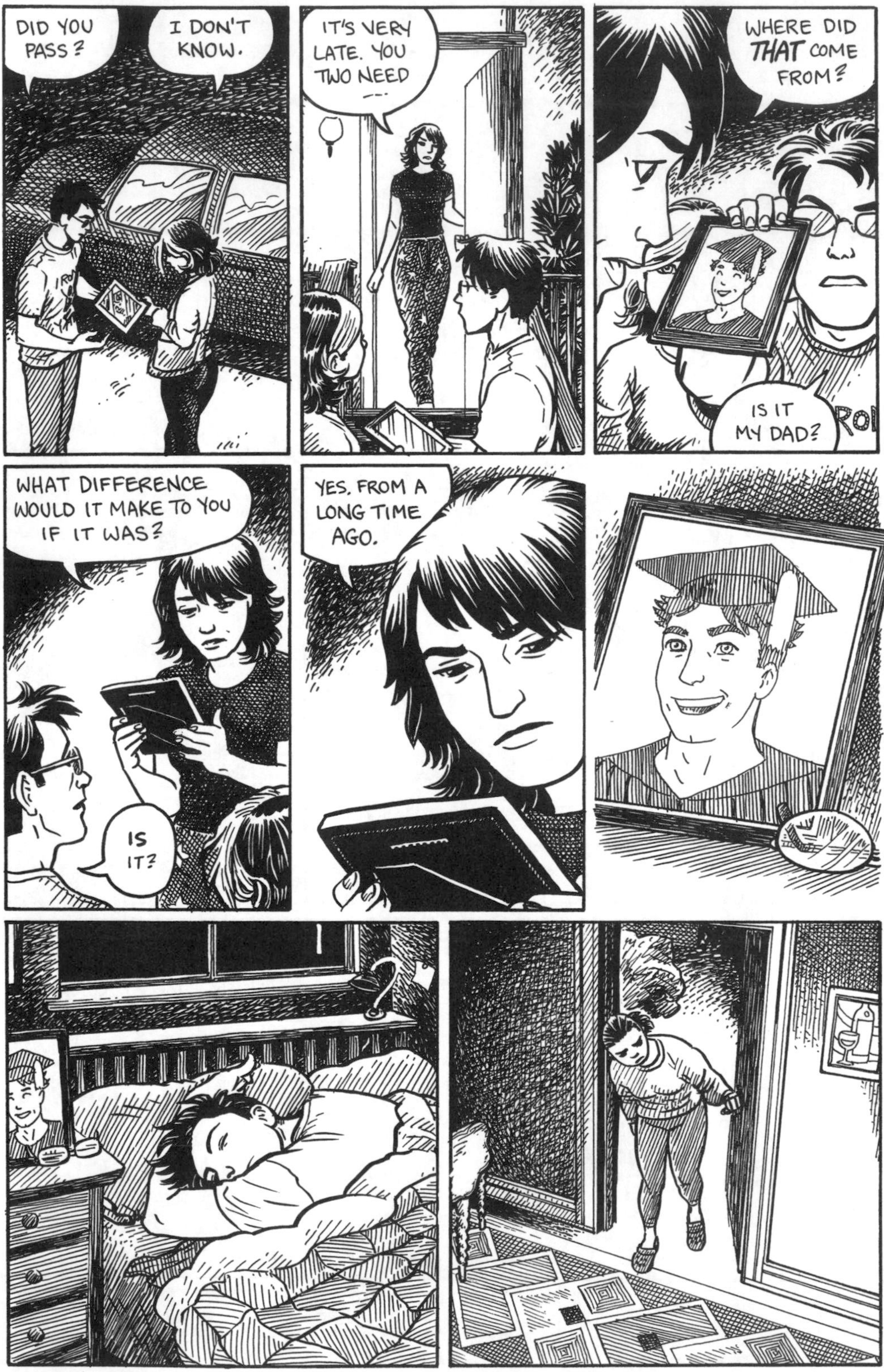
DID YOU PASS?
I DON'T KNOW.
IT'S VERY LATE. YOU TWO NEED --.
WHERE DID THAT COME FROM?
IS IT MY DAD?
WHAT DIFFERENCE WOULD IT MAKE TO YOU IF IT WAS?
IS IT?
YES. FROM A LONG TIME AGO.

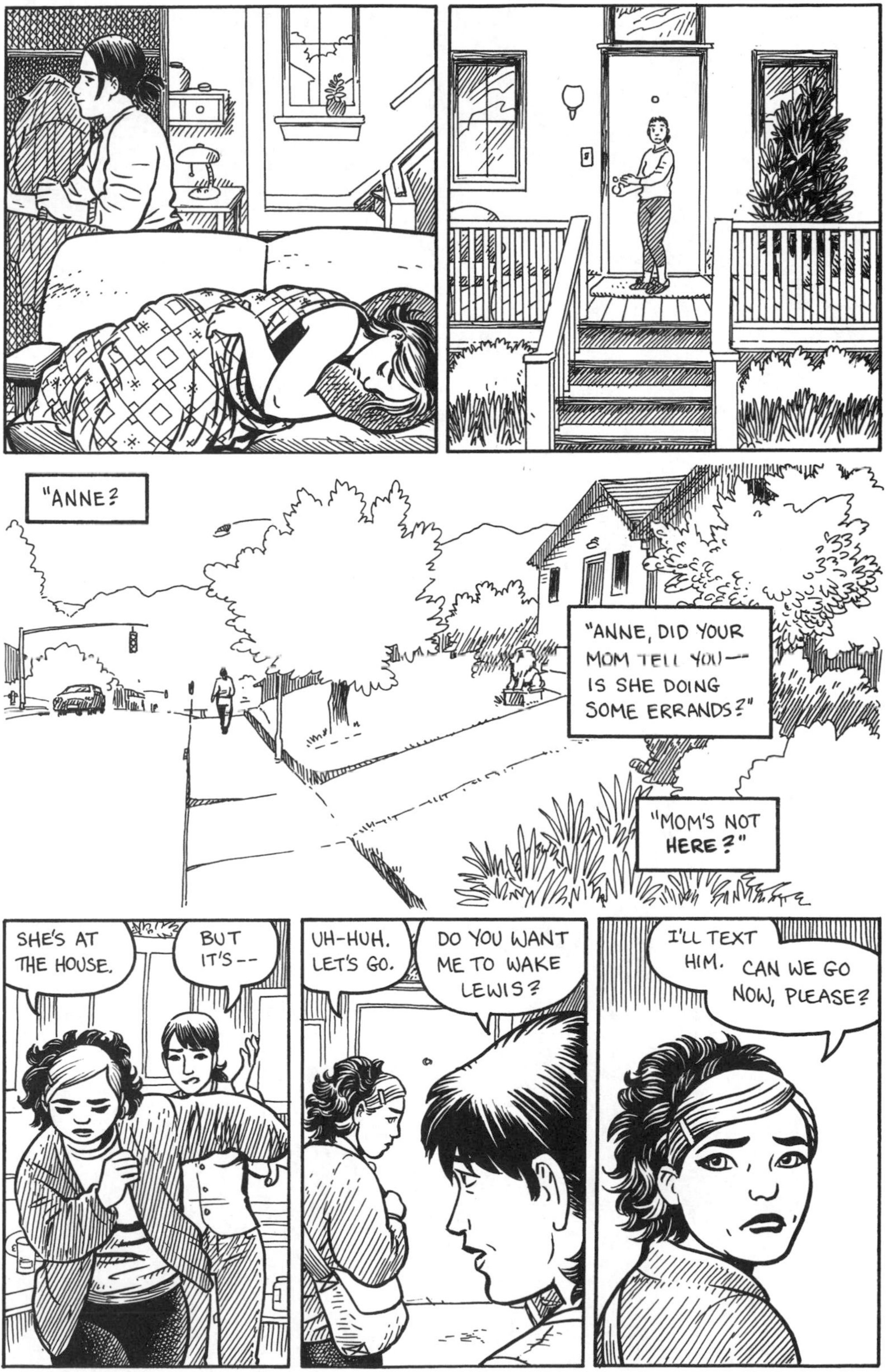
"ANNE?
"ANNE, DID YOUR MOM TELL YOU-- IS SHE DOING SOME ERRANDS?"
"MOM'S NOT **HERE**?"
SHE'S AT THE HOUSE.
BUT IT'S --
UH-HUH. LET'S GO.
DO YOU WANT ME TO WAKE LEWIS?
I'LL TEXT HIM.
CAN WE GO NOW, PLEASE?

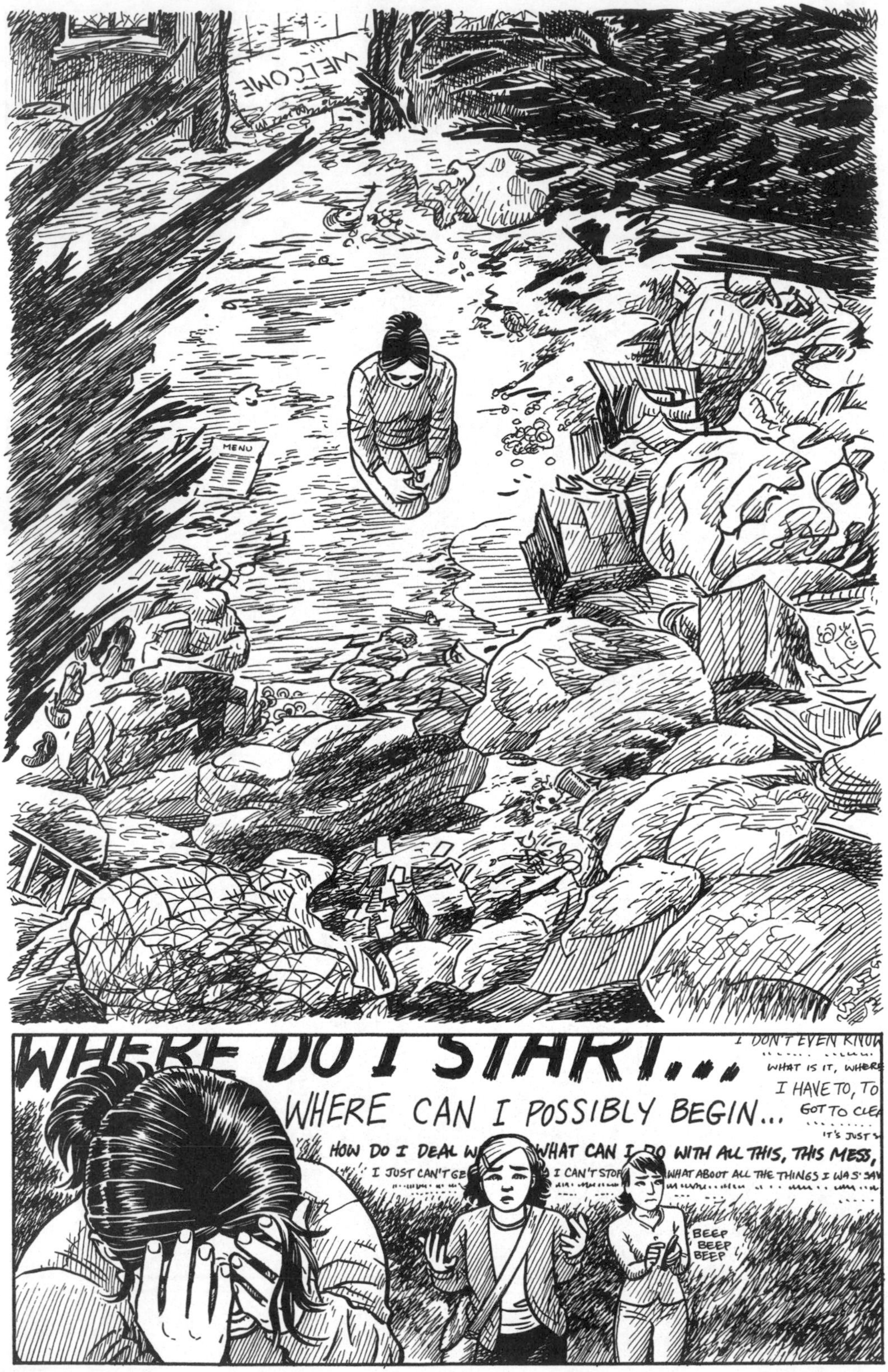
WELCOME
MENU
WHERE DO I START...
WHERE CAN I POSSIBLY BEGIN...
I DON'T EVEN KNOW
WHAT IS IT, WHERE
I HAVE TO, TO
GOT TO CLE
IT'S JUST
HOW DO I DEAL W
WHAT CAN I DO WITH ALL THIS, THIS MESS,
I JUST CAN'T GE
I CAN'T STOP
WHAT ABOUT ALL THE THINGS I WAS SAV
BEEP BEEP BEEP

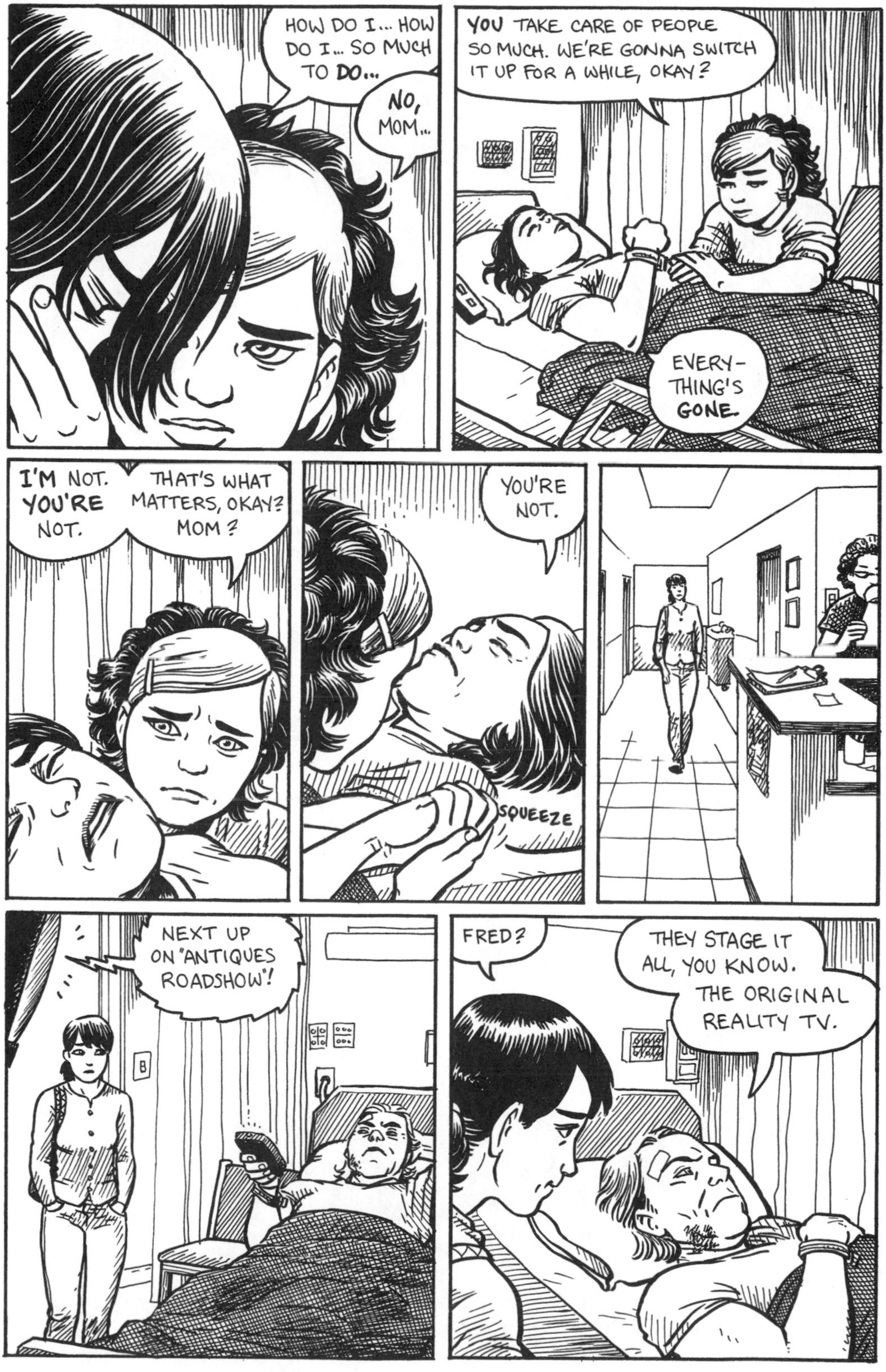
HOW DO I... HOW DO I... SO MUCH TO DO...
NO, MOM...
YOU TAKE CARE OF PEOPLE SO MUCH. WE'RE GONNA SWITCH IT UP FOR A WHILE, OKAY?
EVERY-THING'S GONE.
I'M NOT. YOU'RE NOT.
THAT'S WHAT MATTERS, OKAY? MOM?
YOU'RE NOT.
SQUEEZE
NEXT UP ON "ANTIQUES ROADSHOW"!
FRED?
THEY STAGE IT ALL, YOU KNOW.
THE ORIGINAL REALITY TV.

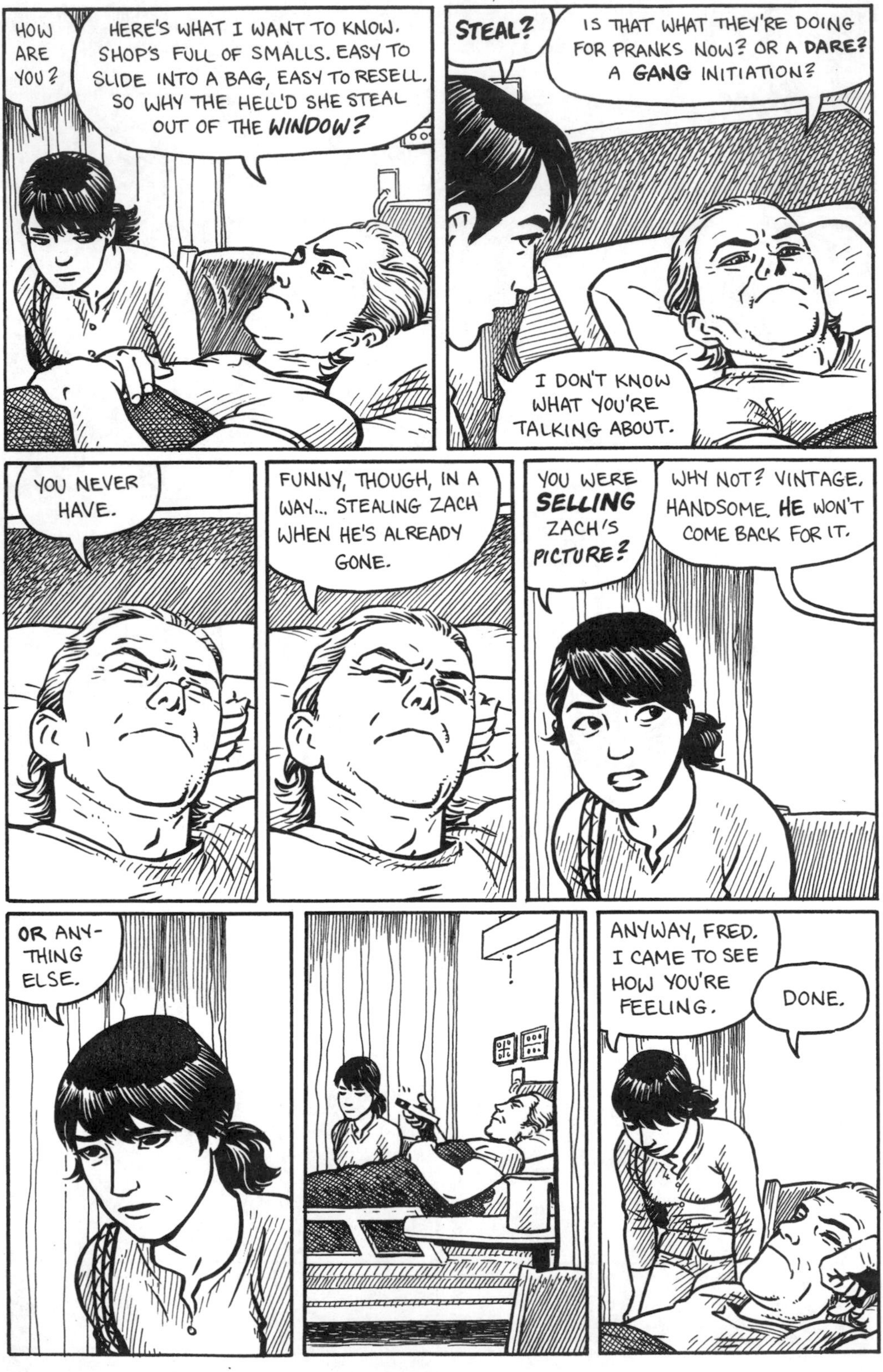
HOW ARE YOU?
HERE'S WHAT I WANT TO KNOW. SHOP'S FULL OF SMALLS. EASY TO SLIDE INTO A BAG, EASY TO RESELL. SO WHY THE HELL'D SHE STEAL OUT OF THE WINDOW?
STEAL?
IS THAT WHAT THEY'RE DOING FOR PRANKS NOW? OR A DARE? A GANG INITIATION?
I DON'T KNOW WHAT YOU'RE TALKING ABOUT.
YOU NEVER HAVE.
FUNNY, THOUGH, IN A WAY... STEALING ZACH WHEN HE'S ALREADY GONE.
YOU WERE SELLING ZACH'S PICTURE?
WHY NOT? VINTAGE. HANDSOME. HE WON'T COME BACK FOR IT.
OR ANYTHING ELSE.
ANYWAY, FRED. I CAME TO SEE HOW YOU'RE FEELING.
DONE.

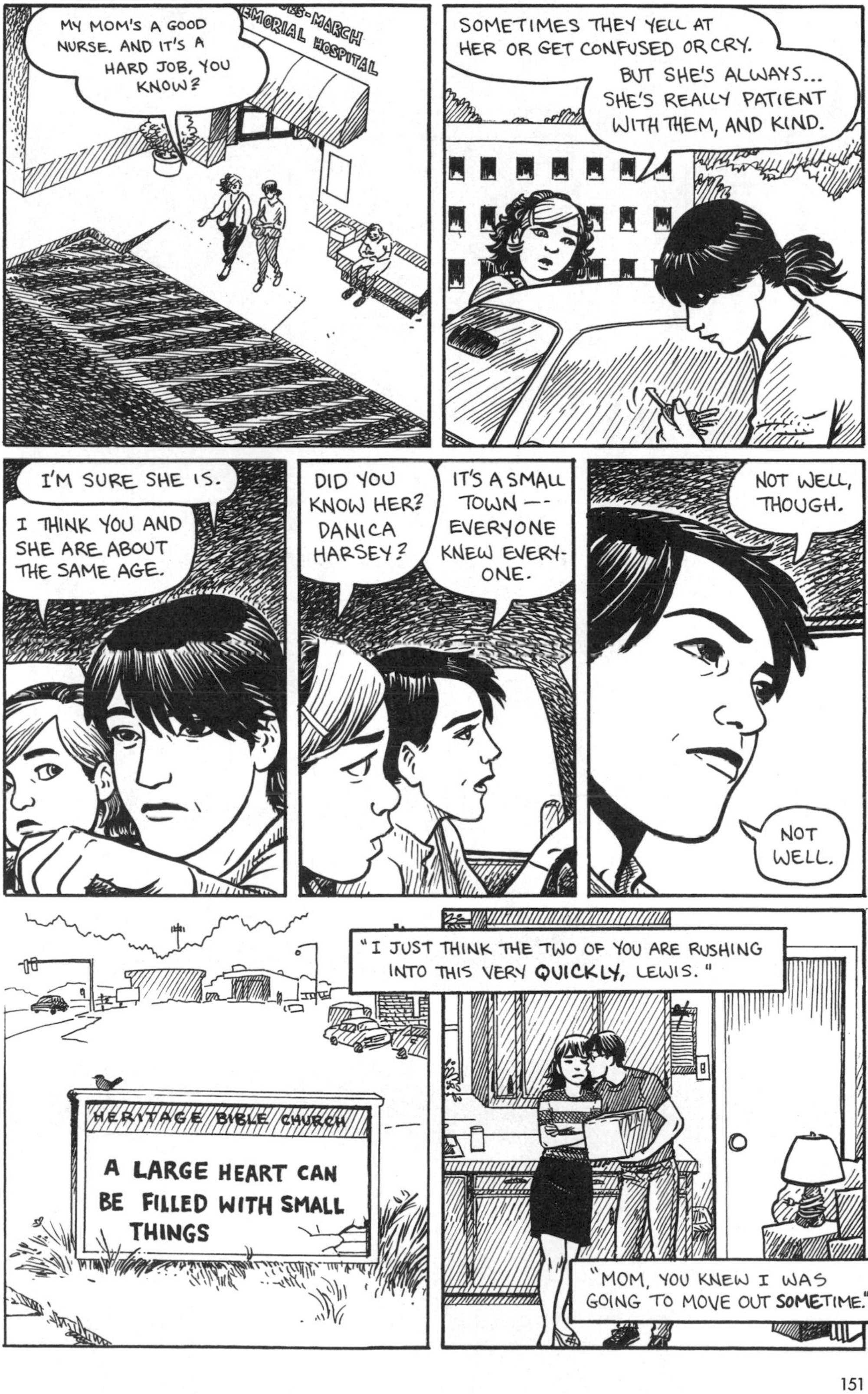

MEMORIAL HOSPITAL
MY MOM'S A GOOD NURSE. AND IT'S A HARD JOB, YOU KNOW?
SOMETIMES THEY YELL AT HER OR GET CONFUSED OR CRY.
BUT SHE'S ALWAYS... SHE'S REALLY PATIENT WITH THEM, AND KIND.
I'M SURE SHE IS.
I THINK YOU AND SHE ARE ABOUT THE SAME AGE.
DID YOU KNOW HER? DANICA HARSEY?
IT'S A SMALL TOWN -- EVERYONE KNEW EVERYONE.
NOT WELL, THOUGH.
NOT WELL.
HERITAGE BIBLE CHURCH
A LARGE HEART CAN BE FILLED WITH SMALL THINGS
"I JUST THINK THE TWO OF YOU ARE RUSHING INTO THIS VERY QUICKLY, LEWIS."
"MOM, YOU KNEW I WAS GOING TO MOVE OUT SOMETIME."

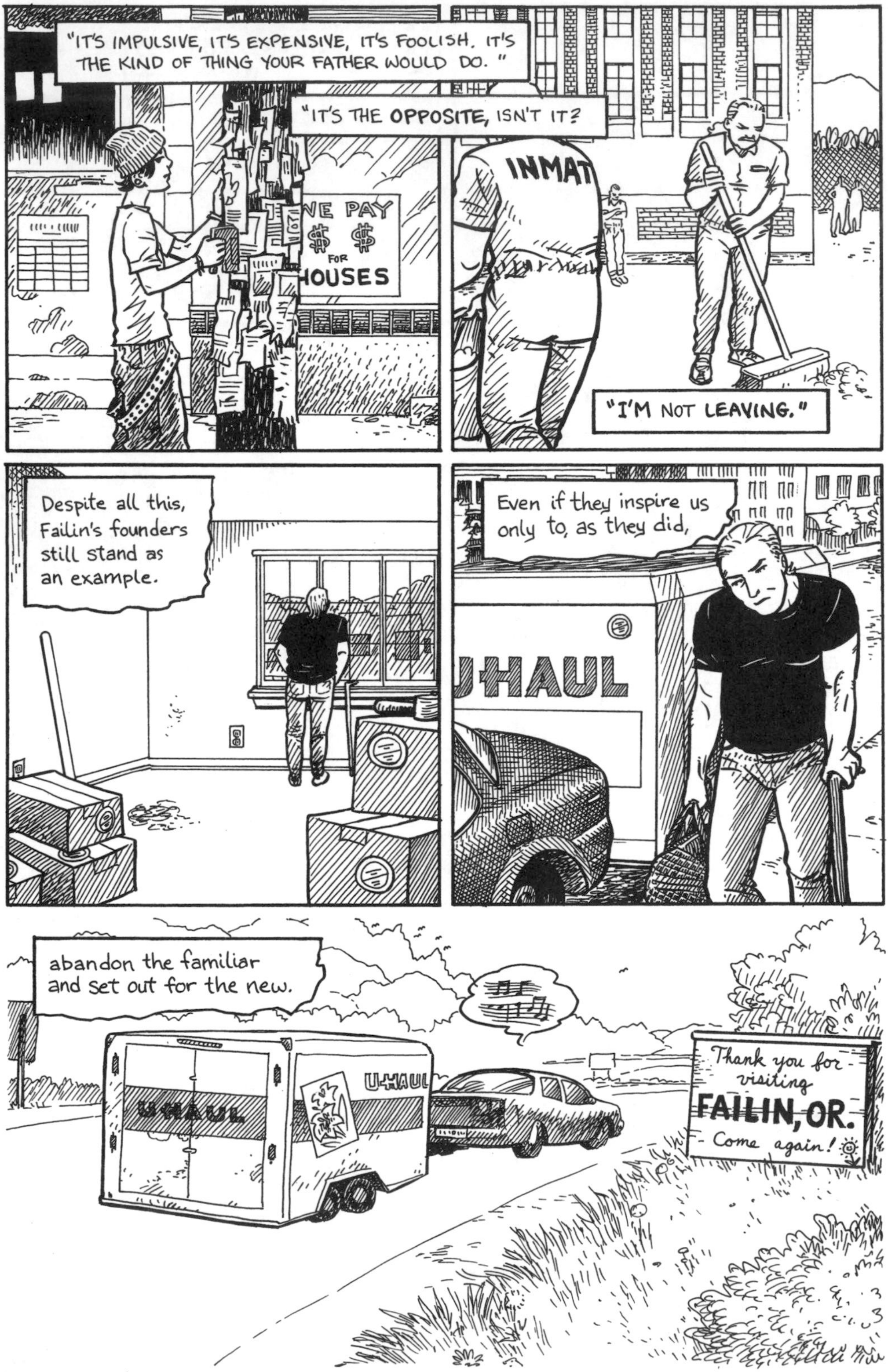
"IT'S IMPULSIVE, IT'S EXPENSIVE, IT'S FOOLISH. IT'S THE KIND OF THING YOUR FATHER WOULD DO."
"IT'S THE OPPOSITE, ISN'T IT?
WE PAY $ $ FOR HOUSES
INMAT
"I'M NOT LEAVING."
Despite all this, Failin's founders still stand as an example.
Even if they inspire us only to, as they did,
U-HAUL
abandon the familiar and set out for the new.
U-HAUL
U-HAUL
Thank you for visiting FAILIN, OR. Come again!

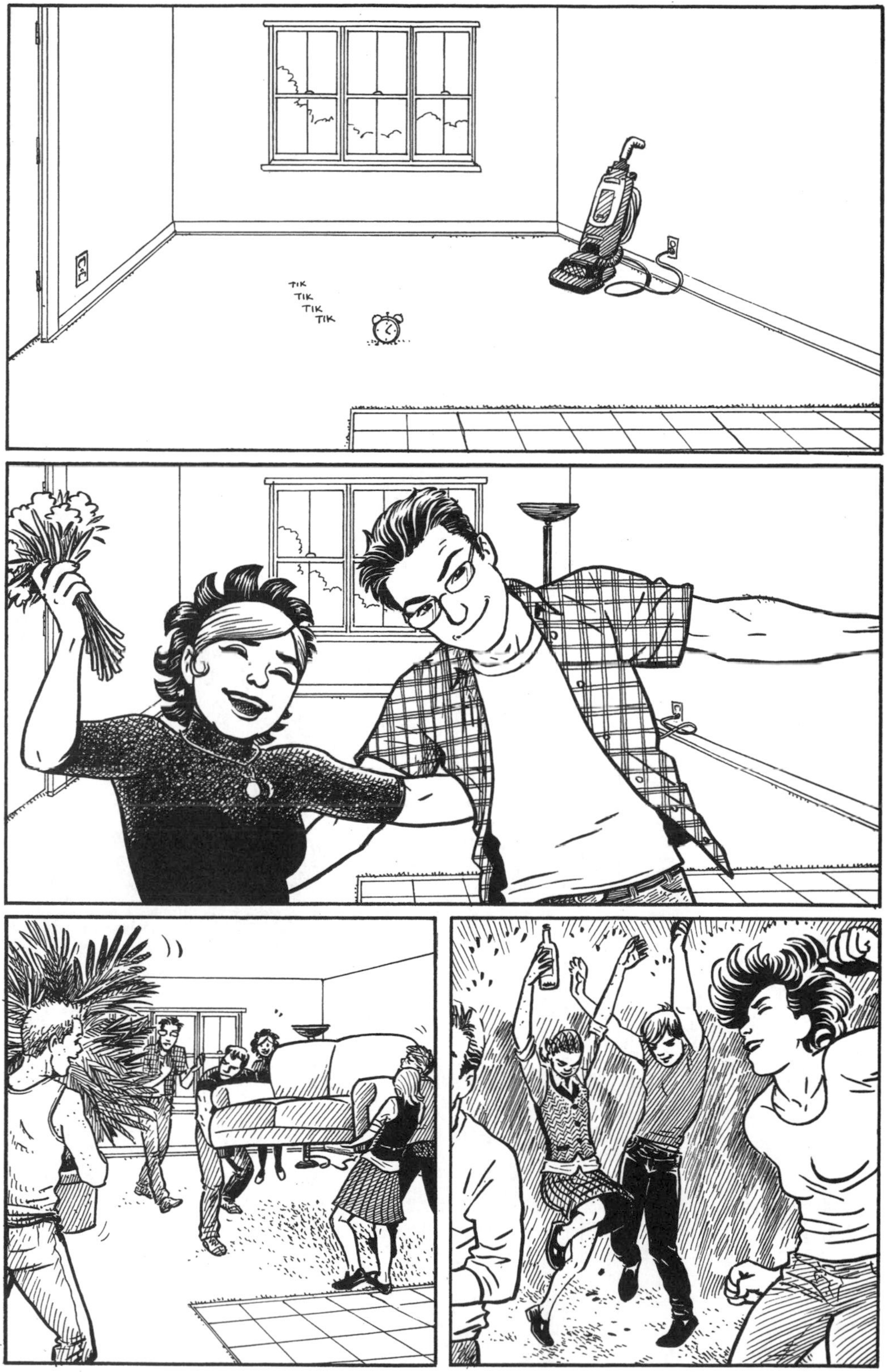
TIK
TIK
TIK
TIK

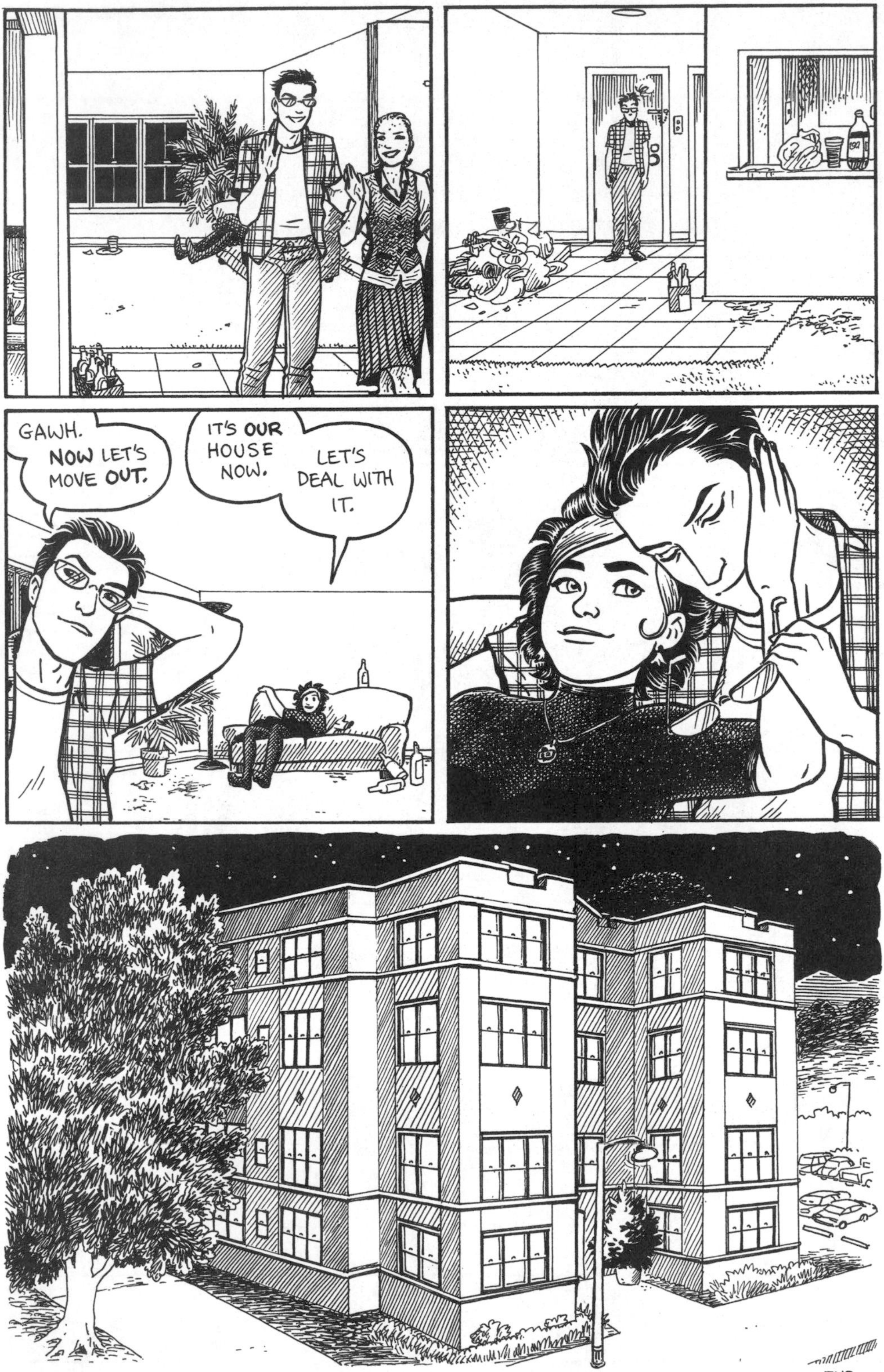
GAWH. NOW LET'S MOVE OUT.
IT'S OUR HOUSE NOW.
LET'S DEAL WITH IT.
END

AFTERWORD

By Sara Ryan

I've been fascinated for years by the ways people invest objects with value—both emotional and financial. I used to go to yard sales for voyeuristic bargain hunting, but once I discovered estate sales, there was no going back. People hold yard sales to raise cash and get rid of things they no longer want. At estate sales, a third party sells the things that someone did want, and kept until they died. Perhaps this accounts for the heightened emotions that come into play. To prevent stampedes when the doors open at a desirable sale, the estate sale employees put a numbered list on the door that—allegedly—people write their names on in the order in which they arrive. Then the employees give out slips of paper with the numbers, and when the doors open, they let in a few people at a time. But sometimes people circulate fake numbers, or even fake lists. While they're waiting, people push through shrubbery to peer in the windows to see the goods. Fights can break out about line placement.

And you can't go to estate sales without thinking about mortality, family, and inheritance. At one sale, I saw a small wooden sewing basket and did a double take. Months before, I'd found its twin in a long-sealed box of things that had belonged to the grandmother I never knew. She died shortly after my father was born. To me, that sewing basket was a singular, highly charged family object. But finding its duplicate (with four-dollar price tag attached) made it clear that it was also a product of mass production. So what, I wondered, was it "really" worth?

What do we hold onto? What do we let go? What's the line between collecting and hoarding? What do we inherit from our parents—objects? looks? disorders?—and does that inheritance doom us?

CHARACTER DESIGNS

By Carla Speed McNeil

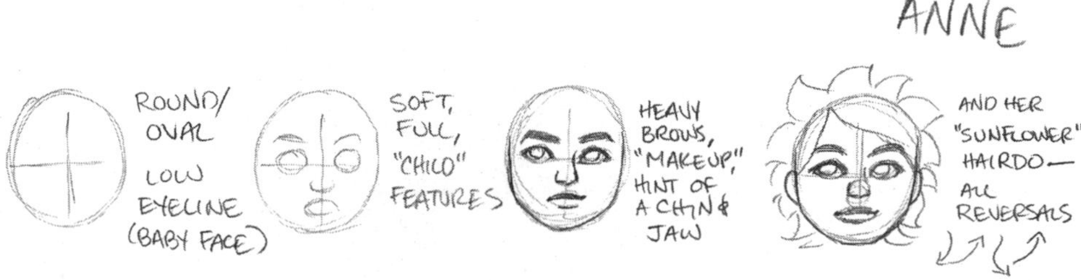
ANNE
ROUND/ OVAL
LOW EYELINE (BABY FACE)
SOFT, FULL, "CHILD" FEATURES
HEAVY BROWS, "MAKEUP," HINT OF A CHIN & JAW
AND HER "SUNFLOWER" HAIRDO—
ALL REVERSALS

POPSICLE-STICK CONSTRUCTION

By Sara Ryan

"Popsicle-Stick Construction" was written by Sara Ryan for the Significant Objects project, a literary and anthropological experiment devised by Rob Walker and Joshua Glenn to demonstrate that the effect of narrative on any given object's subjective value can be measured objectively.

Anne Cole writes:

The summer when I was nine, Mom bought boxes and boxes of popsicles on sale, lemon-lime, some discontinued brand. They looked like fluorescent jaundice on a stick, but they tasted sharply sour-sweet, and I loved them. The first time I ate one, or two, actually, since they were the kind you can break in half to share, but I didn't, I did what anyone would do: tossed the sticks into the trash.

Mom fished them out, rinsed them off, and said, "They're perfectly good."

"For what?" I asked, but she didn't answer.

Our house was already swelling up with things we might need, things we couldn't possibly throw away, things Mom couldn't believe were just sitting out on the curb.

I took the sticks into my room and stared at them. I needed to turn them into something that made sense to me, but I didn't know what.

Soon, it became a ritual. Eat, rinse, take sticks to room.

They were drumsticks until there were too many and Mom said it was too loud when I played.

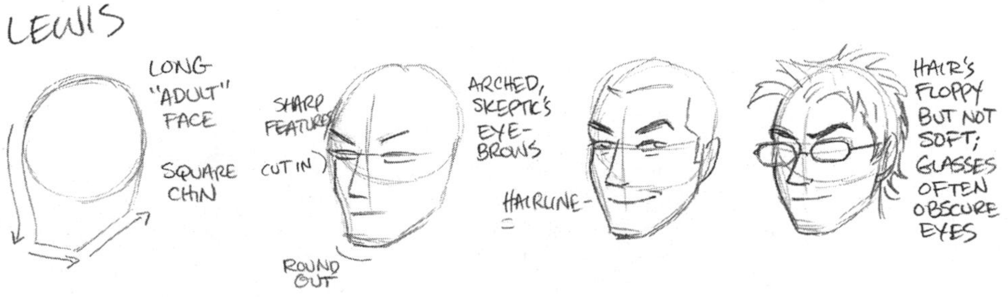

LEWIS
LONG "ADULT" FACE
SQUARE CHIN
SHARP
CUT IN
ROUND OUT
ARCHED, SKEPTIC'S EYE-BROWS
HAIRLINE
HAIR'S FLOPPY BUT NOT SOFT; GLASSES OFTEN OBSCURE EYES

They were bookmarks until they cracked the spine on a library book.

I threw them on my floor and tried to use the patterns they made for divination, but I couldn't make up my mind about what they meant.

I had more and more of them, clustered in a jar on my dresser. Once I dreamed they all came to life like the brooms in that story.

One day when she had to work Mom took me to the Boys and Girls club. The computers and the swings were full, so I went with some lady who said we were going to do art.

First thing, she got out a huge box of popsicle sticks—at least, that's what the box said, but it was clear that no popsicles had ever been attached to them.

At least my sticks had served one useful purpose. What was the point of a box of sticks with no popsicles?

I was going to leave, but you had to stay once you chose an activity. I wouldn't do it, but I watched her and the other kids, and it finally gave me the idea for what to do.

Of course we had glue at home. Of course there was a piece of wood to use for a base. I glued and glued, making up the design as I went.

But when I looked at it when I was done, all I could think is that I'd made a way to perpetuate the cycle, the empty space inside the bowl calling out to be filled with more things. Like the ever-shrinking empty spaces in our house.

I waited until school started, smuggled it out of the house in my backpack, and abandoned it in a kindergartner's cubby.

It was a start.

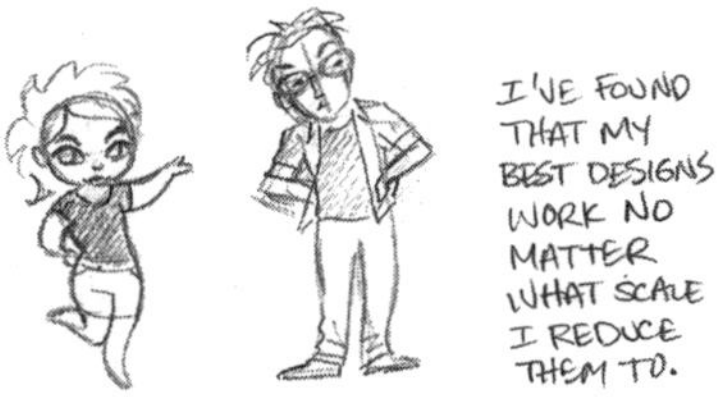
I'VE FOUND THAT MY BEST DESIGNS WORK NO MATTER WHAT SCALE I REDUCE THEM TO.

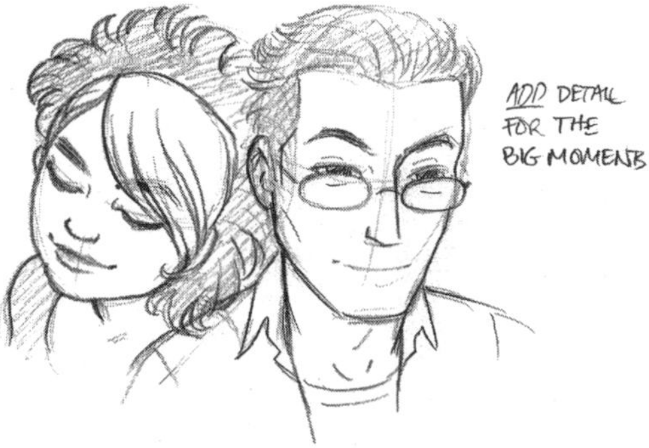
ADD DETAIL FOR THE BIG MOMENTS

SARA RYAN is the author of the novels *Empress of the World*, an Oregon Book Award winner, Lambda Literary Award finalist, and ALA-YALSA Best Book for Young Adults, and *The Rules for Hearts*, an Oregon Book Award winner and Junior Library Guild selection. Her comics work ranges from *Hellboy* to the Tori Amos anthology *Comic Book Tattoo* and the Eisner Award–nominated "Me and Edith Head." *Bad Houses* is her first graphic novel.

CARLA SPEED MCNEIL is the author and artist of the award-winning series *Finder*, published by Dark Horse Comics. In addition to nine printed volumes of *Finder*, she has drawn *Queen & Country* Volume 5: *Operation: Stormfront*, written by Greg Rucka and published by Oni Press; adapted and drawn *Pendragon* Volume 1: *The Merchant of Death* (based on the prose book by D. J. MacHale) for Simon & Schuster; drawn the short story "Here. In My Head" (with writer Elizabeth Genco) for *Comic Book Tattoo* from Image; drawn fan-favorite *Frank Ironwine* by Warren Ellis for Apparat/Avatar; and drawn two pages of *Transmetropolitan*, also by Warren Ellis, for DC/Vertigo. More recently, McNeil drew part of Alex de Campi's *Ashes*. She lives in Maryland with her family.

FINDER

CARLA SPEED McNEIL

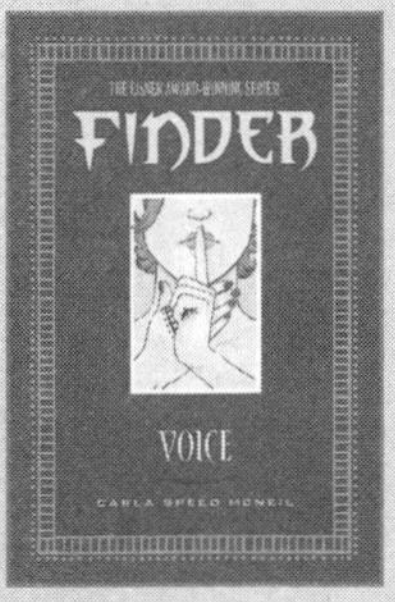
FINDER
VOICE
CARLA SPEED MCNEIL

FINDER: VOICE

ISBN 978-1-59582-651-0
$19.99

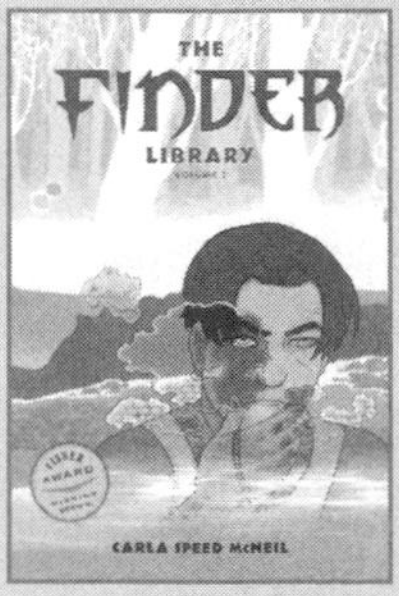
THE
FINDER
LIBRARY
CARLA SPEED McNEIL

THE FINDER LIBRARY VOLUME 1

ISBN 978-1-59582-652-7
$24.99

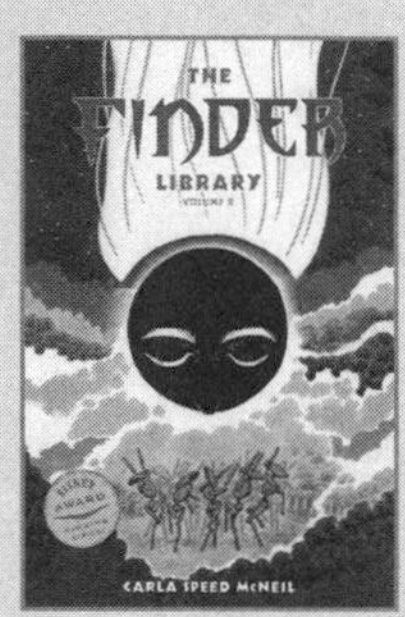
THE
FINDER
LIBRARY
CARLA SPEED McNEIL

THE FINDER LIBRARY VOLUME 2

ISBN 978-1-59582-653-4
$24.99

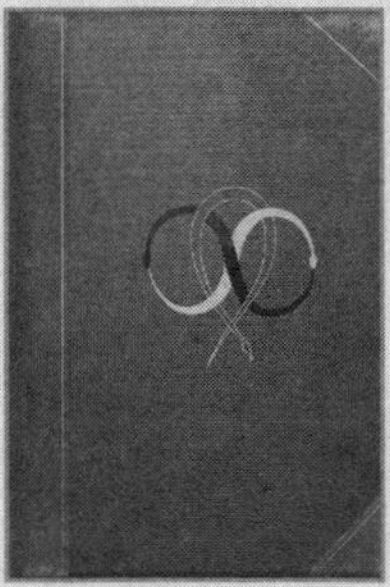

FINDER: TALISMAN
Special edition hardcover

ISBN 978-1-61655-027-1
$19.99

LOSE YOURSELF IN A WORLD BEYOND YOUR WILDEST DREAMS . . .

Since 1996, *Finder* has set the bar for science-fiction storytelling, with a lush, intricate world and compelling characters. Now, Dark Horse is proud to present Carla Speed McNeil's groundbreaking series in newly revised, expanded, affordablypriced volumes!

Follow enigmatic hero Jaeger through a "glorious, catholic pileup of high-tech SF, fannish fantasy, and street-level culture clash" (*Village Voice*), and discover the lush world and compelling characters that have carved *Finder* a permanent place in the pantheon of independent comics.

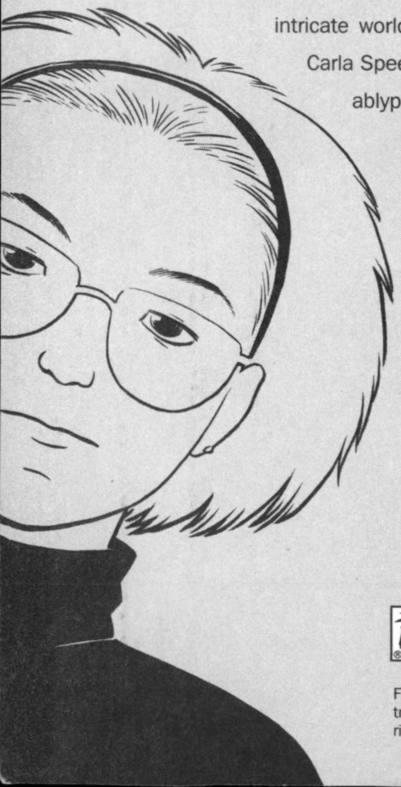

To find a comics shop in your area, call 1-888-266-4226
For more information or to order direct: On the web: DarkHorse.com
E-mail: mailorder@darkhorse.com
Phone: 1-800-862-0052
Mon–Fri 9 AM to 5 PM Pacific Time

DARK HORSE COMICS®
DarkHorse.com

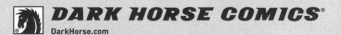